ON A FAR WILD SHORE

MALCOLM MACDONALD

St. Martin's Press
New York

ON A FAR WILD SHORE. Copyright © 1986 by Malcolm Macdonald. All
rights reserved. Printed in the United States of America. No part of this
book may be used or reproduced in any manner whatsoever without
written permission except in the case of brief quotations embodied in
critical articles or reviews. For information, address St. Martin's Press,
175 Fifth Avenue, New York, N. Y. 10010.

Library of Congress Cataloging in Publication Data

Ross-Macdonald, Malcolm.
    On a far wild shore.

    I. Title.
PR6068.082705   1986   823'.914   86-3968
ISBN 0-312-58435-0

First published in Great Britain by Judy Piatkus Limited under the title
Mistress of Pallas and under the writer's pen name Malcolm Ross.

First U.S. Edition

10 9 8 7 6 5 4 3 2 1

for
Pauline and Nicola
and in loving memory of
Ernest and Nigel

CONTENTS

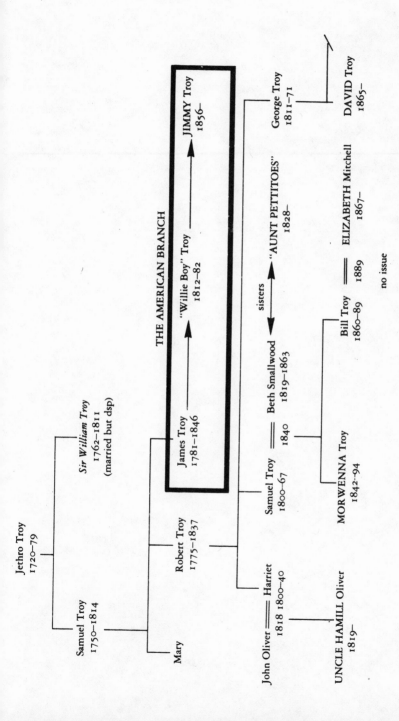

THE AMERICAN BRANCH

Jethro Troy
1720–79

Samuel Troy
1750–1814

Sir William Troy
1762–1811
(married but dsp)

Robert Troy
1775–1837

Mary

James Troy
1781–1846

"Willie Boy" Troy
1812–82

JIMMY Troy
1856–

George Troy
1811–71

DAVID Troy
1865–

Samuel Troy
1800–67

Beth Smallwood
1819–1863

"AUNT PETTITOES"
1828–

sisters

1840

John Oliver
1818

Harriet
1800–40

MORWENNA Troy
1842–94

Bill Troy
1860–89

ELIZABETH Mitchell
1867–

1889

no issue

UNCLE HAMILL Oliver
1819–

The characters marked in CAPITALS are the only ones alive during the course of the story

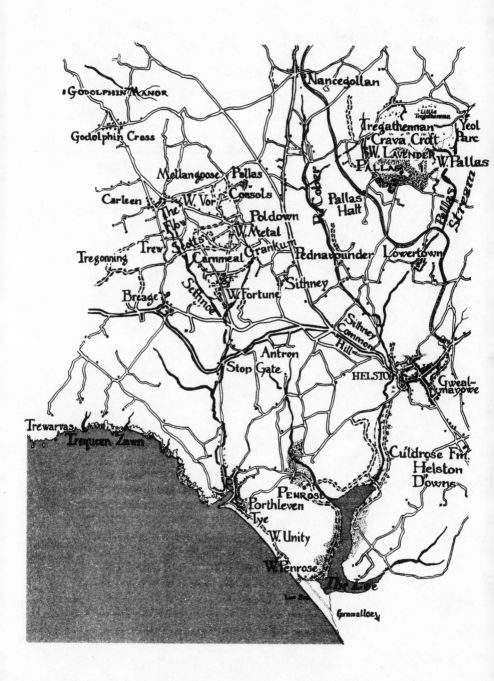

A MAP OF THE HELSTON DISTRICT

PART ONE

THE LOST HEIRESS

CHAPTER ONE

ELIZABETH HAD LOST her way. These Cornish lanes were built with such an absurd respect for private property; they hugged the boundaries of every tiny field, twisting and turning. It was a miracle she had not crossed her own path a score of times this past hour, since her fear had caused her to leave the little branch-line train at Pallas Halt. Not unreasonably she had assumed that Pallas House would be somewhere nearby – somewhere prominent; but it was not, and she was lost.

Still, if she had found the big house at once, she would not have stumbled across this perfect country lodge. The roadside wall yielded to a mixed hedge of privet and escallonia; formerly it had been well tended but now it was running wild. Arching raggedly above the gate it framed a view so perfect that, for a moment, she forgot herself, forget her grief, forgot the dread that had haunted these past weeks.

She had seen many granite houses that day, especially after the main-line train had steamed west of Plymouth, but none had been quite like this. Cornish dwellings are low and stocky, with upper windows that rise to the eaves; in their aggressive plainness they seem to fear any hint of beauty, as if it were a feckless challenge to the gods of the storm. Even on a calm summer's day, like today, they appear to be half battened down against some expected rage of wind and rain.

But this granite house was an essay in elegance. It had high gables whose graceful curves were almost Chinese. The bargeboards at the gable ends were carved in a delicate fretwork that cast fine, lacelike shadows, mellowing the stark gray of the stone walls behind. The windows had arched lintels, with a generous space to the eaves above, where each rafter projected a carved and fluted finial into the sunlight. Bourbon roses grew in profusion beside the pathway, interspersed with bushes of sage and lavender, which laid upon the air a drowsy sense of times forgotten, times foregone.

Neglected it was. Untenanted it was, too, save for a pair of fat doves perched somnolently on the crenellations of the ridge slates. Yet it was

3

perfect. If she had any expectations from her late husband's will, no matter how large they might be, she would gladly renounce them all for this one house, lost in this magical space in this tree-drowned valley, here at the far, far end of England.

Like one possessed she set her hand to the rusted gatelatch and let herself in. The creaking hinges startled the two doves, but they resettled almost at once on a small gable over a window. One or two of the flagstones tilted beneath her feet. Moles had passed this way. The richer flora of the garden, and the profound peace of its neglect, attracted butterflies and birds that were rare in the utilitarian fields around. She had not the country skills to name them, but their variety and abundance were obvious.

She peered in at the dusty, leaded windows and saw bare boards, bare walls, cobwebs. She tried the door. The latch rose on its sneck and the door yielded, but then she lost her courage and closed it again. She made for the side of the house, seeking the tradesmen's entrance. Broad ex-flowerbeds ran along the front walls, skirted by a brick path that led arrow-straight through a hundred yards of garden to a low, woodland gate. At the end of the house the line of its frontage was continued by a series of tall brick pillars, about twelve feet apart. Between them stretched trellisses of roses and clematis, now invaded by bindweed. Her fingers itched to get at this garden; it was still within her powers of rescue. But another two years in the damp, warm, fertile climate of Cornwall and it would need a small army of gardeners.

The trellisses neatly divided the "gentry" half of the garden from its kitchen cousin. The gate between the two had well-oiled hinges. And the kitchen garden, she now saw, was as well tended as the other was neglected. Perhaps the staff of the house were here on board wages? But surely they wouldn't be allowed to neglect the main garden so? She looked along the rows of potatoes, now almost all lifted, cabbages, spring onions, turnips . . . at the frames of lettuce and cucumber . . . at the orderly heaps of compost, manure, and topsoil . . . and wondered who would be allowed to do all this while a once-fine garden went to ruin not ten feet away.

In the yard behind the house someone began to work a pump, five or six strokes followed by a gush of water. She suddenly realized how thirsty the walk and the sun had made her. The heavy black of her full mourning was unbearably hot.

Then she heard a loud gasp, a cry of satisfaction.

The voice was male.

Five more strokes, a lot of splashing and snorting. Then a boyish roar of joy that turned into a laugh.

There was something enigmatic about that laugh — loose, half-surprised, full of self-assurance. Its owner did not fear the sudden appearance of landlord or master.

She rounded the corner as the man was engaged in a third spate of pumping. He was naked.

He was facing away from her, crouched beneath the gushing spout. One lithe arm reached up and worked the handle easily. The muscles on his back rippled and glistened, wet in the sun, which was now falling and reddening in the sky beyond him.

Raising his face into the gushing freshet he blew out a wide whalespout of spray, iridescent against the early evening light. She knew she ought to turn and go, yet she could not take her eyes away. No immodest pleasure kept her there, but sheer aesthetic joy. Thus she would have watched a young tiger, playing beside a waterhole – and, indeed, there *was* something tigerlike about this young man.

He stood and turned, shaking the water from his long, curly hair and puffing the droplets from his hands and lips. Then he saw her and froze. Her stomach fell away inside her. But another Elizabeth, more inward and more secret, continued to exult in his beauty.

Perhaps he saw it, for he broke into a smile. Raising his hands toward her he said, "Why not come and join me?"

He was tall and fair. His gaze, despite his easy smile, was intense. The water plastered his curls to his brow and gave him a wild, dissolute appearance, like a young Bacchus, not yet fattened on debauchery.

He withdrew the challenge of his invitation. "No?" He shrugged and turned away, crouching again beneath the spout and cranking the handle until the water gushed once more, sparkling into the black of his silhouette. The sun poured oxblood over the wet flagstones beyond him.

He rose at last and walked directly to one of the outhouse sheds on the far side of the yard. Without turning to look at her, he said, "Please don't go, Mrs. Troy. I wish particularly to talk to you. Bill was a great friend of mine."

With a hop, skip, and jump he disappeared through the door – a curiously adolescent gesture for a man in his mid-twenties.

When the dark of the shed had swallowed him, the spell that held her broke. She almost ran to the pump and cranked gouts of cold, clear water into her naked palm. Her lips sucked at it greedily; the relief filled her mouth and throat like cool fire. A chill pool of it settled in her stomach. She drank until the water backed up and made her choke and splutter.

"Easy now!" His palm fell lightly, repeatedly, on her shoulderblades. She turned. Through the tears of her coughing she saw him smiling at her, knowingly, full of self-confidence. Not pausing to dry himself, he had simply hastened into his shirt and trousers. His skin glistened wet at his open shirtfront. Damp patches were spreading through the cotton material. He was still barefoot.

Again she had the impression that he was both boy and man, or that the man had not cast off the behaviour of the boy. She said, "You have the advantage of me, Mr. . . . ?"

"Rodda. Courtenay Rodda." He spoke as if the name might already

mean something to her. The sun was warm and golden aslant his skin. The
fresh coolness within her wanted to touch it, as one wants to touch fine
carving.

"Do you own this house, Mr. Rodda?" she asked, turning away from
him. Looking once more at the generous windows, the graceful proportions, she fell in love with it anew.

"That rather depends on your husband's will, Mrs. Troy."

She spun back to him, her eyes wide.

"It's part of the Troy estate. I'm sorry – I should have offered you my
condolences at once."

When she remembered what he *had* offered, she smiled at the
incongruity.

He saw it and was angered. "But your grief is already healing, I see."

"How dare you?" she asked in flat, reasonable tones – so that for a
moment he thought she had asked something like, 'How are you?'

She went on, "How dare you suppose you can measure my grief?"

He lowered his eyes uncomfortably. She saw he did not lose many
skirmishes of that kind.

He seemed on the point of withdrawing. She realized she needed to
talk to him more than he to her. There were so many unanswered questions.
"I saw a stone bench around in the front garden," she said in a more pleasant
tone. "Shall we go there? I have so much I wish to ask you. Or somebody
who lives down here and knows the family."

He nodded. "I have a bar of chocolate." He licked his lips, as if telling
her how to respond, and returned to the shed.

Elizabeth wandered lazily back toward the front garden. It struck her
that this was the first time in her life she had been alone with a man. Of
course, she had walked convalescent officers up and down the gardens of the
nursing home, and she and Bill had often been alone together once they
were officially engaged; but that was different. Those occasions had been
privileged. Now that she was no longer Miss Mitchell, the privilege was
general. She relished the freedom of being Mrs.

Slightly breathless, he joined her before she reached the seat. His hand
poked forward beside her, flat, palm up, framing a jagged lump of chocolate. "Quite clean," he said, as if she had not seen him washing himself.

"Thank you, Mr. Rodda." The water had made her realize her thirst;
now the chocolate did the same for her hunger. As they seated themselves,
her stomach gurgled.

"Have it all," he said, passing the bag to her. "I've already made a pig
of myself." He watched her nibble at the next piece. "Of course you were a
nurse, weren't you!" he went on.

Why 'of course'? she wondered. Then she saw he was seeking excuses for
her calm responses to his nakedness. Was he piqued? Did he find it
unflattering?

"That's how I met Captain Troy. I was his nurse during his convalescence."

Perhaps he was also trying to excuse her lack of outward grief. She ought to have said, *Yes, I'm used to pain and death.*

He asked, "Did you meet after that fall he had on manoeuvres this spring?"

"Yes."

"I understand it was another fall that killed him last month? Funny thing that – Bill was a fine horseman. He and I often hunted with the Cury and the Fourborough, whenever he got leave."

Was he obliquely accusing her of something? Neglect? Failure to cope with Bill's sudden bouts of falling? She felt she had to explain: "It wasn't a fall that killed him, actually. It was a stroke. It was probably a stroke the first time, too, when he was on manoeuvres. We all thought he was completely better. The doctors said he was. Otherwise I assure you . . ."

"But there was a horse. They shot a horse, I heard."

"A pony. I'll tell you how it happened."

She hesitated long enough to provoke him into saying, "Oh please – if you'd rather not . . ."

"No – I'll have to get used to telling it. Everyone'll want to hear. Anyway, we were in a pony and trap, Bill and I. It was such a short drive, you see – only from the church to . . . I mean, I wouldn't even *consider* travelling for our honeymoon, especially as we were already in Brighton. So it was only the drive from the church to the convalescent home, to pick up our bags, and then on to the hotel. Only a mile. And then, when it happened, I was so desperately trying to stop him from falling out of the trap that the reins were just left dangling. The pony must have taken fright and we struck a tree or a bollard or something. Anyway . . ."

"You were lucky to have escaped with your own life."

"I wonder."

His eyes were suddenly inscrutable. She looked for sympathy – or mockery – and saw nothing. He was listening to this account of Bill's death but he was searching her eyes, her voice, for something beyond it. He nodded, rather slowly, and said with great assurance, as if he most particularly wished to persuade her of it, "Oh yes – you *were* lucky!"

"I don't see one bright sign anywhere."

"You're alive. You're young still. You are beautiful. And now you're free to be free."

His compliment excited her, but also gave her a moment of panic, as if she were being uprooted, taken from a safe place. She stared at him and thought, *He has not had much experience of strangers. He wonders how to behave with me and what I think of him.*

He went on, "Also you were a nurse. You *chose* to be a nurse, I presume, so you must feel you have plenty to . . ."

"I didn't say I was a good nurse. As a matter of fact, I think I was awful. I only became a nurse because after my father died I found I couldn't go on living at home, and because there's very little else open to a respectable woman with not much education and very small means."

It wasn't true, or not the entire truth. Life with her mother would have been impossible, but also she had been desperate for some way of life with a discipline to it. Her own disorderly impulses, secret, suppressed inside her, had been frightening.

He said, "You could have trained to be a typewriter. That's the modern thing, you know."

She shrugged.

"And yet you chose nursing. That must mean something."

"Are you a barrister?" she asked.

Her abrupt tone displeased him.

She popped another piece of chocolate into her mouth.

When he saw he wasn't going to draw her back into talking directly about herself he swallowed his annoyance, and became pleasant again. "What d'you think of your new family?" he asked.

"I've not met them yet."

He frowned. "Didn't they meet the train in Helston?"

"I got off at Pallas Halt."

"So that's why you're out here all alone."

"How did you know who I was, by the way?"

"You've been expected for days. And Cornwall isn't exactly Piccadilly Circus. The only visitors we get in these parts are all a bit loony — vegetarians, people who wear Jaeger's woollen underwear all summer – that sort. So who else could you have been?"

"I'm afraid to meet Bill's people, Mr. Rodda. I'm sure they've all formed quite the wrong impression of me."

"Why d'you say that?"

"Isn't it obvious? Bill and I knew each other for such a short while. It was all so fast – you know what a whirlwind he was. And then for him to die like that, between the wedding and the breakfast . . . I mean, even to me it looks dreadful. Suppose he's actually left me some money or something."

"What if he left it *all* to you!"

She looked at him in disbelief and then laughed. "That's out of the question."

"It wouldn't be anything very grand, even so. In fact, you'd inherit a millstone. The grand old days of the Cornish estate, with tin repaying the adventurers at a thousand percent – they're gone these long years."

She didn't even want to think of the inheritance. She shifted her position, preparing to rise. "I suppose I'd better go and find Pallas House. Can you perhaps tell me the way?"

He looked searchingly at her. "Surely you passed a once-fine old gateway back there in the woodland – a heap of rubble now?" She nodded. "Well, that's where you should have turned in. That's Pallas – the 'grand house' of the district. A millstone, as I say." He saw her reluctance and asked, "Are you afraid of your dear sister-in-law? Did Bill tell you about her?"

"Morwenna?"

His smile was malicious. "The Gorgon herself. They went into Helston to meet you, you know. The two women – not Hamill Oliver."

"Oh yes – Bill told me about him, too. His uncle?"

"Not really. Bill always called him uncle because of the difference in age. Actually they were cousins. Hamill is the ruin of a once-fine man." He tipped an imaginary glass down his throat. "So it was only the Gorgon and poor little Pettitoes who went in to meet you. I passed them on my way here. She'll be furious. The whole of Helston will be laughing at it – the Gorgon standing bootless upon the platform! Why did you get off at Pallas Halt?"

"I suddenly realized I couldn't face them."

"You're probably right. Morwenna terrified Bill. He knew – years ago – he knew he ought to come back here and start managing the estate properly. Morwenna is ruining it. But he could never face her."

Was it true? Rodda's assurance annoyed her; but she found it difficult to sustain any emotion these days. Thinking back over what Bill had said – about resigning his commission and coming back here to manage Pallas with her at his side – she felt herself becoming enmeshed in a web of expectations, threads from beyond the grave.

She said, "Considering that Morwenna was more like his mother than his sister, I hardly think that's surprising, do you?" She suddenly felt more alone, or more aware of her loneliness, than at any time since Bill's death. "Were you and Bill close friends?" she asked.

"Ever since I can remember."

"I hope we'll meet again then. I'd like to share your memories of him. What were you doing here this afternoon?"

"I was making a hide."

"D'you mean *curing* a hide? Oxhide or what?"

He smiled. "Come and see it. It'll save ten minutes of explanation." He rose and dusted nothing off his trousers. The damp spots had hearly all dried.

She followed him around to the yard again, to the gloomy shed where he had dressed so hastily.

It was even darker now and the heat was oppressive. The room was a workshop, with the dying glow of a blacksmith's forge at the back. It smelled of coke and male sweat. She felt diminished by it, standing there at the brink of a world she did not understand.

As her eyes grew dark-accustomed she saw on the floor before her a contraption of bent iron rods, welded under the hammer to form a kind of man-high cage. "Now that's a hide," he said. "It hides me from the birds. I take photographs of birds."

She still cloud not see how it worked.

"I clothe it with grass and leaves, of course."

"Ah. It looks enormous. You could practically live inside it."

"I use wet plates, so I need my dark-room with me. Locally, you know, I'm considered a pretty good photographer."

Her mind was blank. What else was there to say? 'May I see your photographs?' But she had no desire to see them. "Is it you who keeps the kitchen-garden so immaculately?" she said at last.

He laughed. "My name means nothing to you, does it."

She shook her head and turned toward the door. "I'd better go. I should think Morwenna's come back from Helston by now."

"Not her! I'll wager she won't be back until supper. The moment she found you weren't on the train, she'll have invented a dozen other reasons for going in to Helston this afternoon. Collecting you will instantly be demoted to something she intended to do in passing. More an act of charity than anything."

His assurance began to annoy her. "How awful to know as much about people as God himself," she said.

He bowed his head, pretending to accept her rebuke. "One day I'll come the most terrible cropper." He stretched forth his hand. "Good evening, Mrs. Troy. I'm sure we'll meet again soon."

While she had been looking at the hide he had rolled up his sleeves. His arms were strong and wiry. The low, slanting light from the doorway sculpted the muscles in high relief. Again that aesthetic joy filled her, as strongly as when she had first seen him at the pump. And because it was so pure, it banished all necessity to think, to speak, to have a response prepared for him.

She shook his hand, only to watch his flesh in motion, to give herself that last pleasure. Then she drifted out into a darkening world.

CHAPTER TWO

THE DRIVEWAY TO PALLAS was rutted and potholed. Briars and blackberries straggled inward from the verges, pruned only by the occasional passing carriage. Trapped between those green ramparts, the air was dank and humid, conserving puddles that would have vanished days ago on the open highway.

In the long-drawn twilight, made almost night by the shade among the trees, Elizabeth picked her path carefully, weaving this way and that, lifting her skirts free of the mud. From time to time she stirred furious clouds of bluebottles, feasting on fresh apples of horsedung. At the ridge came a sudden flood of evening light and she found herself looking down at Pallas and its dying gardens. From here it seemed no more than a larger and older version of the empty lodge, too ambitious, a failure. She was disappointed. Bill had spoken of it so often and with such affection.

He had also warned her of its neglect – the signs of which were everywhere. The croquet lawn was infested with tussocky grass. Thorns and volunteer saplings crowded the feet of specimen trees, littering what had originally been spacious rides. Bill once said, "My heart sometimes sinks at the very thought of Pallas."

How can anyone bequeath love and despair?

The freedom of widowhood began to frighten her. Nursing had filled her life with imperatives from dawn to dusk and round to dawn again. Marriage would have given her a new set – wife, mother, mistress of the household, hostess. But widowhood? It conferred only freedom, which she did not welcome.

Yet, curiously enough, she could envy it in others. She envied Courtenay Rodda and the idyllic life he must lead, photographing birds and sluicing himself naked under pumps whenever he felt like it. Her mind delicately probed the memory of that strange encounter as she followed the winding drive down into the dell. She remembered to pull on her gloves again. Now the cool black silk was luxurious to her fingers.

Where the drive broadened to form the carriage sweep she halted. An elderly man in a beige cotton suit – not a working man – was backing unsteadily toward her, bent almost double. He was dragging an empty wheelbarrow with his left hand. At first she thought he might have lost his right hand but when he became aware of her presence he turned to face her and she saw he was holding a tumbler of whisky.

He smiled and stretched forth his free arm. "Welcome, my dear, you must be Elizabeth."

"And you are Mr. Oliver, I think." She offered her cheek for a kiss but we took up her left hand and shook it warmly, saying, "Welcome!" again and again.

His nose was veined. His pale blue eyes were alert but slack; their lower lids hung free, like miniature cisterns filled with tears. "I'm Old Hamill Oliver to all the world," he said. "You may call me Uncle Hamill. Bill always did." The alehouse air around him enveloped her, too. His eyes looked her up and down but she thought he took in little of what they saw.

"Uncle Hamill, then." She smiled. "He told me so much about you."

Still he held her hand. "How are you, my dear?" he asked. "In yourself, I mean." Immediately he answered for her. "It must sometimes seem as if the grief will never go. But it will." He sighed and brightened simultaneously. "Come in and have a *chota peg*. By the way, where's Morwenna? And Petty?"

Elizabeth practised her lie. "I'm afraid I misunderstood the arrangement. I got off at Pallas Halt."

"But surely Churchill told you – the guard? If he didn't, I'll kick his shins next . . ."

"No, he did tell me. It was so stifling in the carriage, I thought I'd walk."

He stared into her eyes and gave her hand a final squeeze before he let it go. "Funked it, eh? Don't blame you." He turned toward the door and ushered her in.

"Why d'you say that?" she asked.

His answer was reluctant. "You'll find a cool enough welcome here, I'm afraid. I welcome you, of course. Petty, too, I'm sure. And the servants. But we aren't the ones who matter. Have you eaten?"

"I had some chocolate."

"Excellent." He spoke as if a few mouthfuls of chocolate were more than enough. "Morwenna's the one who matters." He smacked his lips in distaste. "She's our alpha and omega. Do say you'll have a drink."

"Are you going to leave the wheelbarrow there?" she asked. The dragging of its legs had scored a couple of shaky furrows in the gravel.

He looked at it critically. "Yes, I think so," he replied at last.

"But it's blocking the drive."

"Just so. It'll give us time to hide the bottles. Now what about this drink?"

"Oh I don't know that I . . ."

"A little one."

"I had a drink of water."

She remembered Rodda, gilded by the sun.

"Water!" Hamill wrinkled his nose. "Never be deceived by water, my dear. Have you *seen* it under a microscope? I promise you, you'd never touch the stuff again, not even if the royal physician himself commanded it. I hope you're not one of these Band of Hopefuls . . ."

She relented. "I do take an occasional glass of wine. Bill taught me that. Perhaps I'll accept a very small sherry, thank you."

Like a puppy off a leash he scampered indoors, delicately, on old man's joints – leaving her to give the façade of the house a final survey. In one respect at least it cheered her. She had been prepared to find an atmosphere of menance clinging to its fabric, the brooding presence of Morwenna. But she found it touched with no more than a genteel sadness, as if a new tenant, a new injection of life, might yet transform it.

The hallway was large, dark below, rising to an airy attic lantern window far above. She had a swift impression of many pictures, fading wallpaper, damp.

"Here!" Hamill called from the room to her left. She found him at the sideboard. "Wine and women," he was saying, "are the earth's greatest bounties, even apart. But *together* . . .!" It was the gallantry of another age, the early Victorian, his youth.

She smiled though she was hardly listening. The sideboard was exquisite – a century old and inlaid with ivory and silver; a craftsman's piece. It clashed with the expectations aroused by the neglected garden and driveway. So did the rest of the furnishings. The walls were hung with silk, printed with elegant, French-looking rural scenes, faded but costly. They were decked with a cobwebby profusion of portraits and landscapes and histories. The fire surround was of marble, carved with swags and classical medallions. On the floor were silken Turkey rugs. Every piece of furniture was a classic of its kind, from Elizabethan oak to modern buhl and inlay.

He nudged her with the glass.

"Here!" she protested. "I said a small one."

"Well, it's only half a glass."

It was, in fact, half a tumbler.

He had observed her scrutiny of the room. "They had good taste once, the Troys. Or perhaps it was just that they had money in an age when there was no such thing as bad taste."

She ran her gloved fingertips over the silken walls. "Toile de Jouy," he told her. Then, between gulps of his brandy, he rattled off the names of the painters. He had a Cornish accent, but educated; at times it sounded almost American. His tone was that of a curator, not an owner: "Rubens, Poussin . . . Wilson . . . Reynolds, Opie, Tintoretto, Zoffany, Gainsborough, Rubens again, ditto . . . another Opie. He was Cornish, you know, old

Opie. And that's his portrait of Sir William Troy, his friend and patron –
and the founder of most of this feast.'

"What relation was he to Bill?"

"Great-great uncle. He was my great-great uncle, too. The baronetcy
died with him." He added, laughing, "And the revenues from tin died soon
after. They've revived once or twice since, but . . . false dawns, all. Enough
to tempt us back to the edge of bankruptcy. You're not drinking."

Even a small sip of the sherry burned her throat, but the aftertaste was
dry and pleasantly cooling. "Are there still tin mines?" she asked.

"Three yet working, but the revenues will hardly keep you in buttons.
Pray for a good long war. Tomorrow, if this fine spell of weather hasn't
broken, we'll go for a stroll in the woods behind the house and I'll show you
what was once the most valuable five acres on the face of this earth. Only
forty years ago, too. You're still not drinking. See what harm water does –
it's quite ruined your thirst."

She sipped again. This time it hardly burned, but the cool, astringent
aftertaste was still there. She began to feel relaxed.

"Yes," Hamill was saying, "the mines paid for all this, the Chippendale and Sheraton, the Wedgwood, the Sèvres, that splendid Aubusson
tapestry out there in the hall. Old Sir William was a great rival, you know,
of that other Sir William – Hamilton – the man who let Nelson take care of
his wife while he took care of Europe's heritage, or of more than one man's
fair share of it, anyway. Care to see the rest of the house? It would all have
been yours. Perhaps it is! We must wait for the will."

"*Wait* for it? Hasn't it been read yet?"

"Oh no – Bill was most insistent that you be there. Morwenna's
furious, of course. But Coad – he's the solicitor – he's saying nothing. Let
me show you the rest of the house. Do bring your drink – one never knows
when one may be glad of it."

With a new void at the pit of her stomach she followed him out.

She lost all count of time as he led her from room to room, or, rather,
from Aladdin's cave to Midas' hoard. In one place alone, a small, dusty
backroom with the mock graining peeling off the woodwork, there lay,
among a stack of paintings, face to the wall, a Rembrandt, a Titian, and a
Watteau. A small, exquisite Donatello bronze was put like a doorstop to
prevent them from sliding. Nearby, on a medieval lectern carved by a
master, lay a folder of paper – drawings by Michelangelo, woodcuts by
Dürer, sketches by Constable and Turner. In the library, what seemed like
an acre of suede and polished calf enshrined the complete education of an
eighteenth-century gentleman. There was fine porcelain. There was
sculpture. There was jewelry. And "furniture enough for a palace," as she
said, not hearing the pun until she had spoken it.

He laughed. "That's the family joke."

She giggled. "My head is swimming from such *richesse*," she said, which was odd, because she had intended to say 'riches.'

She stumbled over a loose floorboard.

"Must get that seen to," Hamill said. "They were all taken up when Bill started to install the electric."

"Electric?" she asked. Vaguely she remembered he had once spoken of it.

"Yes. Only the conductors are there. Great solid rods of copper. More treasures to play with!"

It meant nothing to be told that these riches might have been hers if Bill had lived; no matter who owned them, they would always be just museum pieces. And this house, so burdened by them, could never have been her home. Even the servants' rooms had Chippendale chairs, varnished over in sober black. The old man pointed to a rain stain on the ceiling and said, in disgust, "Water."

She found the remark, and his manner, so hilarious that she had to sit down and laugh until she developed a stitch. The tumbler fell into her lap, but not a drop was spilled, for none was left to spill. She had not felt so relaxed, so entirely freed from her grief, since the day of her wedding and widowhood.

"Your own people now . . .?" Hamill said.

He spoke in that vague, upper-class tone which launches a conversation and then leaves it hanging until the sheer tension forces someone to rescue it.

"My father's dead." Her voice seemed to come from far off.

"Ah."

"Four years ago." Or was it more? A lifetime, it seemed.

"And your mother?"

"She went to live in Italy. She said the legacy would last longer there."

"And you stayed behind? So young? What were you then – eighteen?"

She nodded. "We didn't get on at all well, she and I. I wanted to go into nursing anyway.

It was all true and yet it seemed completely unconnected with her – as if she were rehearsing a life story she might easily forget unless she repeated it aloud occasionally. It shocked her to feel so little continuity between herself, here, now, and that old, easygoing way of life before her father died.

"You look as if you need a drink," Hamill said.

"Good lord, no!" She tried to rise but found it harder than she had expected. Then it was pleasant not to rise; she could sit there all night. Why not! There were a lot of things she could do now. Mrs. Troy, not Miss Mitchell. A pleasing drowsiness stole over her.

"Don't move," he told her. "I'll be back in a trice."

But he was even quicker than that for at the door he paused, slapped his head as if it had let him down, and chuckled. "How could I have forgotten!" He went to the fireplace, stooped, and thrust his hand up the chimney. From its dark interior he extracted a soot-coated bottle of brandy. "My reserve commissariat!" He uncorked it. "Hold out your glass."

"No! Certainly not brandy! I would never drink brandy!"

He winked. She realized that the tumbler he had given her in the first place had not been of sherry. He half-filled her glass again. "Can't bear half measures," he said, pouring himself the full tumbler. She determined not to drink a drop.

He drew up a chair and placed it before her, the wrong way around, with its back facing her. He straddled it, leaning across the back and staring intently into her face.

She intended to let him speak first but was surprised to hear her voice saying, "I'm not going to stay here, Uncle Hamill."

His eyes narrowed. "Go on."

Absently she took a sip. She shook her head, hoping the action might dislodge her into some more wakeful state. "I . . . this isn't *me*. None of it is me. I'm just a . . . just somebody's nurse. I didn't marry Bill for this. I didn't even know about it."

He nodded solemnly. "Perhaps it was the other way around? Perhaps *Bill* married *you* for this!"

She gulped air – then, somehow, brandy. He saw she wanted oblivion from this truth and so he took her glass away. Too late.

He went on, almost intoning the words: "Bill understood the real challenge of this place, and he knew he couldn't face it alone. He wasn't truly a military man, no more than I am, no more than any of the Troys are. He was a squire. He loved Pallas. He loved these people. *His* people. But he couldn't face the challenge. The army was an honourable way out for him. Or, rather, it was a convenient postponement."

She glimpsed a parallel in her own life: Bill wasn't really a soldier; she wasn't truly a nurse; for both it had been their only honourable way of leaving home – evading a personal responsibility in the name of some "higher" cause. But her mind was now too fuddled to chase the insight any further.

"Challenge," she echoed. "Challenge." If she could just repeat the words until they sounded foreign . . .

"That was before he met you, Elizabeth. I'm not saying he didn't love you and all that nonsense, but he also saw in you all those qualities that he needed to sustain him if he was to . . ."

"Challenge," she continued to intone, though it came out more like *shallage*.

"Not the neglect you see all around you. That wasn't the challenge. Nor the exhausted tin lode, the run-down farms, the broken walls, the . . . these aren't the real challenge. They're only symptoms of a disease that runs much deeper. D'you know it's name?" He shook her urgently. Her head shook back a passive *no*.

"The disease is called Morwenna. And love. Every Troy who ever lived has loved the Pallas estate; but Morwenna loves it with a passion that outweighs them all. She'd kill for it. I swear to you – she'd *kill* for it. Or die for it. Every stone and every stick of it."

What's wrong with love? Elizabeth asked herself.

"What's wrong with love?" he echoed. Had she spoken aloud without realizing it? Or had he asked it first and she had echoed him? Her mind was spinning.

He went on: "I'll tell you what's wrong with Morwenna's love. It would fill an ocean. But she hasn't no more competence as would fill a teaspoon." He shook his head angrily at this clash between passion and grammar. "You'll think I'm talking nonsense. When you meet her you won't believe it. Hear her give out the orders – you'd think she was born to command. But it's all a delusion. The tragedy is – the tragedy of Pallas – the tragedy of Bill's death – is that she simply can't manage! She hasn't the first idea."

In her deepening stupor Elizabeth was aware of the urgency of his words. There was something desperate about him. How many years had he waited in bitter, drunken frustration to find someone to whom he could unburden these thoughts – someone who might, just might, be in a position to act?

Part of her mind had remained quite sober. It was watching her with a sort of patrician aloofness. It understood all that the old man said, almost before he spoke. It made decisions on her behalf. She could feel strange resolutions – strange to her – growing within, prompted by his conviction.

Something to do with the deserted cottage, and the pump, and the golden sunlight, and . . . what was his name? A. . .? B. . .? C. . .? Alpha . . . and omega.

The room made several adjustments to its own proportions. There was a rustling at the door. Silk? Bombazine? Water?

Water . . . What was that young man's name? A. . .? Adolph? Adorn? Adorable?

Hamill turned toward the door. "Morwenna!" he said in surprise.

Elizabeth heard the surprise more than the name.

"Adonis!" She remembered it at last.

Happy in the haven of that name, she sank into a profound slumber. Unknown to her, the brandy tumbled from her hand, spilled down her dress, and soaked its way through the cheap and worn linoleum of that servant's bedroom floor.

At the door, a towering galleon of Anglican propriety, dressed overall in black, Morwenna stopped breathing. Her nostrils flared. Her lips vanished in a thin blue line of outrage.

Then a more primitive Morwenna asserted herself, the essential female. She looked down at the drunken, stupefied woman at her feet and she smiled without pity.

CHAPTER THREE

AS HAPPENS SO OFTEN with novice drinkers, Elizabeth awoke next morning feeling on top of the world – until the unfamiliarity of the room nudged her with a reminder of where she was and the shame of what had happened. Then she flung herself beneath the sheets and tried not to breathe. The goosedown mattress closed around her.

She made up her mind there and then – she would not stay. She definitely would not stay. How *could* she stay now? She would stay for the reading of the will, and if Bill had been so foolish as to leave her anything, she'd renounce it, beg some small keepsake of his memory, and go back to nursing – to sisterhood, comradeship, order and discipline, to where she was useful and needed.

She breathed again.

Someone was moving around the room; through the single blanket she heard the clatter of mahogany curtain rings. A paler darkness filled the womb of the bed.

Then it turned to hurtful brilliance. Cool morning air, awash with the eastern sun, invaded her space. An astonished voice said, "Oh my gidge!" The coverings fell back upon her. "I'm sorry, missis." It was the voice of a young woman. "You were lying so squashed-like I never seen 'ee there."

Elizabeth began to crawl out into the morning. Her eyes, rapidly growing used to the daylight, took in a woman of about her own age, dressed in the livery of an upper maid. But whatever gentility this threadbare uniform conferred upon her was spoiled by the rolling-up of her sleeves, like a dairy wench. She had the large, strong arms of a country-woman. "You want for me to bring 'ee some hot water, do 'ee, missis?" she asked in an intense voice that was slightly hoarse.

"I prefer to wash in cold, thank you."

The woman nodded. Everything she did was abrupt and full of energy.

"May I ask your name?" Elizabeth ventured.

"Oenone, missis. They do call I Oenone Beckerleg."

Elizabeth wondered why she was not prettier, for certainly each of her features, taken singly, was pretty enough – cupid-bow lips, high cheekbones, a firm chin, and a straight nose with a slight tilt at its tip. Her eyes were enormous, supernatural, filled with a shimmering, watery light; their quiet intelligence contradicted the rest of her appearance, which was wild, boisterous. The overall effect was of a face put together in haste – the sort of face a flamboyant artist might devise on a bad day, when subtlety had deserted him.

"You work here?" Elizabeth asked.

"Not reg'lar. I belong to come here when they do have people staying. They do have only four reg'lars here. Ti'nt like it was."

She spoke with that same abrupt energy, crushing words together, so that 'do have' became 'dav' and 'belong to' compacted into 'blongtuh.' Elizabeth found it a strain to follow; her own replies were delayed while she worked out what Oenone (or 'Nony,' as it came out) must have said.

Oenone was holding up yesterday's travelling dress. "You gwin put this up'gin, are'ee?" she asked.

It took some time for Elizabeth to translate this as: 'You going to put this up again, are you?' – and to decide that 'put up' must be Cornish for 'put on.' By then the maid had repeated her question and added encouragingly, " 'E in't looking too bad. Not really. That's one good thing about black."

Elizabeth noticed her luggage standing over in the window bay; someone must have collected it from Helston. "If you unpack my things, Oenone, you'll find a lighter one among them. I'd say it's going to be another hot day, wouldn't you?"

"Yes. Very likely."

Her 'yes' came out like: 'ace.' She scampered to Elizabeth's one battered trunk and an equally scarred suitcase; to be allowed to unpack them was obviously a privilege.

Elizabeth cringed when she imagined the woman's reaction to her far-from-splendid wardrobe. Her things were new, of course, being all black, but they were very ordinary – like herself. Oenone, however, was delighted with everything she saw, holding each dress and frock up to the light, crushing it with her strong grip, approving it with a vigorous nod that shook her hair about her face, and then thrusting it into the wardrobe. She made none of those smoothing and cosseting gestures that most women make when they hang up clothes or put them on.

Her delight showed in what simplicity she must live.

The silence seemed to unnerve Oenone. " 'Twas some fine old burying," she said at last, prompted, no doubt, by the sight of so much mourning. "I was bailing like a babby, I can tell'ee."

"You knew my husband? Well, of course you must have."

The woman seemed about to say something but in the end she simply nodded. To Elizabeth it still seemed strange to call Bill 'husband.' They had been married less than an hour when he died. "I suppose you heard what happened yesterday evening," she said ruefully.

"Just gabble, missis.'

'I'm afraid it isn't. It's all true. I disgraced myself."

Oenone shook her head. "You shouldn't ought to talk like that," she said uncomfortably. "Begging pardon. But Mr. Oliver, he foxed you, that's how 'twas."

So they *had* all been talking about it.

"Mr. Hamill he done the same to me when I first come here. I wasn't but a little giglet then. Proper flummoxed I was. But Master Bill he said to me, 'Next time now, you spit in the miller's eye!' " She winked.

Elizabeth laughed. "What does that mean?"

The woman took up the pitcher and poured a helping of water into the ewer. "It do mean, put water in it! That's what."

When she left, the room seemed to shrink, as if her vivid presence had pressed the walls apart. Elizabeth washed herself from head to foot in the cool water. Spit in the miller's eye! Who dreamed up such sayings? Briefly she remembered Courtenay Rodda sluicing himself at the pump.

If Bill really had left her a large bequest, perhaps she could come to some arrangement with the rest of the family — exchange her portion for the beautiful cottage and a modest annuity. Yes — the cottage and fifty pounds a year. She could live happily on that. Seventy pounds, perhaps, and then she could keep a maid, too.

Why not Oenone?

She shook her head in annoyance. It was stupid to let such vague plans grow so specific; they were just half-formed wishes. "Half-warmed fishes," her father once said. There was a smile for his memory.

Still, Oenone was a pleasant enough young woman.

How death changes everything! Suppose her father had lived, what would she be doing now? Certainly not standing here, delaying going down to breakfast, her stomach hollow with fear, not just of Morwenna but of the whole upper-class world of property and money and lawyers and estates.

Yet . . . perhaps she *would* be here, doing exactly these things. There's more than one line through life — another of her father's sayings. And it was true.

What if Bill had lived? He would be in his dressing room now, and she would be rising from a bed in which she and he had passed the whole night together. What would that have been like? She remembered the feel of his arms about her; the sensation was sharp, visceral, urgent. It forced the tears past her usual guard. It was the untutored protest of her body at the continuing agony of his absence. The cry of a baby with whom there can be no reasoning. Her lip trembled. She clenched her fists tight, hearing the knuckle-joints crack. Soon she was calm again.

She knew well enough why her mind rambled so, and pretended to wallow in these self-pitying memories. It was to avoid facing that door, to postpone that moment when she would put her hand to its knob, turn it, and parade herself for all the world to stare at: The woman of the ardent spirits!

She searched the room for one more little chore. Her dressing gown! As she crossed the room to hang it up, she caught sight of herself in the tall looking glass on the wardrobe door. In that flash of a glimpse she did not recognize what she saw; the head-to-toe black was still so novel. There was a flurry of bewilderment; the stranger in the glass was, she saw, quite handsome. This unsolicited testimonial pleased her, encouraged her to pause and gaze at herself critically.

Black was becoming to her. It made her pale skin glow; it gave new lustre to her light brown eyes; it showed off her fine auburn hair.

Her hair – that was the only annoyance. It was still in yesterday's bun, wispy and stale. How had she managed to sleep with it knotted there? She pulled a wry face, knowing well enough how. She caught up the wisps in her widow's snood, a reticule of black silk cord, and pinned it into the top of her bun with a dark tortoiseshell comb; she had expected the effect to be schoolmarmy but the iridescence in the comb made it quite chic. More confident than she had felt for weeks, she opened the door.

She could not have picked a worse moment to enter the family's day. They were all at prayer, ranged at the foot of the main stair. Unfortunately she did not become aware of this fact until she made the turn at the halfway landing, by which time it was too late to go back.

Morwenna paused, as if she had been waiting for Elizabeth. "Good morning, Mrs. Troy." Her voice rang up the stairwell. "I trust you are sober again."

Elizabeth had not expected anything so blunt. "I'm sorry if I interrupt your prayers," she answered.

"Oh, the little daily customs of this house need hardly concern *you*."

The entire household was there, even the outdoor servants. All their eyes were upon Elizabeth. Beside her on the landing was a chair, a fine Jacobean carver. She sank into its broad embrace. "Please continue," she said. Fear had made her unable to complete her descent, but anger now put the colour into her voice.

She had a sudden memory of an accident that had occurred during Bill's convalescence. He had taken her to a concert in Brighton; it was the first evening he had kissed her. Someone had come late and the conductor stopped the whole orchestra – they were playing the overture to *The Thieving Magpie* – he just stopped them at full gallop and then turned round and stared icily at the latecomer until the man had found his seat. She remembered watching the poor fellow, feeling for him, both terror and pity; but the man had turned the tables neatly by acknowledging the conductor's snub as if it had been some ultimate refinement of politeness.

The look in Morwenna's eye now was the same as she had seen in the conductor's on that evening. "You had reached the Lord's Prayer, Miss

Troy," she reminded her sister-in-law.

"We shall begin again from the very beginning," Morwenna said. But she was flustered and immediately went on, "Our Father . . ." Later she slipped in an impromptu prayer for "all who cannot resist strong liquors," but the intention was too naked, the tone too querulous. She had lost the first skirmish. The meeting broke up when she snapped shut her prayer book and turned to gaze up at Elizabeth in undisguised malevolence; their eyes dwelled, each in the other's; war was declared. Morwenna turned on her heel and stalked away into the breakfast room.

Elizabeth rose and descended the last flight, feeling no triumph. "You are not forgiven," she told Hamill sternly as she reached the bottom step.

He shrugged and smiled, implying it was of no importance. "You have given me something I shall always treasure."

"Oh?"

"The sight of Morwenna's face when you collapsed all-of-a-heap at her feet." He chuckled at the memory. "I suppose it lulled her."

"*Lulled* her?"

"Well, she must have thought she could eat you for breakfast this morning. Instead you've quite turned the tables on her. You were the bishop, she the chaplain."

"I wonder . . . perhaps that wasn't so clever? Perhaps I should have allowed her an easy little victory?"

He was shocked. "Never! Who said the best defence is to attack? Caesar probably – which shows what a genius he was because he can't possibly have known Morwenna."

They had reached the breakfast-room doorway. "I don't want a fight," she said.

"The choice is not yours."

Again Elizabeth thought of the strange turns one's life can take, quite by chance. She owed her little victory, in part, anyway, to her memory of that Brighton concert. But suppose she had gone on some other evening, never seen that fellow? Morwenna's rebuke might then have crushed her. The war might already be over and she would even now be packing again. Instead, just that one little flash of memory had steered her toward quite a different path; you could even say it had made her (or anyway made her seem) a different person. And now she could not simply turn back and become the other Elizabeth, the one she truly felt herself to be. She had to go forward in this less familiar guise. And thus, from day to day, we make choices that force us to change, to become someone a little different from our true selves. In the end, perhaps, we forget what those true selves once were.

This new, slightly changed Elizabeth now marched boldly over the threshold. Morwenna was helping herself to fish kedgeree. Elizabeth grasped the initiative again. "I suppose we met last night," she said. "Wasn't I a living sermon!"

Morwenna's eyes narrowed but Elizabeth noticed they now held a glint of uncertainty. She went on, "I have never tasted spirits in my life, so I did not even know it was brandy. I was *told* it was wine." She spoke this last remark directly to Hamill, who joined them at that moment. He grinned.

"Wine!" Morwenna said, implying it was every bit as bad as spirits.

"Let's introduce ourselves properly. I'm Elizabeth, Miss Troy, or do I call you Morwenna?"

"I'd prefer Miss Troy."

Now that she was at close quarters with the woman Elizabeth found her self-confidence beginning to ebb. She could see why even Bill had been in awe of his elder sister, quite apart from the fact that she had been both mother and father to him. (Uncle Hamill could hardly have been any kind of paternal substitute.) She was short, grim, and powerful, with a craggy face and scoured, carbolic sort of skin. She was a fortress under perpetual siege. Her mouth opened like a portcullis, her lungs snatched at the air. Her eyes were small, coal-black, restless; set deep in their sockets they patrolled the very air for insults.

Elizabeth looked away and said, "Yes, I knew wine was all right because it was Bill himself who introduced me to it."

A tall, thin, elderly woman, also in deep mourning, entered the room. "You must be Aunt Petty?" Elizabeth said, going to her and offering her hand.

The old lady took it. With a kindly smile she plucked Elizabeth nearer and offered her cheek for a kiss. "Elizabeth, my dear — welcome to Pallas! But in what dreadful circumstances — poor child, I've been feeling so sorry for you."

"We all share that sorrow," Elizabeth pointed out awkwardly, feeling that her brief acquaintance with Bill, however intense, did not entitle her to any share in *their* loss, which was the accumulation of a lifetime.

In a way, Aunt Petty answered those doubts. "True," she said, "but in our case the grief is added toward the end of lives that are already long and filled with a due share of other sorrows and joys. For you . . . after your father's death, too . . . it must . . ."

"We've been delayed quite enough already," Morwenna snapped. "If we are to engage in this empty chitchat, let us at least do it while we eat."

Aunt Petty gave Elizabeth an apologetic smile. They took up their lukewarm plates and helped themselves. Elizabeth speared one sausage too many and offered it tentatively to Aunt Petty; the old lady looked up at her and nodded eagerly, as if such kindness were rare and had to be snapped up.

They went over to the table. "When my father died," Elizabeth told her, "I sometimes thought I should never smile again. Even though, on the very evening of his death, I went out for a walk with my best friend. It was a Tuesday, you see, and we always walked out on Tuesdays and it simply never occurred to me *not* to do so on that evening. And we even bounced an

indiarubber ball, she and I, which we always did as we walked. Neverthe-less, a day or two later, when the full meaning of his death had entered me –
then I thought I should never smile again. Yet within three years I met Bill
. . . and . . . I'm sorry – am I talking too much?"

Morwenna grunted. "You kept us waiting long enough, I must say."

"I'm sorry about that. When I saw the name Pallas Halt, I forgot all
about the arrangement to meet in Helston, and . . ."

"I don't mean that. I mean for the reading of the will. It's ridiculous."

Aunt Petty intervened. "Talk all you want, my dear. 'Tis a sovereign
tonic against the 'melon colics,' as we call it down here. And you'll laugh
again, never fear."

"I have done, I'm afraid – only this morning – here in this house,
despite all its associations."

"Hilarity . . ." Morwenna began.

"Not hilarity," Elizabeth corrected. "Mild amusement, perhaps. It was
something the maid said. 'Spit in the miller's eye!' She told me Bill . . ."

"What a coarse creature she is," Morwenna said.

"It was a saying Bill told her," Elizabeth continued. Then she turned
and stared straight at Hamill. "The occasion bore more than a passing
resemblance to what happened last night, I may say."

Aunt Petty nudged Hamill and giggled. "A spit in the eye for you, my
lad!" She glanced nervously at Morwenna as she finished.

That glance spoke volumes to Elizabeth. Aunt Petty lived absolutely
at the pleasure of Morwenna; so, too, did Hamill in his different way.
Morwenna was their daily weather.

When breakfast was nearly done, Hamill turned to Elizabeth and
asked, "Shall I show you the woods and the original Wheal Pallas – the tin
mine?"

"The richest five acres on earth!" Fragments of last night's conversa-tion were beginning to return to her.

"You remember!"

Elizabeth was serious again. "The first thing I want to do, before any
of that, is to go into Helston and visit Bill's grave."

"Of course, I'll take you," he volunteered at once.

"Don't think me ungracious, Uncle Hamill, but I'm sure you'll
understand if I say I'd prefer to go alone?"

He nodded. "Well, I'll drive you forth and back, anyway."

Morwenna said nothing. She popped a forkful of rice into her mouth
and chewed it endlessly. All the while she watched her sister-in-law.

Elizabeth was intrigued to discover that she was much less unnerved
by Morwenna's actual hostility, face to face, than ever she had been by her
fears of the woman over these past weeks. She even found herself wondering
whether she really wanted a friendship to grow between them.

Never before, in all her life, had she entertained so cold a speculation.

CHAPTER FOUR

BILL'S GRAVE was to one end of the Troy family plot, a simple mound of new-laid turf. The headstone was not yet carved; only a rude cross of oak stating "William Carter Troy: 1860–89" marked the site of the burial Elizabeth had been too ill to witness. She stood on the churchyard slopes, staring at the ground, and was overcome again by the grief that had almost killed her when the kindly evasions of her doctors and nurses had first alerted her to his death.

There was a dreadful space in her universe, a monstrous, aching emptiness which he and he alone should fill. That absence of him was more real – more solid, in a way – than anything else in her life. It was a treacherous shoal of the mind, a mountain whose long shade fell over each of her days.

She looked up and down the valleyside, framed in narrow slices between oaks and elms and one young Monterey pine. A trick of the vertical perspective caused fine houses and gardens to rise side by side with the garrets and humble cottages of the poor. The day was fine and summery, full of windy bluster in the skies above but sheltered here below. The scene was beautiful. In a remote, abstract sort of way she could appreciate its beauty; but the whole, sunstruck little town was only half-real beside the bodily hurt of her emptiness.

On the other hand . . .

The very fact that only now, standing beside the eloquent mound of clay, did her grief recover all its primal strength showed, paradoxically, how much it had faded over these last weeks of her convalescence. Weeks! It seemed years already. Yet it *was* only weeks, and it *had* needed the actual sight of his grave to revive that portion of her sorrow which had already begun to wither.

Even now, as these thoughts passed through her mind, they worked a delicate alchemy, changing mourning to mere sorrow, hinting that nothing can endure – neither the love that is sworn for ever, nor the grief whose bite seems deeper than the grave itself.

With these thoughts hovering at the rim of her mind, the very act of turning from him was itself a new treachery. She lingered then, wanting desperately to recapture those feelings that had come flooding back the moment she found the grave. "Oh Bill," she whispered. "What did you want of me? What am I to do now?"

The question revived memories of her meeting yesterday evening with Courtenay. For no reason at all she remembered his saying, "And yet you chose nursing" – as if that demonstrated some especially fine quality in her.

"You all think I'm so good and fine," she said bitterly. "But I am not! Whatever you may have thought of me . . . whatever you may expect of me now, I'm not equal to it."

The answering silence trapped her. The breeze nudged at her arm like an unseen finger, dismissing her from this audience with her grief. "I can't do it," she said as she turned and made her way back to the gate, where Hamill waited patiently at the reins of the dogcart. She noticed many graves of young children as she passed, some quite elaborate and all dating from the last half century. Had children become more precious lately, to be memorialized so expensively? Or had such deaths been too commonplace to mark in former times?

Hamill looked like a retired colonial governor in his white drill suit and panama hat. The black armband was a tenuous link between him and her and this doleful place and business. How far could she trust him, she wondered.

"Let's go back to Pallas," she said as he helped her up into the cart.

"You don't call it home, yet." With his tongue he clicked the pony to a walk. "Did Bill never mention coming back here and managing the estate?"

"In a way," she agreed reluctantly. "He hinted at it. You know how Bill always talked in tiny short sentences. Getting everything out backwards." She smiled despite herself and her mood. "I used to tell him he added words to his conversation the way a grocer shakes flour into the scales."

Hamill laughed. "That's very good." He patted her knee, an old man's privilege. "You'll be everything Bill hoped for, Elizabeth. He was never wrong about people."

The burden of his expectations fell heavy upon her. All of them expected so much; a dwindling creature called Elizabeth was drowning in the rising tide of all their needs.

The picture of the lodge came into her mind. If she did stay, she'd certainly move in there rather than face endless breakfasts like this morning's, pegging out her life in ghastly looks and silences.

She suddenly remembered that she had dreamed of Courtenay Rodda last night. The dream itself did not come back to her now; but hints of its quality surfaced – enough to make her flinch from further probing.

Hamill took the long way home so as to show her something of Helston. First they went to the very bottom of the town, a marshy stretch of land full of hovels, some of which had been cleared to make way for the new gasworks; its half-filled holders reared over one end of the ancient market. Dawns were late, dusks early, in that narrow valley.

They crossed the Cober, a mere stream, depleted by summer drought but still flowing. Southward it widened until, in the distance, she could see a great sheet of water confined by green and steeply sloping hills. Plantations of spruce and fir gave it a Canadian aspect.

He followed her gaze. "You'd never believe it, but the sea is just out of sight around the corner there," he told her.

She was surprised. It had such a freshwater smell, a green, damp, unforgettably summery smell. "That can't be the sea?"

"It used to be. Somewhere under all these marshes, I suppose you could find the remains of quite a substantial little harbour. Backalong in the Middle Ages, Helston was a seaport. We got our charter from King John in 1201. We bribed him, of course. Caught him at a weak moment out hunting in Dorset. This town's always been run by crooked knaves and villains. We used to send two members to parliament. A right-down regular rotten borough."

"But what happened to the seaport?"

"A great sandbank called the Loe Bar happened. I'll take you to see it one day soon. The autumn gales are a splendid time. The power of the sea! In a single night, they say, it swept up a great bar of sand, high as a house — higher — a mile long, easily, and almost half a mile wide. Completely barring the mouth of the river. Millions of tons! The power of Nature, eh!"

"Why doesn't it flood?" She pointed back at the stream, which was flowing quite swiftly.

"It does sometimes. In spring usually. There's a ceremony whereby the burghers take three halfpence to the lord of the manor and beg permission to cut open the Bar. It's quite a sight. The water flows out in a great swollen river that stays intact, in the midst of all the salt water, as far as the Scilly Isles — forty miles or more. The islanders can see the different colour of it and one of them told me he'd caught freshwater trout in it — right out there in the Atlantic!"

She noticed then that several of the doors had high thresholds of stone cemented between the jambs. People stared incuriously out from the dark interiors. A few curtseyed or touched their caps.

There was a special Cornish sort of face, she realized — short, dark, powerful — elfin at one extreme, Spanish-looking at the other. It grew brown and wrinkled early in life; the men developed craggy eyebrows and a sidelong way of *not* looking at you. She was surprised at the number of men around in the middle of the morning.

"Is there not much work to be had?" she asked Uncle Hamill.

"Mines seem to close each week. 'Knocked,' they call it. And the agricultural depression is endless. The miners can go abroad, to America or South Africa or somewhere. Australia. There's always work for a good Cousin Jack. But what can a farm labourer do?"

She looked again at the hovels clustered around the gasworks and wondered what it must be like to come home to such a place with not a penny in your pocket and not a crust in the cupboard. She shivered.

"Come to think of it," he said, "one of the Troys must have been among the first Cousin Jacks – my great-uncle, and Bill's – James Troy. He wasn't a working miner of course but he knew the mining business backwards. Worked all over North and South America."

"D'you keep in touch with them?"

"Sadly not. I know he had a son, called 'Willy Boy' Troy, can you believe it! A bit of a wild man by all accounts. But we've heard nothing of that branch for, oh, fifty years."

"That's sad."

Above the market place the way rose on a steep curve to the left, bounded on that side by a long, high wall of whitewashed stone. Beyond it a herd of cattle waited patiently to be let out to pasture. Hamill said, "That's Joel Tregembo. Late with his milking. Late to save his hay. One day he'll be late for . . ."

He left it unsaid, remembering the day and its business. At the bottom of Coinagehall Street, the main street of the town, he pointed to a Gothick folly that formed an archway onto the bowling green. "A memorial to one of the most crooked men in the history of this crooked town," he told her. "I was fifteen when he died. I can just remember him. If he swallowed a nail, they said, it'd come out a screw."

The name carved there was Humphry Millett Grylls.

'What did he do?" she asked.

"He was a lawyer." Hamill spoke as if that were sufficient in itself to support his judgement. "When the Gundry brothers spent too much on the old Wheal Vor mine, young Grylls handled their bankruptcy. Or that's what he was supposed to do. In fact, he secretly bought out all their shares – leaving them with the debt, their creditors with nothing to claim against, and himself and friends with what turned into one of the most profitable mines in Cornwall's history! Oh, a real *Helston* man was Lawyer Grylls!"

"You sound as if you've lost a lot of money in your time, Uncle Hamill."

He laughed. "Touché! My father was one of the creditors. I inherited the claim. The lawsuit lasted thirty-four years!"

"*How* long?"

"Thirty-four years. Until 1850. Judgement was in our favour, but there was nothing left. Nothing workable, anyway. The Grylls faction *raped* that mine. There's no other word for it. They clawed two million pounds' worth of tin out of the ground, but there's twice as much still buried down there. They worked in such haste, you see – to grab it all before judgement could prevent them – they left the mine too dangerous to work."

"Thirty-fours years!" She shuddered.

"A lawyer's paradise."

On up Coinagehall Street they went, avoiding the deep granite kennels, or gutters, at each side, which channelled the tiny Helston "River" down the hill and round the market to join its greater cousin, the Cober. "It used to be no more than an open sewer," Hamill told her. "But the new Board of Works have taken off the drainage and there are even people who drink it now."

Halfway up the street he reined to a halt opposite the brand-new Wesleyan chapel, gaunt and classical.

"Christianity has ruined the Celts," he said.

"Helped by the lawyers," she reminded him.

"Oh, we can survive without money. As the latest recruit to the Troys, you'll soon learn that. But we can't live without our spirit — that Celtic flame." His eyes searched hers. "I wonder if you'll learn that, too?"

"I'm not a Celt."

"You are, you know. I can always tell. You have the blood and bearing of a Celt." His mood changed, lightened. "Talking of money" — he turned to the building facing the chapel — "we Troys bank here. You might as well come in and meet the local agent. A decent fellow. Name of Vivyan."

Bolitho's Bank read the legend over the door.

"Colonel Bolitho owns the Trengwainton estate over to Penzance," he added as he helped her down.

The door was ajar, the bank completely deserted. Flies buzzed; piles of coin lay upon the tables; a cat napped in the window. She thought Hamill was going to stroke it but when he reached the window he ignored the animal and, staring out into the garden, broke into a grin, saying, "Thought as much. Come and look at this."

She joined him.

The sunlit garden was a blaze of roses. Among them, to judge by his clothes, stalked Mr. Vivyan, syringe in hand.

"Carries off all the prizes," Hamill explained.

Vivyan looked up and saw them, guilt moderating to a smile. "You want anything?" he called, dimly heard through the glass.

Hamill raised the window in a screeching of sash pulleys; the cat bolted. "Just to introduce you to Mrs. Troy," he replied. "But another time will do."

Vivyan bowed. "How d'you do, Mrs. Troy. I hope you've recovered?"

"Almost completely thank you, Mr. Vivyan. What beautiful roses."

He shook his head in despairing disagreement. "If they shut down any more mines or smelters we might as well give up." Seeing her frown he added, "Mildew. Are you sure you don't want anything?"

"No hurry." Hamill turned to go.

"You may leave the window open," Vivyan said.

As they went to the door Elizabeth chuckled. "I thought he was going to say, 'If you want any cash, just help yourselves.'"

"But that's exactly what he would have said."

They went back into the street, leaving the door ajar.

At the top of the town, where the way divides into Meneage and Wendron streets, she asked, "Is that the Coinage Hall?"

He looked at her askance. "That's the Corn Market. Good heavens — that was built in *my* time. You'll be asking me next what I did in Noah's Flood. The Coinage Hall has gone. They pulled it down to make way for the Grylls Memorial among other things."

He went on to explain how the tin miners used to be like a nation-within-a-nation, with their own parliament and laws and even their own money.

"How d'you know all these things, Uncle Hamill?" she asked.

"In my youth . . . ." he began jocularly but then fell silent. A wistful look crept into his eyes. "Usually by this time," he went on in quite a different voice, "I've had at least three drinks."

"Instead of which . . .?"

"Not one."

"And you've only just realized it?"

He nodded in surprise.

"But that's good, surely." She touched his arm. "You were saying — in your youth . . .?"

The wistful look intensified. "A long time ago," he said. "Too long."

CHAPTER FIVE

THEY DROVE THE DOGCART straight round into the stable yard and entered the house by way of the kitchen, washing their hands in the scullery. It was not Elizabeth's idea of life in a grand house at all — especially when she saw the blackboard on which the day's menu was supposed to be written out for the cook. Near the bottom a feeble hand — Aunt Petty's no doubt — had scrawled, "Luncheon: parsley pie?" A bolder hand had crossed out this hesitant suggestion in several slashes of chalk, and then, in a script that could only be Morwenna's, it had written "Starry-gazey pie."

I'm like that, she thought. *A blackboard on which other people chalk up their commands, wishes, desires.*

Pilchard pie it was — and a poor one, too. It was served by Polglaze, the old butler, who, on the evidence of his fingernails, had spent the morning in the potting shed.

"Well now, Mrs. Troy," Morwenna said as soon as they were seated, "tell us all about yourself. Your people are from Malvern, I believe?"

There was a warning glint in Hamill's eye. *But what am I to do?* Elizabeth wondered. *If she's pleasant, I've got to be pleasant back.*

"We don't really 'come from' anywhere in that sense, Miss Troy. My mother's family was from Yate near Bristol and my father was from Wotton-under-Edge, which is more towards Gloucester. He was a veterinary surgeon."

"A horse doctor."

"All sorts of animals," Elizabeth said evenly. "He had a way with them all. But he died four years ago when I was eighteen and . . . well, my mother and I never saw eye to eye so I left home and then, through a colleague of my papa's, I trained as a nurse. And that's all, really. Until I met Bill. I suppose he told you about that in his letters home."

"Did Bill ever mention our mother?"

"I'm afraid not, Miss Troy."

"No . . . of course he hardly knew her – no more I suppose than he knew you. I was all the mother he had. I'm sure he told you that much?"

Elizabeth nodded.

"I got on very well with *my* mother. She was never an entirely *well* woman. She needed constant attention, but I never begrudged it. She ought not to have had Bill, not so late in life. She was almost forty. I was eighteen myself then. Mama lingered on for three years but that dreadful confinement was what led to her final decline. However, as I say, I never begrudged it." She fell into a brief reverie but, with a sudden, impatient gesture, snapped herself out of it. She stared intently at Elizabeth. "Some women get on well with their mothers. Some don't. I imagine you've always got on better with *men*, Mrs. Troy."

"Do you really? I can't think why." Elizabeth could stomach no more of the fish pie. Perhaps what Morwenna said was true, though. All the men she had nursed claimed she was a real chum. She'd always found it easy to talk with men – and without having to flirt or be coy or stoop to all those other tricks she'd seen her colleagues use.

"I expect all you nurses were simply thrilled when Bill was brought in," Morwenna said with the sort of warmth that invites woman-to-woman confidences.

"Not especially." Elizabeth stirred uneasily.

"Come!" Morwenna chided, but still in a tone of teasing banter. "You at twenty-two and still on the shelf? And he a big landowner? Proprietor of several mines? Master of Pallas and all its treasures? And a bachelor into the bargain! Surely now . . ."

"I can't answer for the others, but for myself, I did not realize until yesterday what sort of estate he owned. In fact, I still don't – except that I know it's bigger than anything he ever mentioned. From the way he spoke, I imagined a crumbling mansion, a home farm, and one or two tenants."

Morwenna's surprise suggested that this was hardly the Bill she had reared. "So he said nothing to alert you to the sort of life he was inviting you to share? Not one single word?"

Elizabeth tossed her head angrily. "He knew I loved him, not his lands. He knew I'd have married him if all he owned was four acres and a cow."

With apparent reluctance Morwenna said, half to the air, half to anyone who cared to listen, "He can't have meant you to play much of a part here at Pallas, then."

"Or he was absolutely sure of her," Hamill pointed out.

Their tone was so light they might have been discussing the amusing quirks of some distant kinsman.

"Of course he was sure of her!" Morwenna conceded indulgently. "Bill was absolutely sure of every woman he ever fell for. Dozens of them. Even that Beckerleg creature."

"Don't be absurd," Hamill said crossly.

Morwenna's smile chalked up one more petty victory.

Elizabeth racked her brains for something crushing to toss into the other pan of their conversational scales.

Morwenna turned to her. "What d'you suppose Bill had it in mind for you to do, my dear?"

Taking her tone from them, casually, lightly, as if it were very hard for her to recall something so trivial, she replied, "Now that you mention it, I seem to remember his speaking about coming down here and taking up the reins of the estate. He said it was in a lamentable condition . . ."

"I'm sure he said no such thing," Morwenna snapped.

"Indeed, I remembered the words yesterday – the moment I saw that pile of rubble which obviously used to be our main gate."

Morwenna rose and went to the window, throwing it up with a force that took one of the sashcords by surprise; a great loop of it was left trapped at the pulley. For a moment Elizabeth thought, *She's going to throw me out!*

The sashcord parted and the counterweight fell with a heavy thud inside its wooden casing.

"*You* did that!" Hamill said as one fractious child might speak to another. "*You* broke it."

Morwenna swept from the room, almost knocking over Polglaze, causing him to slop a very runny apple charlotte down his suit. He brought the remains of it dripping to the table.

"We don't want that muck," Hamill said. "You can have it out in the servants' hall."

"We shan't want'un eaither," Polglaze said bluntly.

"Give it to the horses then."

The butler's sniff indicated he expected the same sort of response in the stables. But Hamill wasn't listening. He looked straight at Elizabeth and said, "Let's go and inspect the property, eh?"

Aunt Petty, who had sat silent through it all, suddenly said, "Isn't it nice to see some life returning to the house!"

The trees were tall in the valley bottom, reaching for the light. Beneath them they left a cathedral of green air, cool and calming.

"She doesn't often storm out like that," Hamill said. "I think she's met her match in you."

"I take no pleasure in that, Uncle Hamill. She means nothing to me."

"Bill would have been proud of you."

"But he was anyway – as I was proud of him. Were there 'dozens' of other girls?"

"Of course not. Morwenna resented even the few there were."

"And 'the Beckerleg creature'?"

"Puppy love. Did you never sigh after the lad who came round with the milk churn?"

Close to the house the undergrowth was kept somewhat at bay and the woods were open and easy; but farther up the hill the brambles and solomon's seal and snowball bushes had re-established their ancient dominion, forcing the two walkers to keep to one narrow path. Here, too, where the winds blew more fiercely in winter, the trees were stunted and the spreading canopy of green fell to little above head height.

"I remember walks in the Malvern woods when I was young," she told Hamill. "I was no higher than this undergrowth. I used to run and run through it, frightening myself to death, pretending I was lost for ever and ever."

"The same with me!" Hamill answered. "Through these very woods."

"I was never a well-behaved child. I wish we didn't always have to be so decorous when we grow up."

"Who says we do?" Hamill asked truculently. He paused beside an ancient oak. "There's power and magic in all these trees – in everything that grows. We're losing the feel for it in our obsession with being decorous."

"Did you live at Pallas, then, Uncle Hamill? Did you grow up here?"

"No, I grew up at Wheal Leander. The old house."

The direction of his gesture made Elizabeth ask, "Is that the cottage I saw yesterday, in my wanderings?"

"Yes – the villa." He corrected her. "That's the new place. Wheal Lavender. Bill's mother built it and renamed it that. She didn't like the old hunting lodge that used to be there – nor the name Leander, for some reason."

"I'd love to live there. It feels such a happy little place. Bill's mother built it, you say? What was she really like? Do say she was a happy person. I couldn't bear to carry around Morenna's memories of her."

"She *was* happy!" Hamill said, as if that particular aspect of her character had never occurred to him before. "The extraordinary thing is that her name was Elizabeth, too! It never struck me until now. Everyone called her Beth but it was really Elizabeth." He looked quizzically at her. "And she was not unlike you."

"That explains why Morwenna won't call me Elizabeth, of course. D'you mean she was like me to look at?"

"No. But you're alike in temperament. I imagine you'd have quite a sunny temperament – in happier times than these? Local people were heartbroken when she died. Didn't I show you her portrait last night?"

Elizabeth cleared her throat accusingly.

"Remind me when we get back." He took her arm and led her forward once more.

The path wound up over a ridge and then down again. The thick undergrowth made conversation difficult. At the bottom of the next small valley, where the growth was sparser and they could walk at ease again, she said, "It's all very Ancient Greek, isn't it? Troy and Pallas and Leander."

He explained that it was entirely spurious – invented by old Sir William Troy when he founded the estate. Pallas was really *pellas* – old Cornish for oats. Leander was his corruption of *lantic*, which means pleasant place.

"And Troy?" she asked.

That was corrupted much earlier, probably by some medieval English scribe, in a fit of impatience with all these foreign Cornish words. It was originally *trew-iy* – 'village with three roads.'

"You get it still in the name of Truro," Hamill added, "our county town. One of Bill's ancestors must have been head man of a village at a junction of three roads."

"D'you speak Cornish, Uncle Hamill?"

"No one speaks it, my dear. It's a dead language. But once, in my youth, I made a study of the Celts. We knew how to live in those olden times. We were in touch with . . . things – with the forces that shape life itself. We knew how to tap them, until Christianity ruined us. Especially Methodism."

His intensity made her uneasy. "What does Helston mean?"

"New Court Town. See – I'll bet half the population were lawyers even then! Always the confounded lawyers!"

"I prefer Wheal Lavender to them all. What does *wheal* mean?"

"Tin mine. Literally it means work but it's come to mean tin mine. Almost every tin mine is called Wheal something – Wheal Metal, Wheal Vor, Wheal Fortune, Wheal Rose, Wheal Busy . . . the list is endless." He gave an ironic laugh. "Though the work itself is far from endless! *Wheal* means work for precious few these days, I fear."

They rounded a small thicket of coppiced willow and came upon a stretch of valley quite obviously formed by the hand of man. "Wheal Pallas," he announced.

It was a wild tumbling canyon of bare rock, now half-reclaimed by furze. Hewn channels scarred its walls; here and there some mouldering sluice gate could be seen or the sides of a wooden flume for carrying water from one channel to another. A few dozen paces ahead of them, smothered in ivy, reared a derelict water wheel, still connected to a horizontal shaft that led to a simple machine, half eaten by rust.

"Here's where they crushed the ore," Hamill said, leading her past it. He lifted some wild cotoneaster with his foot and revealed the remains of the machine.

"All driven by that one water wheel," he added. "When I was a young man these were working day and night. They couldn't keep up with it! Yet look at it now – Nature soon reasserts herself." He chuckled and looked sidelong at her. "We can't beat old Nature, eh? Try as we will, she has her way with us all in the end."

"It seems very crude, Uncle Hamill. Did it really extract all the tin?"

"It did not! Between here and the bottom of Helston, where the Pallas stream joins the Cober, there were ten families made a living out of 'vanning' the water for tin. And the last family made as good a living as the first! So there. In some future age, I suppose, people will come back to places like this and make a second fortune out of what we call 'halvans' – waste!" He waved his hand over the landscape.

She followed with her eyes. The richest five acres on earth? It looked like any old stone quarry to her. He must have guessed her thoughts for he said, "In most Cornish tin mines, they're content to follow a lode that may be no wider than a foot or two. And the next-nearest lode made be many fathoms away, off to one side. But here at Wheal Pallas the lode was so strong and masterly, and there were so many bunches of it so close together, that it could be mined open-cast like this. That's rare in Cornwall. In fact, there's only ever been one other – up Wheal Fortune – but that had to close just recently." He pointed vaguely westward.

Elizabeth tried to picture the original contour of the land, but it was hard.

"And what you see here is only half the quarry," he went on. "That wall at the end? That's just a rampart they had to leave – because there's a road above it. See those galleries? Caves, you'd call them. Those are where they mined out the main lode. You may walk quite easily through them and come out the other side."

"And what's there? The three mines that are still working?"

"No. They're over to Carnmeal" – another gesture toward the west. "No, beyond that rampart lies a second open-cast tin mine, bigger even than this. It has solid rock on all four sides and there's a conventional shaft at the far end that leads down to the conventional part of the mine. We're standing on top of a great sponge of rock, you realize? Down below our feet there's a maze of twisting passages and levels. The market died so quickly that men were dismissed between one day's core and the next. Their wheelbarrows and pickaxes, many of them, are down there still, abandoned for ever."

She was eager to see this second quarry. "Can we walk through there now?"

He pulled a face. "*You* may if you wish, my dear. All this sobriety, all these memories of childhood are taking their toll. I'll have a little nap in the ling here. Just listen to that furze popping! It's like a shooting party. Good thing you don't have a hangover."

She looked doubtfully toward the end of the quarry-canyon. "Is it safe?" she asked.

"Till the last trump."

"No collapsed floors or anything like that?"

"I promise. It twists a bit, but it never gets completely dark. There's light coming in from both ends. I once led a pony through."

"And what about the sides? Are they all wet and slimy? Will I ruin this dress?"

Hamill laughed. "Take it off if it worries you."

She looked sharply at him, but he went on laughing. "Come on! You're madam now, not miss. None of us need pretend we're numb from the neck down any longer, eh? Anyway, once you're beyond that bush you could take off every stitch and I'll guarantee you could stand there a week and not a soul would see you. This must be one of the most deserted little corners in the whole county."

The idea intrigued her – the thought that this place could be so wild and unvisited.

"Try it," he suggested. "There's power in the rocks . . . and the wind and the sun. You could soak it up."

"Shall we go back by Wheal Lavender?" she asked. "Is it far?"

He had already ensconced himself among the ling but he sat up again and pointed out a pathway that made a vee with the one that had led them here. "Half a mile that way."

She looked again toward the rampart. "Are you sure you won't come with me?"

He settled himself again. "I'll give you an hour. Then if you're not back, I'll come with a rescue party."

Just as she was leaving him he added, without opening his eyes, "By the way, my dear – don't ever trust Morwenna when she's acting all friendly. I don't suppose I need warn you, though – do I?"

She shrugged uneasily. "Warnings are no help to me, Uncle Hamill. I'm a spur-of-the-moment woman."

He opened his eyes and smiled. "You're a true Celt, Elizabeth." He looked around at the landscape. "There's hope for the old place yet."

His confidence seemed absurd to her. What was she? A twenty-two-year-old little girl who knew nothing of life, blindfolded, standing at the edge of a chasm she could feel but not see. Her innards churned with a fear she could not locate or name.

The way to the galleries led down at first, through a winding gully of bare rock crowned with precarious outbursts of vegetation. As the sunbaked walls enveloped her, she began to feel the loneliness of the place, like a sudden slippage in time. It was soothing. The press of unmade decisions lifted from her. She was the last person alive on earth.

She looked down at her skirts. How *did* those women climb the Matterhorn! She could take them off and no one would see.

As an experiment, with no serious intention behind it, she put her fingers to the buckle; but she found she could not bring herself to undo it, not by a single notch. The sad thought struck her that even if she were truly the last person on earth, she would probably go on wearing all her clothes.

What was freedom, then?

The privilege of remaining in self-ignorance for as long as you wished.

Well at least she could prove her own bravery; she could walk into the dark of the tunnel without flinching. Boldly she scrambled up the final rise of the gully, straight to that black yawn of a mouth. Would she lose heart at the last moment? Some detached part of her settled calmly to observe her own behaviour. A spur-of-the-moment woman.

There were, in fact, several tunnels, all cheek by jowl. At the top of each, like a keystone in an arch, she could see the darker line of the tin lode in the ochre face of the rock. She chose the largest and gave herself no time for second thoughts. She was into the maw of it before her heart began to pound at her own daring; by then she might as well go on as retreat.

Except that if she went on, she'd still have to make a return trip through the tunnel.

Yes, but if she'd done it once, she could do it again. A hundred times. The first time was the biggest hurdle – as with everything else in life.

Uncle Hamill had been right – the tunnel never became completely dark. The last glimmer of light faded behind her; the many-faceted walls were reduced to one single blackness; but then that blackness itself began to be silhouetted against a paleness ahead.

Though the floor was dank and slimy, the walls were for the most part dry. Here and there a change in the echo of her footfall and the rustle of her clothing told her that side galleries ran away from this main tunnel.

She teased herself with imaginary horrors – the ghosts of old miners, wild bears like those bones they found in the Cheddar caves, wolves . . .

Which was the quickest way out? Ahead – yes, it must be, the dark was now quite definitely paler ahead.

. . . spiders, bloated toads . . .

If she screamed, would Hamill hear?

. . . foxes, robbers . . .

Foxes, actually, were quite possible. She paused and listened. Nothing.

She took one further stride. Now even the rustle of her clothes was deafening. She halted again. This time it was no abstract fear. She had heard a real noise. Quite close.

There was a metallic scraping sound, ahead and a little to one side.

A miner, exploring some neglected vein of metal?

A badger, brushing against an old, abandoned implement?

There it was again. Someone or something was in the tunnel ahead of her. For an age she stood there, a human stalagmite. At last she could hold her breath no longer; she let it out. In those confines it rang like an explosion.

"Hello?" a man's voice called.

A familiar voice, too. Relief welled up within her.

"Mr. Rodda?" she answered. "Is that you?"

"Mrs. Troy?"

"Yes − oh yes!"

"Are you all right?"

"Perfectly, thank you. What are you doing here?"

"Trespassing, I suppose."

She laughed − with absurd gusto. "To what end though?"

"I'm a leading light of the Helston Naturalists' Society. I've come down here to do some photography."

"A leading light is just what I need!"

"Here." He began walking toward her.

"What can you possibly photograph in the dark? Minerals?"

"No. In point of fact it's *Rhinolophus hipposideros*. I've discovered quite a thriving little colony of them down here. The first ever found in Cornwall." He was close now. "Can you see?"

"Not yet, but I'm beginning to. You're a sort of dark-dark on pale-dark. If I just stand here awhile . . . these rhino-whatsits, they're not vicious, I trust?"

"Not in the least."

"What are they? Earwigs? Slugs?"

"Bats. The lesser horseshoe bat."

She froze: *bats*!

Dear God − bats!

B a t s!

She could not breathe. She wanted to drop to the floor and creep out with her head somehow buried under her hands, but she could not even move.

Bats – entangling themselves in her hair . . .

Bigger than spiders . . .

Mice were bad enough, but mice that could fly . . .

Her flesh crawled. Her heartbeat seemed to come at her from out of the tunnel walls.

"I say, are you all right?" he asked.

"Just . . . please . . ." It didn't sound remotely like her own voice. "Give me your hand and lead me out."

"But . . ."

"*Please!*"

"Which way?"

"The nearest!" she screamed.

His hand found hers. Never had she been more grateful for the touch of a fellow human.

As he led the way forward, the words began to tumble out of her – how stupid she was being . . . she knew they couldn't really hurt one . . . anyway they slept all day . . . probably even goats were more of a danger . . .

All the while the way grew lighter. At the mouth of the tunnel was a brief, sharp incline.

She was still talking when he raised her up into the daylight. There he turned toward her, pulled her into his arms, and silenced her babble with a kiss.

CHAPTER SIX

COURTENAY MUST HAVE EXPECTED some resistance for when he felt none he relaxed his embrace and held her more tenderly. She was herself surprised at her own compliance; but that internal observer was still watching, unastonished, taking no part.

His lips moved. Gently they began to explore her mouth, the tip of her nose, her cheeks. At one point he seemed about to withdraw; but, without her willing it (or without her *precisely* willing it), she pressed her face to him and kept his contact.

Thus encouraged, he allowed one hand to stray below her waist. She stiffened but his other arm was firm about her and his caress was sure. She felt the beginnings of an abdication within, like the devil-may-care entry of wine into the blood.

Then there was panic. She pushed him away, broke free of him entirely. Her moral will closed around her, as the wild sea around a pinnacle of rock, and she was secure again.

Not until then did she feel angry at herself for her quite irrational fear of bats – angry at him, too, for happening upon her weakness.

In him there was a telltale moment of hesitation. It revealed to her that, for all his outward ardour, he had retained more self-control than she had.

Because there was actually nothing there, within him, to control? She observed him closely now; in his eyes she could see that he was actually considering how to deal with this change in her. It was as if he had no feelings to fall back on, only guesses about the way adults behave. Fascinated, she watched him trying to size her up. She saw the decision arrive as his expression hardened. "Still the little girl, eh?" His tone was pleasant but his gaze was flinty, full of chagrin. The total effect was oddly petulant.

She remembered that embarrassing little talk with Matron, at Guy's: "A lady, my dear, should never allow her passions to carry her away. And that is why it is so necessary only to consort with true gentlemen. For if by some stray chance one finds one's emotions roused to that unfortunate heat, one may always rely upon a true gentleman to protect one from oneself."

The idea had inspired her at the time: *Truly, how smooth and well-ordered is our civilization.*

But now she stared about her, at the rock which civilization had laid bare before it fled, at the debris civilization had abandoned.

"In your *mind*, anyway," he added.

"Pardon?"

"You're a little girl in your mind. But a woman in your body."

She felt her pulse quicken again. "You're the one who's being juvenile."

She meant only to ward him off, to put a distance between them; but then she saw the truth of it. There was, indeed, something eternally *not-grown-up* about Courtenay; yesterday she had thought it no more than provincial uncertainty – something she remembered well enough from her own early weeks in London. But now she saw that the boy in him had never withered, never allowed the adult to take over. It was oddly appealing; she suddenly felt much safer with him.

He ignored her remark. "A wonderful woman," he continued. "A beautiful woman. A real woman." He raised an eyebrow.

She wanted to touch his face. She wanted to kiss him again. To make him shut up. Or grow up. "You," she replied, "are not quite . . ."

'What?"

Not wishing to be unkind, she said, ". . . not quite a gentleman."

He laughed, with genuine surprise. "I am arrogant," he agreed —
with pride, though he pretended to deprecate himself. "I assumed you
knew I was here. In fact, I assumed you came here on purpose to meet
me."

"You did no such thing!" She pushed past him and took a few steps out
into the quarry.

Hamill's description had prepared her for the wildness of the place.
Apart from such occasional strays as herself and Courtenay Rodda, no
human ever ventured here. It had that sanctuary feeling, a little Eden of
tumbled rock and rabbit-mown grass, volunteer sallies and dogwood.

She remembered what Hamill had said about power in the rock, the
elements, about soaking it in. It was pure fancy, of course, yet she could
swear she felt a sudden access of . . . what? Energy. Well-being.

"Why *did* you come here?" he asked, following her.

Despite his shallowness he made the air around him alive; when he
stood near her, to her left or right, that side of her flesh tingled with the
knowledge. "Uncle Hamill told me about it. He brought me here. Actually, he's taking a nap by those stamps. He . . ."

"He keeps a bottle of brandy hidden there."

She stared at him in surprise. "Are you making it up?"

"Many's the raw winter day I've been glad of it."

"The old fox!" She returned her gaze to the derelict mine workings.
"He told me this was once the richest five acres on earth."

"Aha? And that attracted you? Does the thought of wealth attract
you?"

His crassness annoyed her. "Of course not. Quite the opposite. It's
just . . . well, if you learned that someone who was once the most famous
man on earth was now living in a cave on Bodmin Moor, wouldn't you want
to go and visit him?"

"Why did he stop being famous?"

"That's beside the point. It doesn't matter."

"It does to me."

"Very well — he just decided there were better things in life than
money."

"Then I shouldn't be interested."

"You would. Anyone would."

She was walking over the trackless grass of the quarry floor, aiming for
the mineshaft at the farther end — not deliberately, but because there was
nowhere else to go except back into the bat-haunted dark.

"I promise you I shouldn't. What would be the point? The whole
purpose of life is *not* to draw in one's horns — *not* to live like a hermit. Surely
it's to reach out, touch more, experience more, feel more, enjoy more, have
more, love more, hate more . . . *everything* more!"

She laughed. "Where did you read that?"

It was his turn for anger. "It's my own opinion. The old ways are no longer enough."

"Bill wouldn't have agreed with you."

He wanted to remind her that Bill was dead: she could see it in his eyes. There was a pause before he said, "You can't play that card too often."

"This isn't a game, Mr. Rodda. Why d'you always assume I'm playing a game?"

"Of course you are. You're testing me in some way – I can feel it. Anyway – life *is* a game. Life has rules. Life has a purpose. There's supposed to be an Umpire up there, watching our every move. We all take it seriously. We all want to win. What's that if it's not a game, eh?"

She was content not to answer.

Believing he had almost convinced her, he added, "This whole business of growing up – it means realizing that Life is the greatest game there is. Only children think games are mere fun."

Loose shale grated underfoot; a blackbird flew up in ear-splitting alarm.

He went on: "Besides, don't think I can't trump you.". She could hear the smile in his voice. "I know I'm different from Bill. For one thing, *he* believed in marriage."

Of course he wanted her to answer, 'And you don't?' But still she held her peace.

As if she had spoken, he added, "I believe in married women!"

She stopped and turned to him in disappointment. "Oh, I see. *That* sort of game! *Fair* game, eh? Open season. Widows might – I've heard all those jokes. D'you really think it's so simple?"

"No." His smile did not waver. "Grown-up games aren't simple." His fingers closed gently about her elbow as he drew her the last few inches toward him. His lips, close to her ear, touched it softly. She shivered. "You are more ripe for love, for that kind of love, than you can possibly imagine, Beth. I could show you. Together we could discover such wonders!"

"Please don't call me Beth."

He went on grazing her skin with his lips, his warm breathing. If she just stood still and did nothing, said nothing, it might simply happen and she wouldn't have to make any decision. She lowered her eyes. His forearms were lean, wiry, strong. She stared at them, willing all her unspoken, unclaimable decisions into them.

But he just went on kissing her ear and running his fingers with infuriating tenderness up and down the back of her arm. He was waiting for her to agree – she could feel it. Her consent, her partnership, was important to him. He wanted a contract; she, a mere surprise.

She shook free of him then and continued her measured walk toward the farther end. The mineshaft, she now saw, began as a cave in the face of the rock. Ling and furze from the moor above had invaded downward, over a small spill of mine tailings. Their flowers almost sang in the sunshine, white, purple, yellow. The breezeless heat began to feel oppressive.

His voice was again close to her ear, murmuring, "Women don't know what they are without men. You'd be little girls for ever – and quite happy, too. Like poor Petty."

His words seemed neither true nor untrue; they were the mere embroidery of a passion she had accidentally blunted for him and could not now discover how to sharpen again.

The floor of the cave sloped steeply down to a sort of rocky vestibule where, out of sight, the mineshaft proper began. He proved it by prying loose a small boulder with his toe. It went smoking down the slope and then fell in a hail of cavernous echoes, culminating in a resounding splash many seconds later.

"That's the level of the adit," he said, "twelve fathoms beneath here. I'm trying to compile records of all the old mines before they pass beyond living memory. People look on me as quite the local expert. Already, you know . . ."

'What's an adit?"

"A horizontal tunnel driven into a mine to allow it to drain out into the nearest valley."

"Like lancing a boil."

"If you say so! When a mine is working they pump the floodwater up to the adit. It's cheaper than pumping it all the way up to grass." He threw in a second stone, again those reverberations and a great hollow splash. "That's the level where it drains out into the Pallas valley. The shaft continues on down for another hundred and fifty fathoms. All flooded now, of course."

The dying reverberations still shook the air around them.

"Tell me how you feel," he said.

"What about?"

"You know what about. Behaving like grown-up men and women."

After a pause she said, "I don't think it's a fit subject for conversation."

"Oh, well done!"

She went on staring into the dark of the cavern; every detail of the rock was crisp and yet, like his words, meaningless. Her answer to his question had surprised her; she was glad he had picked up none of its nuances.

He threw a twig down the shaft but it lodged before it even reached the vestibule. "You may think you're being honest, but you're not."

"Oh, Mr. Rodda, what a demigod you are! Is there anything you don't know?"

He took hold of her arm again, roughly now, making her face him. "Did you just drift into marriage, as you seem to drift into everything else?" he asked. "Didn't you think about it at *all*?"

This time no answer occurred to her. His silence laid the thought like a gauntlet between them.

His expression softened. "You'd better make your mind up to it, Beth. In the eyes of the world Miss Elizabeth Mitchell died on the same day as Bill. You can no longer hide yourself in her skirts."

She looked back along the quarry floor. "If I don't go back soon, Uncle Hamill will send out a rescue party."

He stood aside and made an ironic I'm-not-stopping-you gesture. She hesitated. "I'll see you through the tunnel," he promised. "If that's still frightening you."

As they walked back across the quarry floor he asked, "What d'you think of the Dragon, then?"

"We didn't get off to a good start. Where are your photography things, by the way?"

"The side galleries down in that tunnel are a natural darkroom. She'll never let go of any bit of Pallas, you realize. No matter what the will says. Nor the law. Not even if God himself put fiery angels at the gateway. She'll never loosen her grip on it."

"You're probably right."

"How does it make you feel? D'you want to fight it or turn your back on it all?"

"I don't want any of it. I still feel more numb than anything. I want to wake up and discover that Bill's still alive."

When he failed to answer, she turned to look at him. There were tears in his eyes – not enough to fall but enough to enlarge and darken them.

"What should I do then?" she asked. "Fight or run?"

He took a deep breath and recovered himself. "I was going to warn you . . . if it comes to a fight with Morwenna – well, your habit of drifting may be all very well, but not within a hundred miles of *that* woman. She'll just destroy you."

She nodded morosely and turned to continue their stroll.

He asked, "When's the reading of the will?"

"Tomorrow afternoon, I think." They arrived at the mouth of the tunnel.

"Well, if you need any advice . . . or help of any kind . . ."

She hesitated, staring into the dark. He misunderstood. "The game's over for today," he promised. "You can be the ghost of Miss Mitchell one last time. But leave her in there, eh?" He nodded at the tunnel.

She raised a hand to his cheek, meaning to touch it with her fingertips; but at the last minute her fingers lacked the courage and curled away, so that she actually caressed his jawbone with her knuckles – a gesture that was somehow patronizing rather than tender.

He frowned and backed off.

Because there was no way of explaining her action, she was committed to justifying it instead. "You know nothing about me," she said, wondering what she was going to say next, for this was a distillation of her blood rather than of her thoughts. "I shall never simply say to you, 'I'm ready.' I shall never appear before you and say, 'Now!' . . ." She broke off in dismay, for these notions were the very last she wished to convey to him.

He relaxed and smiled. Angry with herself, she turned and stepped into the dark – never mind the bats. But the swiftness of it confused her, as if she had suddenly gone blind in a world that was still awash with sunlight. Her hands groped wildly for the walls.

"Here." He pushed past her. "Give me your hand."

One final kiss, she thought, would drown so many confusions. But no kiss came. Moments later they were standing beneath the farther edge of the rampart, still hand in hand, blinking out at the day.

"Thus cave-man to his earliest dawn . . ." he began jokingly, making it sound like a quotation. But then the words seemed to evoke some memory in him and he broke off.

"What?" she asked.

He was looking at her with a ruminative stare. "I wonder."

"What?" she repeated.

"Should I show you? Would someone else point it out? In what circumstances? Or would you find it for yourself?"

From time to time he glanced at the rock above her head. She followed his gaze and there, half lost among the cobwebs and the stains of time, she saw a scrawl of letters burned upon the overhang with a smoky candleflame. In the middle there was a crudely drawn heart and Cupid's arrow. To its right was Wm. Troy. And the name to the left – or its initials, rather – was Oe. B.

"Well, you'd have noticed them anyway," Courtenay said defensively. "If not today then tomorrow . . . or sometime."

She looked at him and laughed. "Puppy love, Mr. Rodda. Childhood games . . . and you're still playing them. Really!"

CHAPTER SEVEN

Do you know a man called Courtenay Rodda?" Elizabeth asked Oenone Beckerleg the moment she appeared the following morning.

The maid, who was drawing back the curtains, hesitated; then she pulled with a vigour that was startling even for her. "He's some clever fellow," she said. On her way to the wardrobe she added, "So they do tell I."

"He's a photographer?"

Oenone frowned. "He do own the Helston *Vindicator*."

"A local newspaper?"

The woman nodded.

"Where does he live?"

"Over to Wendron. Well, not hardly so far as Wendron. This side a bit. He do have that big house up above Coverack Bridges. Well, the house isn't hardly *that* big, but still 'tis bigger'n where he was reared." She gave a bark of a laugh.

Elizabeth noticed that the woman had the same habit as Bill of making a positive statement and then immediately qualifying it with something more vague. Had she learned it from him? Or he from her? Or was it a general Cornish mannerism? "Does he live alone?" she asked.

"He do have a sister called Lilian. About eighteen she is."

She wanted to ask about the cupid's heart and initials smoked onto the tunnel mouth at Wheal Pallas but did not know how to broach the topic. When Bill was twenty, Oenone would have been thirteen or fourteen. Too big a gap for puppy love, surely? What about twenty-two and sixteen? Wouldn't he, at least, have been too old by then?

Besides – did it matter any longer?

"I met Mr. Rodda yesterday," she said, making a pause before she added, "over at Wheal Pallas. He was taking photographs of birds."

Oenone turned and looked at her, hesitantly, as if she had at least three things to say and couldn't decide which. At last she said, "Him and Master Bill always belonged to play there. Though there was half a dozen years between them, they always seemed closer, somehow."

"Only they?" Elizabeth asked. "No one else? It seems absolutely

deserted now. Where do the other children play? Where did you play when
you were young? Over there?"

The woman snorted and shook her head, but not, Elizabeth thought,
as if she were saying *no* . . . more as if she found the crowded memories too
complex to unravel. Then she sniggered. Or, rather, she made what in a
woman of more refinement would have been a snigger; with Oenone one
just couldn't tell. Everything about her was so abrupt and energetic.

"So he and Master Bill were great friends then?" Elizabeth asked.

Again that slightly baffled shake of the head – and something new: a
hunted look in her eye. "Two of a kilter, they were," she said. "Silly as a
pair o' waggon 'osses."

"In what way, Oenone?"

"My dad, he always said if they wasn't high-quarter folk they'd of been
put to the assize scores o' times."

Elizabeth laughed, to encourage her. "What sort of things did they
do?"

"May games. Tormentin' folk, mostly. There wasn't no harm in it.
'Twas only daw-brained ol' carrying-on. Not just out Wheal Pallas, mind.
Everywhere."

"I suppose they grew out of it though."

Oenone picked up yesterday's dress. "You going to put this up again,
ar'ee, missis?"

"Yes. That's only a bit of rock dust. It'll brush off. You may put the
underskirt and things to be washed."

Oenone went at the brushing with her customary vigour. A swarm of
dust and black lint flew into the morning sunbeams, causing Elizabeth to
sneeze.

When she was dressed and on the point of leaving the room she asked,
"When were you last out at Wheal Pallas, Oenone?" She searched keenly for
a trace of embarrassment, but there was none.

"Why I don't s'pose I bin out there . . . well, five, six years." She
brightened. " 'E's a proper handsome place for a picnic!"

"That's what I thought. Even on a windy day you could shelter there
and be warm if there was any sun. Perhaps before this summer's out we'll go
there. The only thing I don't like is those tunnels. I'm sure they've got bats
in them."

"And more!" Oenone laughed.

"Oh?"

The maid licked her lower lip. "That's where they couranting couples
do go!"

"I see!" A thought struck Elizabeth. "And you haven't been there for
five or six years, you say!" She smiled teasingly. "Poor you! Or is that
unfair?"

Oenone sniggered again. "Got no call to go out there – not no more.

Anyway, there's as good places close home."

Elizabeth realized that nothing short of a direct question was ever going to resolve her doubts. "And good young men, too?" she asked.

Oenone tossed her head. "I wouldn't go short o' company anytime I'd a mind to it. Which in't often."

"How fortunate for you."

And there, for the moment, Elizabeth's inquiries had to rest.

At half past two that afternoon Mr. Coad, of Coad & Coad, Solicitors, Wendron Street, Helston, was announced; he was shown immediately into the morning room. He was in young middle age. When Elizabeth entered the room he was standing in the window bay staring morosely at the lawn. He was not fat but a certain plumpness swelled his waistcoat. Aunt Petty, who was just ahead of Elizabeth, turned and said, "I like a man to carry a little *importance* before him."

Elizabeth was introduced to Mr. Coad; condolences were offered. Against the fashion he was clean-shaven, like Courtenay; perhaps it was the local fashion among the younger men. He had a round face with full lips and restless, observant eyes, the sort of man, Elizabeth decided, who would miss little of what went on around him – and involve himself less.

Morwenna was last to arrive – a crabby empress who would not deign to appear until her court was assembled.

The ceremony of reading the will was grave, and obscure to the point of being entirely meaningless to Elizabeth. The particular bequests to servants were straightforward enough – fifty pounds here, twenty there . . and so on (though the bequest of "a pair of my mother's white silk gloves to Oenone Beckerleg, late of Lowertown" was tantalizing). But when they came to the heart of the matter – the estate itself – the text became such a thicket of heirs-at-law and tenants-in-tail and remainders and reversions and realty and personalty that she lost the thread entirely.

Morwenna, on the other hand, was listening eagerly and nodding with apparent approval at each clause, as if they vindicated her position in some long-standing argument. She, of course, would know every word of it; she must have been present at the conferences that led up to its drafting. It was from the smile on her face rather than the tenor of Coad's words that Elizabeth understood Morwenna to be the inheritor. The winner.

Her relief was enormous. She began to lose her dread of each new incomprehensible sentence.

Yet something was *not* quite right. A moment came when the lawyer glanced up at Morwenna as if to prepare her for a shock. Elizabeth was intrigued enough to interrupt: "Mr. Coad, I'm afraid all these words mean very little to me . . ."

He nodded gravely. "They are, in effect, a straightforward rehearsal of the title, tracing it back to the original grantor, Sir William Troy, your late husband's twice-great-uncle. The will is also a title deed, you see."

Elizabeth added, "I wonder would it be possible to break off from time to time and interpret for us in everyday language?"

"It concerns you very little," Morwenna crowed.

Coad interrupted. "I'm sorry to have to contradict you, Miss Troy, but it concerns your sister-in-law almost entirely."

Morwenna turned to him. Her face went several shades paler. "But I was there – and so were you – when we drafted Bill's will."

"That was the first will, Miss Troy. But as I'm sure you know, in English law all wills executed prior to a marriage are automatically revoked by that marriage."

"Of course I know that!" Morwenna said testily. "But I'm assuming my brother's head was not turned to such a degree that he entirely forgot his duty. Surely he prepared a new will, to be executed in the vestry of the church immediately after the ceremony?"

"He did indeed, Miss Troy. Here is the very document." Coad gave the parchment a little shake.

"And surely – apart from a new jointure for Mrs. Troy – it simply recapitulates the terms of the previous will?"

"In part, yes."

"Come, come, Mr. Coad. Stop this hedging now. If it does not, then I shall fight it. Be warned!" She gazed at Elizabeth. "I shall fight it, every syllable, every comma!"

Elizabeth turned again to Mr. Coad and raised her eyebrows.

He cleared his throat. "Before I attempt to interpret this document, Mrs. Troy, I regret I have to ask a question that will seem the very height of impertinence. Believe me, it is essential to our present business, or I should not dream of asking it. You see . . . this new will anticipates almost every possible contingency – including a decease without issue, or with female issue only, or with a son and heir. I wonder – could you . . .?"

"The first," Elizabeth said curtly. "There will be no 'issue.'"

"We can be *quite* certain of that? Forgive me if . . ."

"Quite certain. After all, we had been married less than an hour."

"Less than an hour!" Morwenna echoed furiously.

Coad did not seem as reassured as he might have been by this information. He stared at Elizabeth several seconds longer.

"Quite certain," she repeated, angry at his continued hesitation.

Unruffled, he returned his gaze to the documents before him. "In that case," he said, "the will creates a trust . . ." He looked at Morwenna as if to prepare her for a further shock. But she leaped in: "Exactly! A trust of settlement and a jointure for the wife. That's what we all agreed. Why should he go back on that? A jointure for the wife and life tenancy for me. It was a generous jointure, too." She turned to Elizabeth. "*Very* generous. Why did you need to disturb our plans?"

"But I knew nothing of this."

Morwenna gave a disbelieving grunt.

"What is a trust?" Elizabeth asked the lawyer.

"Exactly what it says, Mrs. Troy. But in this case it's not a trust of settlement" – his eyes flickered briefly toward Morwenna – "but what is known as a 'trust for sale.' That is to say, a trust whose sole purpose is the sale of the property. It provides for . . ."

"Never!" Morwenna cried out – it was almost a scream. "He must have gone mad. Oh this is your doing, Miss Mitchell. I see it now. But you shan't win. You shan't sell. They'll carry me dead from this house first, but you'll never sell Pallas."

"Oh dear," Coad said. "This is what I was afraid of. Legal terms are so much more precise. The sale of Pallas is *not* within Mrs. Troy's powers. She is tenant for life, and her interest is vested in the proceeds of the sale. The trust – Miss Troy, if you'd kindly let me complete the sentence – the trust has express power to postpone the sale *sine die*. In other words, indefinitely."

Morwenna stared at him, open-mouthed. "Indefinitely?"

He nodded.

"You mean the sale need never take place?"

"It is entirely at the discretion of the trustees." He quoted from the will. " 'In order that they may secure a good and fair price.' "

"Who are the trustees? Does he name them?"

Coad looked at the paper. "There is myself, of course. And Mr. Hamill Oliver." He gave a tight little smile toward Hamill, who nodded gravely but did not take his eyes off Morwenna.

The lawyer returned to the list: "And Mr. Vivyan . . ."

"The bank agent?" Elizabeth asked.

Morwenna stared at her furiously, as if she had no right to such knowledge.

Coad nodded. "And Mr. Curnow of Treeza. And, ah" – he looked up with the ghost of a smile – "yourself, Miss Troy."

"Of course," she smiled. "So nothing has really changed. I am still the trustee . . ."

"One of them."

"The only one of any importance."

"If you say so. But I have to draw your attention to one vital difference, Miss Troy. The old trust – the trust your father created until your brother came of age – has long since ceased to exist. The arrangement whereby you continued to manage the estate on your brother's behalf was purely . . ."

"But I still have his power of attorney."

Coad shook his head and tapped the document before him. "It is specifically revoked here. The will speaks from death."

Morwenna stared at him; the truth was just beginning to sink in.

He continued, "This new trust is quite a different affair. It is, as I say, a trust for sale. To sell the estate is its sole purpose."

"Or to postpone it indefinitely," Morwenna corrected him.

He quoted again: " 'In order that they may secure a good and fair price . . .' "

Morwenna smiled grimly, much as to say that a 'good and fair price' was in the eye of the beholder.

Coad returned to his original point: "Be that as it may, the *sale* of the estate is its sole purpose. Such a trust can play no part in the actual day-to-day management."

"This is all wrong . . ." Elizabeth began.

But Morwenna cut in, "This trust — do its members have to be unanimous on the point of selling?"

Coad consulted the papers again. "Yes," he said at length. Then, no doubt feeling this was too absolute, he added, "On a provisional reading that would appear to be the case."

Elizabeth returned to her own point by a different route: "I wonder if I might trouble you, Mr. Coad, to read again that part of the will which makes me the . . . something-tenant — what was it?"

"Tenant-for-life. Certainly, Mrs. Troy. It is no trouble at all." He quickly found the place. "It's a rather unusual phrase actually. It reads: 'To my wife Elizabeth née Mitchell provided only that she shall at the time of my death have married me I hereby devise all those lands and easements and hereditaments corporeal and incor . . .' "

"Yes, thank you," Elizabeth interrupted.

He looked up. 'Etcetera etcetera. In short, the Pallas Estate . . . 'as tenant-for-life.' I think I ought to read a little more than that. 'To the said Elizabeth also and upon the sole like condition I hereby bequeath all my remaining personalty.' " He laid aside the document. "The point there is that the portions for Mr. Hamill Oliver and Miss Morwenna Troy and the continuing portion already enjoyed by Miss Pettitoes Smallwood are reserved out of the real estate — the lands. They do not come out of the personalty — which is cash, stocks, shares . . . broadly speaking, all the *movable* items."

"Except the heirlooms," Morwenna snapped frostily.

"Yes. Heirlooms count as part of the realty."

"Forgive my ignorance," Elizabeth persisted. "Do I understand you to say that the four of us all own bits of the estate? What are these 'portions'?"

"She knows nothing!" Morwenna told the family portraits scornfully. "She's quite unfitted to . . ."

"A portion," Coad interrupted, "is a capital sum. In Miss Pettitoes' case it is nine thousand pounds. She is to be paid annually out of the income of the estate what she would have received if she had nine thousand pounds invested in the Funds."

"Two hundred and forty pounds a year, dear!" Aunt Pettitoes said brightly. "Far more than I can possibly spend!"

"The remainder is to you," Coad added.

Elizabeth thought he meant the rest of the estate but Uncle Hamill interpreted: "What he means is that when we three old 'uns peg out, our portions fall to you."

She nodded blankly; perhaps one day it would all make sense. She turned again to Coad. "And what is a life tenant?" she asked.

"That, too, is exactly what it says, Mrs. Troy. You have undisputed ownership and control of the entire Pallas Estate during the course of your natural life. Its tenants are yours. The rents are yours absolutely — except for the income to be set aside for the portions, as I've just explained."

"Bill cannot have meant it," she said. She was dazed.

"Hear, hear!" Morwenna chimed in.

Coad looked at the will. "Determination shouts from every line," he said mildly.

"I'll fight it!" Morwenna promised again.

"It must wait for probate, I suppose?" Elizabeth clung to one small hope.

"There *is* no probate on real estate!" Morwenna sneered, begging patience from the family portraits.

Coad cleared his throat. "In practical terms, Miss Troy is correct. However, in this case . . ."

"What d'you mean — in practical terms?" Morwenna snapped. "Everyone knows wills of realty require no probate. Everyone, that is, who's *any*one at all!"

"Well, in fact, since the reorganization of the courts under the Judicature Acts of 1873, Miss Troy, mixed wills of realty and personalty have actually required probate *in toto*."

"Twenty years behind the times!" Hamill chortled delightedly. "As usual!"

"Oh hold your tongue, sir!"

Coad told Elizabeth, "But, as I say, in practice, in your case, the tenancy-for-life takes immediate effect."

Elizabeth turned to Hamill with a smile. "I'm glad he remembered you."

Morwenna rounded on them both. "You'll drink it! Two drunkards together! You'll ruin the place in a year between you."

Coad went on talking as if Morenna had not spoken. "I should warn you, Mrs. Troy, that the tin mines bring in next to nothing. Not enough for further investment, anyway. And as for the land, much of the estate is in such delapidation that the rents tend to be abated rather than collected."

"Thank you, Coad," Morwenna said heavily. "You may ride your hobby horse with me to your heart's ease. But she has no idea what you're talking about. She's only a horse-doctor's daughter. In all her life I doubt she's ever managed anything larger than a windowbox. Mark my words! Within a year Pallas will be back in trust and I'll be mistress of it once again."

The sneer had the effect of stiffening Elizabeth's resolve. She turned to her sister-in-law with a patient smile. "You are naturally upset, Miss Troy. I shall overlook your hasty remarks and your incivility."

For a moment she thought Morwenna would explode but the woman mastered herself and, with all the patrician dignity she could muster, said, "You are a guest under my roof, Miss Mitchell (for such is how I shall always consider you). An enforced guest, it is true, but a guest nonetheless. Were it not for that, I should say things to you that would prevent our ever meeting again on social terms. I take leave to doubt that you understand such civilities. You were not, after all, born into circles where they are much appreciated. But you are now (by whatever means) legally a Troy and I must accord you the courtesy the *rank* requires, notwithstanding my views of the *holder*."

Despite her fury, Elizabeth could still feel truly sorry for the woman. She made one last attempt to bridge the gap between them: "Believe me, Miss Troy," she said, "I understand your feelings all too well. Bill was both son and brother to you. This house is your lifelong home. How could you feel other than you do? Yet surely you can see that I have a duty, too?"

Morwenna, who had drawn breath to protest, was halted by that unexpected word *duty*.

Elizabeth went on. "A duty to Bill. That must be my life's work, now. I promise you that when I came down here the most I expected was that Bill might have left me a few hundred pounds. And the only thought in my mind was to renounce such an inheritance. I had quite decided that. I would beg some small keepsake of his memory and then return to the only calling I know, which is nursing. But now . . ."

It began to dawn on Morwenna that she had said too much, burned rather too many boats. She now tried her hand at salvage. "I'm sorry, my dear. I've said some unforgivable things. Bill was indeed as a son to me . . . the shock . . ."

"Please — I understand. Don't distress yourself. I've already told you that I shall overlook anything you may have said in the . . ."

But Morwenna went on eagerly, "If such really were your intentions — and I must say, it seems by far the most sensible way out of our difficulties — that we each return to doing the things we know and understand and enjoy the best — though your idea of renouncing your portion is somewhat extreme — I'm sure we could arrive at some arrangement — and as for keepsakes, well!" She waved her hands around her with grand largesse. "Nevertheless, as I say, with me as life tenant . . ."

"But that's what I mean." Elizabeth had to interrupt before Morwenna committed herself too explicitly. "My duty to Bill, you see. If Bill had intended such an arrangement, he would surely have repeated the terms of the original will. But he changed them, and, as Mr. Coad says, he apparently showed great determination in doing so. I cannot simply ignore that — pretend he was mistaken. *I* am the real trustee here — the trustee of your brother's wishes. I must try to observe them. I'm sure you share his desire to see the estate prosperous once again. I'm sure we are not divided in our purpose. And, if it isn't presumptuous of me to say so, I hope I may count on you as my chief support in the struggle that now faces us."

She surprised herself; she had not intended saying anything half so definite. She could see that Morwenna was furious again, but, once-bitten being twice-shy, the woman suppressed it and said, "Well well, we shall see, we shall see."

Elizabeth went on, "As to my status under this roof, I don't think we need inquire too closely into whether I am a tenant-for-life of Pallas House or a guest beneath its roof. In fact, I intend moving into the lodge, Wheal Lavender, at the earliest opportunity. I shall, of course, take some furniture but I'm sure there's enough for both houses — and to spare."

Morwenna nodded warily and held her tongue.

Elizabeth turned back to Coad, flattered by the look of admiring appraisal that he was not quite quick enough to efface. *If only they all knew what a jelly I am inside!* she thought. "It will take me a week or two to complete my removal, Mr. Coad. Obviously there are a million things I must ask you. Perhaps you would be good enough to attend on me, at Wheal Lavender . . . shall we say three weeks from today at around this time?"

He smiled with mock-modesty. "I must not presume that you will continue to favour my partners and me with the custom of the Pallas Estate . . ." he began.

"No, indeed," she agreed firmly — and much to his surprise. "You are quite right. We must take every decision carefully, asking only what would be best for the estate. But in your case I'm sure we shall find no reason to make any change. Perhaps in the meantime you could send one of your clerks out with copies of the last five years' accounts? Just the balance sheets, of course. And the rent rolls. And an estate map."

During the last year of his life she had done her father's books. Simple though they were, they had at least taught her the principles of double-entry bookkeeping — and the appropriate words.

Coad looked uncertainly at Morwenna, who said sullenly, "I have them here."

"Oh good. And would it be possible to cast up the present year . . . roughly?"

Morwenna gave a tight little nod.

Elizabeth smiled at Hamill. "Well now," she said. "I think we might all enjoy a *small* glass of port before Mr. Coad leaves us."

Hamill chuckled and rose to pull the bell sash.

Morwenna rose, too, and said in a stage aside: "It begins already!" Then speaking directly to them she added, "I have business to attend to, if you'll excuse me." At the door she turned. "You may enjoy the income, Mrs. Troy – for what it is – but remember this: you can't sell a single brass candlestick!"

"Oh, but I'm determined not to," Elizabeth told her.

One last withering look and Morwenna was gone, leaving a silence.

"I hope she'll soon realize I'm not her enemy." Elizabeth spoke to no one in particular.

Polglaze appeared – in clothes so filthy that even Hamill was shocked. "I'll get it myself," he told the man in disgust. "Go and tidy your livery, for heaven's sake! I never saw such a jakes."

"Drains is not a fitty job for a butler," Polglaze grumbled as he went away. "Not in any house but this."

Aunt Petty leaned right across the table and gave Elizabeth's hand a squeeze. "You were wonderful, dear. I see exactly why you captivated poor dear Bill."

"Thank you, Aunt Petty. You know you're welcome to move to the lodge with me as well if you wish."

But the old woman shook her head. "This is my nestle now, as we say. I'm close home." She looked skywards.

"Nonsense, Miss Troy!" Coad said jovially. "You'll see us all upalong yet."

Hamill returned with four glasses of port – far from small.

"If economies become necessary, Uncle Hamill," Elizabeth said sternly, "then I'll give you one guess where we're going to start!"

Coad relaxed still further. He even laughed. "Drabbit, Oliver – if we haven't all met our match here!"

Elizabeth watched the lawyer. In the corner of her eye she had seen him frown when Morwenna had warned her not to sell a single brass candlestick; she knew he disagreed. Yet he'd volunteer no information. She'd have to ask – every step of the way. In fact, her task was not even as simple as that. First she'd have to know *what* to ask.

She wondered how much a lawyer really cared about his clients – how much he could afford to care. When she put it to herself like that, she saw it was not really so different from being a nurse. You cared about your patients, of course, but there was a limit beyond which you could not afford to go or you'd be weighed down with all the pain and death.

When the time came for Coad to leave, Elizabeth went with him to the front door. As the dogcart drove away, Hamill said, "Morwenna will not approve."

"Of what? Or of what in particular?"

"Your seeing Coad to the door. You'll give the man ideas above his station."

She looked about her, at the grand staircase, the paintings, all the trappings of ancient wealth. "This entire house is above my station," she said .

Hamill chuckled. "Let's go and look at Wheal Lavender, eh?"

She brightened. "Home!" she said.

CHAPTER EIGHT

OENONE BECKERLEG!" Hamill chortled. "*Of Lowertown!* I liked that! How many other Oenone Beckerlegs d'you suppose there are in all the world, never mind Helston."

Elizabeth's amusement was less hearty. "And why 'a pair of white silk gloves once belonging to my mother'? What's behind all that?"

They were approaching the backyard of Wheal Lavender, where Elizabeth had first seen Courtney Rodda sluicing himself. A vague unease stirred in her mind, not that he might be there again but that something, some small evidence of that episode, might still linger here and proclaim itself.

"Does the gift offend you?" Hamill asked.

"Of course not." She was surprised. "Bill wouldn't do anything that might possibly offend me."

"I'm glad you say so."

The remark puzzled her. "Why?"

"Oh it might have crossed your mind that this entire bequest is just an elaborate kind of revenge against Morwenna."

Elizabeth stopped dead, her mouth open.

"Of course it's no such thing," Hamill went on. "Bill loved Pallas far too much to treat it that way. And you, too. He loved both of you far too much."

But now that the question was raised she had to pursue it. "Why do you think he did it then?"

He sized her up. "How d'you feel about it?"

"Numb." She sighed. "I *shall* renounce it, of course – despite all my brave words to Morwenna . . ."

"But you mustn't . . . you can't . . ." He became most agitated.

"Oh, I'd make the most fearful mess of everything."

"You couldn't possibly do worse than . . ."

"What do I know about land and farming and tin mines and all those things?"

He relaxed. He even smiled. "Is that what you think it amounts to?"

"Well, doesn't it?"

"Of course not."

She drew breath to press him with questions but he fended them off before she could say a word. "Listen, dear girl — it'll take you three or four weeks to get this place all shipshape and Bristol-fashion. I'll pop over from time to time and tell you what it really takes — and why I think you, above all, can do it."

In one way he was like Courtenay Rodda. They both had a trick of introducing a topic, pursuing it a little, and then abandoning it. But no sooner did she make the comparison than she saw how shallow it was. Hamill dropped his points the way a farmer drops seeds. But Courtenay was still too juvenile to know what points to push . . . and where and when and how far . . . and what he might win if only he persisted.

She wondered what he was doing at that moment. And would they meet again soon?

The backyard was empty. The base of the pump was dry.

"All the same," she said, "I'm intrigued by that bequest of the gloves."

"We draw up our wills in circumstances that are so different from those in which they are read. I've no doubt it seemed an amusing little joke at the time. Bill always loved a good practical joke. You should ask Oenone. She's suffered from it over the years. Perhaps it was his swansong in that line." He looked around at the house. "Well — there you are. Home sweet home."

Grass was growing in one of the gutters. There was a damp stain of green on the granite at that point. She wondered she had not noticed it last time.

"Are you really going to move over here? Lock, stock, and barrel?" he asked.

She dug him playfully in the side. "Not the barrel — I'll leave that for you. And as for my stock, I've precious little of that, so I'll hardly need the lock, will I!"

"In point of fact, I don't believe there is one. Pallas has locks, of course, though we never use them. I should think they're rusted solid." His smile turned to a frown and he strode across the yard to the door of the shoeing forge. "Talk of the devil," he said. "Here's a rum thing." He tapped a bright brass padlock, obviously new, securing the door.

"I think I saw it here last time," she said.

"But we've never locked *anything* here. This is none of our doing."

"Could it be Mr. Rodda?"

"Rodda? Courtenay Rodda? How do you . . ."

"When I came here, I found him making up some kind of . . ."

Hamill exploded. "I should have known it. The confounded cheek of the fellow! The arrogance!"

"I thought he had permission."

"Thinks he owns the county. And half the people in it. You want to steer clear of that puppy, Elizabeth. Fancy locking this property, as if he owned it!"

"He spoke about Bill. He told me they were good friends."

Hamill collected his thoughts before he went on: "One thing you have to understand about Bill — he was a most tolerant fellow. Not an ounce of *side* to him — you know what I mean?" He saw that she did not. "Bill was no snob. No tufthunter. Not lawdydaw, as we say in Cornwall. He'd as soon hobnob with his hedgetrimmer as with the Duke of Cornwall himself. From one point of view you could say he was a saint, but from another you could as easily say he lacked all power of discrimination."

He saw she was ready to contradict him and added soothingly, "I know. I know. Speak no ill of the dead and all that. But where Mr. Rodda is concerned, I'm afraid it's the truth."

She changed the subject slightly. "The inheritor of the white gloves tells me he owns the local newspaper."

Hamill darted her a shrewd glance. "Oh? You've been discussing him, then!"

Elizabeth blushed. "Only because he was rude to me. Well — not so much rude . . ." She had to laugh.

"What now?" he asked, giving the padlock an angry tug, to show he hadn't really dropped the subject.

"Nothing. It's just that I seem to have caught this Cornish habit of saying something positive and then immediately watering it down. Even Mr. Coad did it, if you noticed." She walked over to the back door of the main house.

"Cornish habit you say? It's news to me." Hamill gave the padlock one last angry punch and joined her. "Just steer clear of Mr. Rodda," he said. "That would be my advice. He may have a fine big house now, but it was a much humbler cottage that saw him through childhood."

"So his family didn't always own the newspaper?"

"Certainly not! It was Bill who lent him the capital . . ." He paused. "What?"

He laughed. "I suppose that makes you part-owner. Not just for life but 'in fee simple absolute,' as Coad would no doubt put it. Bill's share of the paper would be part of his personal estate, not of Pallas. Well, well,

well! I'll lay wager the brave Courtenay Rodda never mentioned *that* possibility to you!"

Elizabeth grinned; the news excited her far more than her inheritance of Pallas.

They went inside. It smelled of baked floorboards and must. Dying flies limped up the dusty panes or buzzed among the heaped corpses of their forebears on the sills.

Hamill looked around. "Doesn't it daunt you?"

"You mean all the work to be done?"

He nodded.

She shook her head. "I'll be glad to toil through each day until I drop. I crave that sort of exhaustion."

His jaw dropped. "You mean to do it yourself? Labour with your own hands?"

"Of course I do. My muscles are crying out for it."

"Oh, you and Morwenna are never going to see eye to eye. She'll be horrified."

"Then it's as well I'm moving out." She opened the tall cupboards, aimlessly. All were empty. "Exhaustion is a sovereign remedy for many ills," she added.

"You mean you don't have to face yourself. Or if you do – if it accidentally happens – then you're much too tired to *do* anything about it!"

"In my case there isn't a real self to face. I'm just the remains of what everybody else has tried to make of me."

His eyes encouraged her to go on: "I've never told this to anyone. But when I was a little girl, I used to wonder if I'd ever really been properly born – I mean all of me. Everyone spoke of my soul and all I could think was, *I haven't got one of those.*"

He laughed.

"I was the wickedest girl they'd ever had at school, you know," she added. "They asked my parents not to send me back. And I wanted to explain that it wasn't *real* wickedness. I just wanted to feel my soul hurting. So I'd know I was entire."

"And did it?"

"No. But I stopped being wicked. Then I thought I'd live entirely by other people's rules, to see if that would fill the gap."

"Did you think of becoming a nun?"

"Yes, but I knew that rebellious streak in me. It's still there. It's what made me talk to Morwenna like that. If she'd simply congratulated me and said she'd do everything in her power to help, I'd probably have burst into tears and renounced the entire bequest on the spot." She laughed. "Poor Morwenna! And poor me – we're all trapped by our . . . by what we are. Anyway, I could never have become a nun. I wanted rules that I'd ultimately be free to rebel against. So I chose nursing."

"And now this new life's work has chosen you!"

"Actually, I'll tell you what daunts me."

"What?" he asked.

"Conversations like the one we had just now. About Mr. Rodda and . . . oh, the past in general. In a way, my life is just beginning down here. I mean, it's like starting a new life. But everyone else is halfway through theirs. Or a third of the way. Or . . ."

"Say it, I don't mind – 'Or they're almost over.' "

"There's so much to catch up on. So much that all of you know about each other and that I might only ever hear by accident . . . only hear the half of it . . . jump to all sorts of wrong conclusions."

"How strange," he said.

"Strange? Why?"

"Strange – and also very encouraging. From what you said earlier, I supposed you'd be worried stiff about managing the estate. Morwenna's choice of words was cruel, I know – about your having managed nothing bigger than a window box – but there's an undeniable truth in them, isn't there?"

She looked at him askance. "You're changing your tune rather smartly!"

"Yet the actual business of managing it isn't what frightens you."

She realized it was true. "No, what really frightens me, I suppose, is my ignorance – of this place, these people, all these settled lives. These buried histories." The words revived a recent memory. "Upalong in the churchyard the other day . . ."

He smiled at her adoption of the Cornish idiom.

". . . I noticed a grave, nearer the church than Bill's. There's three people buried in it, all at different times: a woman of thirty-five; another woman of eighty-seven, and a baby boy of ten months. And all three have different surnames."

He nodded, smiling, "Elizabeth Jane Tracy, Elizabeth Pappin and William Henry Martin."

"Yes. I noticed it because of the two Elizabeths, of course. But I wondered what possible chain of circumstance could account for their being buried in the same grave? All in different years."

He drew breath to tell her but she raised a hand to stop him. "No – I almost don't *want* to know. Can you understand? There are so many local lives and stories I'll never know about. That's the most frightening thing about this bequest – my ignorance about the people, the tenants, the farm servants, the bankers, the lawyers . . . everyone. All those lives."

It pleased him enormously. "Believe me, my dear, if you can say that, then you already understand more about the management of Pallas than Morwenna ever will. You have it in your bones. Morwenna thinks it enough to be born to the appropriate rank in Society. That's why she's all but ruined us. Bill was right. Hold fast to that thought. He was never wrong. If anyone can salvage Pallas, you can."

She stretched forth a hand and gave his arm a squeeze. Her smile was solid, twenty-six carat disbelief.

"It's true," he insisted.

She opened the kitchen range, a new monster of black iron and neglected brass. *Toy of Helston* it proclaimed in an arc of letters on the oven door. Toy was another name she had noticed in the churchyard. She wondered idly if they and the Troys were related. Pipes led from the firebox to a large hot press beside the window, showing that it heated the water for the taps, too. That was good.

She went out into the hall. Dust lay thick upon everything in sight. It made her long to be here – with Oenone, perhaps – boiling endless buckets of water in that lovely big range and scrubbing everything until it gleamed. She'd bring the portrait of Bill's mother over here. She began to plan the future in absurd detail.

He took her through the house, describing each room as it had been in Bill's mother's time. His tone was warmer than it had been on his conducted tour of Pallas House; there was no trace of the impersonal curator.

But the effort made him tired. "I'll go and sit in your garden," he told her. "You wander around a bit on your own. Make your own plans."

"Have a drink of water," she suggested. "The pump is sweet."

"I said I'm tired, not sick." He paused at the door. "By the way – just so that you know – the Pallas Estate comprises some two thousand, two hundred and fifty-six acres of arable land, one hundred and fifteen acres of demesne, and one thousand, two hundred and seventy-seven of croft and mine country. You have one hundred and eight tenants, most of them smallholders. The rental on the arable land is, on average, thirty-five shillings an acre, bringing in slightly less than four thousand pounds. The three mines bring in another six hundred or so, and income from other sources is over a thousand – making a total of nearly six thousand pounds a year in all."

She stared at him aghast.

He smiled "Now the rest of the news: The three portions – for Morwenna, Petty, and me – take nearly a thousand. And you have to find for all the repairs, all the new buildings, all the upkeep of the demesne, any new investment in the mines. So there's very little left over at the end of the day. In proper hands, however, and with a bit of luck at the mines, an estate this size should be capable of yielding fifteen to twenty thousand a year. That should be your goal."

He left her to digest the news. Moments later, peering down through the dust-shrouded windowpanes, she saw him hobbling across the uncut lawn to the old stone seat. His mind was so combative, his voice so firm, one could easily forget his age and the long abuse of his liver. She wondered how many years he had yet to live.

She turned from the window and looked about the dusty, cobwebbed room. The fact that this would be hers had far more immediate meaning than anything Hamill had just said. Her mind sought refuge in it. There was where Bill's mother had her bed. A memory of her own mother entered her mind; but she instantly shied away from it. Her mother was in Italy, did not reply to letters – probably did not read them, even. Her mother never wanted to see her again. So be it.

The thought of Bill's mother was far more comforting. She tried to picture the room again . . . there a little escritoire . . . there a wardrobe. The carpet had been blue – lavender blue. She would re-create it all. A safe world for a woman alone. A coccoon of warmth and peace.

Unless . . .

In a new imagining she saw rich turkey rugs on the floor, which was of polished cedar – not these plain boards of pitch-pine. Jewelled tapestries bedecked the walls, illumined dimly by flickering oriental lamps. Damask and velvet cushions were scattered all about her. Twisted, fluted columns soared to impossible heights . . . incense wreathed the air. She saw herself at languorous ease among it all, one cushion here in the small of her back, one behind her head, her arms snaking out among a heap of silks, burrowing, emerging, jewels on her fingers, gold bangles on bare skin . . .

She ran from her fantasy, laughing at it, to the next room and tried what fresh picture her mind might probject upon its fading papers and bare boards.

She was free to be anything now. But here the confusion of self-images was the same.

In a way the emptiness of the house was her own emptiness – which was something more than the familiar, aching hollowness, the absence of Bill. As she laboured to clean it, to refurnish it, to fill it once more with new life, her own, that inner emptiness would vanish, too.

What would fill it?

She did not know. She did not know herself. She was still only partially born.

Her fingers touched her bare forearms. The flesh burned but the burning was like ice. She remembered Courtenay's arms when he held her in the quarry. She remembered her wish that those arms would lift the burden of decision from her.

Could she ever love him? She doubted it. Yet he could be a good friend.

Suddenly this house frightened her. It was no longer a haven from the world, from grief; rather it was a whispering grotto, a temple haunted by all her futures – smiling, beckoning, promising . . . disturbing.

Her throat was dry. She wanted crystal pumpwater, golden with the sun.

She longed for the taste of chocolate.

END OF PART ONE

PART TWO

INDEPENDENCE

CHAPTER NINE

HEN COURTENAY'S PADLOCK prevented their using the shed, Elizabeth said, "I'll drop by his place and get the key." She'd been hoping for days for some casual way of discovering precisely where he lived.

But Oenone said, "Hell to that!" and smashed it with a hammer.

After that they were too busy cleaning the house and arranging the first pieces of furniture for Elizabeth to notice, much less worry about, his continuing absence. The summer days seemed endless but already there was a golden edge to the sunlight, an autumnal angle to its rays. Then one day, toward the end of August, Courtenay suddenly appeared in the garden. Elizabeth saw him from an upstairs window. She was just about to call out to him when she thought better of it and simply watched. He was approaching the back yard, where Oenone was drawing a pail of water at the pump.

He leaped a decaying trellis into the vegetable garden. "Hello!" he called jovially.

Oenone looked up; his face fell. The woman stared at him briefly and then resumed her pumping.

"Oh, Oenone," he said, drawing near, "are we never to be friends again?"

He flinched as if he thought she were about to chuck the water over him, bucket and all. Then she turned on her heel and went indoors.

"What a civilizing influence Mrs. Troy is having on you!" he called after her.

Elizabeth poked her head out. "It's Mr. Rodda, isn't it? Have you come to collect your things?"

He laughed. "Why am I so welcome!"

"They're still in the forge. Quite safe. We had to remove the padlock, I'm afraid."

He shrugged. "I've brought the chocolate – if you'll supply the tea."

"Oh, all right. I want a talk with you, anyway." She withdrew, leaving the window open.

He entered the kitchen. "You should've got that chimney swept," he told Oenone. "The woods reek of hot soot."

"The earth-dog do smell his own hole first." She was drawing a pail of hot water from the tap.

"Don't be coarse. Can't you see I'm only trying to be friendly. We can't go on spitting at each other till we're put upalong."

"Oh, shave your head and go east!" She picked up the pail and a cake of soap and walked out of the room as Elizabeth was about to enter. "I aren't staying, not with he there," she said. "Kick un out if you've any sense. He's dagging for a fight. I can see it in his eyes." She went upstairs to continue scrubbing the floors.

Elizabeth shrugged and came into the kitchen. "*Spoiling* for a fight, I suppose she means." She stared at Courtenay. "And are you?"

He laughed and shook his head. "We have a word for a woman like her — *bufflehead!*" He filled the kettle from the pail of cold water and set it on the hob. "You're looking well," he told her. "You've put back a little flesh. It suits you." He was staring at her hands, which were red and lined from the scrubbing. First she curled them up and hid them in the folds of her pinafore; then she thought better of it and forgot them.

"And what does Miss Troy say to your becoming a washerwoman?" he asked.

"She hates it, of course. But we're on the last room now. The paperhangers left yesterday, thank God. Cornish men have no domestic sense at all, I've decided."

"You don't let the old Gorgon browbeat you then? That must be a new experience for her." He raised his eyebrows approvingly.

"I've been wanting to talk to you about the newspaper. Where do I stand?"

His nod suggested that her interest was entirely reasonable, yet he did not answer her; instead he said, "What a surprise you've turned out to be!"

"Bill owned part of it, I gather?"

"Outwardly you're so self-possessed, with your sensible, down-to-earth looks, your businesslike manner . . . and those rather severe clothes — no concession to fancy there! No one ever suspects, do they, what's going on inside."

She laughed — despite herself. "You're like a little boy," she told him. He behaved as if that were a reward.

"Where've you been?" she asked reproachfully.

"Oh? D'you mean you've missed me?"

"Well, I need to talk to someone — someone who knows me through and through, as you seem to."

To her surprise he took her seriously — either that or he wasn't going to allow her to commandeer his jokes and use them against him, even in play. "Harvest days . . . busy time," he said vaguely. "Clearing up old accounts, soliciting new ones. Newspapers don't grow on their own."

"Talking of which, what are we worth?"

His disappointment was intense. "Is that all you're interested in now?"

"Well, the estate's income seems to be all *out-go*. I'm not accustomed to running up debts. I have to seize my chances where I can. Now if I could be sure of meeting you more often . . ."

He glanced away uneasily. "My question about the Gorgon wasn't just empty. I was trying, as delicately as possible, to discover if you're aware of what's going on?"

A little knot of fear began to curl in her stomach.

"Tell me?"

"It is said — now this may be only talk — Helston is a great sounding board for every bit of idle gossip — but it is being said that Morwenna intends to sue in the courts to have the will set aside, have your marriage declared invalid — something like that."

Elizabeth put down her cup and slumped into one of the kitchen chairs. "Oh Lord! Now it begins!"

From far off came the sound of a huntsman's horn.

"They must be out cubbing," he said. "Look, I'm desperately sorry to be the bearer . . ."

"On what possible grounds? No, I'm grateful — truly. Is this just one of her vindictive ideas or has she any solid legal backing?"

"Coad is handling it, they say. A bit awkward for you." The horn sounded nearer. "They're heading this way," he added, crossing to the window.

"Do lawyers just take orders from clients — whatever their own view of the matter?"

"If Morwenna is determined to throw money away, I don't suppose her lawyers would feel an altogether desperate need to discourage her. Shall we go out and watch? It sounds as if they're coming dead this way."

Not being in the least inclined to watch, yet wanting to go on talking to him, she followed him across the yard and through the forge, where a solid wooden door gave out into a little paddock, now an ocean of weeds.

They were just in time to see the fox, a blur of russet and white, half lost in the mist of red dock stems and last season's thistlebeard. The hounds were hard upon it and gaining. In its panic it threw away what small chance remained by doubling toward the house. The pack, hunting by gaze now rather than by scent, veered across the angle, gaining still further. At the last minute the creature saw the two humans and turned. The hounds were only yards away. Moments later the whole yelping wall of them fell upon it, turning it like flotsam in a wave. As it went down its eye briefly caught Elizabeth's. In that moment she saw neither terror nor anger, just an enormous upwelling of disbelief. Nothing the creature had done in life had prepared it to die like this; its incredulity was the closing anaesthetic.

"You don't mind?" Courtenay's voice, hard by her ear, fell from afar.

She became aware that he was watching her rather than the drama before them. She shook her head to show that the business was more complicated than that.

He whistled, uneasily and only half in admiration.

She knew he had misunderstood. He wanted her to be more womanly, squeamish; her coolness threatened his. But there was no way of explaining why she was so outwardly calm.

That final, baffled gaze of the fox, not to the world in general but to *her* – from its eyes directly into hers – had assumed an almost magical meaning, beyond the power of reason. It still held her in thrall. She knew the precise quality of that bewilderment; it had lain within her, all her life perhaps, so that when she had seen it there, bared and unmistakable, she had for an instant become that fox. Or become interchangeable with it. To the blind forces of the world it was a matter of indifference which one of them went down. If the hounds had stormed on, ignoring their original quarry, and had overwhelmed her instead, she would have looked up at the fox in just such disbelief, neither angry nor frightened.

Something within would accept her doom with that same passive bewilderment. She shivered at the revelation. Courtenay misunderstood that, too, for now he laughed contentedly. She turned to him with a smile and gave the moment of new gloss, not untrue in itself, yet irrelevant to what had really passed. "Isn't it strange – I cannot throw a log with loose bark onto the fire for fear of incinerating whole families of woodlice. I make them strip all the bark off before we burn anything. Yet that" – she gestured toward the gory pack – "doesn't disturb me at all."

"Even though a fox has much more feeling than a woodlouse?"

"I know. Don't ask me to justify it. Except that this is somehow natural and a drawing-room fire isn't."

"You should join the hunt," he told her. "The Troys have always been in the Fourborough. In fact, here's the man to see. He's membership secretary this year."

Since this was only cubbing time, the "hunt" consisted of the master and a few privileged friends. They were reined in beyond the pack. The whippers-in were trying to get among the hounds to stop them breaking up the corpse entirely. One rider circled the melee and reined in before Courtenay, who lightly grasped the bridle and began to pat the horse vigorously, calling it by name. Its great eyes were still wild with excitement.

"Let me present Mr. George Ivey," Courtenay said. "I'm sure you know Mrs. Troy."

"Indeed, indeed. Good morning, Mrs. Troy. I hope this hasn't distressed you."

"Mr. Ivey." She nodded, and suddenly felt her lack of headcovering. "We just ran out – as you see. Don't I know you? Haven't I seen you in Mr. Coad's office?"

"I'm flattered." He dismounted.

"He shouldn't stand still," Courtenay warned.

Ivey grinned. "Push him round a bit if you wish."

Courtenay needed no second invitation. Moments later he was trotting off toward the rest of the hunt. Elizabeth had a strange intimation that the two men had conspired to bring about this meeting – yet how could they have prearranged the line the fox might run?

She wanted to take up Courtenay's disturbing news but was afraid it might not be the done thing to talk shop at a hunt.

Ivey was watching the pack. The whippers-in were having little success. The rending and the tearing went on amid excited yelping, almost hysterical. "There but for the rule of law go you, go I," he told her.

He was older than Courtenay – more like Bill's age. One day, she thought, he would be fat; he already had the "importance" so prized by Aunt Petty.

"I don't know much about the law," she replied.

It was a first step, anyway.

"If you can imagine those hounds as men – our ancient forebears – and young Reynard as some outsider, then you know the single most important fact about the law."

"I'm the outsider."

"Exactly."

"No, I mean I shouldn't be standing out here, hatless and bare armed. Also I left a kettle boiling. May I offer you a cup of tea, Mr. Ivey?"

He accepted gratefully and, with a wave to Courtenay, who waved back but did not break out of the circle in which he was trotting, followed her through the forge and back into the house.

"It'll have to be a cup-in-hand in the kitchen, I'm afraid," she told him.

"Country lawyers see many kitchens."

The words just tripped off his tongue. He had a ready answer for everything. She decided to go at it directly. "It's extremely fortuitous your turning up like this."

"Oh?"

He knew what was coming; she could see it in his eyes. "Only moments before we heard the hunt approaching, Mr. Rodda was telling me some disturbing gossip he's picked up in Helston."

Ivey licked his lips, uncertain what to say. There was obviously a form of words, some particular abracadabra, that she needed to utter before he was released to speak. She tried again: "It concerns my sister-in-law and the younger Mr. Coad, so I don't know how much you're free to say."

He cleared his throat.

"But it sounds as if I shall need a lawyer myself."

"There *are* other firms of solicitors in the town," he said, but his tone suggested that was not the answer to her case. "Indeed," he went on airily, "one could say there are not *sufficient* other firms there. It is, after all, an expanding town now that the railway has arrived."

She poured out three cups and took one to the foot of the stair. "I'll leave it here, Oenone," she called.

"Right, missis."

Ivey was standing in the doorway, smiling. "How very democratic," he said.

"If democracy saves time, I'm all for it."

He laughed. "I stand rebuked. Well, I imagine you want to know the grounds for Miss Morwenna's action – and her chances."

"You're free to discuss it? I mean, you could represent me if I chose?"

He nodded – with just enough uncertainty for her to understand that though there was some small element of disloyalty in all this, more a matter of etiquette than of straight professional conduct, he was not in any way a disloyal person. She admired him for his ability to convey these small nuances – though she did not like him any the more as a person. One could peel him like an onion, discovering layer after layer of different sorts of behaviour, but would one ever find a heart?

On the other hand, would one ever need to?

"Her grounds," he said, "are somewhat technical. They rely on the fact, which you apparently confirmed to Mr. Coad when the will was read, that the marriage was never consummated. And that there had been no . . ."

"But surely it's still a valid marriage?"

"Oh yes, its validity isn't in contention. Not directly. But the laws relating to the disposal of property after decease are ancient, dating back to the days of the Conquest. Our Norman ancestors had such a different outlook . . . well, the Conqueror himself, as you probably know, was born on the wrong side of the blanket. I find it fascinating – the way in which the law pretends to enshrine only the grandest principles of pure justice, while all the time it's merely helping the ruling classes to go on nibbling away at the best end of the bone."

"What has this to do with . . ."

"Ah yes – husband and wife. Well, in Norman law they were called *baron* and *femme*. The single woman was *femme sole*; the wife was *femme covert*. In some ways she was a coparcener with her baron but chiefly she was his fuedal vassal. Isn't it bizarre!"

"But surely it's all been superseded long ago? Wasn't there a Married Women's Property Act recently?"

"Of course, of course! And yet it's not *quite* a dead letter, you know.

Nothing ever quite dies out in the law. The notion of coverture, you see, is still very important in deciding whether or not a true marriage exists."

It sounded too indelicate for her to pursue – and yet she desperately wanted to have it explained.

He went on, "I know nothing of your sister-in-law's intentions . . . I mean I have deliberately kept myself in ignorance." He stared pointedly at her. "But I assume she's being advised to challenge your inheritance on the grounds that there was no coverture. If so, I have to say I consider it most unsound."

Elizabeth could feel reality dissolving about her – Bill, their marriage, his intentions, the desperate need of the estate for management, the whole new shape of her life . . . all these would be set aside to make room for dry old men to dance their sarabands with a clutch of ancient, cobwebby books. "But the will," she said, "surely that takes precedence over everything? The wording . . ."

He nodded. "That's our hope – *your* hope, I mean. The wording is beautifully precise. I take my hat off to those Brighton solicitors – 'provided only that at the time of my death she shall have married me . . .' – brilliant! Now if it had read, 'provided . . . etcetera . . . that she shall *be married* to me . . .' – that would be quite a different kettle of fish."

"If you say so."

"I do, I do. To marry is an action. To *be* married is a state. The *state* of marriage undoubtedly involves coverture. But the action of marry*ing* may not. I can find no case in which the point has been tested."

"Surely the wording of Bill's will doesn't allow more than one construction?"

He stared jovially at her. "*Construction*, eh? Construction! Someone has been reading a little law on the sly!"

She smiled. "Only the *Encyclopaedia Britannica*. Surely it doesn't allow two constructions?"

"If you let an expensive barrister loose on it, it might. After all, if a barrister can't prove that hell is heaven, or life is really death, who on earth would employ him?"

She took her half-consumed cup of tea to the sink and poured the rest away. "It isn't even as if I *want* the damned estate!" she said bitterly.

"Oh?"

She turned to him. "Of course I don't. I'd happily vegetate on my portion or jointure or whatever you call it, here, in his house, for the rest of my life."

"Really?" He was not so much intrigued as alarmed. This was obviously the last thing he had expected – for she was now certain that, with or without Courtenay's collusion, he had ridden out today of a purpose to see her.

"It's only that I know what Bill would have wanted – and as I hope to

be reunited with him in the life hereafter, I have to honour his wishes. I
have to plough that furrow."

He was relieved. "I couldn't imagine your not fighting it."

It was the one thing that mattered to him. She saw that he was
interested in people's motives only insofar as they served him or gave him an
immediate purchase on them. Perhaps that was all any good lawyer needed;
too much understanding might even choke the mills of action.

She sighed. "I still don't follow it, but I suppose there comes a point
where one simply has to take legal advice on trust."

He laughed sympathetically. "Yes, if the law were simplified, everyone would be at it. The world would be full of litigants-in-person."

"Like a pack of hounds! I see what you were driving at."

His eyes gleamed. "You are quick, Mrs. Troy. The glory of our
English law is its uncertainty. In the first place, we have no written
constitution to hinder us. Parliament can change its mind – that is, the law
– any time it wishes. And then, as if that weren't enough, our judges have
carte blanche to rewrite what Parliament sends down – almost at their whim.
It's called 'making case law.'"

Behind his cynical review she sensed there lay the remnants of some
old idealism. Her feelings toward him were not strong enough to be called
dislike, or anything else; yet this realization softened them. She veered –
slightly – toward actually liking him. Not wishing to encourage such a
feeling too much, she said, "There's one thing you'll have to do, Mr. Ivey, if
you ever wish to become a truly great lawyer."

"Oh?" He was amused.

"You'll have to hide this blatant streak of idealism."

She had meant it half-seriously, to show him that his cynicism had not
deceived her; but again he was interested only in the appearance of things.
He laughed hugely.

"So will you represent me?" she asked suddenly.

He became serious at once. "For the moment, Mrs. Troy, I would
prefer you to think of me as an informal advisor. A friend of a friend. I
would need to consult with Mr. Coad – to persuade him of the wisdom of
keeping your representation within the firm, and *without* any conflict of
interest. Also, now that I know something of your mind, I would need to
make a thorough and serious study of the precedents in the case. Also the
actual law. There is much new legislation on the subject of estates. You've
become tenant-for-life at a most interesting time, I may say. A life tenant
has more powers now than ever before in history."

She saw Courtenay crossing the yard on foot. She rose to pour him a
cup of tea.

"We'll say so, then?" Ivey concluded. "I'll speak to the Coads."

She nodded. "Is it going to be a long battle?"

He shrugged. "It could be all over within a few months."

"Or?"

"I'd dread to put the upper limit to it."

When she and Courtenay were alone again he asked, "Did you bring up that business I mentioned?"

"He doesn't yet know which of us has chosen the sinking ship. Morwenna or me. So he's left me to simmer. And also, I'm sure he wants to lull the Coads' suspicions while he prepares to set up his own practice — naturally taking as many of their clients as he can along with him."

"Oh Beth!" He was shocked. "Where did you learn to be so cynical?"

She wanted to tell him not to call her Beth but somehow the fight had gone out of her. "Why did you really come here this morning, Courtenay?" she asked.

Her use of his Christian name pleased him.

"It's hopeless trying to hide things from you," he said ruefully. "The gossip made it urgent but actually I had another reason. My sister Lilian, who's been away with cousins of ours in London, is coming back next week. I'm going to give a welcoming party, that's all. And I wanted to ask you. You'll be into half-mourning next week, or jolly nearly, so that's all right. I rather think you and she might get on. I know that's always a risky thing to say . . ."

"Oh but I'd love to come. I must give a housewarming, too, when the six months are up. We must all give lots of parties. Tell me about Lilian. That's a good name. How old is she?"

He took the request as some kind of challenge. He sat in a chair, composing his answer before he gave it. "I suppose in many ways she's the exact opposite of you. In fact, just as you seemed to belong here from the moment you stepped off the train, I'm surprised that Lilian's coming back at all. I imagined that once she and London met each other, they'd stick like leeches. But perhaps they're *too* similar."

"I remember now. Oenone mentioned her. She's eighteen?"

"Twenty, actually. You know how London's all gaiety and charm, yet underneath it's cool and . . . calculating?" He became impatient with himself "No, not calculating, but you know what I mean — worldly-wise, not swayed by emotion? Lilian's like that."

"Describe her — tall, short, dark . . .?"

"That's hard for a brother. I suppose looking at her objectively, as a journalist perhaps, I'd say her features are angelic, except that she has those large, sultry eyes."

Elizabeth laughed. "That's 'as a journalist,' all right!"

He pointedly ignored her. "One's impression of her is that she's all curves and frills and fluttering gestures and new perfumes — the ultimate sort of feminine woman. But I know her. I've watched her from the moment she became aware of herself in that way. She uses these attributes like weapons, with all the skill and care of a general. Cool is the only word one can use about Lilian." He smiled. "But don't think I don't like her – I do!'

"And that's the very opposite of me, eh? I can't wait to hear what the journalist makes of me!"

"Oh you!" He rose and, putting an arm around her shoulder, took her to the window. "If Lilian's like London, you're like Cornwall. Look at it!" His hand made a conjuror's discovery of the landscape. "Confused . . . full of chaos . . . wild . . . always trembling on the brink of returning to her primeval roots. But look at her on the outside – all sober granite and Primitive Methodist prohibitions, filled with the dread of all excess."

What a strange mixture he was, she thought. Sometimes so juvenile, sometimes so perceptive.

She leaned her head against his. "Come and talk to me," she said. "Soon. Don't leave it for weeks and weeks."

He drew breath. For a moment, she was sure, he was about to say something dismissive, flippant; but all he did was kiss her ear. "I won't," he whispered.

"You could also bring the newspaper accounts," she added, as if the words were a continuation of her endearment.

"You!" His grip tightened to the threshold of pain.

She remembered the dying fox – that look of bewilderment and resignation.

And resignation? Yes, that had been there, too.

CHAPTER TEN

YEOL PARC, COURTENAY'S house beyond Coverack Bridges, was larger than Wheal Lavender. But, as one of the guests told Elizabeth with an amused satisfaction, "it would never make a manor."

The outward style was severely Cornish, with none of your modern taste for ornament. The interior decoration made it very much a man's house – but not Courtenay's kind of man. There was a fleabitten old elk head in the hall, so obviously bought at some country auction that to hang it there could only be a joke. The same was true, surely, of the elephant's-foot umbrella stand in the porch; and, at a subtler level, of the brown varnish stain used almost everywhere. Indeed, the longer Elizabeth studied the place, the less she saw in it of the Courtenay she knew. A foreigner in love with England, and armed with a humorous book about the English Gentleman's Home (and unaware that the book was intended to be funny), would create such an interior, slavishly putting every little paragraph into practice.

But was Courtenay joking? Or was he, as it were, wondering in public what he might be one day?

Uncle Hamill cut short her speculations, saying that as he had been the first man to see her into full mourning down here, he wished to be the first to see her out of it. Courtenay, about to claim that priority, caught Elizabeth's eye and yielded.

"Never mind the pianist, I'll teach you the Hal-an-Tow," Hamill said, rhyming it with *cow*.

"Don't tell me – a Celtic dance?" She laughed.

"A troop of urchins and one man of rank who should know better," Hamill answered, with a mock-malevolent smile at Courtenay.

"He's quoting what I wrote about him last Flora Day," Courtenay explained.

"Furry Day," Hamill corrected him contemptuously. "I'll explain it to her if you don't mind."

"I'm surprised to find you here," she told him as he led her away to the area that had been cleared for dancing.

"Our host has been wonderfully attentive to me of late," he replied enigmatically. "Last Furry Day – have you heard about Helston Furry Day?"

"Vaguely. Each spring, isn't it?"

"It's the ancient druidic rite of the vernal equinox, where the people hold hands to form a long serpent and dance in a tighter and tighter circle, winding themselves up with the mad new energy of Mother Earth in spring . . ."

His dance was beginning to suit his words. It was like no dance Elizabeth had ever done. He gripped both her wrists in his hands, forcing her to clasp him in the same way, and spun himself and her around in a wild, ecstatic caper – for which the flounces and hobbles of her skirts were not designed. "Heel and toe!" he cried. "Heel and toe!" Every step was at the threshold of disaster. Yet the combination of his encouragement and her fearful deceleration somehow kept them steady, until his age and the heat of the room forced him to be calmer.

"I see what you mean," she said when they had drawn fresh breath.

"No you don't, my lass! I'll show you what I mean come Furry Day next May. They cancelled the whole dance last year! Can you imagine it? Something that's probably gone on for three thousand years! And they go and cancel it, just because Miss Grylls up and died. Damn their miserable Methodist souls! We'll revive it, you and I. All the ancient glories!"

Hamill was the life of that party, at least until around ten o'clock, when fatigue forced him to retire for an hour or so.

"In medieval times," a later partner in a more sedate two-step told her, "they had a name for a man like him: the Lord of Misrule."

The title was so apt that it struck her almost physically: the Lord of Misrule! He dispensed chaos and confusion into everyone's lives; but more than that, he lifted the veil on ancient, elemental powers, dark and deep, beyond the curbs of reason. He gave Chaos a seat of judgement; he put a goad into Confusion's hands. Until this evening she had seen his Celtic infatuation as a harmless, romantic eccentricity.

The Lord of Misrule.

It gave a name to everything she found disquieting in him – the sense that he unfailingly discovered the thin ice in her soul and then seduced her into skating upon it.

"Well," Courtenay said later, "who haven't you met?"

"I think I've met everyone. I'm so grateful you invited me, it's just what I've needed."

"I'd have cancelled it without you."

"Who's that man over there? Standing alone, staring into the fire?"

Courtenay followed her gaze. "Pascoe," he answered. "Richard Pascoe. Owns Chym Manor. You been over to the Lizard yet, have you?"

"Yes. Hamill took me a few weeks ago. What a wild . . ."

"You must have passed Chym. Down in a little dell – a bit gloomy. Full of monkey-puzzle trees and dark cypresses. The most haunted spot in Cornwall, they say."

She remembered the place; Hamill had given it the same reputation.

"D'you want to meet him?" Courtenay asked.

"Not especially. He looks a bit morose."

"Well between you and me I think he's rather overspent himself on his estate. He's improved everything except the income to pay for it all. That's the whisper, anyway."

She gave a grim laugh. "Whispers! What do they say about me, I wonder?"

"That you keep yourself to yourself. The general tone is one of approval. They all expected you to come a cropper and you haven't."

"Give me a chance!"

He turned to her with sudden interest. "Oh? Do you intend to make big changes then?"

"Things can't go on as they are. The fields are small enough, heaven knows, but even so, some of them are subdivided even further and rented out to two or three different farmers. I'm still only learning the horrors."

"Cheer up! Wait till they all turn on you and say, 'Oh, but it's always been done this way!'"

"And then there's this dreadful court case . . . the awful accusations. I'm sure Morwenna's going about saying the most dreadful things."

He smiled encouragingly. "People know her of old. Every last syllable that woman may utter in the next twenty-five *years* has already been discounted."

At times like this she welcomed his shallowness, which enable him to pooh-pooh important and serious threats to her. But, for that very reason, she saw that she would never be able to rely on him entirely.

He said, "Tell me what you think of Lilian?"

"We've only exchanged a few words."

"Well the night is young yet. But" – he consulted his watch – "just about old enough, perhaps, for us to start doing our party pieces."

She was alarmed. "You didn't say anything about party pieces."

"But this is provincial society, you know. We make all our own amusements. Surely you can knock out one or two tunes on the piano?"

"Of course I can, but not without a bit of practice. I haven't touched a piano in months."

"Oh well, you can do a dumb crambo with me. That's all I ever do. And, come to think of it, I need a partner for the word I've chosen."

"What word is that?"

"We'll try *wedlock*, I thought."

He got Lilian to help her with the costume and make-up. Elizabeth had never known any woman like her – well, perhaps one: a very pretty, frail-looking nurse called Alice, who was actually hard as pickled oak. Alice had set her sights upon the senior surgeon at Guy's, a recent widower. The poor fellow hadn't stood a chance. Now Alice was Lady Something and queen of one of those snobbish little villages up the Thames beyond Richmond.

Had it not been for her memory of Alice, Elizabeth might not have grasped Lilian's nature so quickly; yet it misled her in one way, for it caused her to dislike the young woman, mildly, but for no good reason.

As an impromptu costume designer Lilian was amazing. She took an old damask tablecloth and wound it about Elizabeth, somehow fashioning it into a costly-looking bridal gown, with a fold here, a pleat there, and pins all over the place. Elizabeth's wedding to Bill had been a quiet affair. She had merely worn her best everyday suit; the only concession to the occasion had been a pale grey net over her face, making-do as a veil. So this transformation of herself was almost shocking after the starkness of full mourning.

Lilian was a little martinet, plucking her this way and that, telling her to stand still, lift this, put her thumb on that, turn about. Only when she had done the job to her satisfaction did she soften and indulge in a brief spell of girlish admiration.

Bill had once told Elizabeth she was the only woman who never scared him, the only one who had put him at ease from the very beginning. Most men, he said, were afraid of women. Now she understood what he meant.

She saw in Lilian all those feminine attributes she herself seemed to lack.

Lilian gazed at her approvingly. "You've got pretty fine features, you know." She spoke with a hint of surprise. "Let's see if we can't make something of them."

Elizabeth didn't know what she meant until she saw the tray of make-up bearing down on her. 'Paints,' Matron would have called them. 'Painted Jezebel . . . painted harlot . . .' the associations hovered in the mind. Yet Lilian had obviously 'made something of' her own features with these same paints, and the result was angelic rather than devilish. She was like a flower; her skin had that fine, delicate bloom of petals. Her eyes were bright, alive with the fiery green of wet young moss. But the angel who drove Man from Eden had such a gaze, verdant, cool, watchful – pitiless and wise at once. It disturbed Elizabeth, every aspect of this young woman's femininity disturbed her, like a standing challenge.

While Lilian worked – whenever she wasn't ordering her about, "head up . . . look this way . . . close your eyes!" – Elizabeth gazed at the array of woman-paints in wonder. "What's this for?" she asked at last, picking up a pear-shaped bottle of fragrant pink cream.

Lilian laughed. "You're just like Courtenay – except that I know why *he's* curious. I don't understand you at all."

"You're more like him," Elizabeth was stung into replying. "You're both of you blunt to the point of rudeness."

Lilian winked at her and went on with her work. It was a curiously manly gesture – the way men wink to show that despite all appearances they have the situation well under control.

"Why is Courtenay curious about your paints?" Elizabeth asked.

"Because he thinks women are out to trap him. He's at war with us all. He's round me like a spy, for ever sniffing out the enemy's weapons. Now," she said, picking up her own metaphor, "for your lips, what would you say to a touch of my Mark Ten Howitzer?" She waved a bottle of red stuff.

Elizabeth laughed and felt the first stirrings of liking – that is to say, of kinship – with this strange, alien creature whose perfume was so faint, so nameless, it might almost be her own natural aura. She began to understand why her encounters with Courtenay had an aspect of battle about them.

From a newly washed cheesecloth and a few glass beads Lilian conjured up a bridal veil, which she draped around Elizabeth's face, rearranging it several times before it met with her approval. "Now come and look at yourself," she said, leading her to a long looking glass at the farther end of the room. She turned up the oil lamp and stood back like a sculptress with her newest creation.

Elizabeth raised the veil. Her heart beat faster at what she saw. She had never in her life attempted to look like that, so the sight of her ought to have been strange beyond measure. Yet it was not. On the contrary, there was a shocking familiarity in that image. Somehow Lilian had stripped away all her protective outer disguise and left her face to face with her true self, revealed in those white acres of frills and tucks and flounces, exposed in the skins of paint. She had never seen that self before, yet, like the mother and her long-lost son in one of Oenone's penny-dreadful novels, she knew it at once.

"Well?" Lilian asked, disappointed at the lack of hysterics, protests, giggles.

"I can't," Elizabeth whispered. But how could she explain that it would be like going naked on stage? How could Lilian – she above all – be made to see that the paint now exposed as real what in others, in Lilian herself, it could only promise to simulate?

"Too late to back out now," Lilian said cheerfully. "I think you look spiffing. I wish I hadn't done it."

"D'you live here?" Elizabeth asked, looking at the make-up tray and thinking a woman would hardly have brought over all those tubes and jars and bottles just for one party.

Lilian followed her gaze. "Oh no. I just keep my war paint here. Our parents are . . . well, not terribly understanding about that sort of thing. They're self-made people, as I expect everyone's told you. They never had time for such frivolities. Actually, I want to move out. You wouldn't want a lodger at Wheal Lavender, would you? No, why should you. Come on – let's see if the dear bro is ready."

Elizabeth thought it strange she should ask such a question, almost begging the answer "yes," and then immediately answer it herself in the negative. Then she realized that the technique actually left the question open, while it took the sting out of any possible rebuff.

Becoming suddenly businesslike again, Lilian snapped, "Pull your veil back down."

"Why?"

"Well . . ." Reasons did not come easily. "You mustn't let Courtenay see you like that until you've started acting. It'd spoil the surprise."

This simple suggestion of a ruse, something that was such second nature to Lilian that she had floundered in explaining it, transformed the evening for Elizabeth. A door closed behind her; a new one, a secret one, opened up ahead.

Courtenay was delighted with the transformation Lilian had wrought, but all he saw was the outward show, the dense veil, the gleaming bridal gown. In any case he was eager to tell her the simple actions they were to go through. He gave himself all the best bits, she noticed. When they were miming *wed*, he would fumble with the ring, he would drop it he would lose it. Carrying her across the threshold, he was the one who would find the door *lock*ed, he would make a hames of using the key. It was he who'd make the audience laugh. And when they came to mime the complete word, he was the one who'd sit by the fire and have his slippers and pipe fetched, while she would kneel before him, taking off his shoes, and looking up at him in dumbstruck admiration.

Lilian listened to these instructions in sour disapproval and whispered to her, "You can do better than that! Make it up as you go. I'll give you a piano accompaniment. Take your tone from me."

There were gasps of admiration from the audience, sighs from some of the women. Uncle Hamill, revived again, was grinning like Mr. Punch.

Lilian's piano accompanied Courtenay's orthodox script until the moment when he had to raise Elizabeth's veil. Lilian anticipated his shock and modulated swiftly from Mendelssohn to Wagner, to the climax of the Siegfried idyll.

The power of it, of her appearance and what it suddenly did to Courtenay, both frightened and thrilled Elizabeth. She had read of men being "smitten" like that. Her own father had told her how, walking down a quiet lane in the village of Yate, he had looked over a garden hedge, saw a young girl, and fell in love with her at once. That young girl had, of course, grown up to become Elizabeth's mother. But until this moment, until she saw the change in Courtenay's face, she had never believed it could be quite so simple.

They bowed and curtseyed gravely to indicate the end of the first syllable. When the applause died away, Courtenay picked her up to carry her over the threshold. She was as heavy as he yet he managed her with ease. His strength excited her, the firm embrace of his arms. He tried the imaginary doorhandle and found it locked. His clowning was good; people weren't just laughing because he was their host, or out of embarrassment. Refusing to put her down, he fumbled for the key in several pockets; she played along, kicking in alarm at her precarious position. He produced the key with melodramatic delight, and then found it wouldn't work. He scratched his head. He looked at the number on the door. He looked at his watch. He even looked at her to see if he'd married the right woman. His timing was perfect; he milked these simple acts for every last chuckle.

At the piano Lilian, annoyed to see him having so much of his own way, and doing so well at it, changed the mood to Gathering Storm. Elizabeth took her cue and struggle free. He looked surprised but when the audience turned to ribaldry – "Watch out, Courtenay, old bean – she's got the measure of you already!" . . . "Don't let her wear the trousers!" . . . and other helpful advice – he saw the comic possibilities and encouraged her with his eyes.

She thrust him aside with a boomps-a-daisy of her hips, risking the collapse of her bridal gown, and grabbed the imaginary key from him. The piano played Sweetness and Light. The key turned easily. The audience cheered. An inspired Elizabeth surprised both of them when she managed to pick him up and carry him over the threshold. The audience went wild. The pair of them bowed and curtseyed again; the second syllable was done.

"Splendid!" he whispered. Yet there was anger in his eyes.

For the miming of the whole word Lilian went straight into the Revolutionary Etude. Musical thunder and lightning filled the room. Courtenay's script was in shreds. The violence of the music dictated a new story to them both. Elizabeth stood like a fishwife, hands on hips, looking at him truculently.

"Oh, oh!" cried the audience. And, "Here's a pretty change!" And, "Yes! Yes – they always do that!"

The fishwife became a proud, fiery Spanish dancer, not in her steps but in her stance. Magnificent in her pride and anger, she tore off her cheesecloth veil and trod it into the ground. The audience groaned and hissed – and then the women counter-cheered her. She flashed her eyes at them and then, with withering scorn, upon her miserable husband, who now took all his cues from her.

All the time she was thinking, *is it really me doing all this? What has happened to me? I have never behaved like this in all my life.*

She began a finger-wagging harangue, first with one hand, then with the other. He skulked about the stage in fear.

"Be a man! Stand up to her," the guests all cried.

He looked at them, weighed up the advice, and turned to her with a new purpose. The music changed sides. Lilian Iscariot! The storm from the Pastoral encouraged the slumbering giant to awaken. He approached her. She became afraid and the fear was real. Courtenay, not the comic, key-fumbling husband of the mime, but real-life Courtenay was advancing toward her, bent on some revenge, a wicked, laughing fury in his eye. In vain she went on wagging a finger at him; she had no other repertoire.

"Teach her a lesson!" the audience bayed. Even the women shouted, "Show her who's master!"

Elizabeth turned and ran. He sprang like a tiger. The watchers cheered to the echo. He bent her over his knee and pretended to spank her. The audience stood and, like the quartermaster sergeant at a military flogging, began to count the ration: "One! Two! Three! Four! . . ."

At ten he stopped and became their host again, all smiles and good humour. She alone felt the stinging glap of that final spank; all the others, from one to nine, had been mere acting, but number ten had been in earnest. She was filled with confusion. The sting of that slap was not painful. Indeed, the afterburn, the tingle of it, was one of the most acute pleasures she had ever experienced. At the height of it her eye had met Hamill's. He knew, too.

And now they stood there, casually smiling at their friends, waiting for the guesses to roll in. Lilian, never one to be left out when admiration was going the rounds, joined them. Instead of taking the symmetrical position, putting her brother in the middle, she took Elizabeth's hand, making her the prima donna. "Spiffing!" she said.

Elizabeth felt on top of the world.

Naturally, everyone knew the word was wedlock; the game was to have fun in *not* guessing it.

"Milton!" a wag shouted.

Everyone looked at him.

"*Paradise Lost, Paradise Regained*," he explained.

Groans.

"*Forty years of Wedded Bliss*," another said. It was a popular song of the day. So was "*Ten of the best, my lads!*"

"*Cheeks as red as apples-oh!*"

"Ah, damnation — I was going to say *Red Cheeks at Eventide!*"

"*And the Dealer dealt her a Darlin' Hand!*"

"I say — steady there."

"Was it *Spick and Spank?*"

"Or 'spare the *rod* and spoil the *bride?*' "

"Here, I say, Steady the Buffs you know!"

The guessing and the laughter petered out at last, by which time no one was crass enough to say, "wedlock!" It was left to Courtenay to announce — whereupon everyone pretended to have great difficulty in seeing how it fitted, and then came the most exaggerated congratulations for his wit and intellect.

The other party pieces followed. Willie Bettens sang *Goin' up Camborne Hill Comin' Down*, with all his customary vigour. Miss Ivey played a sentimental Scottish ballad. Her brother George did a quickfire sketch-and-patter act in which he drew a glowing sunset at sea, with a cliff in the foreground, and then, just by adding a few lines, turned it into a vulgar view of a washerwoman scrubbing the floor. He drew brilliantly, much to Elizabeth's surprise. And so the limelight played around the company until it reached the traditional climax — an old Cornish ghost story from Uncle Hamill.

All were appreciated by all, yet they were agreed that theatrical custom had on this night been breached: the top of the bill had come first.

"That was the quickest marriage and divorce *a mensa et thoro* in legal history," George Ivey told Elizabeth at supper. They sat without precedence, as they came to the table; she felt he had been waiting this chance to put himself beside her. "I thought you, Mrs. Troy, were quite . . ." he sought the word and settled for, "excellent."

"Thank you, Mr. Ivey. And you have a great facility for drawing."

The compliment appeared to disconcert him. She wondered what it was about him that she could not bring herself to like. He was personable enough, his manner pleasant in a neutral sort of way. And yet . . .

"Mr. Rodda mentioned you might wish to join the hunt?" he said; a clumsy change of subject.

'Well . . . I should be honoured."

"On the contrary, you would do us the honour. There's always been a Troy in the Fourborough."

"Next season, perhaps? I'm hardly settled yet."

"It's a capital way of keeping an eye on one's estates, you know, to ride over them a couple of times a week."

She answered with a short laugh, not humorous. "I've seen all I wish to see of the Pallas Estate for a while, thank you very much. I'm ashamed. I think I've managed to get around every farm . . ."

"Every field – or so I'm told," he interrupted admiringly.

"There's not one I'm proud of."

Richard Pascoe came in at that moment. Ivey nodded minutely toward him and said, under his breath, "As this man would tell you, the other extreme is worse." Then, raising his voice, "Come and join us, Pascoe. I take it you've met Mrs. Troy?"

"Not formally. How d'you do, Mrs. Troy. May I?"

"Please do. The game pie is highly recommendable." When he was seated she went on, "I believe I passed your place the other day, on the way to the Lizard? In a charming little dell. You keep it immaculately."

"Thank you."

She laughed. "I know it's a compliment you could not truthfully return where Pallas is concerned. I was just saying to Mr. Ivey how shameful it is."

"Ah – you mean to do something about it, then?"

"If I'm still in a position to. The future has lately become highly uncertain, as you may have heard."

"The future is always uncertain," he said darkly.

"Yes. Of course." She felt rebuffed.

"Well now, I don't believe it's as uncertain as all that," Ivey countered.

She turned to him. "In my case, or generally?"

"Well, certainly in your case, Mrs. Troy. I believe you may face it with confidence. One doesn't want to talk shop on such an occasion as this, but perhaps I may attend on you one afternoon next week?"

She saw Pascoe raise an eyebrow. This was a fairly public declaration of allegiance in a man as discreet at George Ivey.

"Monday," she told him.

Pascoe smiled at her directness. "It wasn't just a dumb crambo, then!" he said.

"Sorry, am I begin autocratic?" She laughed.

"When a lawyer says, 'May I attend upon you,' instead of, 'Will you kindly attend upon me,' then you know you're among the elect, for whom autocracy is mere mother's milk."

They all laughed. Pascoe began to shed some of his dark reserve. The conversation turned to local affairs – not gossip but prices of land and livestock, new machines, improvements to the buildings down in the cattle market, drainage. . . . They spoke without apology to her, assuming she was as absorbed in these things as they.

In a sense she was. Yet part of her — the woman whom Lilian had revealed — held aloof and watched. When Pascoe spoke, she listened, for he spoke with an inner conviction. But when George Ivey replied, she heard only a speech by rote. She found herself staring at his stiff white shirt. Most of the men wore the narrow-fronted fashion of a decade ago but Ivey showed a fashionably broad expanse of dazzling white. Jokingly she imagined how, when he took that shirt off at bedtime, it would remain stiff even after he threw it down. Indeed, it would bulk itself up again, as if his body were still inside, and climb back into the dinner jacket; it would move about, and seat itself at table, and go on talking sagely to its neighbours about the price of land, the depression in the markets. But the real George Ivey, the *person* behind that acre of white starch, remained an enigma.

"You certainly cheered old Pascoe up," Courtenay told her later.

"George Ivey will 'attend upon me' next Monday. Full of promises and good cheer. There's something about him that reminds me of a preacher. I feel he's trying to cajole me into litigation the way a preacher promises salvation."

Courtenay laughed. "Oh, no one's ever going to trap *you* with flattery and sweet words!"

Gently she jabbed his arm with her wrist. "Indeed not."

"Talking of preachers, you know one of the Troys is gaining quite a reputation in that line?"

"Hamill told me. David Troy, I think? One of the 'Poor Troys,' as he calls them."

"Bill's first cousin — and Hamill's, come to that."

"If they weren't Methodists, Hamill says Morwenna would be looking into the possibility of their inheriting Pallas instead of me. But the Anglican Troys have never forgiven the Methodist ones."

"Have you forgiven me?"

"For what?"

"I couldn't resist that last smack in earnest — but I ought to have. I can't think now why I felt so annoyed at you."

"It wasn't hard. Not very. In fact, there was a funny sort of pleasure in it. Like being children. My father whacked me once — only once — when I was . . ." She hesitated, not really wanting to pursue the memory.

Courtenay's eyes were closed; he sighed in a kind of amused bewilderment. "In some ways you are so artless, Beth!"

"Compared with Lilian, I suppose you mean." She remembered Lilian's saying how he thought all men and women were at perpetual war with one another. "No rest for the wicked," she added.

"Oh? D'you feel especially wicked tonight – says he in a voice full of hope?"

She laughed and, shaking her head, walked away from him.

The strange thing was she *had* felt 'wicked' – in his sense – the moment he revived her memory of that smack. Perhaps if he had not tried to turn it into a joke . . .?

CHAPTER ELEVEN

ELIZABETH WAS SLOW to bring the less essential furniture over from Pallas. She liked the emptiness of Wheal Lavender, the simple rooms, echoing floorboards, the clean smell of varnish. She and the house were one in spirit, beginning again, casting off the ancient clutter. She chose the bedroom that had once belonged to Bill's mother, farthest from the lane. It looked out toward the sunrise, the woodlands between the house and Wheal Pallas. Oenone slept in the old housekeeper's room at the other end of the L-shaped passage. It was strategically sited at the head of the servants' stair – a real old Cornish staircase, with a central stringer and half treads, and far too steep for comfort. But then comfort couldn't sell cushions in Cornwall.

"How they girls lugged pails and slops up and down they steps do beat I," Oenone said. She would only use them last thing at night, and only for the upward journey; otherwise she used the main staircase in the front hall – more democracy for the Roddas and the Iveys of the world to sneer at.

On their first day in the house Oenone had told Elizabeth of a notoriously lazy family over at Gunwalloe. They had a steep old staircase, just like this one, but they chopped it up for kindling one bitterly cold week when none of them was willing to go out and gather driftwood; and now they swung themselves up and down by a rope – granny and all.

Oenone was an invaluable source of talk and local information.

Lilian, who was now a frequent visitor, thought Elizabeth was mad to take old Mrs. Troy's bedroom – the room where Bill had been born. She herself, of course, would discard her entire past each day if she could. She was eager – at times desperate – to get out from under her parents' thumb and come and lodge there. At weak moments Elizabeth almost relented but there were too many uncertainties. She and Oenone got on well; Lilian's arrival might upset that subtle balance. And the rest of the district would probably call her a meddlesome homebreaker. She had never known such a community for having opinions and taking sides. She couldn't afford to risk such antagonism yet. So the head ruled the heart.

It was Oenone's brother, Henry Beckerleg, who had tended the vegetable garden so effectively. He paid no rent for it, but he kept the house supplied with produce. "Half-'crease," he called it, meaning he'd pay half the increase or half the crop. He came one or two afternoons a week, a thin, cadaverous man, always sucking on a bent, wet cigarette tucked away at the corner of his mouth.

"Has he no work?" Elizabeth asked.

"Nothing reg'lar." Oenone, who usually bristled with scurrilous opinions about all the world and his wife, never had much to say about her brother. Hamill remarked vaguely that Henry had had a troubled past but was "straight 'nuff" now. The man grew splendid vegetables, anyway.

The week after the party, George Ivey paid his promised call. He and the Coads had agreed upon a *modus vivandi* whereby he might represent her (if she were willing) while the younger Coad continued to represent Morwenna. Naturally she was perfectly at liberty to reject the arrangement . . .

She accepted it. That cool ambition of his would serve her well, she guessed. It complemented her own, which daily grew stronger, not just to salvage the Pallas Estate but to make it the most prosperous in West Cornwall. Yet, while his ambition was evident, she kept hers well hidden. Morwenna had interpreted this move to the lodge (or, as she saw it, the yielding of Pallas House to its rightful owners) as a sign of submission. There was no point, yet, in correcting so useful and comforting a delusion.

In any case, in all matters of business, Elizabeth was cautious by her very nature. So far she had made not a single change in the running of the estate; instead, she spent the long evenings reading all the books she could borrow or buy, touching the business of agriculture, mining, and the management of lands.

As to the mines, she had asked for a report from her mine captain, William Body. She received it that November:

Madam: The sittuation you asked of is thus:-
All of the Levels below the adit is abandoned on account of the water. The mine was forked dry untill 5yr. ago. There are presentley being worked above the adit — at Deepwork, 4 Levels; at Wheal Anchor, 2; at Wheal Tor, 3. There are 40 men on tribute work at 2 shilling to 4s/3d on the £, and just presently 12 pickmen rising a winze at Wheal Tor at £7 a fathom tutwork and 8 similar driving the Five Fathom West (above the adit) at Deepwork at 15s/fathom. No steam is raised for underground work; the old horse whim being just adiquate for the shallow winching. But the old 54inch is sound and could fork out dry to sump bottom inside three month. The new 36inch

is in steam for the bal machinery. Captain Monteith is your grass captain. We raise to grass sufficient water for dressing the ore, which is performed by 8 day laborers at 41s/month and 12 bal-maidens at 35s. There are in addition 4 Tradesmen at 60s.

The pitches are very well, throwing up metal of good quality. At Wheal Tor in the Four Fathom East (above the adit), where the slide has gone under the lode, there is a very flattering bunch of tin on a softish gozan, very pretty. The older tributers say this is certainly the same lode as formed the Great Floor of tin at Wheal Vor 50yrs ago and which payed near two million in her time. With us it is a steep caunter lode but at Deepwork sump level, near on 200 fathoms, the dip must be mild or it would never level to a floor at Wheal Vor, which is but 450 fathoms west of here and only 16 fathoms lower. The 170 Fathom West at Deepwork would only need drifting a further 20 to prove this lode, for they all run east-and-west in this country. If we proved it at the same assay as we already got at Wheal Tor, we could then to my certain knoledge sell 100 shares at £1,000 apiece, even with tin at these depressed prices. There never was so pretty a lode as the Wheal Vor. The outside cost of forking dry to 170 fathoms below the adit, plus 10 for margin, plus drifting the old gunnis to meet the lode, is £800.

There is also 10 tributers picking over the old halvans around the bal for metal neglected in the glory days, at 13 shilling on the £.

At presentley, seeing as you are the only venturer left in, the total profit on the three mines is all yours at £600 per anum."

"Couldn't have put it better myself," Courtenay commented drily when she showed him the report. "It's good to know the old skills are being kept alive."

"Mining?"

"No! Writing glowing mine reports for the venturers and the mineral lord. I never yet knew an abandoned mine that didn't have the world's richest lode just a few fathoms beyond the point where foolish and shortsighted owners abandoned the levels."

"But according to him this same lode was actually mined at Wheal Vor, only half a mile away. It's not an absolute myth."

"It never is. But Wheal Vor made more money for the lawyers than ever it brought to the adventurers."

"So I've heard – thirty-four years!"

"You and Morwenna may yet beat that."

"Oh don't joke about it!"

"Well, if you want my serious advice, Beth, just tell Cap'n Body that your six hundred pounds (through whatever orifice they may be paid) are sweeter to you than the thought of having to pay *through the nose!* Per nostrilum – or whatever the medical term might be."

For the first time she noticed the misspelling at the end of the report. She blushed and laughed.

That evening she replied to Captain Body that she would give his suggestion her deepest consideration. She fell asleep that night, dreaming of finding a huge new lode. But then – such dreams hover in the very air of Cornwall.

On most days she spent an hour or two in tackling the garden; Lilian often came to help, proving surprisingly strong and resilient to the weather. More often than not they wore sou'westers and men's oilskin trousers and thigh boots against that heavy drizzle so characteristic of the Cornish winter. They began by tearing the ivy off the trees and pulling down the strands of what Oenone called "convulsions." A damp, perpetual fire, daily revived, hung a pall of steamy smoke over the place and gave their clothes a kippered, gipsy reek. Lilian wore soft leather gloves to guard her hands. Elizabeth's only protection was goose grease. She loved the touch of the wet plants, the raw feel of nature.

She knew the scientific theories about plants – minerals, sunlight, sugars . . . all that – but when she saw the fat green shoots of creeping buttercup, or nettles, or ground elder, come thrusting up out of the decay, even now, with winter upon them, she could not help feeling that Hamill was in touch with a deeper truth. There was a mighty force down there, in the earth, tyrant to the whole of life, dooming it to fruitfulness. Nothing could thwart it for ever.

One day, quite suddenly, out of the gray, as it were (for blue skies seemed to have been banished for the season), Lilian asked, "Beth, have you fallen in love with Courtenay?"

"Lilian!" she was shocked.

"Well, it's a reasonable question. He's the right age. You're free. He's . . ."

"I'm still in half-mourning!"

"But you'll be out of it in less than six months. That's no time at all. You've got to lay your plans *now*."

"Well, they don't include Courtenay."

Lilian stared at her; she tried to stare back but flinched. Lilian smiled. "You're not absolutely sure, then."

"If you must know, I think it's the other way round. Ever since we did that dumb crambo at the party."

Lilian eyes narrowed. Her solemnity was comic. "You don't welcome it?" she asked at length.

Elizabeth shrugged and continued heaping the sodden weeds upon the fire. "He has his life to lead. I have mine." She laughed suddenly. "I know how to keep him away, though. Just ask him about my share of the newspaper! He suddenly has urgent calls to remote parishes on the Lizard or up Redruth way."

"And how many times have you asked him lately?" Lilian came back.

Elizabeth didn't answer.

"Once? Twice? How many?"

"I didn't count."

Lilian smiled, as if that were all the answer she had sought.

"I enjoy talking to him, silly!" Elizabeth wished she didn't sound so querulous.

"Of course."

"He has an interesting mind."

"I've always known it." The annoying little smile did not waver.

After a longish silence, Lilian returned to the subject. "Actually, if you *aren't* madly in love . . ."

"Which I'm not."

". . . then you'd be perfect for him. I've always thought that what he needs is someone *he's* madly in love with but who doesn't love him back. Fond of him, yes. But not in love with him."

Elizabeth tried to deflect the conversation. "He says you have the looks of an angel and the soul of a hangman."

"So if you do love him, never show it. He'll only take the most scurrilous advantage of you."

"Did you hear what I said?"

"Yes. It's much better to keep *him* guessing. He must never be sure of you – so that he has to go on courting you for ever."

She gave up. "Thanks for the advice, my dear." Later, feeling genuinely curious, she asked, "Lilian, don't you think it would be necessary in any marriage for the parties to be in love? Both of them, I mean."

"With each other?" Lilian asked, as if the idea were both novel and slightly distasteful.

"Of course."

"Absolutely not."

Elizabeth was disappointed. "Oh, this is some book you've been reading. You just like to be perverse. You enjoy shocking me – or imagining you shock me, which you don't, I may say."

But Lilian was quite serious. "I promise you! I certainly don't intend to love the man I marry. I'll pick a good father, a good provider, a good man, a steady man with definite prospects. We'll get the brood-mare business over and done with before I'm thirty, by which time he'll be working flat-out at his career or business or whatever it is, and he'll be rather glad I've ceased to hang on his lips and pester him for affection, and that I can *amuse* myself discreetly. Then I shall be free to have the most passionate affairs with young poets and prizefighters and all sorts of extraordinary people."

Elizabeth listened in fascination, tinged with a certain horror at finding herself half-convinced. Why did everyone else's ideas about life seem so attractive?

Lilian summed up: "Every woman would *adore* to be Lord Byron's mistress, of course. But which of us would even cross the road to become his wife?"

"To be Caesar's wife . . . but Byron's lover," Elizabeth mused. "Are you sure this isn't out of some shocking book? Have you really thought it all out for yourself?"

"Of course. Listen — who are all the world's most famous lovers, eh? Abélard and Héloïse. Dante and Beatrice. Venus and Adonis. Romeo and Juliet. Antony and Cleopatra . . ."

"All right!" Elizabeth laughed.

"Well, don't you see what they all have in common? The *only* thing they have in common?"

"What?"

"Not one of those women settled down and lived happy-ever-after with her lover. They'd all have saved themselves a lot of misery if they'd married some good, sensible bourgeois and kept their lovers for their ripe middle years. You must agree I'm right, Beth."

"You make it sound plausible, but I could never work it all out like that. Or even if I could, I'd never trust my own reasoning enough to follow it. Or, come to think of it, my own self-discipline."

There were footsteps in the lane. Elizabeth recognized them at once by their limping gait: Hezekiah Gilbert. She had never met him but Oenone had told her the name. He was a labourer. She had observed him several times recently from one of the upstairs windows. He was, in fact, a tenant of the estate. He had a cottage farther up the road, toward Tregathennan, where he bred a very hardy strain of white chickens that were said to be excellent layers. Elizabeth had often meant to stop him and ask if he'd sell her some, but she had always been in the middle of washing a panel or hanging a curtain or something of that sort.

Gilbert was also known as an excellent stonemason. She wanted to ask him how much it would cost to restore the main gate at Pallas, which she hated passing on her way to Helston.

When the footsteps drew close, she walked over to a gap in the hedge. Gilbert was limping slowly toward her, bending his head against the steady drift of drizzle from the west. He saw her when he drew level. "Mornin', missis," he said with a flick of his head that showered dark, silvery drops around him. Then, catching sight of Lilian, too, he added, "Mornin', maid!"

"Morning, me 'ansum!" she called back. "Not at work then?"

He spat at bad luck and turned to face them full square. "Patching a hedge over to Antron. But they do want fresh stone, and the hosses are poaching the ground more'n he's worth. So I thought I might so well come home and have me croust." He looked up at the sky, briefly, malevolently. "See how he is after dinner. He might not be so damping then." He peered through the hedge and saw what they had been at. "How are you working out in this skew-rain if you don't have to, then?"

"It's not so bad if you're dressed for it," Elizabeth answered. "Actually, Mr. Gilbert, I'm glad I've met you at last. I wonder if you've any pullets for sale? Good layers, mind. I'd want them on a week's approval."

"One week on approval wouldn't hardly be fair, missis. They'm in lay now. You move them and they'd go off for a week."

"All right, two weeks' approval. Oenone Beckerleg says you have some way of keeping them in good lay all through the winter?"

"He in't no great secret. You just put a little oil lamp in the henhouse, see, up where they can't scat'n. Keep'n shining there till seven or eight each night and they do think he's summer still. You won't have no trouble. Bit o' pepper and spice and that do help, too. You want to come upalong now and pick out what you like?"

"All right."

Lilian came too. They joined him in the road. The sight of his crippled foot was a shock. The boot was specially made. It formed an almost perfect circle, as if he had a cart-horse's hoof in there rather than a foot with toes. He saw her reaction and laughed. He laughed at almost everything.

She felt she had to refer to it in some sympathetic way. "Did you get that at work?" she asked.

He looked down proudly. "Best lesson ever I learned," he said. "That taught me a proper respect for stone. That's what."

"I hope you got proper compensation, too."

He laughed. "Well, missis, that leg is two inches short. So the other one is two inches longer – to make up for 'n, like." He stopped dramatically and fixed her with a solemn gaze. "That's what you do call proper compensation now." He laughed uproariously at his wit. And then, as seemed to be the local custom, he repeated it as a dying fall to his laughter. "Yes – that's proper compensation."

Crava Croft, Gilbert's place, lay at the end of a blind, narrow lane, tucked into the western flank of Tregathennan Hill. His own front gatepost, Elizabeth noticed, could do with the touch of a mason's hand. The doctor's children get the worst medicine.

For a labourer the dwelling was large – two limewashed cottages knocked into one, and with a little cowshouse behind it, farther up the hill. Beyond the cowshouse, uphill yet again, was a small stonewalled yard, or mowie, for the hay. Here the chickens scratched and fretted for their corn.

"Pick out which ones you mind to, Mrs. Troy," Gilbert told her.

They picked out a dozen. Lilian showed her the three-finger test for whether a pullet was in lay or not. Gilbert watched with tolerant amusement. "You get that old henhouse ready, I'll bring they down to'ee tomorrow morning." They were just above to take their leave when he added, with a sideways sort of grin, "Course, I don't only keep chicken, you know. I got other beasts here. You want to see a lion, do'ee?"

"A lion?" Elizabeth stared in disbelief.

"Yes. African lion. Black as a devil. Great mane o' hair out here. And he's got some loud roar when you do ballyrag 'n a bit and get'ee ramping angry."

Elizabeth suspected she was being teased. "Oh yes! And where d'you keep this creature?" she asked.

He pointed to a two-storeyed outhouse – a miniature barn – whose wall formed the western end of the little mowie. Three rough-hewn steps led up to a stable-type door. "He's in there," he said. "Behind that hepps door."

"I just know this is some joke." She looked at Lilian, whose face gave nothing away as she replied, "Oh no. Mr. Gilbert really does keep a lion here. He's famous for it all around."

"No, it's just some kind of trick. Come on, let's be off." She took only one step before Gilbert said, "If you'm so sure there i'nt nothing to it, you wouldn't be 'fraid for to open that door now, would'ee!"

"Of course I'm not afraid. It's just so silly. A lion! The authorities simply wouldn't permit you to keep such a creature."

"Then how are you so feared for to go up there and open 'n?"

Elizabeth laughed uneasily. "I told you – I'm not."

"Well – 'tis easy said, missis."

"It won't hurt you," Lilian promised.

"Don'tee open but the top half, mind," he warned. "Don'tee stir they bottom bolts or he'll pull at his chains and hurt hisself."

Elizabeth gave an impatient shrug, to show them she was only humouring their childishness, and began to walk toward the door. But with each step her confidence ebbed away and the beat of her heart grew louder and faster. This was such a strange county, so unlike anywhere else in England, it was quite possible the pair of them were telling the truth after all.

For the last two paces she seemed to be more floating than walking. The oilskin sou'wester picked up every flutter of her breathing and amplified it into her ears; she was frightening herself, now.

She reached an ear toward the door and held her breath. Suddenly she felt very cold. The hair on her neck stiffened. There *was* something inside the barn. It made a curious noise, half-snuffle, half-groan. She strained every fibre to catch it again. But now there was only silence – except for her heart, which was going like a water hammer. Then she heard a new sound – not a snort but the distinct rattle of a chain.

She looked back at the other two. They were smiling their encouragement.

"He's held fast, missis. He can't hurt'ee. Just slip back the top bolt and open up, nice and slow. He's some friendly little cooze, really."

Elizabeth took a huge breath and set her hand to the bolt. The creature within, whatever it might be, was roused at once. It rattled its chains like one of the damned and gave out a deep-throated growl.

CHAPTER TWELVE

ELIZABETH RAISED THE LATCH, intending to pull the door gently toward her; but the moment the sneck was lifted, something struck the upper half a violent blow from the inside. Its swinging edge flew past her face, missing her by a whisker.

She gave out an involuntary scream.

A great foul hairy creature sprang at her. Not a lion but an ape. A huge ape, big as a man, but with a vast mane on it indeed like a lion. Only its chain restrained it — inches from the doorway. It stood there and slobbered and made strange chatterings through its nose. The stench of its den was overpowering.

Gilbert and Lilian howled with laughter.

As her shock subsided, Elizabeth saw that the creature was not, after all, an ape but a human being — an idiot, strong in body but stooped and ungainly. As these facts dawned upon her, the fear subsided. The creature saw the change in her and grew more calm. Their eyes met. She recognized there the faint glimmer of intelligence. She had often seen it in the eyes of idiots, a pained bewilderment at a world that could treat them so. "You poor creature," she said aloud.

Her eyes fell, as if he saw himself through her and could not face the revelation.

Behind her the laughter died.

"Lilian," Elizabeth called, not taking her eyes off the poor fellow. "Come and look at this."

"I've seen him before," she answered with uneasy truculence. "Old Tom's been around here all my life."

"Nevertheless, do as I ask."

Lilian obeyed. "It was only a joke," she began to explain. "Old Gilbert plays it on everyone. The new postman was furious. He refuses to deliver here."

"I should think so, too."

Lilian stood beside her now. "What a stench! Don't say you're angry? I thought you had more humour than that."

"I am angry – but not at the joke you both played on me." She raised her voice so that Gilbert should hear. "I'm angry to see any fellow human treated in so vile a fashion."

She turned to Gilbert. He looked away, uphill, up to Tregathennan moor, whither the spirit of his "joke" was fleeing like the shades at dawn. "What's he to you?" she asked.

"He's brother to the old woman."

"Your uncle, you mean?"

"I 'speck so."

"Do you have to keep him out here? Can't you keep him in the house?"

"He do bite a body's legs when we do have company. I do have to whip 'n all the time. He do come in when there's no company and when 'tis cold."

"And d'you never wash him? Never change his clothes? Surely your pigs are better kept than this?"

Gilbert did not reply.

"Bring me soap and water, then," she told him. "Warm water if you have it. And a change of clothes for him."

Now it was Gilbert's turn to be shocked – and Lilian's. "Beth!" she said, scandalized. "You can't! It wouldn't be decent."

Elizabeth turned on her. "You, I suppose, could quite happily walk away from here and leave that poor fellow in such a condition!"

"But I mean . . . well . . . surely you can't intend to wash him yourself! Not all over?"

"And why not? When I was training at Guys we all had to take our turn in the madhouse. I've strip-washing more idiots than the ones you've danced waltzes with." She turned to Gilbert. "And what's keeping you?"

He stirred uneasily. 'Well, I aren't 'zackly sure now."

"Mr. Gilbert, if you want to stay on terms with me, you'll do as I say."

"Well . . . Miss Morwenna, she . . ."

"You'd do well, Mr. Gilbert, to remember who is your landlord now."

The man swallowed all his Wesleyan misgivings and shuffled away through the cowshouse.

Lilian watched, open-mouthed. "You're a revelation!" she said.

"Heungh schleeugh!" Old Tom chortled, rattling his chains gently.

Elizabeth went to him and, talking all the while in soothing tones, unscrewed the turnbuckle that held him fast.

"No!" Lilian said, half-turning to run.

But Elizabeth paid no heed. "Don't be afeared, Tom. No one's going to hurt you." She stroked his cheek with the back of her fingers, forcing herself not to flinch from the vermin that crawled there. Again there was that passing flicker of comprehension in his pale, sad eyes.

Lilian relaxed but still kept her distance.

When Gilbert returned with her requisitions she told him to get another pail of water, and a yardbrush and shovel, and to give the barn a good cleanout. Then she took a pinch of Tom's shirt between thumb and forefinger and led him like a lamb down into the cowshouse. He was barefoot but the straggling brambles worried him not at all.

Lilian followed up with the pail and soap, and the clean clothing. "Lucky we were wearing our oilskins," she said.

Old Tom loved being washed. He loved the warm water. They eased off his shirt and scrubbed at his body quite hard. His frame was large and muscular; he must have spent many hours off the leash. The moment came to pull off his stinking trousers. Lilian demurred but Elizabeth told her not to be so absurd. Tom just giggled and drooled all the time. His member was atrophied and shrivelled. Lilian stared at it. "Is that what all the fuss is about!" she asked.

Elizabeth saw a certain humour in the situation – that she, who had no reservations whatever about pulling off the man's trousers (given the circumstances), should be unable to talk about what was then revealed, while Lilian, who had been shocked at the very idea of stripping a man, had no qualms about the rest.

"Or is it like a stallion?" Lilian went on in the same matter-of-fact voice. "What does warm water do?" She squeezed a spongeful over his groin and began soaping him. "That's what the stud grooms do if they have to."

Tom gurgled merrily and lay back across the bale. Lilian's stimulation had the predictable effect.

"*Just* like a stallion's!" she said contentedly.

"Lilian! For heaven's sake. Where's your shame?"

"Shame? But he's no more than a baby. You talk as if he was a grown man."

Elizabeth almost pointed out that one part of him certainly was like a grown man – *and* it was still growing.

"Anyway," Lilian went on, watching with aloof fascination as it grew larger and larger, "it's all very well for you. I expect you did this every day when you were a nurse until you were heartily sick of it. But I'll just bet you were as curious as me the first time."

Tom began to play with himself. Elizabeth slapped his hand. "No, Tom! Bad! Don't do that!"

He snarled and grabbed her arm and bit hard. She did not flinch or cry out. Lilian was now horrified. "What can I do? What can I do?" she asked.

"Get that pail of cold water by the door there," Elizabeth said quietly, "and dash it . . . well, where you put the hot water that started all this." The pain of his bite was now intense; she wouldn't be able to stand it much longer.

Lilian ran to obey. The cold douche did the trick; Tom curled up into a ball and hugged himself, whimpering.

Lilian looked at Elizabeth's arm. "You'll have the king of all bruises there."

"Pain is like love for him. Gilbert feeds him. Gilbert whips him. His mind's not big enough to separate the two acts. I wonder if we'll ever be able to teach him."

Lilian pulled a dubious face. "I'm jolly sure I wouldn't be so philosophical if he did that to me."

"We can't do anything about that hair," Elizabeth said. "I'll come back tomorrow with a good pair of scissors."

There were a couple of miller's sacks hung over the rafters. They did their best to dry Tom with them before they helped him into his clean clothing. He was delighted; all trace of anger had gone.

"I've often wondered what it is that's different about idiots," Lilian said. "Even if they look quite normal, you can still somehow tell. Now I know."

"What?"

"They don't do up their own buttons. Their clothing always looks as if it's just on loan."

When they returned Tom to his newly sanitized den, Gilbert didn't thank them – indeed, he dismissed them with a curt nod and a gruff promise to bring the fowl down to Wheal Lavender in the morning.

On the way back down the lane, Lilian said, "Can I ask you a very personal question, Beth? Strangle me if you want."

"I don't promise to answer."

"I know it's different with an idiot. But when you're a nurse and you have to strip a normal man to wash him, a handsome, young man, isn't it just a teeny bit embarrassing?"

"Yes. Well – in the beginning. But you get used to it, of course."

"And isn't it also just a little bit – well, doesn't it make you . . . you know?"

"Oh Lilian my dear – one is just too busy. Have you ever been in hospital? Have you ever seen how much work there is to do in just . . ."

"All right. Not at the time. But after. When you're just lying in bed and dreaming about this and that – about the dashing young marquis who drives off a gang of desperadoes when they were on the point of doing unspeakable things to you and then he falls in love with you. Doesn't he look awfully like the handsome young fellow you stripped and washed that morning?"

Elizabeth laughed. "Ah Lilian – you're a cure for dull aches!"

"That's no answer, Beth dear. Everyone has daydreams."

"Well I'm not denying that. Of course I have daydreams. But only about people I know. And *that* sort of daydream I would only have – only be able to have – about someone I actually loved. Otherwise it would be horrid, surely. Or just silly. Like expending all your best nursing skills on a dummy made of wood."

Lilian was now as baffled as Elizabeth. "But the whole point about daydreams is that they're *not* like real life. Sometimes they're the only thing that can make real life bearable."

"D'you find real life unbearable?"

"Sometimes."

"Then why not change it?"

Lilian simply laughed.

They returned to Wheal Lavender to find George Ivey waiting. "Splendid news!" he called.

"Can you tell me out here? I don't want to struggle out of these oilskins only to struggle back into them again."

He looked at Lilian. "Why Miss Rodda! I certainly didn't recognize *you*."

Lilian's face hardened. "I'll go and tend the fire."

"Stay if you wish," Elizabeth called after her. "I'm sure it's not secret."

But Lilian did not turn.

"Put my foot in it there," Ivey said. "What are you doing to the district – Miss Rodda in men's oilers! I've never seen her dressed for under ten guineas."

"What's the news? You can stay for luncheon if you wish."

He nodded toward Lilian, who was pulling the stubs of burned branches and tossing them into the heart of the fire. "Is she staying?"

"Does it make any difference?"

"I'll go back to Helston then, thanks all the same. I don't think she altogether cares for me. Anyway, the news is that the opposition has decided, after all, not to challenge the will on grounds of non-coverture. That form of words – 'provided only that she shall have married me' – has beaten them. They've decided instead to go for a frontal assault on the matter of undue influence and Captain Troy's soundness of mind."

"I can't see why that should please you so much."

"It's the strongest challenge they can mount – and even so it's pretty feeble stuff."

"You seem very sure."

He raised a warning finger. Why did all his gestures seems *borrowed*? "I can be as cautious as the next man when it's called for. But in this case I don't believe it is. Any man who makes a will has to be pretty gah-gah – as we lawyers say – before the courts will overturn . . ." He voice tailed off.

"What?" she prompted.

"Look at that colour! The smoke . . . and the oilskin against it . . . the shapes they make!"

"Black and gray," she said.

"Black and gray? Is that really all you can see? Dear God!" He shook his head pityingly.

It was so transparent. All he actually wanted to do was admire Lilian. "When will it come to court?" Elizabeth pressed him.

He sighed and returned to the business in hand. "End of Hilary term, with a bit of luck. April."

"Oh, why does it take so long?" she asked crossly.

"That's not long. That's quick."

His eyes kept edging back toward Lilian and the fire.

After he had gone Elizabeth joined Lilian and they began heaping wet greenery on the rekindled blaze. Soon it was all covered and they had to retire coughing.

"Did you and Ivey ever fall out?" Elizabeth asked.

"Ivey? I don't think we've exchanged more than a few dozen words in our lives. Why?"

Elizabeth saw a chance to tease a little, get her revenge for Old Tom. "Well, it proves to me that you weren't really sincere when you boasted about picking a husband who was so engrossed in his career he'd be quite complaisant about your lovers – once you'd given him a good little family."

Lilian frowned in bewilderment.

"If you were even half-way sincere," Elizabeth pointed out, "you're bound to have considered George Ivey. Doesn't he *exactly* fit the bill?"

Early the following morning, but not so early that Elizabeth was still abed – as he had hoped – Gilbert came down the hill on his way to work. On a little sprung handcart he'd fashioned for carrying stone, he brought an orange crate crammed with the promised pullets. In fact there were thirteen. "I giv'ee one for luck," he said.

But in his eye she could read the true reason – a compound of regret at the trick he had played and of gratitude for what she had done.

She risked saying, "You know, I think Old Tom could be a help to you."

"He can draw a plough so good as any hoss," Gilbert admitted. "And you can fix he 'tween the shafts and he'll pull a pony trap up over Sithney Common Hill."

"I'm sure he can. He's very strong. He needs work. He needs to be exhausted, otherwise all that unused energy just builds up inside him and comes out as wickedness."

But Gilbert shook his head. "I tried, missis. Backalong, years agoo. But he in't no good."

"We'll see," Elizabeth told him. "Sometime soon, before the spring, I'd like you to rebuild the main gates at Pallas. I'll come down and help with Tom – teach him to tend you." She could see him wondering what she might know about either building gates or teaching idiots. "Didn't you know I was once a nurse?" she asked. "I've nursed simpletons in a far worse condition than Old Tom. You'd be amazed at what they can do if you just go about it the right way. What d'you say? When you've finished this wall up at Antron, we'll make a start at Pallas. Is it a bargain?"

"Done!" he said and laughed.

It pleased her to have restored the old, laughing Hezekiah Gilbert and to see him go limping jauntily away, as if his limp, too, were just another jolly addition to his character.

CHAPTER THIRTEEN

As ELIZABETH LEFT THE CHURCH that Sunday morning, the rector, Canon Lucey, said to her, "I hear you're at last doing something about poor Old Tom, Mrs. Troy."

Morwenna, who was near enough to overhear this, interrupted: "At last?"

Elizabeth seized her chance. "Yes, I'm glad you mentioned it, Canon. It's been on my mind all week to ask Miss Troy." She turned to Morwenna. "After all, you know so many more people than I do, people who might help us. What Old Tom needs is castoff clothing. If he were kept clean, I'm sure he could be taught proper care of his clothes, too. It's no wonder he destroys whatever they put on him. It gets verminous within a day, the state he was in. I'd see to the cleaning and so on if you'd help gather in the clothing? Would that be possible? Now that you no longer have the burdens of the estate, time must hang heavy."

As she spoke these last few words she turned again to include the rector in their conversation.

"What a capital idea!" he said cheerily. "Working together, eh?"

Morwenna was beside herself with fury; but, with the minister there, she was forced to contain it. "As you know, Canon," she said, "I've wept over the scandalous treatment of that poor old fellow for years. But there was no one to help me *do* anything about it. One simply can't take the whole burden of the world upon oneself."

"Ah, but now . . ."

"I'll do what I can, naturally."

"Otherwise, if you'd rather not, the Parish Women's . . ."

Morwenna drew herself up. "I wouldn't dream of it, Canon. Old Zakky Gilbert is *my* tenant, after all."

"Capital, capital!" He beamed at them both and turned to greet other departing worshippers.

Elizabeth let her get half a dozen paces away and then called out, "Miss Troy!"

Morwenna turned.

"May I drive home with you?" Elizabeth asked.

A score of neighbours were carefully not looking and not listening. Morwenna had no real choice but to agree. "I don't know what you're hoping for," she hissed under her breath. "You'll never persuade me to drop the case."

"I wouldn't expect it," Elizabeth answered. "I fully understand why you feel you have to pursue it. I know you love Pallas. Even after fifty years I don't suppose I'd develop as strong a feeling for the place as you . . ."

"Not that you'll have the chance," Morwenna said stoutly.

"Well – that's for the courts to decide. But the reason I asked if we might drive home together is that I believe there are matters which only *we* may decide – and they oughtn't to wait until April."

"April?" Morwenna could not help brightening. "I was told next autumn." Her tongue lingered on her lip, restless with delight at the prospect of resuming the reins of power so soon.

Hamill was waiting with the carriage; he almost fell out of his seat to see the two women, side by side, and Morwenna smiling. Elizabeth asked him if he wouldn't mind driving her dogcart behind them as she had particular matters to discuss with Morwenna. He was plainly reluctant to leave them, until her eyes promised a full account of all that passed between her and Morwenna.

"Did Bill write and tell you about resigning his commission?" Elizabeth began as soon as they were on their way.

Morwenna looked as her askance. "And if he did – what's it to you?"

"Did he tell you we were coming back to take up residence at Pallas?"

The woman stirred uncomfortably. "I suppose he did. He must have done. It was all so swift – he'd hardly been introduced to you before he was leading you to the altar. Or," she added as if talking aside to a third party, "*one* of you was leading the other."

Elizabeth ignored the provocation. "It must have crossed your mind, then, that he might wish to take over the management of the estate?"

Morwenna snorted contemptuously. "Why should he? Hadn't I managed it all his life? I don't see where this conversation is getting us."

"Tell me this, then," Elizabeth went on "At the time he died, were you considering making any changes in the estate?"

The response was guarded. "I don't know what you may mean by changes."

"*Any* changes. Great or small."

"Well – an estate is always, by its very nature, changing."

"Yes?"

"But I don't know how I might explain it to you – any more than a train driver could explain the mechanism of his engine to me. May I ask what is the purpose of these questions, Mrs. Troy?"

"Oh, it's just that I've reached certain, rather tentative decisions . . ."

"Concerning the estate?" Alarm, anger, amusement, ridicule – all were in her tone.

". . . and I rather hoped to hear you had reached them before me."

"Reached them and discarded them, I shouldn't wonder. Give me an example."

Elizabeth looked all about them as if for inspiration. "Well, take that field over there. Little Hendren." She pointed across the valley. "Not quite three-and-a-half acres and yet it's divided among three farmers, John Curnow, Joseph Faull, and Harry . . ."

"My dear young woman – I knew them before you were born!"

"And was that field divided among them even then?"

"I expect so. Them or their fathers."

"And is there a reason for it?"

Morwenna's sigh begged patience of the heavens. "Their predecessors decided it that way."

"Why?"

"I don't know. Why are the hedges where they are? The reasons are lost in antiquity. Ask Hamill – if you can catch him sober. These things are as they are."

"Joseph Faull farms forty-three acres split up into fifty-six patches in forty-nine fields. There are six fields in which he has two separate patches and one where he has three."

Morwenna smiled. "To a furriner it must seem strange, I know. But such are our ways, Mrs. Troy. We're used to things as they are. And if, when this case is settled, *if* you decide to remain down here, you'll come to understand it in time."

"So you had no intention of redistributing the land on a more rational plan?"

Morwenna merely laughed.

"Good," Elizabeth said in tones of finality, as if they had just had the most pleasant chat.

"What's good about it?" Morwenna asked uneasily.

"I didn't want to puzzle out a plan of my own if you had already devised one. I'm sure yours would have been much better."

Her calm tone and assumed humility gave Morwenna's anger no real toehold. "You wouldn't dare!" she challenged.

Elizabeth made no response.

"Fortunately – if April is indeed the date – you won't have the chance. You couldn't even begin until Quarter-day." She pulled up, turned around, and beckoned Hamill forward with her whip. "Miss Troy will return to her own . . . conveyance," she said tartly.

Elizabeth winked at Hamill as they changed positions.

When Morwenna had promised to help gather castoff clothes, she had not the slightest intention of keeping her word. But by the time she and Hamill reached Pallas, calmer and wiser counsels were beginning to prevail. It would be a fine chance – and a rare one in her life – to go about *showing* people how charitable she was, instead of just telling them. Next day she was seen in a dozen places in four parishes.

"I've wept over the scandalous treatment of poor Old Tom for years," she repeated at each household. "But, of course, there was no one to help me *do* anything about it. One simply can't take the whole burden of the world upon oneself. But little Miss Mitchell . . . well, the minute I put it to her that she could help me do something about poor Old Tom at last, she was ready to fall in with whatever I suggested. It'll help distract her mind from her *little trouble*, too."

"Little trouble? Do tell!"

"I oughtn't to, really. The same thing as with Hamill." She tipped an imaginary glass down her throat. "Quite shocking. One couldn't have her going round the neighbourhood bothering all one's friends. No telling *what* condition she'd be in when she turned up on your doorstep."

"I had no idea!"

"Well, I suppose you heard about her disgraceful behaviour at that atrocious smoking party given by the unspeakable Rodda . . ." And so on.

Or perhaps the question would be: "But aren't the pair of you supposed to be at daggers drawn?"

Then, with a light laugh, she would answer: "Good gracious – whatever gave you that idea? I feel no personal animosity toward her, I assure you. I hope I may say I'm above *that* sort of thing. No – it's just that there's an important point of law to be determined. That's what the entire case is about – a simple point of law. As to our personal relations, well honestly now, how could I, in all conscience, how could I leave her to flounder? Poor little creature – she's never managed anything larger than a window box. No – one must simply put one's private feelings to one side and do one's Christian best . . ."

Morwenna was surprised to discover that what their friends called "castoffs" were often superior to what Hamill wore around the house. And there was so much of it, too – for naturally she had to tell her tale in as many households as she could think of. Her collection was far too big for one wretched simpleton, so to disguise their origins she bought packets of black dye and mordant and gave the choicest of the castoffs a thorough soaking.

Hamill began to go about the house and estate looking like a retired clergyman – "as befits my reformed character," he told Elizabeth.

"Reformed?" she said scornfully. "It's the best disguise you could wish for, Uncle Hamill."

He pretended to be hurt.

"I know you," she went on. "You're the Lord of Misrule."

He laughed delightedly. "You mean I say yes to life. Only a rationalist would call that misrule. Or a Christian."

She told him of her conversation with Morwenna. He agreed that it would be eminently sensible to redistribute the Pallas tenancies on a more rational plan, but told her she had no idea what a hornet's nest she'd be stirring.

She told George Ivey, too. He looked dubious, not at her plans for the estate but at the news that she and Morwenna were collaborating, even in so small a matter as Old Tom's welfare. "It's uncommon," he said, "for people who are supposed to be fighting each other in the courts to engage jointly in charities like that."

"Does it matter?"

He was unable to say that it did; he spoke vaguely about their lordships' dislike of anything that smacked of collusion.

"Does it still look like April? Morwenna was told autumn."

"We're ready now. I've written to your husband's surgeon and commanding officer – and to the solicitors he instructed. All are absolutely sure of his soundness of mind."

"And until then I continue to have absolute charge of the estate?"

"Of the land, yes. It's annoying not being able to touch the personalty. You're foregoing an income of about six hundred a year, you know."

"You don't think they might be delaying it deliberately – Morwenna and your esteemed partners? Just to make life harder for me? The pleasure she showed on hearing it might be April – that could all be bluff."

"If it starts looking like that, we'll apply for an interim judgement allowing you at least to draw the income during the *lis pendens*."

She laughed. "Now why didn't I think of that!"

Part of each day she went up to Crava Croft to tend Old Tom. She taught him to perform his functions outside when he could, and at least to use a pot when he couldn't. She bathed him every week and changed his clothes when they needed it.

At first, Flossie Gilbert, Hezekiah's wife, would have nothing to do with "all this loustering." She'd give Elizabeth a cup of tea and a cut of heavycake, but that was the limit. Usually she was not even there. Hezekiah would set off for his work whenever it suited him, for he was paid by the piece and could please himself, and an hour later Flossie would set out after him carrying a billycan of tea and a pasty or some kind of pie for his "croust." So the cottage was usually deserted and Elizabeth had to go in and find for herself whatever she wanted – soap and a cloth or some hot water off the hob.

The Gilberts' kind of simplicity did not appeal to her. It was soulless. It revealed them for exactly what they were – the sort of people who could keep a relative in the condition Tom had been in on that dreadful day.

Yet they were not cheerless folk. Hezekiah was always laughing, always telling jokes, usually about local characters and always at their expense. And Flossie was a great bearer of scurrilous tidings and voluble in asserting her own opinions – from the colour of the preacher's socks to the state of the tin-mining industry. Nevertheless, she and her husband shared a drabness of soul that all this surface colour could not mask.

On New Year's Eve Courtenay gave another party, this time to welcome in the last decade of the century. It was fancy dress. *Fin de siècle* was the theme. Elizabeth went as the Spirit of *Liberté* from the French Revolution. "All centuries end in revolution," she explained. Actually, she liked the freedom of the flowing draperies.

Lilian came covered in what looked like fallen leaves. She had spent the whole of Christmas in great secrecy, stitching the costume together. The leaves were actually cut from scraps of silk and felt, brown, red, amber, and russet. They were artfully arranged to seem revealing, but – as the menfolk soon discovered – they were not. Her justification was that the last ten years of the century must, by definition, be *decay*dent.

Courtenay was in ordinary evening dress but he had hung around his neck a placard on which there was a larger-than-life-size photograph of his own face, with huge, surprised eyes and a mouth like an O. Into that open mouth he had carefully inserted a real, ticking fob watch, telling the correct time. "I'm the man of the moment," he explained.

"But a decade can hardly be called a mere moment," they protested.

"Ah, but to those of us accustomed to taking the long view in life . . ." he replied portentously.

The same crowd was there. When it came to the party pieces, Willie Bettens sang *Goin' up Camborne Hill Comin' Down* with undiminished vigour. Miss Ivey played a sentimental Irish ballad. Her brother George did some more artistic-joke drawings, and very good they were, too. And so on until Hamill told another old Cornish ghost story.

But this time he was no longer top of the bill. That spot, by universal request, was dedicated to a repeat of the dramatic mime, "Wedlock," by Mrs. Troy and Miss and Mr. Rodda. Though she was not expecting his spanking to have any sting in it this time, Courtenay performed it exactly as before – the first nine slaps were staged, the tenth was real. Again she felt that sting of pleasure, acute, disquieting.

Richard Pascoe was there, too, this time with his wife. They arrived late, their coach having shed a wheel at Carnkie. From the moment they entered, Elizabeth knew something was amiss. The man had been morose enough last time but now . . . she had never seen anyone so dispirited. Some time later, while passing the library door, she noticed them both in earnest conversation with George Ivey. Later still, at supper, Ivey sat beside her, as he had the previous time.

"You're a man of habit," she told him.

He laughed. "I always seem to have something urgent to discuss with you."

"Our case?"

"Not this time. No, it's the Pascoes. You remember I told you he was pretty deeply in . . ."

"I remember."

"Well, it seems the bank has foreclosed at last. Things must be bad because Mrs. Pascoe is distantly related to the Bolithos, who own the bank. That is, of course, why he was allowed to get in so far in the first place – way over his head. He was killed by kindness. It's a tragedy."

"What'll he do now?"

"He'll have to get out of Chym. I think he intends to rent a house from our host."

"Mr. Rodda? I didn't know he owned any land."

"He's bought some quite recently, between here and Relubbas. Part of the Pengellys' old estate. The Pengellys of Trenethick, that is. There's quite a decent house with it, just beyond Wendron. Not as big as Chym, of course, but it won't be such a dreadful crash for them – not as if they had to move into a shepherd's cottage."

"Yes, but what'll he *do*?"

Ivey, as always, chuckled at her directness. "That's why I thought I might talk with you, Mrs. Troy. Pascoe knows as much about estate management as any man living. Granted he *borrowed* unwisely, yet I think anyone would agree that he *spent* well, if one can draw that distinction. He . . ."

"Yes, I do agree. After you praised him last time I went out and had another look over the Chym estate – or what one can see of it from the road. It's a splendid achievement. D'you know how much rent he'll be paying for the Pengellys' old place – hasn't it got a name?"

"Trebere House. Why d'you ask?"

"D'you know how much?"

"I do, as it happens. Nothing!"

"How generous of Mr. Rodda!"

"Yes and no. I think Rodda has the bargain. Pascoe will act as manager . . . steward . . . bailiff – whatever you'd like to call it – of the new Rodda 'estate,' such as it is. Of course, he'll be able to do the entire job any wet Saturday evening with one arm in a sling."

"And you think he might spend the other seven days of the week managing Pallas for me?"

"Would that be out of the question?"

"Have you made any suggestion to him along those lines?"

"Of course not!" She could see he was telling the truth.

"If his carriage is broken down, where will he and Mrs. Pascoe spend the night?"

"Here. That's already arranged."

"Good. I'll come over and have a word with him tomorrow, then." She smiled at the lawyer. "And thank you. It was a splendid thought."

At midnight Hamill revived another piece of ancient Celtic lore. He sent Courtenay, being a dark-haired man, outdoors and made him carry a bucket of coals back in over the threshold; then he told him to kiss the unmarried girls to give them the luck to find a husband during the coming year.

Before Elizabeth he paused.

"Yes! Yes!" everyone cried.

But he said, "No – I have a different surprise for you."

She mimed alarm.

"A nice one," he promised and passed on.

After that, they all joined hands and sang Auld Lang Syne. Courtenay manoeuvred himself to be next to Elizabeth. His hand was hot, his grip fierce. Now that no one's eyes were upon him he was filled with a buccaneering sort of wildness; it excited her.

If he can just stop himself from turning his wants into jokes . . . she thought.

When people called for their carriages he said, "I'll see you home."

"And Lilian," she told him. "She's stopping the night with me."

"Of course," he said, but with an air of disappointment.

He carried a carbide lantern with an incandescent mantle. It made a hissing island of daylight all around them. They linked arms, Elizabeth in the middle, and took the long way around, by the road through Tregathennan village. They sang as they walked; Courtenay and Lilian could do the harmonies to many of the new revivalist hymns. Elizabeth sang the main tune where she knew it. With Lilian's clear, flute-like soprano to her left and Courtenay's rich baritone to her right, the air was dark and vibrant. She hugged his arm, feeling unaccountably happy, filled with confidence for the future.

They passed the lane to Crava. A light snow began to fall. The flakes spat and vanished as they touched the lamp chimney.

"I hope they think to bring Old Tom indoors," Elizabeth said. The ground was so cold the snow settled at once.

When they reached Wheal Lavender all Elizabeth could offer was a cup of tea. Courtenay declined and, leaving his lamp with them – saying he could see better in the dark than with its aid – he took the short way home through the old Wheal Pallas workings. He did not turn and look at Elizabeth as he set off. She was filled with disappointment, though what else she might have expected she could not say.

Half an hour later she put out her light and settled to sleep. She cried for Bill's memory only very briefly these days. Life was opening out again. It grew longer with each passing week.

The room had not been dark for half a minute when she heard a tapping at the window. She knew it was Courtenay even before she wiped the meagre tears from her eyes and drew back the curtains. He was standing on a ladder, his head a little way below hers. She had never seen him from above; he was all out of proportion. She opened the casement a crack and whispered, "What d'you want?" – knowing well enough.

He pointed to himself and then toward her bed.

"No," she said quickly. "I'll get dressed. Wait for me in the yard."

He could not argue for she locked the window and drew the curtains again.

To him in the frozen outdoors – and to her in the heat of her impatience – it seemed an age before she let herself out into the yard and quietly closed the door.

"What's the point of all this?" he hissed angrily. "Why didn't you just let me in?"

She put her finger to her lips and pointed up at Oenone's window. Then she took his gloved hand in hers and led him toward the wood. "The ladder?" she asked.

"I put it back in the shed."

It was still snowing; she hoped it would go on long enough to obliterate their traces. Even in the short time since it had begun, it had laid a soft mantle over everything, deadening their footfall.

As soon as he dared he said, "What on earth are you doing?"

"I'm doing what I once told you I never would. I'm saying I'm ready. I'm saying, 'Now!' So there!"

He gave a little laugh, bewildered, delighted. "Where?"

"I'm going back with you to Yeol Parc."

All the joy went out of him. "You most certainly are not!"

"Oh." She paused, looked at him. "Oh, very well." She turned to face the way they had come.

He caught her arm. "Beth! This is most aggravating, you know. Why didn't you just let me in?"

She put her arms about him and said, as if her words were words of tenderness, "Never! That's *my* room. Not you – not any man – will ever be allowed in there. You're always going on about women being free at last. You think it means freedom to please you. Well, now you know!"

He held her tight. For a long moment the only sound was his breathing, which was strained, restless. She could almost hear the argument raging in his mind.

"Then I shall have to see you back before dawn," he said crossly, pushing her away and resuming their walk. "Two journeys. Twice the risk of being seen. You're mad."

She smiled to herself. "I needn't come creeping back in the small hours," she said. "I left a note."

"The devil you did!"

"I said I'd got up early and gone for a walk. Oenone will think I went to see about Tom. Later, I'll tell them the truth . . ."

"Ha ha!"

". . . that I went to Yeol Parc to have a talk with Pascoe."

He stopped. She pulled him forward.

"What about Pascoe?"

"I want him to be my agent for Pallas."

"Oh, indeed!"

"Oh, come on, Courtenay, you don't suppose a man of such ability will be content to manage *your* few fields for the rest of his life? And even if he were, how long d'you think it would be before half the big landowners in Cornwall would be knocking at his door with more tempting offers?"

Courtenay was silent – morosely so.

"Did you ever hear a word against his ability?" she challenged.

"I suppose not. Lord, but you dip your oar in quickly! Is this really why you're coming back to Yeol Parc with me."

"You know why I'm coming back with you."

Her tone calmed him. "You're a strange one. You don't love me, I'm sure of that. Still . . . I mustn't . . ."

She cut him short. "What I want you to do now is to print a . . . feature? Is that the right word? An article, anyway, in the *Vindicator*, all about how Bolitho is foreclosing on Chym and saying what an excellent . . ."

"Beth!"

"Pointing out what a bargain someone is going to get when the place is auctioned. That's the point to stress."

"Beth? Don't you want to talk about . . ."

"What?"

"Well – us, of course. Why we're going back to my place – my room?"

"We could get an artist to do a birdseye view of the whole estate. George Ivey? He's very good with his pencil. I want something that will . . ."

He stopped dead, and this time he braced himself against her tugging hand.

She relented and leaned her head against his chest. "Don't," she whispered.

"Don't what?"

"Ask me to talk about it. Talk about anything else, even fatstock prices. Tell me you'll print this article about Chym."

They resumed their walk. Yeol Park was almost in view by now.

"What's so important about it?" he asked.

"Don't you see? The place will probably fetch a good price anyway, but if it looks to Pascoe as if *we* helped him get it, he'll feel in our debt for life. I mean, suppose we puff the place so well that his debt is actually cleared! I want a free man working for me. Don't you? What was your 'nice surprise,' by the way?"

"A dividend from the newspaper. It's a bit awkward . . ."

"How much?"

"It's a bit awkward, considering where we're going and . . . I mean it seems to create a relationship where . . . ."

"How much?"

"Six hundred and forty pounds, eighteen shillings and fourpence."

She laughed, partly in delight, partly at his comic exactitude. "Why not just six hundred and forty?"

"Because that's what I gave for the land I bought."

"Oh, I see! In other words, it bears no relation to the profits of the paper."

"It does in a way."

"In what way?"

"I mean, the paper can afford it. Aren't you pleased?"

They had reached the short drive up to Yeol Parc. She answered in a whisper: "Two things I must do tomorrow. One is speak with Pascoe. The second is call an extraordinary shareholders's meeting of the Board of the *Vindicator*."

When he remained silent, she added, "I take it that's just you and me?"

"Yes," he said unhappily. "Just you and me!"

CHAPTER FOURTEEN

ELIZABETH WOKE EARLY next morning. The bed had shrunk, though a few short hours ago it seemed to hold all the universe. She stared bleary-eyed at Courtenay, unshaven, deep asleep. Dreaming still? His lips moved. She no longer wanted to kiss them.

What had happened since last night? Where had all that longing

gone? She had never known such intensities of pleasure. She could admit
that – and yet she never wanted to do such a thing again. She was afraid of
becoming its familiar, of understanding it, of ranking it among the
ticketed recreations of everyday life. She feared the death of its elemental
mystery.

He stirred uneasily. She slipped from his sheets, from the man warmth
of him, and out into the cold dawn of the new decade. Her skin tingled with
sensations – sweet, seductive memories. It was new skin, burnished bright
with his touch and scent; it dulled her kinship with an earlier, inviolate
woman, a fortress-Elizabeth, an only child to herself. From this hour there
would be a second tenant; she must share her life, her hearth, her hours,
with another self, formed by Courtenay and part-loyal to him.

She broke the thin ice on the pitcher and plunged his flannel into the
water below. Its frigid touch set her body on fire again. Even the pressure of
her clothing felt different. Overnight, new and secret channels had opened
up between her body and her mind. Parts of her that had been vague,
vestigial, bewildering – mere smudges in her own self-picture – were now
poignantly sharp. Her breasts felt larger, firmer, more definite . . . her
thighs had new muscles . . . everything had grown more purposeful, more
ardent. And more demanding.

Yet it was a new birth, a successful one this time: she had at last been
delivered in her entirety.

Dressed again she slipped downstairs and walked out into the sunrise.
No servants were about. None saw her but Cato, the mastiff. He raised his
head at his kennel door, sniffed, and whimpered, but was unwilling to
disturb the scratched-up straw beneath which he lay. She patted him,
accepted a few warm, grateful finger licks. Could he taste Courtenay there?
She went on down the path, taking care to walk in last night's footsteps
wherever they were visible in the snow.

The world was only half clad in its new white mantle. The black lines
of drystone hedgerows networked the rise and fall of the almost treeless
hills. Dark windbent thorns and blasted scrub oaks leaned eastward, toward
her, toward the new day. The rising sun was a ghostly circle, silver-gilt in a
cold, gray, breezeless sky.

South and west of Yeol Parc, protecting the house from the prevailing
winds, but not dwarfing it, there reared a wild little brother of Tregathennan Hill, a haunt of goats and rabbits. Toward its modest crown Elizabeth
now turned her feet. She had first to cross one small field, tenanted by three
elderly Guernsey cows, who stood in morose boredom and watched her
approach. Their breath hung in airless wreaths about their long, sad, amber
faces. She felt sorry for them, out in such cold; could they remember
fly-tormented summer days when they would have longed for such weather
as this? The nearest cow delayed until the very last moment before she
moved out of the way. Elizabeth was astonished to hear the creature's hip

joints crack and squeak like a rusty old door.

On she went, over the far hedge where a sloping ladder of projecting stones must have given many a sportsman quiet access to the wilderness killing-ground beyond. Up the goat paths she climbed, to a natural rockery at the summit. And there she sat awhile and looked down over Pallas, her millstone-realm.

The heart of the estate lay before her like a model, from her own darling Wheal Lavender, away to her right, to the two quarries of Wheal Pallas, not a half-mile to her front. The sun, just beginning to strengthen into red, touched the ochre stone with its fire. It also, she noticed, picked up the pale brick chimneys of Pallas House, otherwise lost in its valley of trees. Only the manors and estate houses of Cornwall had such woodlands now; elsewhere they had all been devoured by the mines, for pitprops and fuel.

Down there Morwenna, too, was awakening to a new decade. Would she, Elizabeth wondered, survive this century that had shaped her – and which, in turn, she and her kind had done so much to shape? What difference would it make? She had a feeling Morwenna would not allow anything so trivial as death to ease her grip on the Troy inheritance. A thousand years hence her awesome shade would still be caught hovering around the house and its treasures. Even if they were split up, scattered over half the world, she would continue to inhabit them and curse the generations that had disturbed them – beginning with Elizabeth herself. There would be no release in death.

The farms of the Pallas estate did not form one neat island of neglect amid a sea of relative good-stewardship; yet, concealed though they were by the snow, their patchwork of shame was plain enough to see, from Breage in the west to Gweek in the east, from Porthleven cliffs, beyond the hills to the south of Helston, to Nancegollan, a mile or two north of Tregathennan behind her.

Pallas fields had grass that grew in tussocks, like hillside land suddenly flattened. The dark scratch of each Pallas hedgerow was thicker, where untended gorse and blackberries encroached upon the pasture. Pallas pastures bore fans of brown earth, poached by the cattle, not just at the gateways but here and there along the hedges, where tumbled stones gave casual access to the next-door field. The unwhitewashed buildings of Pallas farms besmirched the snows in which their gleaming neighbours almost vanished.

It was a fitting day on which to see them, the first of a new decade. Her decade. She vowed she would return here every New Year's Morn and if, even from this distance, she could discern no obvious improvement, she would count that year her failure. She rose, filled with a new purpose, and returned to Yeol Parc.

She picked up a yard besom and roused the household with her cheerful din, battering away at a new zinc bath that hung outside the back door. Two windows flew up, protesting in unison. Mr. Pascoe was at one, Courtenay at the other.

"Give a poor travelling woman some breakfast?" she asked gaily. "It's a thrilling day. Why aren't you up yet?"

Courtenay groaned and shut the window. Moments later, clad in dressing gown and slippers, he let her in. His body, normally so lithe and straight, looked collapsed. She felt that all his strength had passed to her.

The servants were up by now. Fires were crackling, kettles singing, porridge bubbling on the stove. Her senses, honed so keen by the cold, picked up the fustian tang of raw bacon as the cook sliced the rashers for breakfast.

"How can you be so spirited?" he asked morosely.

"Mind over matter."

He did not even smile.

"Don't get pompous, Courtenay," she warned. "You're nowhere near old enough."

"Pompous! That's the last word I'd use. Oh Lord – what have we started?"

"Nothing we can't as easily finish."

It stung him. In his eyes she was surprised to see something very like hatred, for himself as much as for her. She understood then that he had grown as fond of his freedom as she had of hers; he, too, now faced a life shared with a second Courtenay, shaped by her, bound to her; and, like the old, single Elizabeth, the old, single Courtenay resented the prospect.

"Perhaps that would be for the best," he said.

"I certainly think so." Her tone was level, amazing to herself.

"Why did you come back then?"

"I told you – to see Mr. Pascoe."

"Oh, damn your good sense!" He ran away upstairs.

She was strangely, pleasantly void of feeling as she turned to the buffet. The difference between love and passion was never more clear to her. Love can never rest. It must create its beloved anew each day. It reaches outside, beyond itself, wanting the universe. Passion is a closed circle. It seeks only itself, is fulfilled by itself, desires no change. Passion can never be faithless.

Betty, the maid, brought in the bacon and egg, the porridge, the devilled kidneys, the toast. They wished each other a happy new year. Hunger filled that emptiness within; Elizabeth piled her plate high.

Pascoe was the first down; another happy new year. Elizabeth wasted no time – as if she needed to convince herself that this was, indeed, her only reason for returning. "I was so sorry to hear about your loss of Chym," she told him. "But everyone says you'll rebuild your fortune and own it again before long – that or something even better."

The opinion seemed to take him by surprise. "Everyone?" he repeated. She saw a skeptical eagerness in him; he wanted to believe it.

"Everyone I spoke to – which is about one and a half people, actually." She didn't wish him to think his misfortunes had been *the* topic of the party. "Still, I'm sure they were right."

He smiled wanly. "You're very kind, Mrs. Troy. But perhaps your sister-in-law has the best idea, after all. When the rents go down . . . put up the leather patches!"

She stared hard at him, unsmiling, angry, until the change in her alarmed him. "No," he said awkwardly, "to be serious about it . . ."

She let the sentence hang a bit before she rescued him. "On my way over here," she said, "I walked to the top of Little Tregathennan to watch the sunrise. I had never realized you can see the whole of the Pallas demesne and most of the estate from there. How dreadfully run down it all looks, even hidden under the snow."

He nodded. "Perhaps I'm not one to talk, but there must be a middle way between outright neglect and" – his eyes fell – "well . . . excessive improvement."

"How would you like the chance to prove it?" she asked.

He knew what she was driving at but, she saw, did not dare believe it.

"I mean exactly what you think I mean," she told him. "Be my bailiff . . . steward – whatever you want to call it. Manager! Help me *manage* Pallas Estate. I know you're promised to our host, but you can still look after his few acres any wet Saturday evening."

He chuckled. "Is this your idea?"

"George Ivey thinks he put it into my head, so don't ever tell him otherwise. Actually, I thought of it weeks ago."

"When you first heard I was in difficulties – I see."

"Yes, I must confess there *is* the whiff of the ambulance chaser about it. But still, I'll bet I'm only the first of half a dozen who'll be knocking at your door with similar offers over the coming weeks. So if I were you, I shouldn't make me any too hasty an answer."

"You're pretty candid with me, Mrs. Troy. I admire that." He closed his eyes awhile in thought. "Whatever I did next it'd have to be in this part of the world. I wouldn't be happy anywhere else. And down here there's nothing half so challenging as Pallas, is there!"

He looked hesitantly at her, afraid she might take the comment amiss. She smiled. "Be as rude as you like about it, Mr. Pascoe."

"What terms?" he asked.

"Generous."

He laughed. "By Harry, you're on!"

"I'll still give you a week to think better of it. Now" – she rose from her seat – "stay where you are and start planning while I fill your plate for you. A little of everything?"

There was a new sparkle in his eye. "A little of everything," he echoed. "Now that's a good recipe."

CHAPTER FIFTEEN

THE WINDFALL "DIVIDEND" from the *Vindicator* was earmarked for the forking out of the mines in preparation for a new exploratory drift in search of the great Wheal Vor lode at the 180 level.

"Are we going to find useful bunches of metal at the higher levels?" Elizabeth asked. "Something to help pay for this exploration?"

"That's a good point there, missis," Captain Body replied. "Maybe we will now." He did not tell her he had already assumed as much in his calculation that the "outside" cost would be no more than £600. After all, venturers and minerals lords were the salt of the earth – nothing but the best was good enough for them, especially when it came to news and forecasts.

The days drew out. The primroses came and went, and the little dog violets. The daffodils lingered while the grass rose to drown them. The hedgerows, the unweeded corners of the garden, the woodlands, all burst into new growth – with green frills of honeysuckle and hawthorn, green spears of nettles and ground elder, green dabs of coltsfoot and primrose leaves. Yet it was not spring, it had not the feel of spring as Elizabeth had always known it. The air remained wet and cold. She never walked along a lane without seeing, amid all that thrusting green, the black-of-winter twigs silvered with clear drops of ice-cold water. Nothing ever dried. Salt congealed in the cruet and on the pantry shelf; envelopes sealed themselves in the writing desk; speckled moulds flourished wherever the draughts did not actually howl a half-gale – behind curtains, in cupboards, under carpets. The hens stood stubbornly in the horizontal rain and went off lay. If she kept them cooped, they turned broody instead.

Every excursion out of doors was a dash through driving drizzle. Bending double into it did not help. The disturbed and rushing air swirled the fine droplets into every cranny of her clothing; the very atmosphere was a cold, wet, questing tongue.

So it was not spring. The green was mockery. She remembered she had told Gilbert they would rebuild the main gate at Pallas before now, but he was tactful enough never to remind her of it when they met. Anyway, he had a job that would take him almost into summer, rebuilding and extending the wall at Clowance, four or five miles away on the Camborne road. On three days a week Old Tom went out with him, and was proving a great help. It was enough to exhaust him and take the edge off his wickedness. She went up to Crava and saw to Tom only once or twice a week these days. He had become so amenable they allowed him into the house more often, and Flossie was finding him far easier to cope with. She had discovered a threat more potent than the whip: no visit from Mrs. Troy! She never had to carry it out.

Elizabeth, now almost out of mourning, began to go about more. Each week she and Lilian took the horse-bus from Helston into Penzance. They rarely bought anything there. A pair of gloves, perhaps, the odd dress length in a sale. They took sandwiches for lunch, which they washed down with ginger pop in a shelter on the new esplanade if the weather was bright, or by the fireside in the waiting room of the Scilly packet boat when it was wet, which was more often. From there they could look out across the tidal harbour at the hundreds of fishing boats, or – in the floating harbour – at the dozens of tramp steamers, carrying everything from coal to Portland stone.

The two of them came to town not to so much to buy things as to keep in touch, however vaguely, with the outer world – to look at the local variants of last year's London fashions . . . or just to stare at the railway line and remember that the metropolis existed some three hundred miles away "up there."

On their Penzance days Elizabeth would go early into Helston so as to tend Bill's grave. It now had its proper headstone of Cornish serpentine from Kynance, as Bill had directed. As she worked away with her trowel and fork, she told him how she had passed her week – but not about herself and Courtenay. Did he know, anyway? Or care? Would he not be far beyond all passion now – beyond jealousy, anger, even love? She tried to imagine such an existence but could not.

Then, hiding her implements in the three-inch gap between the grave of Trevanion Westlake, "Died on June 22, 1863, Aged 8 Years," and his now indecipherable neighbour, she would walk through the foot of the town to meet Lilian. She often wondered about little Trevanion, "sainted companion/Of Cherub and Seraph on high . . ." Aged eight years. She pictured him with tousled fair hair and pockets full of string and knives and earthworms. Would she ever have a son, she wondered. Or a daughter?

The bus was a brightly painted horse wagonette. Bold showman's letters all around its canopy declared that it was owned by Matthew Polglaze (no relation to the Pallas butler) and ran daily from Helston through Porthleven, Breage, Ashton, Perranuthnoe, and Marazion to Penzance. And then back again. It also (and quite illegally) bore the royal coat of arms among its many decorations.

At the market place, where Elizabeth and Lilian joined the bus, it left the turnpike and made a detour via Porthleven. Matthew Polglaze identified each village by its public house, running the name in with the command to his horses – "Harbour House hooback! . . . Queen's Arms hooback! . . . Lion and Lamb hooback! . . . Falmouth Packet hooback!" Without Lilian to guide her, Elizabeth would have known every pub by name but their respective villages only by sight. What would Morwenna have made of that!

She grew to love those journeys; they united her spirit with that of the land and people in ways that would not otherwise have been possible. The variety was astonishing. Every quarter-mile or so the bus seemed to pass into a different landscape. First it rose to a bald, broad hill south of Helston; then, by the gates of the Penrose estate, it plunged into steeply winding the wooded valleys. But swiftly, over the brow of the next hill, it dropped to the quaysides of the new fishing harbour at Porthleven, built from massive blocks of a strange kind of granite, warm in colour, almost orange when wet. The stench of pilchards was all-pervasive – and utterly appalling – there were times when the oil ran down the streets and the paving had to be sanded for fear the horses might slip.

Then came a long, green valley that could have been twenty miles inland. There, at the cunningly sited tollgate, the bus rejoined the turnpike to Penzance, turning left on the long, uphill climb to Breage. The climax of the journey came at its half-way point, at the Ashton tollgate, where the road wound over the flank of Tregonning Hill and one could see, eight miles away, the entire Land's End peninsula. Far away to the north was a glimpse of the Atlantic, while to the south and much closer, came the mighty sweep of the Channel in Mount's Bay. Later came the romantically Arthurian silhouette of St. Michael's Mount at Marazion; and finally, approaching Penzance itself, the bustle of the present century, the salt-blown railway tracks, the goods yards, the terminus of the Great Western Railway, all practically on the seashore.

She could understand the attraction of this place for those people about whom Hamill had once sneered, faddists of one kind or another, vegetarians, believers in woolen underwear, rational dressers. There was a remote, foreign, tucked-away feeling about the whole of West Cornwall. It held the promise of withdrawal from the bustle and pressure of the industrial world, even here in Penzance, where one might have supposed the railway would be king. In fact, it barely penetrated the town. The terminus was on the extreme eastern fringe. The shops and houses closest to it seemed to draw back in distaste from the invader and scurry away uphill to the west. From the town hall at the centre you could not even see the station, though it was only a few hundred yards away. Someone with no eye for fashion could have taken the year for 1790 rather than a full century on. Surely it was that sense of timeless withdrawal which brought such a strange handful of visitors down the line each summer.

Not that the locals were any less strange – though in a different way. Lilian used to beguile the journey with their tales.

Joel Treloar used to live in an empty pigstye on a farm at Higher Kenneggy, but he left that employment and went to another farm at nearby Prussia Cove "because they 'ad a better pigstye."

Zachary Body was summonsed to Penzance police court for driving a horse and cart at night without proper means of illumination. "Dammee," he told the magistrate, "I didn't need no lamp – I had a white horse."

Old man Andrewartha used to farm up White Alice in a frock coat; Barney Williams, his neighbour over the valley, used to roar across to him, " 'Wartha – where d'ee get that old coat!" and then fall down and roll about the hillside in helpless laughter – every day of his life.

Vic Rogers used to go about selling sand for the housewives to strew on the floor. "Go on!" he used to say. "What good's a hap'orth? Have two-pennyworth!" He was famous for it. He put quite a bit of money aside, which eventually he was persuaded to lodge in Bolitho's Bank in Helston. After he retired he used to sit all day on a bench across the street, in front of the Wesleyan chapel, just to make sure no one robbed the place.

Other passengers broke in with their stories.

When the first bicycle came to Porkellis, Jim Opie of the four-cross took off the back tyre, stood the whole thing upside down, and used it as a hand-cranked winding engine for pulling rabbit skins up the hillside, chased by mongrel dogs on whom the miners placed bets.

The Trethewey choir was not very good. An adjudicator tactfully told them, "I've heard *sweeter* – but never *louder*." They went about for years repeating the judgement under the impression that it was the highest praise.

Of course, the stories did not flow so thick and fast as this simple recounting of them must make it seem. Between each there was much genealogy and local history to be set in order; and every passenger was a specialist in both subjects. No one could mention "Jim Opie of Porkellis four-cross," without someone saying, "Didn't he belong to farm over to Constantine?" Someone else would reply, "No, that was his brother. His father had the corn chandler's in Praze-an-Beeble backalong." Another would chime in, "Old Jim, he married that widow woman out Carharrack. She had some old foreign name. Her sister was sister-in-law to" – turning to another passenger – "your cousin Mary, I b'lieve."

Cousin Mary was, to be sure, a leading member of the Trethewey choir – which was how *that* story came to be retold.

And so, as the bus trotted smartly among the hills and valleys in which these events had all (so folk swore) taken place, Elizabeth came to see it with new eyes. Superimposed upon the crisscross patchwork of tiny fields, she now felt an invisible network of relationships, events, human follies, all the flotsam of rural life. Though invisible, it breathed an extra vigour, a new reality into the passing scene. She could no longer view it in mere picture postcard terms.

In the evenings, though, when it approached the hour for the return journey, the bus ran on human time that took no account of Greenwich or the moon. It would set off dead on the appointed minute, but it would halt after no more than twenty yards.

"Where's Mrs. Tresidder then?" Old Matthew would say.

"I seen she down to Widow Priske, being measured for her new stays."

"Well go and fetch her to once then! Anyone else not here?"

" 'es, master. Thomas Penaluna, he had a tooth pulled. I b'lieve he got drunk."

"Just so well to leave he, then. Where's Peter Caddy?"

"Having his watch mended."

And it would be another half-hour before they were all rounded up and safely stowed aboard.

And *then* Matthew would say, "Well that was thirsty work. We might just so well stop for a dish of tea now as later on."

And there went another half hour, if not more.

In the evenings, after their first experience of the return by bus, Elizabeth and Lilian went home by train.

But thanks to the slow, insidious alchemy of those Penzance days, Elizabeth started to belong down here in Cornwall as she had never belonged anywhere else in her life.

CHAPTER SIXTEEN

IT TOOK RICHARD PASCOE a month or so to grow familiar with the entire estate; Elizabeth quite expected him to conclude his tour with the announcement that he was, regretfully, taking up some other post; she did not doubt he had received offers in plenty. But the worse he found the state of things, the happier he seemed. "It's like the day you discovered Old Tom in those dreadful conditions," he told her. "I'll bet at least part of you sang at the prospect of cleaning him up and putting all to rights."

The fragmentation of the farms was only the most obvious sign of the estate's decay. Others ran deeper. The farms, their buildings, their methods — and in some cases even their tenants — were straight out of the last century. Time had passed over the Pallas lands and left them a living museum to tradition and ineffectiveness. There were too many smallholders, part-time farmers who had once been able to eke out their living with work in the mines. Now that the mines had largely gone, some of them had taken up "lobster fishing," a euphemism for smuggling; others lived by what casual work they could catch. All were desperately poor, so the rents were paltry.

"Yet the land is sound," Pascoe said, "or could be made so. It isn't just a matter of reorganizing the fields. It's the holdings themselves that need amalgamating — in groups of four or five. Then we'd have decent little farms to offer — and the prospect of a fair return on the capital they represent."

"But we can't just turn the tenants off," Elizabeth objected.

"One must sometimes be cruel to be kind, you know, Mrs. Troy. No omelettes without eggshells. In any case, the men themselves would have better prospects . . ."

"But Miss Morwenna's just waiting for me to do something like that. She'd have a field day. I'd be the heartless . . ."

"Are we to manage this estate with *her* at our backs!"

"I'm afraid so, Mr. Pascoe. At least until this wretched court case is done with."

He looked at her in bewilderment. "But the amalgamations I'm talking about will take years. It'll take us until summer just to plan them. I'm sorry if I gave the impression we could manage it overnight."

Elizabeth thought over his words for a few days before she returned to the subject. "What worries me is that the farms don't seem to employ many labourers. Just a few lads to scare the crows — lads who'd be far better off in school. If we displace a lot of the smallholders, where will they find work?"

He replied, "The lack of employment arises because they're all in the wrong type of farming — as I said — a century out of date. You'd think the railway to Helston had never been built."

"But how would that affect the type of farming? Apart from getting produce to market quicker and more . . ."

"Oh, but it completely changes things. Everything! That was my purpose at Chym, you see. If a farmer carries a box of lettuce into Helston station before breakfast, then fifteen hours later it can be on sale in Covent Garden, in London. If maps showed time rather than distance, our land would appear on the inner fringes of the home counties. People haven't woken up to it yet, but it's so. We could now start producing an entirely different range of crops. Indeed, we are now *better* placed than any of the market gardens near London. Thanks to our mild climate, we're a month ahead of them in most things. I'm sure we could even do cut flowers. The Scillies are already doing spring bulbs. Why can't we?"

As he spoke, the last pieces of a puzzle fell into place in Elizabeth's mind — something that had been bothering her, almost without her recognizing it, for months past. Filled with excitement she tried out the idea on him. "All this time, Mr. Pascoe, ever since I realized that the estate must be drastically rearranged, I've had this one nagging thought pulling me back. And you've just shown me the answer."

"What thought was that, Mrs. Troy?"

"I was irked by the fact that whatever I did, I would be goading the tenants into a situation full of risks while I stayed in relative safety. But I couldn't see any other way."

"And now you do?"

"Yes – you've just suggested it. Instead of leading from behind we'll go ahead and beckon them forward to join us. We'll put aside all thought of reorganization for a year. For two, if necessary. And meanwhile we create our model farm, our farm of the future – a sort of living, working demonstration of your ideas."

He laughed at the simplicity of it. "Of course! Of course! But where? I could manage the place easily enough, but . . ."

"Oh, I don't think that's a good idea – for *you* to manage it."

He bridled.

"Don't you see?" she continued. "They'd only say, ' 'Tis well enough for *you*, Squire Pascoe – man of eddycation. But the likes of we could never do'n fitty like.' "

He laughed at her mimicry but conceded the point. "What then?" he asked.

"Me. I'll manage it."

"You?"

"Aren't I the obvious choice? Which of them would be willing to admit he'd fail where some ignorant foreign woman who never saw a haybaler in her life had succeeded!"

"By George, Mrs. Troy!" he said admiringly. "But it'll take all your time, especially . . ."

"Especially as I know less than nothing about it! You needn't say it."

"No, I was thinking of your legal problems. You'll be fighting on every possible front."

"I have no other choice, though, have I."

He was pensive again. "Pity there's no home farm. Who are we going to turn off? Joseph Faull? He's nearest, but the shame of it is he's one of the better tenants."

After a few moments' thought she turned down the idea of taking any existing farm at all. "They'd only say I was profiting from what my predecessor put back into the land over the years. Even if he'd been the world's worst, they'd suddenly claim he was a second Jethro Tull. I think we ought to make it really difficult for ourselves. Let's assemble our farm out of a patchwork of all the spare little parcels of unused land lying about the place. For a start there's three acres below Helston, along the river, by the new sewage farm. We could put up some glasshouses there and do cucumber and lettuce . . ."

"And tomatoes. I think tomatoes could really *take* as a soft fruit in the years to come. But" – he sucked at a tooth – "glasshouses cost money."

"And there's four acres of south-facing spinney behind Wheal Lavender here, remarkably free of frost. The timber is all mature, all good oak. I happened to be over in Penryn the other day so I thought why not call in on Fox's timber yard for a word with their manager? I may have got my sums wrong, but it seems to me that the timber could pay for the clearance of the land and leave several hundred for investment in the crops and machinery."

"What are the terms of your tenancy? Are you liable for delapidations?"

"No. I've checked that."

"The hunt won't be pleased. They draw that spinney every season. They never find it blank, either."

She smiled. "They may draw the Home Wood instead."

He burst into laughter. "Miss Morwenna will be delighted, I don't think."

"We must all make our little sacrifices."

His laughter redoubled. "So you just 'happened' to be near Fox's timberyard the other day! You never stop. I don't suppose you just 'happen' to have a plan already drawn out of this bits-and-pieces farm of ours?"

They took down the estate map and within the hour assembled a scattered holding of around fifty acres. She looked at it and laughed. "You'd imagine we just dropped an inkwell and saw where the spots landed."

"What on earth do we name it?" he asked.

"Let's keep up the classical tradition and call it the Archipelago."

And for the rest of that day, indeed for much of that week, they planned the Archipelago to its last detail, beginning with the new early crops made marketable by the new railway, right through to the cabbage, the sprouts, and the root crops that could be left standing for harvest all through the winter. The need to give year-round employment for the men, with three or four seasonal bursts for their womenfolk between Easter and the fall, was a consideration every bit as important as wringing the last penny out of the soil – if they were later to encourage a voluntary enclosure of the smallholdings.

They decided to confine themselves entirely to arable and market-garden operations – no livestock to begin with. Elizabeth had always had green fingers; the prospect of cabbages and flowers did not seem daunting, even though the crops were to cover acres rather than just a few backgarden beds. Nevertheless, the cost of it all was beyond her present resources – until she could claim Bill's personalty, or at least the interest upon it.

"We'll just have to content ourselves with half of it for this year," Pascoe said.

She saw that for all his knowledge and self-assurance he was not at heart a fighter. "It's all or nothing, Mr. Pascoe," she said. "We must find the money somehow."

"You could owe me some of my salary? Or put me in for a percentage of the final profit instead? I could get by, you know. We'd not starve."

He really was an exceedingly nice man, she thought. Why were all the nicest men flawed by lack of that final ounce of ruthlessness? Courtenay would never have considered making such a gesture.

"I'll bully it out of someone," she promised. "That's assuming the case will drag on and on. If it's finished quickly, our immediate money worries will be solved."

But he tapped his lean forefinger on the map. "Even if you win the legal point, Mrs. Troy, the real battle with your sister-in-law will be here."

CHAPTER SEVENTEEN

THE COURT HEARING came at the end of Hilary, as George Ivey had predicted. Within a very short while Elizabeth decided that, compared with the organization of English Law, the arrangements on the Pallas estate were already a model of efficiency. Her bafflement began even before they entered the Law Courts, when she learned that George Ivey himself was not there to speak for her. No matter that he knew her case inside out, knew the estate, the plaintiff . . . every last detail — the rules of the court prevented him from saying so much as one word. Instead he had to hire (or "retain," as he called it) another lawyer, a Queen's Counsellor, to speak for him. This was a man she had never met, who had never seen the estate, and who had no continuing interest in her future. His name was Dudley Montague and everyone assured her he was most eminent.

They met for the first time in the corridor outside the courtroom. He was tall, handsome in a fiftyish way, slightly dishevelled — probably a bachelor, she decided. He had a habit of consulting his watch, or any clock in sight, not as other busy men are wont to do but with a yearning intensity, as if it were about to yield up secrets that had always eluded him.

This most eminent legal personage required, in turn, the support of something called a "junior counsel," a Mr. Jervis Conyngham, who was actually Mr. Montague's senior in years, though not in inches. He managed to be both remote and irascible, sourly interested in everything and everyone except his immediate surroundings and company. His left hand had developed a mind and will of its own; it kept up an endless patrol of the openings to all the numerous pockets of his trousers, morning coat, and waistcoat, inserting the tip of a finger here, the knuckle of a thumb there . . . counting, smoothing, patting, and occasionally transferring their contents.

Both men were barristers, the only kind of lawyer permitted to plead in the High Court.

"You should have told me as much in the first place," Elizabeth grumbled privately to Ivey. "Then I could have gone directly to them."

"Barristers can't take instructions from the public — only from solicitors."

"But that's extraordinary. Do they think you're incapable of pleading our case?"

"Of course not. It's just the way things are done here, that's all."

"And why must there be two of them?"

"Because Montague's a very eminent man. He probably has at least a couple of other cases, apart from ours, coming up today — all in different courts. Conyngham's here to cover for him if he can't appear for us."

"Ah, I see! It's for Montague's benefit, not ours. So I take it Montague's paying?"

"I'm afraid not. It doesn't work that way. We're paying for both of them."

"*We* are! I like that."

"We're extremely lucky to get Montague, you know. He's one of the very best."

The same lavish system of triplicate employment ruled on Morwenna's side, too, Elizabeth was glad to notice. But Morwenna's expenses did not stop there. She had splashed out on a new dress, a galleon-like creation of watered silk in dark mauve. Her hat must have consumed half a tropical aviary. She eyed Elizabeth, who was dressed in provincial simplicity, once and once only, smiled with acid contentment, and then stared about her like a Roman general in triumph. If the contest depended upon which of them *seemed* more like the true mistress of Pallas, Morwenna was already past the finishing line.

They were waiting in the Great Hall, two hundred and thirty feet long and more than eighty high. To the judges and counsel who had transferred here from the ancient Westminster Hall it must have seem like home from home, though it was barely ten years old. To all other visitors it already seemed the most abysmal anachronism. At last came the moment to file into court, a much smaller room than Elizabeth had anticipated.

A few moments later the president, the Right Honourable Ogle St. Clair Gonne, Baron Northcott, wandered in, like a man seeking a lost bookmark; indeed, he appeared not to realize it *was* his court until he arrived at his bench and peered down over his spectacles at the small gathering that now awaited his pleasure. Sitting with him were the Hon. Sir Gavin Dunlop Uthwatt and the Hon. Sir Fergus Turnbull Bennett. The president sighed and nodded, much as to say, 'Well, since you're all here, we might as well go through with it.'

When the introductions were over, and the distribution of papers, and the coughing, and the general crossing and uncrossing of legs, Mr. Dudley "Lucky-to-get-him" Montague QC permitted Morwenna's counsel, a Mr. Royston Meredith QC, to recite the facts of the case.

Elizabeth was forced to miss these preliminaries because Montague, leaving his junior to hold the fort, called her and George Ivey outside for a conference.

"It's the wording of this will that puzzles me," he said. "It only occurred to me last night or I'd have mentioned it earlier. I was looking over the document when that sentence struck me most forcibly: 'To my wife Elizabeth née Mitchell provided only that she shall at the time of my death have married me I hereby devise . . .' etcetera. It's a strange form of wording, don't you think?"

Elizabeth looked at Ivey. "You also commented on that."

"Why d'you think they chose such a wording?" Montague pressed.

"To make quite sure," George replied. "To avoid any question of femme sole and femme covert."

Montague nodded. "My thought exactly. Rum, what!" He paused and turned to her. "May I be entirely frank, Mrs. Troy?"

"I wish you would. You're all like doctors here. You seem to think the less we laymen know, the better."

He ignored the comment. "Do you suppose that Bill might have had some intimation of his death?"

The notion shook her, but the more she considered it, the more she had to allow its possibility. She nodded and said, reluctantly, "He'd had one mild stroke earlier in the year — I mean, that's why he was in hospital. That's how I came to be his nurse. Who knows what little episodes he might not have experienced during his recovery?"

"Did he mention any such thing?"

"No, but he wouldn't have. When he was in pain, or even when he was just uncomfortable, you'd never get a word of it out of him. But I've nursed stroke patients who've recovered from a second stroke and afterwards — those who could speak still — they've said they knew the second one was coming. Little syncopes — fainting — whirrings in the ear . . . spasms. Bill would never have mentioned such things but he might have experienced them nonetheless."

He nodded, as if her words confirmed his thoughts. "You see, if I were a solicitor drawing up a will, it's a form of words I might just hit upon if a client intimated to me that he thought he could die at any moment. Literally *any* moment. Otherwise the word *wife* would surely be sufficient. As you say, Mr. Ivey, it's as if he wanted to make absolutely sure from the moment of leaving the church – no matter what might happen to him – absolutely sure you, Mrs. Troy – and not his sister – would inherit."

He and George exchanged glances. "I think we must call that Brighton solicitor, whatsisname – Haskins," George said.

They seemed about to settle on that when Elizabeth interrupted. "Just a moment. Is Haskins likely to say Bill was desperate to prevent Morwenna from continuing to manage the estate?"

Montague nodded. "That would seem to be the clear inference. Why?"

"If so, I'd almost rather lose the case. I just want . . ."

"For heaven's sake, Mrs. Troy!" Ivey protested.

"I only want to destroy Morwenna's argument, not Morwenna herself."

The two men exchanged a further glance. Elizabeth knew its meaning well. It said, 'Let's humour this silly, emotional young woman for the moment, but we'll go our own strong, manly way in the end.'

They went back into court, where Morwenna's evidence was about to begin. But Elizabeth found herself so torn between the argument she had just had outside and the presentation of the case in court that she lost the thread of both. Fortunately, it was all summed up most crisply the following day in *The Courts Gazette*. Elizabeth and Oenone, taking breakfast in their rooms in a small private hotel in Paddington, read the summary with incredulity:

High Court of Chancery
In re: *Troy vs. Troy – a Disputed Will*

The hearing opened today before The Rt. Hon. Ogle St. Clair Gonne, Baron Northcott (presiding), The Hon. Sir Gavin Dunlop Uthwatt and the Hon. Sir Fergus Turnbull Bennett. The plaintiff, Miss Morwenna Troy of Pallas House, Helston, Cornwall, moved that the will of her late brother, Capt. William Carter Troy, DCLI, be set aside on the grounds that he was not of sound mind, memory, and understanding at the time of making it; alternatively, she claims that Capt. Troy, even if of sound mind, was subjected to undue influence by the defendant, Mrs. Elizabeth Troy of Wheal Lavender, Helston, who married Capt. Troy on the day of his death.

The captain died on Saturday 15th April, 1889. By the terms of the disputed will, which was executed in the vestry immediately after the wedding ceremony, a discretionary trust for sale is created; Mrs. Troy is tenant-for-life; a portion is allotted to Miss Troy, who is also made a trustee for sale; other portions were left to two older members of the Troy family, both alive. The remainder on the portions, and on the rest of the estate after its eventual sale, is to Mrs. Troy.

An earlier will, drawn up when William Troy came of age in 1881, provided *inter alia* that in the event of his dying married but childless, his wife should have a portion and Miss Troy should be tenant-for-life with remainder to the issue of George Troy, the testator's paternal uncle.

In evidence the plaintiff introduced a number of letters from the deceased in which the following passages were, in particular, relied upon:

"I am beside myself, almost mad I think, to be married to her."

"She has me in such a turmoil that at times I hardly know my head from my heels."

"This love is a kind of insanity."

Mr. JUSTICE UTHWATT: Is it plaintiff's contention that no sane man, in the days leading up to his wedding, has ever written of his beloved in such terms?

Mr. ROYSTON MEREDITH QC (*for the plaintiff*): It is plaintiff's contention that Capt. Troy had never before written and spoken in such terms and that they are indicative of his disordered state of mind. Taken together with the stroke he had suffered in January of that year and the one which we now know killed him on the day of his wedding, it is clear that his mental state during that final week of his life was, to say the least, far from normal.

Elizabeth's eye skipped down the dry, neat columns of the report. "They leave so much out, Oenone," she said. "All the facts are there, but . . . well, it's nothing like what actually happened."

Oenone took the paper, looked at if briefly, and said, "I calculate you'd have to be burr and educated to know what to leave out."

"The trouble is we've got no way of knowing what they think is important or not. Look at this." Elizabeth read out a passage in a neutral tone: " 'Miss Morwenna Troy: All his life he was a most careful, thoughtful lad . . .' "

"Master Bill?" Oenone asked incredulously.

"Yes, but listen."

"Him – careful? Thoughtful? That's louch, that is!"

"Listen, she goes on: 'His military training, too, taught him to think of the consequences of his actions. Anyone who knew him well would tell you it was utterly uncharacteristic of him that he should hazard the Pallas Estate in this way. By his insistence upon this form of words he was, in effect, saying that if he died, he wished his family heritage – two and a quarter thousand acres of arable land, one and a quarter thousand acres of croft, invaluable mineral rights, and the finest art collection and library in the county – all that – he wished it *all* to pass into the hands of a pretty young nurse whose breeding had barely fitted her to manage a small suburban household. No man of William's class and upbringing could contemplate such a possibility. How anyone could believe such a will to be the product of a completely sane mind, defeats me.'"

Elizabeth shook her head. "I don't even remember her saying any of that."

Oenone pulled a face. "I do. 'Cept it never sounded like that when she stood up there and said it. Don't you remember? That's when she was spitting and that — when the judge had to ask her if she wished to sit down, when he called for a glass of water? You do surely 'member."

"Oh yes — I recall the glass of water. Yes, she was almost in a frenzy. That's why I didn't recognize it, because you don't get any of that in the words as they're reported, do you?" Her eye fell down the page. "And also here where it says I married him on the day of his death — as if I *knew* it at the time! But it makes the whole thing look so calculated. It worries me. Do the judges go by the words or by what they actually see and hear?"

"They aren't no fools, those old fellers."

"I hope not. But, as George Ivey says, they don't deal in truth, only in permissible evidence. And they don't hand out justice, only legal verdicts."

"The Dragon's had it all to herself so far. Who've we got today?"

"Our best witnesses, I think, will be Colonel Treadwell, his old CO, who entertained him in the mess the night before our wedding. And above all, Mr. Rawlins, Bill's surgeon. He's one of the world's leading specialists on the brain. And Ivey says we could also call Mr. Haskins, the lawyer who drew up the will. He's in no doubt Bill knew exactly what he was doing and was determined not to leave Pallas in the Dragon's tender care. But I don't want to call him."

Oenone looked at her in surprise. "Why not?"

"I'd rather win by other means. I just want to refute Morwenna, not crush her."

Oenone looked as if she were about to argue but Elizabeth said, "Go and ask them to call a cab, there's a dear."

When they arrived at the Law Courts for the start of the second day, Elizabeth was surprised to see, alighting from the cab ahead of her, the Brighton lawyer himself.

"Mr. Haskins!" she called out.

He recognized her and paused. "Good morning, Mrs. Troy."

"Good morning. I hope you are not here in connection with my case? I gave specific instructions that you were not to be called."

He nodded gravely. "Mr. Montague believes I may serve your purpose without being called — not into open court, that is."

"I don't like the sound of this."

"Shall we go inside? I'm sure he'll explain it to you."

"I doubt it. He and George Ivey both belong to the Ignorance-is-Bliss brigade."

"Oh really?" Haskins looked at her in bewilderment.

"*You* tell me."

"Very well. If you insist. You remember the papers I brought to the convalescent home for you and Captain Troy to sign?"

"The ones he covered up with his gloves so that all I could see was the blank space for my signature?"

"That's the fellow. Well, that was to give you Power of Attorney in case he was incapacitated. He kept it secret from you because he didn't want you distressed. He didn't want you to know that the thought of his possible incapacity was very much on his mind."

"I see. And what present bearing . . ."

"Montague believes that if we privately approach the other party with this information, they'll realize that it virtually undermines their entire case. And so . . ."

"When you say the other party, you mean only the legal advisors — Coad and Mr. Meredith? Miss Morwenna needn't know?"

Haskins cleared his throat delicately. "There is more," he said.

"What, pray?"

"You'd better read it." From his briefcase he drew forth a letter, addressed to him.

It was in Bill's hand.

He passed it to her with his black-gloved finger on a particular paragraph. "That's the relevant portion," he said.

It read:

> Having taken the coward's way out and left the estate in my sister's hands, I have had to watch it fall yet further into rack and ruin. Now I can bear it no longer. I have found the perfect partner for such a perilous venture, and have resigned my commission. I am resolved to return forthwith to Pallas and "clean out the Augean Stables." But, as I have already suffered one stroke, I must in all prudence guard against a recurrence, whether it might lead to my incapacity or to my death.
>
> To cover the case of incapacity, I would like you to prepare Power of Attorney for Elizabeth Mitchell, my wife-to-be. Tell me what particulars you need and I shall supply them. She is not to know of this yet. After we are married I shall explain to her that I would wish her to sell the estate and devote the proceeds to my medical expenses, also, of course, to herself and the surviving members of the family.
>
> In the event of my death, I wish Elizabeth to be made life-tenant. My sister, together with others whose names I shall give you, will be made trustees for sale. I know Morwenna well enough to be sure that, once she sees the reins firmly in Elizabeth's hands, she will not be able to sell the estate quickly enough!

Thus in both eventualities my purpose is achieved. The estate will be quickly sold and my dearest Elizabeth will have the burden of it for the least possible time.

There was more but she had already seen enough.

"Such a letter cannot possibly be made public, Mr. Haskins," she said. "Miss Morwenna must never see it or even know of its existence."

George Ivey joined them at that moment. He saw the letter and overheard her final remark. "For what reason?" he asked.

"I told you yesterday – it would break her heart. It would destroy her."

"She's doing her level best to destroy you!"

"No. The two cases are not equal. Even if she won hands down, I'd still be left with a lovely home and a comfortable portion. I wouldn't call that destruction. But show her this letter and the rest of her life will be in shreds."

"Go on! She's as tough as fresh granite."

"I disagree. Anyway, I refuse to take the risk. But perhaps if there were some way of showing it to Coad – or Meredith – and swearing them to secrecy?"

Ivey looked dubious. "I don't know how ethical that would be."

"Good heavens, Ivey – where's your horns and tail now?"

Haskins looked at the pair of them askance. Montague joined them at that moment. After yesterday there was no need to explain Elizabeth's scruples to him.

"I commend you heartily, Mrs. Troy," he said. "Yet I must also counsel you that no case in law is ever so certain that one can afford to leave one's best ammunition lying in the locker."

"How ethical would it be to approach Meredith?"

All this talk of ethics was beginning to give Haskins cold feet. He said, "I'm not even sure of the propriety of producing a client's letters in court – dead though he may be."

She fanned his doubts: "I'm sure it would be a scandal, Mr. Haskins."

Ivey looked miserable but Montague brightened at once. "There we have it!" He beamed. "We'll approach their lordships in chambers, counsel for both sides. And I'll ask their opinion on the ethics of introducing the letter. We'd surely do that anyway, wouldn't we? Just to cover ourselves. Then Meredith will know what ammunition we have – but, er, in circumstances that would make it quite proper for me to ask him not to divulge . . ."

"Isn't there an offence called 'Conspiracy to pervert the course of justice'?" Elizabeth asked.

They ignored her.

"Our big gun could burst on us," Ivey cautioned. "What if their lordships rule that it *would* be unethical?"

She interrupted again. "Let this conversation stop now! This minute. I absolutely forbid you to introduce that letter – or to call Mr. Haskins in evidence as to Bill's intentions."

"Then you must face the possibility of losing, ma'am," Montague said crisply.

"I'd sooner live with that than be responsible for the utter destruction of Miss Morwenna."

They began drifting toward the courtroom, shaking their heads at her foolhardiness.

"You wouldn't hurt that old dragon," Oenone assured Elizabeth. "Whatever's in that old letter, she'd just say 'twas another 'zample of Master Bill being wiffle-headed."

The evidence followed its predictable course that morning. Colonel Treadwell spoke of Bill's utter normality not only on the eve of his wedding but ever since his recovery. "If anything," he said, "the poor old chap settled down somewhat as soon as his engagement was announced. Not that he was a wild sort of fellow before, but junior officers . . . bachelors . . . well, one doesn't expect them to be old before their time, eh!"

Everyone knew exactly what he meant.

One or two brother officers corroborated their CO's opinion. Elizabeth passed a note to Montague: *See! You're doing splendidly. We don't need Haskins.* And then it was time for lunch. Mr. Rawlins, Bill's surgeon, was to be called immediately after.

Elizabeth hastened up to the public benches to join Oenone. They were just about to leave when Oenone pointed down and said, "Well! Just look at him!"

The only person remaining on the floor of the court was Mr. Meredith. He was standing rigid, immersed in some reading.

"That's Master Bill's letter, isn't it?" Oenone went on. "He just stooped and picked 'un up. Bold as brass."

Elizabeth was on the point of shouting at the man when Montague's clerk came breezing back into the court in great agitation.

"Looking for this?" Meredith asked innocently.

"I'll strangle that Montague!" Elizabeth was furious.

She had worked up a fine lather by the time the court reassembled. But a shock awaited them: Mr. Meredith rose at once to announce that the plaintiff was withdrawing her suit.

And that was it. The unbobbed tips of quill pens shivered in brief, medieval flurries, recording the non-decision; the screech of them, though it lay beyond the hearing of those who had speaking parts in the drama, excruciated Elizabeth. The ensuing silence left the air heavy with the stench of costly litigation, as two senior counsel, two junior counsel, and two solicitors, trooped out to fresh courts and triumphs new.

Elizabeth swivelled around and looked at Morwenna. The older woman, though well aware of her sister-in-law's gaze, continued to stare directly ahead of her.

She knows! Elizabeth thought. Without hesitation she walked among the counsels' benches to reach her; still Morwenna did not turn.

"I told them *not* to reveal that letter," Elizabeth said.

The woman appeared not to hear her; she was shaking with some emotion.

Elizabeth tried again. "I'm so sorry. I'd rather you had won than that."

At last Morwenna turned to her. "If Bill could see you now, if he could see how you intend to ruin Pallas, he would *spit* upon you."

"Morwenna! How can you say that – especially . . ."

"He expected you to be guided by me, of course. He loved me. He respected everything I did at Pallas. And he thought he knew you. He thought you'd ask my advice every step of the way."

"You mean . . ."

"Instead of which you have spurned and despised . . ." Her voice broke. She pursed her lips together and stared directly ahead of her again.

Elizabeth understood then. Meredith had not told her of the letter. Out of concern for her pride? Or his own? No matter – he had found some other way to dissuade her from her suit. "Well," she said in as conciliatory a tone as she could muster, "at least all this wrangling about the will is now behind us. Perhaps we can begin to mend . . ."

Her voice tailed off. The Dragon turned and froze her with the iciest, most superior smile – such a smile as no woman could give if so damning a fraternal opinion had just been conveyed to her.

This smile said, 'I have not even *begun* to deal with you yet!'

CHAPTER EIGHTEEN

THE EASY WIN, where she had expected a long, untidy, dispiriting, and probably inconclusive fight, left Elizabeth filled with an angry steam that had no simple outlet. She felt ready to burst most of the time. She tried to apply herself to the business of the estate, especially to the Archipelago farm, but it did not help. Nature was too slow, even now, in spring, with all the world burgeoning around her. She had never seen anything so prolific, so breathtakingly lovely, as these Cornish hedgerows bursting into the new year's growth. By contrast, the cultivated part of Nature, the part from which the estate drew its income, was a slow old clodhopper. It offered no channels for her sudden excess of energy.

She thought then of the mines. She really ought to be more involved in their day-to-day operations. And then there was the *Vindicator*, as well. In her view it was as much in need of reform as the estate; it, too, had not caught up with the railway age.

But then came the cold water: What did she know about mines and newspapers! Wasn't the creation of the Archipelago work enough for one ignorant woman over the next few years? The sensible course would be to come to some arrangement with the trustees to sell off the mining interests and devote the proceeds to the land. And she should do the same with her share of the paper. She had too many irons in the fire.

But no sooner had she reached these excellent resolutions than the pendulum would swing back the other way and she would see the three different ventures as three potential throws of fortune's dice. If the depression in agriculture continued, then all the improvements in the world would not make the estate prosperous, as Pascoe often reminded her – and who should know better than he! But then she would still have the mines and the paper as her safety net . . .

And so, as she swung from one extreme to the other, her restlessness increased. One day, about two weeks after she returned from her High Court "triumph," she called on Courtenay at the *Vindicator* offices; at least she could find out what her share was worth. She wasted no time on ceremonies. "What'll you give me for my interest in the paper?" she asked.

"Thank you, I've been very well. A slight cold, but I'm over it now. And you?"

"Never better. How much?"

He relaxed. "Lord, Beth! You're a lovely woman."

"How much?"

"I was in Bristol a couple of weeks ago – while you were wiping the floor of the Law Courts with the Gorgon. Went to the zoo. Saw a pair of tigers there, in cages side by side. Two solitary carnivores. Couldn't help thinking of you and me. That slumbering aggression between them. Those calm, lethal eyes. Yet there comes that inevitable season when wise old Mother Nature stirs the juices and . . ."

"I didn't come here to talk about that."

He looked closely into her eyes. "I'm sure you believe it."

She sat down with a sigh. Why was she so easily deflected? Why did her firmest purpose prove so volatile? Her fingers drummed the table.

He reseated himself, too. "Joking apart, Beth – what's up?"

"There are so many things to do, I don't know where to start. Yet everything's so slow, too."

"What you need, my lover, is a holiday. Go to Italy. Look up your mother — let her hear what's happened. D'you think she knows?"

"She never answers my letters. I don't suppose she reads them even. But *that* isn't the answer." She despaired of being able to explain it to him.

He went on: "It's all of a piece with your determination to scrub the floors at Wheal Lavender yourself. You could have hired a couple of women to do it in a fraction of the time, but no — you have to roll up your sleeves, get your own skin red and raw."

She smiled ruefully. "I can't help wanting to work. My idea of hell is all eternity on a sunlit beach."

"It's so idiotic. You've got the best possible manager in Richard Pascoe, why not leave it to . . ."

"I'll tell you something about Pascoe. He's a wonderful manager. I wouldn't argue with that. I'd be finished without him. But he just lacks that ultimate . . . I don't know — electricity. He needs *me* to give him that final bit of a spark. And if you're about to say I've got Cornwall's best mine captain in Captain Body, again I'll agree. But again I'd have to add that he needs *me* to argue with, to cajole for more investment. Without that, he's lost."

Courtenay straightened two pencils with finality. "There you are then. Problem solved."

She stifled a scream in her head. "But those two roles, vital though they may be, consume about an hour of my time each *month*!"

He smiled, narrowing his eyes. "Bill really knew what he was doing when he chose you." He grew solemn. "God, what a tragedy. You and he together — you could have . . ."

He sighed and let the rest of the sentence hang. He had spoken sincerely, even a little thoughtlessly, from the heart — but she could see he was also testing her, noting the depth of her response.

She gave away nothing. The shade of that particular grief had passed too frequently across her soul to make so shallow a revelation now. "I don't think he knew me at all. Neither me nor the Dragon. When I was in London his solicitor, the one in Brighton, showed me a letter he'd written. In it he said that once Morwenna realized she no longer controlled Pallas, she'd sell it at the first opportunity. Bill's idea was that I'd never actually have to take up the life tenancy but merely enjoy the proceeds of it."

"How d'you know she won't? She's only had a couple of weeks to grasp the fact that at last she's lost control of the estate. When she's drained that cup to its bitterest dregs, perhaps she'll prove Bill right after all."

"I'll bet my share of the paper against yours that she'll die rather than sell a single acre. Are you on?"

With a slow smile he shook his head.

"And, talking of the paper," she went on, "what *would* my share of it be worth? To you? I'm sure you'd pay handsomely to be rid of me?"

"Are you serious? If you need money, you know life tenants can now mortgage their lands? George'd tell you."

"I'm not saying I'd sell. But I'd like to know where I stand."

He shrugged. "For a quick sale? Sixteen hundred. If you wanted to convert your interest into a debenture? In round figures . . . three thousand."

"Is that all?"

"Oh yes – everyone thinks newspapers are goldmines."

"But Courtenay – that's shocking!"

He bridled. "Don't you think you ought to stick to something you *really* know nothing about – like Pallas?"

But now, in her anger, the words just tumbled out of her: "You're every bit as blind as my tenants, Courtenay. They have no idea what the coming of the railway has meant – and nor have you."

"Oh but you'll tell me!"

"Someone has to. This paper still serves the area reached by horse and cart. If we used the railway for our circulation, we could reach from Land's End up to Truro. Or why not all Cornwall? People are moving around much more nowadays. Oenone was telling me about the last church social – how they all went by train up to St. Austell for the day. Most of them had never been farther than Long Downs before that. I think the time is ripe for a paper to cover the whole of West Cornwall. If we don't do it, someone else will."

All the while she spoke she watched his jaw muscles ripple as he chewed on his teeth; at his temple it looked like the throbbing of an angry vein. There was something thrilling about his anger.

"Finished?" he said at last. "It so happens that I've edited and managed this paper from the very first issue. There's nothing you can tell me about it. Our readers expect certain standards and they respect me because I maintain them. We shall never kowtow to fashion."

"Respect is not negotiable at the bank."

There was a knock at the door. After a pause Courtenay called, "Come in!" His tone was surprised, as if he had never before had to say such a thing.

Beresford, the chief (and only) reporter, brought in a few sheets of paper. "The market prices," he said.

Courtenay glanced at them and then, to give the impression that all was calm, said to Elizabeth, "Be thankful you're not in sheep, Mrs. Troy."

"Shall I bring you the keys, Mr. Rodda?" Beresford asked.

"Just leave them in the door. We shan't be long here."

He went, somehow taking all their anger with him. Their eyes dwelled in each other's and they laughed.

Elizabeth looked at the clock and asked, "Isn't five somewhat early to be closing the office?"

"Alarmed?" he laughed. "You'll never get used to it, will you – *Mrs. Troy?*"

"But isn't it?"

"On the day before publication, yes. On the day after, however, it's quite usual. Did you imagine I'd tipped Beresford to leave early any time you called?"

She rose. "I must go." Her voice trembled; her heart was racing.

He noticed it, and the effect on him was immediate. All his superior humour vanished; his face was suddenly pale. He rose and came around the desk. "I'll see you to your carriage."

"It's only the dogcart." What a strange, remote voice she had. "I left it behind the Angel . . ."

His hands touched her shoulder as he resettled her wrap. Her shivering grew so violent it frightened her. She wanted her feet to move but his grip tightened, pulling her toward him; his breath on her neck.

"No, Courtenay."

His fingers spoke for him.

"We mustn't."

This time the flesh was more knowing; their entanglement almost too sweet to bear.

Afterwards he seemed unable to look at her.

"That must never happen again," she said

He nodded.

"From now on," she added, "we must make sure we are never in danger of meeting alone."

Again their eyes dwelled in each other's. They both knew how impossible it was going to be.

CHAPTER NINETEEN

GEORGE IVEY LOOKED UP in surprise. "Oh . . . but this is indeed an honour. *I* could have called upon *you*, Mrs. Troy."

"I needed the exercise," she told him.

His eyes went wide. "You don't mean you've walked?" He went to fetch a chair from across his office.

"No, I've taken up riding again. One can do a lot of thinking while one rides."

"One can also do a lot of falling off while one's thinking. Anyway – what is the fruit of all this brainwork?" He placed the chair under her and went to the cabinet. "Sherry and biscuits?"

"I'd love a sherry. There's been no fruitfulness, I'm afraid. Just this question that goes on and on in my mind: What will *she* do next?"

He stopped in the middle of pouring her measure.

"That's enough for me," she told him.

He brought it to her and returned to pour his own. She knew then why she had come here instead of summoning him out to Wheal Lavender. His office was so solid and reassuring. The dark oak of the panelling and furniture, the high polish, the comfortable leather of the chairs, the small, well-ordered pile of documents on his desk – here the whole world was under control. Rampant, disorderly fields were reduced to neatly bound title deeds; all the fury and rancour of personal strife was rendered down to dry, cool sections and sub-paragraphs. Here the problems of life withered like leaves on the forest floor; and in their decaying litter, the answers grew and flourished.

"I know the feeling well," he said, toasting her with his glass. "Ever since you came down to Cornwall, the future for you has been focussed on that one point – who will win, Morwenna or you?"

"Morwenna or Bill," she corrected. "I'd hardly call it *my* victory!"

"Whatever you say. But now the trial is no longer in a court of law, where it's all done by the rules; instead, it's out there, in the big, nasty world where the rules are few. Yes, I know that feeling only too well."

She had a passing intimation that he was talking about something else. But then, completely changing the subject, he inquired whether she had seen the latest *Vindicator*.

"Is there something about Morwenna?" she asked.

He opened a drawer and took out a copy. "Page four," he said, passing it to her. "It's the only item of interest in the whole wretched rag."

She turned to the page in question and her eye was at once caught by a large drawing – a balloonist's view of the Chym estate. "Bolitho's Bank has at last decided to put it under the hammer," he explained. "Next month."

"Did you draw that?" she asked. "It's beautiful."

He grinned. "Modesty forbids . . ."

"I hope Rodda paid you well for it?"

He struggled for some flippant reply but seriousness overcame him. "I did it gladly, for nothing. Every now and then I *need* to do something like that, you know."

The accompanying text was a thicket of superlatives.

"When I read the article, it almost got me wondering if I couldn't raise the wind to buy the place myself," he went on. "Pity your circulation's so small."

She leaned forward. "Tell me . . . I'd welcome your opinion. What d'you think of the *Vindicator*?"

"Dull."

She waited for more.

"I've known Courtenay Rodda all my life. Dear fellow! Wouldn't hear a word against him."

"But?"

"But who is he? I think you'd have a better paper if he could answer that question. At the moment, the *Vindicator* is the only firm, solid thing about him. It needs changing – you and I can see it clearly – and so, probably can he. But he daren't do it. I think it's because he doesn't know who he is. Is he a retired colonial administrator (which you'd imagine from the way he's decorated Yeol Parc)? Or a landowner? Or a photographer? A naturalist? A local historian? Or is he, after all, a newspaper proprietor? To put it bluntly – what is the dear boy going to be when he grows up?" He smiled. "Don't tell him I said so."

Elizabeth nodded grimly. "I'll have no difficulty in passing off the opinion as my own, believe me."

They sipped their wine and sat a moment in silence.

"As to your question," he said reluctantly, "I don't know Miss Troy well enough to answer you with any confidence. Can't old Hamill Oliver tell you anything?"

"I don't want to put him in the position of informer. Unless he comes to me of his own free will . . . of course."

"Scruples again! I've no doubt it's bankable in heaven but it's not much good here below."

"What would you advise her – if she turned to you – professionally?"

Ivey sank his forehead to his hand and massaged hard while he spoke, as if the words would stick but for this easing. "Bill was able to leave the land as he liked because the original entail was broken. Well – never mind the legal niceties – the fact is, he was the owner in fee simple, the outright owner. The first thing I'd do is check back along the line of succession just to make sure that everything is in order."

"Shouldn't we do that then?"

He shrugged and looked up. "If you've money to burn. But I shouldn't worry. If they found anything, we'd still have bags of time for our own research."

"What else would you advise her?"

"I'd let her in on one of the great legal secrets. I'd tell her that lawyers have done more harm by telling clients of their rights than they ever did by simply keeping quiet. Take a look at this!" He fished in his drawer again and came out with a little wood engraving of the kind that tradesmen put at

THE LAWSUIT.

the head of their correspondence. "I wish I had the courage to use this on my own letterhead."

"The lawyer's the scroundrel in the middle, of course," he went on. "You may be quite certain he advised both those peasants of their every last little right." Idly, while he was speaking, he sketched in skirts and bonnets over the two contending peasants; like everything he drew they had an amazing life and reality. He handed the result to her with a flourish. "I'm sure I needn't hang name cards around the necks of those two women."

It ought to have reassured her, but it failed. He sighed and went on, "In fact, I don't think her best attack is on the legal front at all. And I'm sure she's known it all along."

"What then?"

He hesitated before he said, "Social."

She didn't follow.

"Miss Troy will do her level best – or, rather, her considerable worst – to keep you out of local Society."

Elizabeth laughed. "As if I give a fig for that!"

But he was not amused. "Now there you would be mistaken, if I may say so, Mrs. Troy."

"I have not the slightest desire to 'go about,' as they say."

"It isn't a simple matter of being At Home and being seen in the right places and wearing the right clothes and opinions – though that's all you see of Society from the outside. The view from inside is quite different, I assure you." When he saw she did not believe him he put it more bluntly. "To be one of the county's largest landowners and yet to be cut off from its richest springs of inside information . . ."

"Gossip, you mean!"

"Gossip *is* inside information. You don't just need to know what way the local lawmakers are thinking, you need to play a part in shaping their thought. A word here, a nod there, a nudge somewhere else. You need a friend on the Highways Committee . . . someone who owes you a favour on the Board of Works . . . someone who daren't cross you among the Harbour Commissioners."

"But what have harbours to do with me? Or, come to that . . ."

"You never know! You might be able to do someone a favour. And he, in turn . . . well, you see how it goes. And these matters are all arranged at dinners and tea parties and regattas and Sunday School prizegivings and all the other occasions you say you don't give a fig for. If you're excluded from them, you'll be managing Pallas blinded, hobbled, and with one hand pinioned."

She looked morosely at her empty glass. "I should have asked for more sherry." But when he rose to obey she waved him back to his seat. "No – that's Hamill's answer."

He grinned wickedly to prepare her for his next suggestion. "Under the new Settled Lands Acts, you know, you're at liberty to grant a tenancy for a fixed term which, even if you decease, would have to be honoured by your successors. In the old days a life-tenant's death cancelled all such arrangements, so, of course, they weren't worth a bean. Now they're worth good money. What do you say, eh?"

She laughed. "I say get thee behind me, Satan!"

"It doesn't tempt you?"

"Of course it does. But I'd have to live with myself afterwards. I'd have to explain such cowardice to myself every single sunrise until I die. No – if Morwenna wants to move the battle to those fields, I'll have to join her there." She pulled a face. "Talk about David and Goliath!"

For some reason her words heartened him; she began to suspect he had anticipated this conversation for weeks past and hadn't been sure how she would take it. "You have some formidable weapons of your own," he said.

"I can't think of one."

"Your youth and the energy and beauty that go with it . . . your position as landowner . . . your eligibility as a widow still of breeding age . . ."

"Oh stop!"

"And let us not forget your part-ownership of the *Vindicator!* Potentially that is your biggest trump of all."

She put down her glass with finality. "I can't tell you, Mr. Ivey, how glad I am we had this talk. For the first time in almost a year I have a clear idea of what to do next – or what I ought to do next. I shall go and see Courtenay Rodda at once."

"Give him my regards." He went to open the door for her. Then he added, "And his sister, too."

The afterthought struck her as odd. Her feeling must have shown in her face for he added, "I saw her going into the newspaper office on my way here this morning."

The old imp made Elizabeth say, "Indeed, Mr. Ivey, I'll be especially glad to pass on your regards. For some reason she believes you don't particularly care for her."

He was stunned to hear it. "I can't for the life of me imagine why."

"Can't you? I can."

"I'd be obliged to hear . . ."

"She's smitten with you, and is angry with herself for it." Elizabeth winked. "Like me, she treasures her independence."

CHAPTER TWENTY

IN THE OUTER OFFICE of the *Vindicator* she met a most soberly dressed Lilian.

"What's all this?" she asked.

Lilian explained that Courtenay was taking her to lunch at the Angel. "You come along too, darling. I'm sure he'd rather take you than me. Especially as he knows I'm going to pester him about money." She made a grand gesture. "My salary, I mean."

"Salary?"

"Hasn't he told you? I'm to have a job on the paper. I've spent the morning with Beresford, my fellow galley-slave."

Elizabeth laughed.

"I'm serious," Lilian's eyes gleamed. "Actually, perhaps I'm about to pester the wrong proprietor. Don't *you* own more of it than him?"

"I don't know. He always shies away from that subject."

"I'm sure you do. I seem to remember him once mentioning – no, *his* once mentioning – must be careful of my grammar now! He once said Bill Troy owned more of it than us. Than we. No – than us. Oh dear."

At that moment Courtenay emerged from his office. He was delighted to see Elizabeth and at once included her in the luncheon invitation.

They walked up the steep, broad street to the grandly porticoed doorway of the old inn. The Angel, which had once been the town house of the earls of Godolphin, was the gentry's "pub." It sold more claret and brandy than porter or ale. Inside it was still very much a gentleman's house, with oak panelling, a minstrels' gallery, and gleaming copper ornaments hanging everywhere. Indeed, the atmosphere was so clublike that many men kept on their hats while they dined. The tables were of deeply polished cherrywood and mahogany. The fare was a plain, three-course table d-hôte: brown Windsor soup, steak and kidney pie with turnip and carrots, and a pudding of spotted dick and custard.

"The old traditions, eh!" Courtenay said vaguely.

Elizabeth had never seen Lilian go all out for something she really wanted. It was fascinating. She flattered, she smiled, she charmed – not blatantly, but with a contained sort of exhilaration that suggested more, more, more was being withheld, could be drawn from her, would be lavished . . . if only he responded in the right way. And although Courtenay was only her brother – and knew exactly what was happening, anyway – she still managed to bend him, gesture by gesture, smile by smile.

At last he said, "I ought to make you fight for it, young'un. Nothing worthwhile is gained in this life except by fighting. But, it just so happens, you've caught me on the best possible day. I've been doing a lot of thinking about the old rag these last few months and it strikes me it's time we joined the railway age."

Elizabeth stared at him open-mouthed but he didn't bat an eyelid.

He said there was a firm of printers over to Hayle who had a Linotype machine going cheap. He could adapt his own photographic apparatus to make line-block clichés. Then they would be all set to raise their circulation. They could appoint local agents in every parish between Truro and Land's End and do four editions – Penzance–St. Ives, Camborne–Redruth, Truro-Falmouth, and Helston–The Lizard. Each edition would contain the same all-Cornwall items; only the local news would change. The new name would be the *Penwith Vindicator*.

"And you thought all this up by yourself!" Elizabeth said.

"Over the past few months," he said evenly.

"Why didn't you say?"

"I had other things on my mind."

Lilian stared from one to the other. "What's going on? Is there something I don't know?"

Elizabeth looked at him, "Will you tell her? Or shall I?"

"You seem to know it all."

She kept her eyes fixed on Courtenay as she answered. "It's because he's obviously been planning improvements for months, and I spoiled it all by walking in last week and telling him I thought the paper could be a lot better. Or, to put it more simply: It's because your dear bro hasn't quite reached maturity yet."

Lilian slapped her brother's arm and laughed: "See! I'm not the only one who thinks it!"

For the rest of the meal it was mostly Courtenay who did the talking, with occasional interjections from Lilian. The main idea was to run a number of regular columns: hearth and home, women's features – "That's why he's brought me in," Lilian explained – gardening; sport; naturalists' notes. He described each one in detail.

He had obviously been working on the idea for months. Why, then, had he been so silly about it last week?

"Perhaps we could even have a short story," he concluded. "The idea is, you see, for each page to develop its own character. Then the paper itself will come to seem like an old friend. What d'you think, Beth?"

"She could do a nursing column," Lilian suggested.

"I'd rather see a column on new ideas in farming."

"Written from debtors' gaol, no doubt," Courtenay said.

"Some jokes cut too near the bone to be funny," she told him. "Instead of a short story, I'm sure Uncle Hamill would do a splendid column on Old Cornwall. He has material enough to last fifty years."

Lilian thought that a spiffing idea.

"Any more pearls?" Courtenay asked, miffed that his baby was turning into general property.

Elizabeth took her chance. "The Helston *Vindicator* hardly needed a point of view. But the Penwith *Vindicator* won't get by without one. May I ask what it'll be?"

Courtenay spread his hands as if there were only one possible answer. "Liberal, of course. Mildly liberal. What else?"

"I was just thinking – there isn't a good Tory paper this side of Plymouth."

"Is it any wonder! Ever since the repeal of the Corn Laws . . ."

"Which was almost – if not more than – half a century ago. Now, especially with the railways, the county's bound to get more industrial. Don't you think there might be room for a Tory rag? Mildly Tory, of course?"

He drew breath to argue but Lilian said, "She could be right, brother dear."

Just before they rose, she was fishing for her handkerchief when she discovered she had absentmindedly tucked George Ivey's little vignette into her bag. She showed it to them.

"Oh, doesn't he draw beautifully!" Lilian commented.

"I didn't take to him at all in the beginning," Elizabeth told her, "but now I'm so glad he's my lawyer." She turned to Courtenay. "I'm so grateful for your introduction."

"Extraordinary fellow," Courtenay said. "I wonder how long this town will hold him."

Lilian was still staring at the drawing. "May I keep this?" she asked.

"By all means."

"Nothing important — just . . . someone I want to show it to."

On their return to the office they were distracted by a great commotion toward the bottom of the long, sloping street. There was a deal of whistling, in strange, piercing tones. Boys ran excitedly up the hill, calling their friends out of doors. Dogs barked. Curtains swayed and faces appeared at windows.

"It's Will Tyacke," Lilian said. "You must stop and watch this, Beth. I'll guarantee you've never seen anyting like it."

"Men must work and women must weep," Courtenay said as he left them.

A carthorse appeared from around the corner, followed by a pair, then another pair, then another, another, and yet another — all hitched not to a shaft but to a monstrous manilla rope, stout enough for an ocean clipper. The lead horse went so wide it almost brushed the stone of the Grylls Memorial.

Of the carter there was no sight. But the draught horses kept on appearing. Ten pairs . . . twelve, thirteen . . . sixteen, seventeen . . . there seemed no end to them. All other traffic was brought to a halt. Bill Tripp, the driver of one of the St. Keverne buses, which was parked close by the two young women, was having great trouble controlling his mare; he had to enlist the aid of several passers-by to hold her and pet her and talk to her.

"She belonged to pull for old Tyacke," he explained. "Ten year ago. I should o' thought her would o' been over 'n by now. Gusson, damm'ee — look at she!"

The shivering mare was a-sweat from her neck to her tail.

"Left she in the stall once when he passed by. Dam'ee if she never kicked the whole durn place to fletters!"

In all there were twenty-one pairs of horses going up the street before the cart came into view — though cart was hardly the word. It consisted of a single stout treetrunk connecting two of the most massive axles and wheels Elizabeth had ever seen. Disappointingly (for the number of horses had promised a titanic load) it was empty. However, it was not the cart that held everyone's attention, but the man who drove it.

Will Tyacke was a short, powerful fellow, dark, unmistakably gipsy. He had that magical rapport with horseflesh, that uncanny, frightening gift which enables a Romany to buy a horse from a farmer and walk off without a backward glance or word — and, no matter if that horse were hand-reared, or fierce as a lion, or never saw another human soul, the gipsy would know it was there, walking meekly at his heel. And no familiar call or curse from the farmer would ever bring it back.

Will Tyacke took his forty-three horses up through Helston main street guiding them entirely by calls and whistles. Traces would have been useless; a whip even worse than useless. It was a royal progress. The people marvelled still, though they must have seen it scores of times; they cheered and called out his name. And he acknowledged it with a knowing superiority, a twinkling eye; he was the best man with a horse in all the world. Yet the greatest tribute to his skill that day was not his management of that enormous team but his gentling of Bill Tripp's mare, which had once been his. Before he drew level he saw what a state she was in; and the nearer he came, the wilder she grew, whinnying like the damned, kicking over her traces.

He gave one piercing whistle; it brought his team to a halt of which a Guards drill sergeant would have been proud; then, taking up a short baton, he leaped from his seat and walked regally toward the mare. She was beside herself with frenzy by the time he reached her. One hand shot up and grabbed her mane. Then he leaped to her side and, with the baton, dealt her a thwack about the rump that rang among the houses.

At once the mare became gentleness itself. It seemed impossible – a blow that would have set any other creature wild had transformed her into the very picture of docility.

"How does he do it?" Lilian asked.

Elizabeth stood there, transfixed, forgetting to breathe, knowing exactly how he did it.

Tyacke stuffed the baton into his belt and began to fondle the mare with both hands, talking to her in a strange cant, incomprehensible to the onlookers but full of comfort and goodness to her. "Give us her nosebag then," he told Tripp. The man complied. Tyacke hung it around her neck and sorted out the traces; then, with one final pat, he let go of her.

"I can't understand it," Lilian said.

"Can't you?" Elizabeth asked.

The man heard her and grinned. He let his eyes rove up and down the crowd before he casually fixed them on her. "Any other filly need a bit of gentling then?" he asked.

Everyone laughed, but Elizabeth barely heared. The man reeked worse than all his horses put together. The dirt of his childhood was engrained in his skin. He had the nose of an old soak. Yet from his eyes there seemed to radiate an awareness that was majestic, elemental. He need just crook one finger . . .

He knew it too. The power of it was in his laugh as he turned and walked back to his vehicle. The mare did not even look up. Elizabeth began to breathe again. She and Lilian watched the long procession wind its way up the hill until it passed into Wendron Street, beyond the offices of Coad & Coad.

"Well!" she said, recovering her normal self once more.

"He's a masterman," Lilian agreed – and then added, "He gets drunk every night, you know. But it doesn't matter – the horses know the way home."

"Which is where?"

"Carleen, right by Wheal Vor. When the horses reach Trew they break out in a gallop. Can you imagine it? Forty or fifty huge shire horses — all galloping, and him drunk as a lord!" She laughed. "Isn't that right, Mr. Tripp?"

"Yes, my lover!" The bus driver nodded and chuckled. "Last fall, you know, he got took up by the Penzance police for being drunk in charge. Threw he in the cell all night — and put his dog in with him. And when he wakes up next morning he opens one eye and dam'ee, the first thing he sees is that li'l ol' dog. 'Hello,' he says. 'You too, eh!' "

The bystanders roared with laughter.

The two women resumed their walk. "What does he carry on that . . . *thing?*" Elizabeth asked. "You can hardly call it a cart?"

"All the heavy gear for the mines. Big boilers from Harveys of Hayle. Those huge calciners . . . tilting beams. Just lately he's carrying a lot of stone for the extension to Porthleven harbour. There are large granite quarries up Long Downs and he . . ."

"Long Downs? Isn't that above Penryn?"

"Yes. About three miles. Why?"

"So he fetches the stone here — and goes back empty?"

"I suppose so. He's certainly empty today."

"Then he's the man to carry my timber cheap to Penryn."

Lilian laughed. "Don't you ever stop, Beth?"

"I daren't," Elizabeth told her. "Once the hand is to the plough . . ."

"Why don't you come and work on the paper with us?"

"Not until pigs fly. I thought I was going to have battle royal with Courtenay — over improving the paper. I wonder if all my other problems will dissolve so easily?"

"You? What problems do you have now the case is won?"

Elizabeth told her of her conversation with George. "It looks as if I ought to think of finding a husband," she concluded, "whether I want to or not."

"Did George Ivey actually tell you to?"

"Not in so many words. He spoke of 'position in Society,' but we all know what *that* means."

"Do you want to marry again?"

"Not particularly."

Lilian grinned. "If I were a rich and handsome young widow, I'm damned if *I* would."

CHAPTER TWENTY-ONE

THE LAST THREE MINES of Pallas, Wheal Tor, Deepwork, and Wheal Anchor, stood cheek by jowl some four miles northwest of Pallas House, almost hidden in that rough hinterland between Higher Pednavounder and Drym. Their separate names were historical; many years ago they were, indeed, individual mines but for as long as anyone could now remember their labyrinthine galleries had been interconnected to make a single enterprise. In fact, their official name on the share certificates was "Pallas Consolidated," or Pallas Consols for short.

They marked the northern end of the great Carnmeal elvanstone country whose fabled mines include Wheal Vor, Wheal Metal, and Wheal Fortune, all now abandoned.

The landscape was so wild, so cut about by generations of mining, so despoiled by waste and by runs of muddy, greasy water – in general, so utterly unlike the soft, green acres given over to farming – that Elizabeth visited her mines as rarely as possible. One occasion, however, could not be avoided – Tribute Day, when all the miners are paid their share of the mine's earnings over the past month and the mine venturers give a supper in one or other of the mine buildings. Everyone who works at the mines attends these affairs – captains, tributers, tutworkers, boys, bal maidens, dressers, firemen, carpenters – and all the other artisans whose wages make the business of mine ownership seem as profitable as climbing steadily up a ladder whose foot was just as steadily sinking in a morass.

The Cornish miners' fortunes swing wildly between long bouts of poverty whose depths would be hard to match anywhere else in the land and brief spells of sudden riches that few of them are able to cope with wisely. Superstition and depravity are twin gods of their meagre hearths. Their acolytes are drink and recklessness.

This was especially apparent at the Tribute Day supper. The wild drinking began after the last dish was cleared away; Elizabeth and the bal maidens always departed at that point.

The ordinary drinking and fighting was bad enough but the worst usually followed when men began to boast of their knowledge of ancient underground galleries, some of which had not been worked for a century or more. All the once-great mines of Carnmeal join up with their neighbours in several places, making it possible for gangs of drunken miners to engage in a suicidal form of gambling. With a dozen or so pints of strong ale inside them, one will say, "Bet I do know the quickest way from Wheal Tor whimshaft to the south adit on the Blueborough shaft over to Wheal Fortune."

Another will reply, "I'll lay I know a quicker then."

And the race is on. Gangs of men, some hardly able to stand, will quit the supper and swarm below ground. There, lighted only by candles, they leap like goats through levels and drifts, and climb or descend by shafts and winzes, which twist and turn to follow the lode; and for added excitement there is the frequent random pitfall where a forty-foot stope below has burst through its "back" or ceiling into the level above.

The wager may be for anything from a kitty collected by the onlookers all the way up to the right of the winner to work the loser's pitch in the mine. Or it may all end in accusations of cheating, followed by a fight that will leave several men a thousand feet below ground with broken bones, bleeding half to death.

Everything to do with the mines repelled Elizabeth – their arcane jargon; their alien customs; their secrecy (for nothing would induce her to go within a quarter-mile of a working shafthead); their wild, unwashed and reeking workers, men and women both; and above all, their cost.

But late that spring an amazing change took place. There was, as it happened, a rally in the price of Cornish tin, and as a result, Pallas Consols actually began to yield a profit over and above the pitiful £600 they earned from the levels above the adit and from picking over the old waste. Elizabeth was forced to take a greater interest.

By then the mines were forked out to 190 fathoms below the adit – which gave a ten-fathom margin of safety below the new 180 Level that was to be driven westward in the hope of meeting the legendary Great Lode of Wheal Vor. What with the rally in tin, the tributers were keen. As the waters fell, revealing level after level of the old mines, new landings were placed across the manshaft and new ladders build between them, and the men swarmed down to study the lodes that had been abandoned anything from five to fifty years earlier. At these new, favourable prices about a third of all the possible pitches could be tributed for – which was just as well, because Captain Body had left the cost of renewing the ladders and platforms out of his original calculations.

"But why didn't you include them in the price?" Elizabeth asked.

" 'Cause the ladders is part of the permanent mine, see. Not of the exploration. They should be charged against the metal we're *going to* win."

"But what if we find none?"

"We already have, missis."

"But if we hadn't?"

He shrugged uncomfortably. "Then that'd of been pure loss."

"Yes – and guess whose!"

It was a real lesson in "Mine Captain's Accountancy."

"Now we got a bit extra coming in, we should ought to rebuild that man-engine," the captain added.

She laughed grimly. "I thought I wasn't going to be allowed to *save* it! What's a man-engine?"

"Ten years ago, we belonged to have one here at Deepwork. But we took the timber out and sold it afore we let her flood up to the adit, see?"

"Yes, but what is it?"

" 'Tis a treetrunk going forth-and-back like a piston. If the shaft is vertical, then the treetrunk is hanging in the man-engine shaft and it do go two fathom down, wait for more steam, two fathom up, wait again, down, up . . . ten movements a minute. But usually the shaft is on the slope – what we do all *caunter* – like here at Pallas Consols. Then the treetrunk do slide forth and back on huge great rollers. 'Course, one tree-trunk wouldn't get'ee very far, so we do put another fast the end of it – then another fast the end of that . . . and so forth, all down to the bottom . . . thirty or forty trunks joined end-to-end. There's footrests and handholds let into the trunk, so, if you'm going down, you do step on at the top of the stroke, go down twelve foot, step off on a little old platform, wait while her do go up again, and then step on for the next downstroke . . . and so on, all the way down. We do keep the man-engine running all day."

"All day! That must burn a lot of coal!"

"No, she'm counterbalanced, see? The weight of one man on the tilting beam is enough to move'n either way. He don't burn much coals at all."

"Why don't we just send the men in and out in the kibbles we use for fetching up the ore?"

" 'Cause that would interfere with raising the ore. Also the men would all want different levels . . . start-stop-start-stop. Think of that for a couple of hundred at the start and finish of each core! You'd never raise no metal up at all!"

She sighed. "Well, no doubt it's very convenient for them to be wafted up and down like that, but the money for it has to come out of *my* purse."

He sucked a tooth. " 'E'd pay for hisself inside a month." He winked "Inside two at the most."

She saw the point readily enough. To have to climb a thousand feet up fifty flights of ladders, lighted only by a single candle stuck to your helmet, is gruelling work – especially after long hours in narrow, ill-ventilated galleries with the temperature well into the nineties and the humidity close to a hundred. Small wonder that few miners worked – or even survived – above the age of fifty. Without a man-engine, in a hot, wet mine like Deepwork, a man's core below ground cannot last longer than five hours;

but *with* one, he can work eight. It might pay for itself inside a year, she supposed. *If* the new price of tin held out that long . . .

The captain was relentless. "Most of the old rollers is intact, missis. They don't need no more'n a dab o' grease. And all the old mortices in the rock, for the platforms, they're already cut. And the caverns for the counterbalances, too – they'm all there. That's all the expensive part of the work ready and done. 'Tis only the carpentry now."

Elizabeth weakened sufficiently to ask for a bill of quantities; Captain Body "happened" to have one ready. But when she saw it, she nearly had a fit.

"That's half of Norway!" she complained.

"Why, he isn't hardly so bad as that, missis."

"Bad enough! If that's what you have in mind, we'll do it when we've earned the cash to pay for it."

"If we done it first, we'd earn it quicker."

But she remained firm on the point. The most he dared do was rebuild the old flat-rods for transferring power across the fields between the engine house and the man-engine shaft. He had called it a field, but in fact the area was a quarter-mile tract of scrub and wasteland. When he had finished, it was spanned by a long train of timber rods – really just rough-hewn treetrunks – swinging back and forth not on rollers but on ten-foot-high levers, to allow free passage of men and traffic underneath them – a string of metronome arms all joined at their tips and swinging in unison. From a distance it was hard not to think of them as alive – a team of tug-o'-war automatons, losing, winning, losing, winning . . .

Elizabeth meanwhile used the new mining profits to start paying off the estate debts that had accumulated since she had inherited. The merchants were delighted, for previous owners of Pallas had not been so tender of their creditors' purses. Morwenna, cheated of her favourite grumble about the alarming rise in Pallas's debts, unashamedly took the opposite line. "When were gentlefolk ever afraid of owing a fortune to the tinkers and tailors and candlestick-makers of this world?" she asked. "In every day, in every way, that common little woman's origins shine through more clearly."

Next time Elizabeth went to the mines Captain Body beckoned her into his office with a smile. "What's that old saying?" he asked. " 'If the mountain won't go to the comet, the comet must come to the mountain.' " He whipped an old sheet off a bulging heap that covered his desk. "There!"

Her first thought was that he had gone mad. It looked like a pile of rubbish – five ragged, motheaten, wooden shelves standing almost upright on their long edges, shaved thin in some places, swelling out in others, connected by horizontal bits of dowelling and pierced by two or three vertical bamboo canes.

" 'Course," he added, "what's shown solid here is empty air in the mines themselves. And conversely like, what's empty air here is solid rock in the real mines — otherwise you couldn't see nothing."

Once her mind accepted that switch between solid and space, she saw it all in a flash: a model of Pallas Consols!

"I made everthing fatter than he should be in scale," he explained. "Else 'twouldn't hardly stand up. 'Twouldn't be more'n sheets of paper and card. And that dowel wouldn't be no more'n thin copper wire. But the vertical scale is right — one to a thousand."

"How big is a man on that?"

"So big as a grain o' salt."

The model was almost fifteen inches high. She tried to imagine herself no bigger than a grain of salt, standing at the bottom of one of those "shelves," which were really slices of mined-out lode sandwiched between two vast walls of rock — fifteen-hundred feet of emptiness towering above her, and never the kiss of the sun. She shivered at the thought.

"Why all the holes?" she asked.

"We do have to leave bits of lode unmined here and there, to support the walls, keep they apart. Else the hanging wall'd collapse in on the foot wall."

She saw that each of the lodes had a name. From north to south she read: Troy, Junket, Devil's Kitchen . . .

"The man who found that one," Captain Body explained, "why, he come up to grass with eyes so big as soup plates. He swore 'twas 'so wide as the Devil's kitchen!' So that's how they named that one."

. . . Sago . . .

"That was found by a miner called Jago. But 'tis a wet ground, see — the walls is all soft and slimy. So the men do call'n Sago instead."

. . . and the last lode was called Hallelujah — found during one of John Wesley's evangelizing tours of the district. " 'Tis all history," the captain said. "History everywhere."

"What do these bits of starched gray flannel stand for?" she asked, noticing them for the first time.

Without blinking an eyelid he answered, "Bits of lode no one hasn't yet discovered."

She noticed that the hoped-for Great Lode of Wheal Vor was there, as thick in its scale as a church and steeple.

She laughed. "You're such optimists! Experience counts for nothing, does it! Optimism is to a Cornishman what whisky is to the Scotchman."

He said nothing. She looked at the model again. "It must have taken you ages."

"Funny things, missis. I already knew everything that's there, yet I learned as much again."

"What are these different coloured lines?"

"The different ages of the workings — so near as I could guess. To be sure, there's been li'l drifts and adits all along the lode since Roman times. But most of the work was done in living memory – or in the last four generations, anyway. Every foot could tell a story, now. This whole level here" – he pointed to a section near the top of Troy – "that's the bit as once made old Sir William rich. If he never owned that, why you wouldn't be here now. That's worth thinking 'bout!"

"He also owned Wheal Pallas," she reminded him. "He got the best of it."

"That's true. That's true. The best o' everything. Why, this section here, 'tisn't no more'n a fathom of drift, but I'll lay odds 'twas enough to buy that grand hoss-painting beside the fireplace in the drawing room over to Pallas House."

"The Stubbs."

"No. 'Tis a black hoss. And they do say that was the same bit of drift as almost killed Cripple Billy Tresidder. He was some famous old fella. He begged his living forty years on the steps of Coinagehall – afore they pulled it down. He had some brave old voice. Why he could sing like a nightjar."

"Don't tell me – you heard sweeter but never louder."

He laughed. "Something like that. Still th'old feller, he outlived all his mateys – so you might say the rockfall saved him, really. Now this next section, that could have paid for your gatelodge. That's the way I do like to look at it."

"And yet today, you know," she said, "that painting of the black horse alone would probably fetch enough at auction to buy out the mineral rights to the entire Pallas Consols for the next ninety-nine years!"

The Captain sucked at his unlit pipe. "Why that's a deep question, Mrs. Troy. Are the mines there for the sake o' Pallas House? Or is it the other way about?"

"I'm sure Miss Morwenna was never in any doubt."

"That she weren't!"

He looked at Elizabeth and gave her a flattering smile.

"I know what you're working round to, Captain Body. So you may just as well spare your breath."

"Five hundred pound," he sighed. " 'Twouldn't want no more to fix up that man-engine proper-job." He looked at her, speculatively. "Tell'ee another thing, missis. Over to Wheal Fortune, down below there in the valley by Sethnoe Farm, they got an adit that would cut through Deepwork at nineteen fathom below *our* adit. That's a good deep valley there, see." He pointed out the present adit level on his model, and then this other level, a good inch below it.

"I know I'm going to regret asking this, Captain Body, but what d'you mean when you say it *would* cut through Deepwork at that level? If it was extended toward us, you mean?"

" 'Zackly so, missis. 'Zackly so!"

"And now you're going to say it'll only cost ten shillings to do it?"

He sniffed. "Well – bit more'n that. But 'twould pay for hisself inside a month – two month, mebbe – what with the saving on coals, see?

The trouble was, she did see.

She saw that a man who went down a thousand feet by man-engine could hew twice as much ore as one who had to climb up and down by ladders.

She saw that a pump twenty-four thousand gallons of water an hour, the average winter rate from Deepwork, up only one hundred and fifty-odd fathoms instead of a hundred and seventy would be as good as the gift of two new engines.

"What do I do, Uncle Hamill?" she asked as he drove her into Helston, very early on the eighth of May, Furry Day, for that year's celebrations. "No sooner is there a sniff of money in the wind than the begging bowls begin to tremble in every neglected corner of the estate. They all have the most plausible tongues, too."

"You could invest your last penny up there and then see the bottom drop out of the market again. You'd lose it all. Mind you – if the market holds, and the man-engine was working again, this would be one of the most profitable mines in the county. And if, on top of that, you find the Great Floor . . . well! You'd have the world at your feet!"

"My instinct is pushing me elsewhere – toward investment in the land. I'm sure Pascoe and I are right, you see. There *is* a new market for us to reach, opened up by the railways."

He squeezed her arm. "Then that's what you must do, my dear. If you fail, at least you'll have only yourself to blame."

"The trouble is, I don't feel comfortable up at the mines, so maybe that's what's prejudicing me. I find it hard to think about them calmly. It's all so big and alien and . . . huge! So full of power and menace. Those greedy boilers, gulping down hundreds of bushels of coal each week. I always feel they're on the point of exploding. The way they hiss and sizzle at every strap and rivet; and the heat you can feel just pouring from them! I sometimes dream about them, you know – that there's a furious, peppery giant penned up inside, endlessly straining to burst them abroad, those black bands of iron, and come roaring free."

Hamill revelled in her fantasy. "Yes! And when you watch the sumpwater come gurgling up that two-yard-wide liftpipe, eh? All warm and seething. And oily. It makes me think of those thousands of gallons trickling and running and joining together, gathering pace and power, through that vast, dark labyrinth below. Oh, the power that's locked away inside this Earth! You'll feel it today in the dance."

She shivered. "How *can* men consent to go down there! I can't bring myself to go near any of the shafts."

"You will one day. They'll call you down."

His very intensity broke the spell; she saw how absurd it was. "Yes, well, I don't know about that. But the point I'm making is that perhaps all these feelings are preventing me from investing the money there, when it's really what I ought to be doing. Perhaps, after all, I'll tell Captain Body he may have three hundred pounds plus whatever credit he can get above six months at the lumberyard – and do what he can with the man-engine."

Hamill roared with laughter. "Ah, you're a gambler at heart, Elizabeth. A true Cornishwoman – one of the best!"

Her spirits sank. "Is it a big gamble?"

"Of course it is! A grand gamble. But what isn't?"

"At least tell me I'm right about the land? I *am*, aren't I?"

"I'm sure!"

She gave a dour nod. "I know what you're thinking. So was every failed investor who ever lived. They were all of them *sure!* Oh, I just wasn't made for this sort of life."

In a light, conversational tone, he asked, "D'you often think of Bill now?"

She turned sharply to face him. He smiled but removed the challenge of his gaze. "No one can hear us," he told her.

"Well I do as a matter of fact – but . . . differently, somehow. He's become a sort of unseen partner in . . . heavens! I'd never admit this to another soul. I'd be carried off to Bodmin. D'you think it sounds fanciful? I feel Bill's become a sort of partner in what I'm doing. He wants it, too – the way I'm doing it. I don't mean I hear voices or see his ghost nodding away in satisfaction. But I feel his presence there. I feel a kind of . . . *bathing* of his approval. I'm sure it's what he wants, too." She gave a nervous laugh, afraid of his disbelief. "At least I'm no longer paralyzed with fear."

"I don't believe you ever were, Elizabeth."

"Oh, but I was! Those first weeks. I could feel him wanting to do all sorts of things through me – wanting me to start tackling the estate. But I just couldn't do it. Now it's different."

"In what way?"

She thought before she said, "I suppose it must be that I'm enjoying it now. In the beginning I had no idea I could do any of this. What? Run an estate! Say yes or no to the spending of thousands of pounds on a tin mine! Help change a newspaper from a dull old rag to something you'd be proud of! Fight an old dragon like Morwenna!" She laughed. "Yes, I had no idea. But here I am – actually doing it. And enjoying it. Why not!"

"Why not indeed?" Hamill let a silence grow before he went on. "This feeling that Bill's somehow around you – is it all the time?"

She knew that seemingly casual tone of his by now. "Why d'you ask?"

"He wouldn't prevent you from taking up with some other young fellow? If the chance came?"

She dug him with her elbow but said nothing.

"I mean it," he told her.

"Well, I think Bill has passed beyond that sort of passion, Uncle Hamill."

"Good," he answered. "You took the words out of my mouth."

The Furry Day dances were even more desultory than they had been last year, when Courtenay had written his disparaging paragraphs about Hamill's singlehanded attempt to keep the old customs alive. The respectable townsfolk wanted to abolish the festival because, in their view, it had degenerated into an excuse for idleness and debauchery. By ancient custom, no one was supposed to work on Furry Day; anyone caught at it had to pay forfeit of a gallon of ale or cider, or they had to attempt an impossible leap over the Cober; so gangs of ruffians roamed the town, seeking out the industrious and threatening to cart them off to the river for a ducking unless they bought drinks all round. Hamill's argument was that the respectable people could turn it back into a respectable festival, a day when all classes could unite and rediscover their ancient tribal kinship. But the respectable were not interested, indeed, all the Sunday schools held special tea meetings on Furry Day, to keep the children and their parents free of such pagan scandals.

The pagan scandals this year consisted of eight couples dancing to the music of the rifle corps band (or most of it) up through the streets to Gwealmayowe — the site of an ancient ring fort. In the afternoon, a handful of servants and tradesmen danced the Hal-an-Tow up one side of Coinagehall Street and down the other, more as a lark than anything else. In the evening there was a ball for the gentry in the Angel Hotel, indistinguishable from the Hunt Ball, the Police Ball, the Summer Ball, "and all the other Balls in our social calendar," as Hamill later wrote in his Old Cornwall column in the *Vindicator*.

This fine and ancient festival, commemorating as it does the slaying by St. Michael of the Dragon, the triumph of Virtue over Vice, of Summer's Light over the Dark and Dread of Winter, of Flora's spring flowering, of our own awakening to all the joys and beauties of this Great Earth, seems doomed to extinction by our pettifogging, mean-hearted, penny-sparing, clock-watching, black-bibled generation. But the Folk Memory is long; our dead forefathers are not mocked; they bequeathed us these Rites of Spring and we shall keep the Faith. The Earth-Force that drives the life-fuse through bough and twig to explode in every bud of leaf or flower cannot be prisoned for ever. It will out. When the last stale hallelujah has risen from the last weary Sunday School bench, when our children burst forth, laughing and dancing into the sun and air, it will out."

Elizabeth, who had actually witnessed the giggling, self-conscious little group go galumphing up the street to the excruciating arrhythmias of flute, bugle, and drum, thought his words a triumph of Hope over Experience.

Not unlike tin mining, in fact.

END OF PART TWO

PART THREE

DISASTERS

CHAPTER TWENTY-TWO

MORWENNA WAS SHREWDLY aware that her display of Christian charity in the matter of Old Tom's clothes, not to mention her saintly forebearance in withdrawing her suit against Elizabeth, had won her sympathy in quarters where she would not formerly have looked for it: from families she had snubbed in grander days, from professional people whom she had at various times dismissed with contempt. Ancient wounds healed; many of her former victims believed they saw a new Morwenna.

Tradition, too, was her ally.

People said, "One can't deny she has a much greater right to Pallas than this new woman."

"Yes, can't help pitying her."

"I think she's taking it surprisingly well."

"Poor old Bill must have been going off his chump for months without anyone realizing it. Fancy his making this little slip of a woman the life tenant!"

"Obviously there are more ways of going gah-gah than painting your arse blue, shinning up a tree, and baying the moon, what!"

"Listen – he had one stroke in the spring, another on the day he married – you're not going to tell me his brains weren't already half-addled."

Those whose memories could not be so conveniently curtailed might object that Pallas had been going to rack and ruin for many years under Morwenna's bungling thumb.

There was an answer to that, too: "Yes, but old Morwenna has *style*. You can't deny it. That's what's coming out in her now – breeding. After all, who *is* this Elizabeth Troy? A horse-doctor's daughter! What does anyone know about her?"

"We know she hasn't let the inheritance go to her head."

"Only because her head lacks the room to hold it anyway! We've heard a lot of talk about how she's planning to regenerate the estate, but what has she actually *done*, eh? Scratched up a few scattered acres here and there all over the place. Where's that going to get her? A jumped-up little ignoramus holding hands with a failed landowner: the halt leading the blind, that's my opinion."

Not since the glorious days of old Sir William had Pallas and its affairs so dominated the local dinner tables. And Morwenna was both surprised and gratified to find herself taken to the collective local bosom in ways quite novel to her. As George Ivey had predicted, she made the most of it.

"I hear that when your sister-in-law first met old Hezekiah Gilbert," said Squire Wilson of Culdrose, "you know – the fellow with the funny foot – her first thought was to ask him if he got proper compensation." Zakky had acquired his "funny foot" while working at Culdrose, so Wilson was sensitive on the topic.

"Oh, she's quite the little socialist, I believe," Morwenna replied. "I never argue with her, of course. She can be extremely belligerent after a glass or two, and in any case, no matter what the provocation, one has to do one's best to stay on amicable terms. But you've seen her yourself – out in the garden without gloves – and wearing men's oilskins! Oh yes, an out-and-out socialist!"

"Socialist?" Maud Veryan chimed in, alarmed.

"Indeed. You've no doubt noticed she always goes to Penzance by common omnibus, when she could more easily take our carriage from Pallas. I've heard people say she's too proud to come and ask me – or too mean to wear out the wheels! But they wrong her there. She's not mean. She can spend money like water when it pleases her. No, the simple fact is she *enjoys* hobnobbing with the common people."

"Ah! How like Hamill!" Maud said incautiously. "And Bill was just the same."

"Bill never lost his dignity," Morwenna replied with crushing insistence.

"Only his heart!" Mrs. Trerice trilled sweetly. She was from the faction that was enjoying Morwenna's demotion.

Morwenna was also shrewd enough to realize that this constant sniping at Elizabeth was all very well in its way, but many a big landowner had survived far worse. The woman's position as mistress of Pallas would guarantee her an entrée where even the most scurrilous blackguarding of her character would hardly be a barrier. Something bigger and deeper was called for. But what?

She racked her brains but came up with nothing. There seemed no point on which the Mitchell woman was vulnerable. She hadn't even put a penny on the rents; the tenants all spoke highly of her – naturally! For a while Morwenna had hopes of a scandal over the Rodda person, but that turned out to be a shallow sort of business acquaintance derived entirely from Bill's former ownership of the paper. She was more friendly with Rodda's sister, and *that* little minx was so cool and self-possessed there was no hope of a scandal there.

But Morwenna's chance came – how or why or in what shape or form, she did not know, yet she felt it in her bones – the moment she ran across her cousin David Troy, one of the "poor Troys." Normally the circles in which they moved were so far apart they were as likely to meet the Tsar of all the Russians as each other. David was a lawyer with a somewhat radical reputation, a local preacher, an ardent Methodist, a Liberal – the very opposite to everything Morwenna professed and practised.

It was a shipwreck that brought them together. The *Santiago* ran ashore at Praa Sands with a cargo of, among other things, brandy. Morwenna, like half the countryside, went out in her carriage to watch the spectacle of a fine clipper breaking up in the waves. David Troy went to smash the brandy casks and preach temperance. When it was over they met on the Germoe road. Dusk was falling; he was walking home to Penzance, she being driven toward Helston.

She looked at him in astonishment, not having seen him in years. He had certainly grown up into a handsome young man, strong and dark, with the most intense and piercing eyes. He reminded her almost poignantly of Bill – but Bill as the world's most flattering portrait painter would have depicted him.

The moment this likeness struck her, she thought of Elizabeth. In some way, she knew, she simply *knew*, this young man offered her the chance to bring Elizabeth low once more. Without further thought she poked her head out of the carriage window and called after him – they had by this time passed each other.

The coach stopped. He turned and came back. "Miss Troy?" he asked. "Cousin Morwenna?"

Her answering smile startled him. "The Lord has caused our paths to cross," she said. "So often lately I have thought of you."

He put his head on one side; his eyes narrowed.

She went on. "However much our parents may have fallen out, I have lately begun to feel it wrong, sinful even, for us to perpetuate the rancour. How long has it been now? Sixty years?"

He nodded. "Sixty years, come next year."

Again she smiled. "Don't you think that's rather too long a time?"

"I've made a life for myself without any thought of Pallas Estate."

"You have Troy blood. You'd triumph no matter what the adversity."

"I have God's Word, cousin. That's my triumph over adversity. May I ask the purpose of this conversation?"

"You look hungry," Morwenna answered. "And not a little wet and cold. May I invite you to eat with me at the Falmouth Packet?" It was an inn less than a mile away.

Intrigued, he accepted, climbing up in the coach beside her. "Were you at the wrecking?" he asked.

"Piteous."

"Blasphemous! I came out to stop the drinking and found all Marazion Band of Hope, who should have been helping me, drunk as lords on the sand!"

"You needn't tell me, David! I've shared me home with a drunkard these forty years and more. And I've had to watch the estate pass into the hands of a young woman who's very little better."

"Oh? Bill's wife? I hadn't heard that of her."

"Well . . . she does make an effort to fight it. I'll say that for her. She is not beyond salvation."

"No one is beyond salvation."

"But you know what I mean. It's even harder for those who are young and beautiful and rich. I was most touched by your letter of condolence, by the way."

"Too touched even to reply?" he commented drily.

She patted his arm. "That is the sort of arrogance of which I am now thoroughly ashamed. Are you going to strew our reconciliation with these cruel little reminders, David?"

"I wish I knew what it is you really want. I'm not a fool, you know."

She sighed. "Why should you believe me? I shall just have to persevere."

"If it means you'll keep buying me dinners, then persevere all you wish."

She risked saying, "You're a strange mixture of simple faith and the most advanced cynicism, you know."

He nodded. "I didn't start preaching yesterday. I've stared into the murk of many a soul – not least my own."

They went on sparring in this gentle way, and catching up on the minutiae of family news, through most of the dinner. Toward its conclusion, though, she felt emboldened to ask, "What is it you really want in life, David? Suppose, for instance, you had inherited Pallas and could now apply its wealth in any direction you wished?"

Without pausing for thought he answered, "If I had inherited Pallas on a Monday, I'd have given it all away by Tuesday. Inherited wealth on that scale is an abomination."

Morwenna felt dizzy; it was too good to be true! If she could somehow bring Elizabeth and this ardent young idiot together, she was sure that the disgusting alchemy of sex would wreak its usual havoc between them. Then if he infected her with these preposterous notions, why – the way would be open for the trustees to step in and resume control. Too much to hope for, perhaps? Well, even if he did no more than unsettle her, make her lose her way . . . it wouldn't take long for the whole business to collapse.

She smiled tolerantly at his outburst. "Perhaps it's as well that your line was barred from the succession." Then she grew philosophical. "Although . . . I don't know . . ."

He eyed her warily. "What don't you know?"

She weighed him up, as if wondering whether he was quite ready to hear what she was about to say. "Perhaps it would have been for the better after all. We are such prisoners of our upbringing, aren't we – for better or for worse. I was brought up to believe that the barring of your family's line was the best thing that could ever have happened to Pallas. Never questioned it! Or never until now."

"What's different now?"

"Well, your proposed end for the estate would be *glorious*, wouldn't it! We'd got out in a blaze of glory. But as things stand at present . . ." She sighed.

"Do drop the other boot, Morwenna."

"It'll go out in a trickle of foreclosures and mortgages. You mark my words. I think your end is far more preferable – if end there has to be."

"Only God can know that."

"True – yet He can only work through us, David. We can't just sit back and leave it all to Him."

CHAPTER TWENTY-THREE

ECHOES OF MORWENNA'S gossip were quick to reach Elizabeth. Sometimes it was a lady's maid who passed it to a lady's maid who passed it to Oenone's mother. At other times it came to Courtenay, who would either tell Elizabeth directly or convey it via Lilian. One way and another, she came to hear whatever Morwenna said about her, often within hours of the utterance.

In June, Zakky Gilbert finished his stint on the wall over at Clowance and, as promised, came down the road to rebuild the main gate at Pallas. Tom came to help him every day. Elizabeth, knowing that Zakky was the acknowledged local master in all branches of stonemasonry, stayed around to watch and to flatter him with questions; she wanted to know what to look for – how to distinguish sound work from bad . . . where a tricky workman would try to cut corners . . . that sort of thing.

"There's tricky masters, too, missis," Zakky said, and went on to tell her how, when he began rebuilding the wall at Clowance, he was so much faster than all the other masons that he was making twenty-five to thirty shillings a week while they were clearing only twelve to fifteen. After two weeks of this, the clerk of the works had told him they'd have to cut his rate because he was making too much money.

Elizabeth was furious. "How despicably mean! I hope you gave him a piece of your mind."

He shook his head and laughed. "Wouldn't be no point, missis. He'd only of turned I off."

"You mean you just accepted it?"

"Well now! You do get paid tutwork on a job like that, see. They do come out and measure each week's progress. And that's how they belong to pay. Well this clerk-of-works, Cecil Waverley, he's some eddycated man, see. He wouldn't know blue elvan from granite – so that'll tell'ee how eddycated he is! So each week like, I just moved back the measuring stone – eight . . . ten yards – just enough to get I back to the proper rate, see. I never cheated they. Just took me proper rate."

While he was speaking, Tom picked up a stone and held it against the nearby wall; then, giggling and drooling, he ran a dozen paces along the wall and held it there. His giggling rose to near hysterics.

She laughed. "And he never noticed, this Cecil Waverley?"

Zakky winked. " 'Course he noticed! But he could see I'd beat him at his own game. Retired hurted you might say."

She realized that he bore no resentment because, at heart, he himself was just as dishonest and unscrupulous. If the situations had been reversed, he'd have tried the same mean trick on some other mason. It put her on her guard.

"So you must have quite a bit of money saved," she said. "What'll you do with it?"

He gave her a sidelong glance. "Well now, missis, there's a thing I meant to say to'ee. Helston Guardians is asking tenders for laying hardcore on the drive up the union workhouse. I thought as I might put in for 'n. And if I could carry the hardcore from they old halvans out Wheal Pallas, I could mend this here gate for'ee for nothing."

"How many cartloads will you be needing?" she asked.

The question seemed to take him aback. He had obviously not expected her to trouble to inquire. "Why – mebbe forty. No more'n fifty, anyroad."

He had quoted forty pounds to restored the gateway; it did not add up. "A pound a load?" she asked. "Isn't that rather high?"

He shrugged and looked away.

"Perhaps you want more like a hundred and twenty loads?" she suggested.

Tom stood nearby and snuffled; he sensed conflict.

Zakky bent down and tapped the mortar off his trowel, wiping it clean in the miller's sack that was tied around his waist. "You leave that to set and the trowel's ruined, see," he explained.

She ignored the distraction. "It so happens I've been carrying hardcore lately for the foundations of my greenhouses in Helston. So I know the price very well – ten shillings a load. So eighty loads for forty pounds would be quite fair. Why did you try to make me believe you want half that much?"

He moved one of the stones with his foot. "Well now missis, you do seem to know 'n all."

"I think I know this one. Tell me if I'm right. You're hoping this roadmaking contract will be the first of many. You've had your ambitions awakened out there at Clowance, Mr. Gilbert – and who'd blame you? You want to get out from the bottom of the heap where some ignorant clerk-of-the-works can tell you how much you may or may not earn. Bravo! So you hope you'll be coming to me for hardcore for years and years – until all the mine waste at Wheal Pallas is gone. And you know jolly well I'll never put a man out there just to count your carts in and out. So you wouldn't at all mind if I thought your hundred or more loads bite was a mere forty. Now isn't that the top and bottom of it?"

He shrugged again and looked about him for a rescue that was never going to arrive.

She was relentless. "Did you honestly take me for such a simpleton?"

He sniffed. "Anyway . . . would you be agreeable, missis?"

She gave it a moment's thought. "I'll go better," she told him. "If I'm right – if you are developing ambitions to go into the civil-contracting business – I'll strike a bargain with you that'll make your path to riches ten times easier. Are you listening?"

He nodded. His eyes now met hers without wavering. No conscience skulked behind them.

"As I said, I'm never going to put a man out there to count every load. So I'll let you take as much as you want over the next three years. Take the lot if you can use it!"

His eyes bulged.

"For your own use, mind – on your own contracts. Not for resale to other contractors. And not for carrying away and storing in some other quarry. Is that understood?"

He still could not believe it.

"And in return," she said, "you will, during those same three years, by certain fixed dates that we'll agree between us – you'll rebuild these gates, restore that gatelodge, reroof the three derelict stables behind Pallas House, and build me a pretty little drystone wall all along the roadside at Wheal Lavender – one I can plant out like a rockery."

He was waiting for more.

"I know," she told him with a generous smile. "You're getting much the best end of the bargain – *if* you can make use of it. If you can't, you're saddling yourself with promises to do a lot of unpaid work. So think it over carefully."

He screwed up his brow almost as if he were in pain; the risks were worrying but the potential rewards were huge.

Tom saw his consternation and giggled.

She waited until she judged it right to add, "If you can't make a success of it with all that free material, you'd never manage it at ten shillings a load."

He looked at her and nodded grimly. "If you was a man, missis, I'd say you was some proper old feller. Hard – but burr and braw."

She laughed. "Burr and braw? I hope that means something good."

"The best."

At that moment Morwenna came bustling down the Pallas drive in the open landau on her way to someone's At Home. She stopped the carriage as soon as she saw them, intending to ask what was going on, but Elizabeth took the initiative: "Miss Troy!" she called out in apparent pleasure. Then, since she considered it open season between them, she added, "Maud Veryan tells me you think I'm the most raging socialist. I wish you'd convince this man here! He considers me the most desperate grasping capitalist ever."

"Drive on!" Morwenna ordered sharply.

Elizabeth thought this was entirely the effect of her words. But as the carriage disappeared in the direction of Helston, she turned to find Tom bent double with his arse facing the spot where the carriage had been. His trousers were around his ankles.

Later that evening, when Elizabeth was sitting out in the arbour at the heart of her revived and burgeoning garden, Lilian called by.

"You've put the cat among the pigeons!" she said gleefully. "I don't know what you told the Gorgon but she went off in a lather, straight to the Veryans', and now there are writs flying like" – she flapped at the air around her – "like these midges, actually. Why do they attack me and not you?"

"It must be the perfume."

Lilian tossed her head. "It's because they can't even see you. Your skin's all burned by the sun. Look at you! How can you – it's horrid!"

They sat awhile, enjoying the cool-of-the-evening sunlight and talking of this and that. Oenone brought out some ginger ale and then went to close up her brother's cucumber frames.

There was the sound of someone approaching on horseback, from the direction of Helston; a moment later the figure of a man came into view, head and shoulders above the hedge. It was George Ivey.

He did not notice them in the arbour; by habit rather than necessity, for the sun was behind him, he shaded his eyes and peered at the upstairs windows of the house.

Elizabeth was about to hail him when Lilian put out a hand to restrain her. "No – let's see what he does."

"Why on earth?"

Lilian was watching him with a strange intensity that began to fascinate Elizabeth, especially when the girl asked quietly, "What d'you think of him?"

"He's a good lawyer if you can stay two jumps ahead of him."

"You're going to be one of those awful, frank, crabby old women, Beth."

"What makes you say that?"

"You're almost there already."

"Why all this interest in George Ivey?"

"You've probably forgotten – but I owe it all to you."

"Owe what?"

"I think George Ivey may very well be the next man I marry."

Elizabeth lowered her head to hide her smile.

Ivey saw them at that moment. "Oh hello!" he called. "May I join you?"

"Business or pleasure?" Elizabeth asked.

"With you, Mrs. Troy, there can be no such distinction." He dismounted and, easing the girth, left his horse tied to the hedge on a long rein.

"Never short of an answer," Elizabeth murmured.

Without waiting to be asked, Oenone brought out a third glass and another bottle. She had a great liking for George Ivey, who (as far as Elizabeth could gather, for it was a sensitive subject) had once defended her brother Henry on some never-mentioned charge before the assize in Bodmin.

"To what do we owe this honour?" Elizabeth asked.

"To a fine evening, a tractable mare, the lure of your never-failing hospitality and charm," – he turned briefly toward Lilian – "but to find Miss Rodda here as well is like cream on butter."

"Oh, I adore flattery," Lilian said.

How does the girl do that with her eyes? Elizabeth wondered. They burned with a sudden, lambent intensity that rocked poor Ivey on his heels. Smooth words he had been about to speak were choked to little gurgles in his gullet. He almost collapsed into his seat. "Flattery?" he managed to say at last. "It would take the brush of genius to flatter you, Miss Rodda."

After a decent interval, when they had exhausted their small talk, Elizabeth made an excuse and went indoors. An hour later the pair of them were still in earnest conversation. Watching them from her window Elizabeth suddenly felt unbearably lonely. She decided to slip out and walk through Wheal Pallas to Yeol Parc, to see if Courtenay were home.

The solace she found with him was not exactly what her soul was longing for, but until that came along – whatever form it might take – he would have to do.

CHAPTER TWENTY-FOUR

IN LATER YEARS Elizabeth always maintained she had an intimation of the disaster moments before she actually saw the rider turn into the lane that led along the bottom of the valley and up to the site of the greenhouses. His excited words, flung to her upon the evening winds, did no more than confirm it.

" 'Tis the man-engine, missis!" he yelled. She recognized him as a surface worker called Tom Gillan. "He've come abroad . . . at the top and . . . fell back . . . down the shaft . . ." He fought his own words for breath.

One of the masons came running up to hold the horse, which was lathered to a fright.

"Get your breath back and then tell me calmly," Elizabeth said. To one of the hodcarriers she added, "Get my pony and trap ready." To the carpenter: "Go to Doctor Reeves, he's the surgeon to the mine – in fact, go to every doctor you know" – she broke off and asked Gillan, "Are many hurt?"

"Burr and many. They aren't 'zackly certain, but there was a hundred and twenty or more below ground."

She turned back to the carpenter. "Go yourself to every doctor you know in the town and tell him he'll be needed out at Pallas Deepwork tonight."

She waited for no further details but, the moment the trap was ready, set off for the mines. It was hard not to whip her pony to a gallop but the long haul up Sithney Common Hill lay ahead and there was no point in tiring the creature before they gained the crest of it. On her way through St. Johns she reined in beside James Trevose's, the miller's house; she recognized his wife at an upper window.

"There's been an accident, Mrs. Trevose," she called out. "Up at Pallas Deepwork. I'm Mrs. Troy. Please let me have all your spare sheets for bandages – they'll be replaced, of course."

The woman nodded and vanished indoors. Trevose himself came out, having heard her request. "You might want sacks for to make stretchers. What is it – a heave?"

"They say it's the man-engine."

He hunched his shoulders and shivered. "Is someone gone for the doctors?"

"Yes. Frank Blewet."

"Well, you drive on, missis. I'll come on behind'ee with all the sacks I got. I cut some withies last week, too. They'll be fitty for poles."

"Bless you! I'll wait for the sheets, anyway. There's nothing I can do without them. Have you any kindling wood cut? I can make tourniquets with short bits of wood." She held her fingers a foot or so apart.

"I'll have a look-see what there is."

Moments later she was once again on her way, carrying six laundered sheets and a creel of kindling wood.

Never had the way to Pallas Consols seemed so long and so tortuous. The evening was already late. She reached the top of Sithney Common just in time to see the sunset beyond Tregonning Hill. Dusk was gathering fast as, ten minutes later, she turned off the Camborne road toward Godolphin. She was still afraid to demand too much of the pony because the final stretch up Poldown Hill, though short, was also steep. The poor beast was at the end of its strength as they turned into the long, narrow lane leading to the workings.

She arrived as twilight was fading into darkness. Even in the western sky there was little light, for ominous clouds were massing to the northwest, forming a pall above the dismal scene that now met her eyes.

The near-silence was eerie. Somehow she had expected shouting, the cries of the injured, the miners' womenfolk pressing around with questions; but from a distance the only sound was the profound sighing of the steam engine and the gurgling of the pumps, an endless cycle that now seemed imprinted on the very air of that bleak moorland height. Missing was the shunting clank of the flat-rod power train as it swept back and forth across the fields; they must have disconnected it as soon as the accident happened.

All across the moor people were converging on the mines, carrying lanterns. At the workings themselves a trail had been marked out with carbide lamps. There was a cluster of them around the man-engine shaft, which Elizabeth now dared to approach for the first time. By their light a crew of carpenters was working like demons to construct a winding gear to span the shaft and allow rescuers to be lowered and the victims raised.

Captain Body saw her approaching and came running to meet her.

"I sent Frank Blewet to rouse every doctor in town," she called. "John Trevose is coming out with sacks and poles for stretchers. And I have the makings of bandages and tourniquets with me here. Have you managed to get anyone out yet?"

There was no need to hold her pony; not a yard of movement was left in its exhausted muscles.

"We shall have to bring they out by the whimshaft," the captain answered. "The sides of all the sloping shafts is too durn rough. They'd shake theirselves to fletters."

"This is so awful . . ."

"Terrible. Terrible."

Their eyes met but could not hold each other.

"How much of the man-engine had you rebuilt?" she asked.

"Down to sixty below the adit. That's beyond the change in the dip. We been calling down to they men who was working the upper levels. They do say there's bits of it broken and lying wedged this way and that across the shaft. If we just dislodged one of them we could start up a fresh fall and kill anyone who's survived lower down. That's where our trouble is to, see. We shall have to work from the sump up."

"The ladders in the manshaft are all still there, I take it?"

He nodded. "But we shall get in quicker if we go down one of the whimshafts. Wheal Anchor whim – that's the handiest. We can go down in the kibble. We'll see, anyway. I'll put up a rope and go down the man-engine shaft so far as I can afore I decide."

"It's going to rain. Have we a tarpaulin? Or a rick cover – or anything? If we could rig up a shelter . . . I must get some of these women tearing up the sheets for bandages. Can you possibly spare me a couple of men?"

He frowned, thinking she meant to have them tearing bandages, too.

"I want them to cut some light, straight branches out of the hedges," she explained. "We're going to need splints. Ash and sycamore – there's plenty of it."

He turned to go. "I'll send you a pair. Tell them what you do need."

"One more thing," she called out.

He paused.

"Can you get me a pair of moleskin trousers? Someone who knows what they're about will have to go down there and splint any broken bones before you try moving them. And I'm certainly not going down in these skirts."

He walked the few paces back toward her. "You don't never mean to . . ."

"There's no time to argue, man. Please just do it."

He caught the glint of combat in her eye. "There's a spare pair of me own should fit'ee," he mumbled as he went off to fetch them.

She called several of the women over and showed them the various widths into which she wanted the sheets torn. They all shared with her the opinion that it was, "turr'ble . . . turr'ble."

Two men came out of the dark; she told them what sort of splints to cut.

The resignation of the people amazed her. If Bill were still alive, and trapped somewhere down there, she'd be beside herself with anguish and worry. Even as it was, she felt poised at the edge, not of hysteria but of a screaming-crying rage at the monstrous unfairness of it all. This disaster had no *right* to be happening to these fine people, to her.

Leaving the women to tear the sheets she dared to approach the edge of the man-engine shaft itself. A low protective wall of loose stone ringed the very lip, though it rose no more than knee height. A miner came forward and held his arm in front of her like a railing. She clutched at it. The sharp reek of his sweat carried her back to the casual wards of Guy's Hospital. It had the curious effect of reawakening the nurse in her; until how she had been playing out a memory.

Of the man-engine there was no sight. Only the remnant of the broken swivel pin, madly twisted in its housing at the end of the tilting beam, was there to explain what had happened. The shaft looked like any other, a large, empty hole, sloping away into blackness among the furze and ling. "Gone," she murmured.

"She'm gone right 'nuff," the miner said.

"How many men were on it at the time?"

"Can't rightly say, missis. 'Twas end of day-core – could be fifty . . . sixty? Could be more."

She closed her eyes and breathed a prayer. What must it have been like to be clinging to that column when it broke? That terrifying moment of rumbling downward through the pitch dark . . . ten, twenty feet – it would take no more than half a second – you wouldn't realize what was happening until you felt the thump as it began to crumple between the hanging wall and foot wall. Even if you were on a platform, you'd hardly be safe; the whiplash of those vast trunks, the debris falling from above – they'd smash the platforms and everything on them within moments. Men would be shaken off like so much ripe fruit, like woodlice – falling, bouncing from rockface to rockface, hurtling into the tumbled diagonals of the dismembered engine, smearing themselves down the man-polished wood.

The rain, which suddenly began to fall in large, warm drops, released her from those terrible images. She turned from the shaft to find herself staring straight into the dark silhouette of an unknown man. His head precisely eclipsed the nearest carbide lamp; its light, shining through his wild, unkempt hair gave him a bright halo.

"Damnation!" he cried. It was a religious ejaculation, not an oath. "This is the wages of sin, Mrs. Troy – the sin of greed, the sin of every Pallas Troy who ever lived."

The sentiment was so inappropriate to the occasion that she wondered why no one cried out in protest. Yet even she was tongue-tied. Something about the interloper compelled their attention.

The stranger continued: "You've plundered these workings for centuries to build your fine houses and fund your grand lives – and now the Lord has come with his swift wrath to smite you!"

At that moment Captain Body returned with the promised pair of trousers. Glad of an excuse to get away from the accusing stranger, she stepped past him and, taking the clothing, asked, "Where may I change?"

"What do'ee want, missis?" the miner asked.

"There are men lying down there with broken bones. Someone must go below and splint them before anyone tries to move them."

"You?"

"I've been trained as a nurse. Come on – this is wasting time. Isn't there a shed or something? Do I have to go all the way back to . . ."

The miner laughed and gave a piercing whistle. A pale ring sprang up all around them as several dozen faces turned in their direction. "Curtis! Jones! Strike! Thomas . . ." he called them forward, big men all. "We got half Redruth rugby club here," he told her cheerily. "Listen mateys – we got a new player on the field." He nodded toward Elizabeth. "Needs a change of togs now."

At once they formed themselves in a circle around her, facing outwards; they linked arms and shuffled inwards until they were so tight-packed that not an inch of light could pass between any man and his neighbour. In that oasis of black, with the rain now pouring down, Elizabeth stepped out of her skirts and into the moleskin trousers.

"Done!" she called.

The ranks broke up again.

"Blasphemy!" the stranger shouted when he saw what emerged.

Now Elizabeth ignored him. "What's your name?" she asked the miner.

"Clifford Chigwidden of Carleen, missis."

Reluctantly Captain Body handed her an oilskin jacket, which, on her smaller frame, became a half-coat. She was used to oilskins that reeked of compost and smoke; this one had an almost acrid tang, a blend of blasting compound and wet rock dust.

"Where's this other shaft?" she asked. "The Wheal Anchor whim?"

"You'd never go down there," the captain said. "You was afraid even for to go near the shafts before."

"Where is it?"

"The men won't like a woman going below."

"Oh go on!" she shouted scornfully. "You'll be telling me next it's bad luck!"

It *was*, of course, but he could not say it.

"I could lead she in by the old Mellangoose adit," Chigwidden suggested. "That's dry, anyway. She could nearly walk down the Long Stope. Then 'tis just they two short winzes to the Seventy East."

Captain Body shrugged and resigned the decision to him. "You'd best take this here carbide lamp. He's only now been filled."

She went to get a supply of bandages. The splint cutters returned; she

took an armful of those, too. A bunch of farmers arrived with half a dozen
rick covers. She pointed up to the flat rods and told them to make a sort of
tent, using them for a ridge. It was uncanny. She said things and people
obeyed her without question or discussion.

There was a shout from across the moor, by the Wheal Anchor
whimshaft. "Light! Bring light!"

Men ran toward the sound. Lanterns picked out a bedraggled party of
miners, carrying two colleagues. They were the first to have made it to the
surface, winched up in the kibbles.

The injured were, in military terms, mere "walking wounded."
While she examined them, questions were flung at the other survivors, so
thick and fast there was no time for their replies – until Captain Body took
command. He soon drew out of them what they knew of the situation
underground. The stout timbers of the man engine had been reduced in
many places to splinters; quantities of rock had been dislodged from the
wall of the shaft and had fallen among the debris; here and there it was
wedged tight – even hundreds of feet from the bottom; elsewhere these
chance lodgements of stone and wood were so precarious that the slightest
movement could create fresh falls. The four lowest levels from the shaft
were completely blocked, unreachable either from above or from the lode.
Most of the dead would be buried there for weeks, perhaps for ever. But
there were survivors at the 30 level and – by some miracle – at the 70; some
were still stuck in the shaft, marooned on the remnants of those platforms
that had survived.

"What level is this Mellangoose adit?" Elizabeth asked.

There was surprise from the newcomers, who, until that moment, had
taken her for a man.

Chigwidden explained that ancient exploratory drifts from the Long
Stope cut through many of the levels of the three mines, allowing access to
everything between the 40 and the 150.

"We'll start at the Seventy, then," she told the captain, "where they
say there are definitely some men injured. You may send any doctor willing
to go underground there."

She nodded to Chigwidden, who set off at once into the teeth of the
rain, ahead of her. She raised her lantern the better to guide his feet. By the
light of it, as she turned from the group, she saw the face of the stranger, the
man with the obsession about the sins of the Troys. His eyes were black as
anthracite and large in his face, which was sharply etched on the night,
strong, angular – yet somewhat elfin, too, delicate . . . vulnerable. The
harsh judgement of his words was absent from his features. He was staring
at her with such troubled intensity that she found it hard to turn from him,
turn into the dark, into the rain – turn and face the unimaginable carnage
waiting there below.

The stranger's face went with her into that dark. Her fantasy blended his image with older memories of Bill. Yet, now she came to think of it, there *was* a passing similarity. An affinity, even.

She tried to avoid looking directly at the lantern but whenever her eyes scanned the black rim of the moorland, ghost afterimages of its piercing flame danced around the edges of her vision. They faded, not to blackness but to subtle and disturbing hints of that strong, pale, haunted visage with its deep-dark eyes; Bill's eyes, not softened by Bill's good humour. At last she could bear it no longer.

"Who was that man who was shouting about sin?" she asked her companion.

"Weeel! You do know *he*, surely, Mrs. Troy!"

"I'm certain I don't."

"Why, that's David Troy the preacher-man, that's who."

CHAPTER TWENTY-FIVE

THE MEDIEVAL MEN who built the Mellangoose adit must have been small. It was a mere five foot high and just two foot broad. Her hard whalehide hat saved the crown of Elizabeth's head many a nasty bump until – having walked what seemed like half a mile although it was, in fact, a mere furlong – they emerged into the grander cavern of the Long Stope. The bigger acoustic proclaimed a new sense of space. Only then did she realize she had not once thought of bats.

To call the angle of the Long Stope "shallow" was something of an exaggeration; it was all of two-in-three, or about thirty-five degrees. One slip and it would be hard to stop oneself from rolling all the way down. However, a little to one side of their point of entry, a series of steps had been cut into the foot wall, which made the going much less precarious.

Chigwidden's steady, echoing footfall soon became hypnotic. From time to time she risked staring about her, wondering at the massive face of the hanging wall, which loomed above them and vanished into the blackness on all sides. It was seemingly unsupported, either by "horse" of unmined rock or by pit-prop of wood. She was about to ask what kept it from falling when ahead of them she made out the first glimmerings of a rock wall. As they drew nearer, she saw that it ran diagonally across the space of the stope, uniting both walls. But not until they were almost upon it did she see that a tunnel had been cut into it, running at right angles to the path of their descent.

"What happened here?" she asked Chigwidden. "Why did they stop mining all of a sudden?"

" 'Tis a slide see, missis. What they do call a heave. A section heave." He put his hand against the wall, which, now that the candle was close to it, she saw was made entirely of quartz; its gleaming white face was suffused with blushes of blue and pink. "This here old quartz slide now, he've like cut the lode in half, see? Us'll find the other half of 'un two or three fathom below here, where we'm now standing."

He led her into the passage, which almost immediately gave way to a winze with a ladder poking up from its gaping mouth. She looked at it in dismay.

"Only three fathoms, Mrs. Troy," he told her as he tied a hank of line to the handle of the lantern. "I'll go first."

"Are there many of these slides?" she asked.

He started down the ladder; his voice rose to her out of the dark. "No, we aren't too badly off that way. Not like up St. Agnes. They do get section heaves every two fathoms. And 'tis nothing to find a fifty-fathom difference between one side of the heave and the other."

She lowered the lantern to him and started to descend the ladder. Three fathoms seemed a long way. "It's getting some warm," she said. "Or is it just the exertion?'

"He'll get warmer yet!" He helped her to find her foothold. The dip of the floor had increased; the carved steps were shorter.

"It's strange," she said. "You can walk across the moors above, and you'd have no idea all this was going on below."

He chuckled. "That's 'cos you don't hardly know what to look for, missis. You might see a line of red sicklegrass now, and ladies' bedstraw – well that's a sure sign o' quartz. And that'd be where a heave do reach the surface. Or common bedstraw, now, with like a sooty-yellow flicker in the leaf. That's what they old miners belonged to look for, 'cos that's a sign of cassiterite – the best black tin, see?"

By the time they had worked their way down to the horzintal drift that led to the 70, she knew the signs of tungsten, lead, copper, and iron, too. Chigwidden's knowledge amazed her, not least because the man himself hardly thought of it as knowledge at all. In his own way he was as learned as old Hamill, yet you could pass him on the roadside and think him nothing but a common, ignorant labourer.

The drift was modern, fully seven foot high and all of thirty inches wide. By now all her fears of being underground had evaporated; it seemed the most normal thing in the world to be walking a tunnel carved through the rock over five hundred feet below the moor. The world she had left behind up there – the engine houses, the fires, the flapping tarpaulins, the shouted commands, the warm, heavy rain – now seemed remote and unreal. She had the first inkling of that strange camaraderie which unites all miners the world over – to the bafflement of outsiders – and which keeps drawing them back to a labour whose agonies and dangers no rational man would contemplate for five minutes.

But nothing she had seen on that subterranean walk could have prepared her for the first breathtaking glimpse of the mine at the 70 Level. The lode at this point had been almost twenty feet wide; its dip was just eight degrees off the vertical. The two rock walls soared away almost directly above and below them, from blackness into blackness. The ore had been completely mined away, so the "level" was, in fact, a long wooden bridge that clung to the foot wall, resting on joists that spanned the entire gap. To their east, almost beyond the reach of the lantern, the bridge ended on a "horse" of rock; to their west, it vanished in utter darkness.

"Now," Chigwidden said, "which way is the man-engine shaft?"

"Don't you know?" she asked in surprise.

"You was up there," he reminded her. "You seen it yourself. Haven't you got no li'l ol' compass in your head?"

She wanted to tell him there was no time for games, but she was hot and out of breath. The air was stifling. She could feel the sweat running in rivulets down her back. So she was ready for a moment's pause. She looked about them, hoping for some sign, some clue, but finding none; then, because the bridge was shorter that way, she pointed east.

Chigwidden laughed and started off in that direction. "Us'll make a miner of'ee yet, missis."

He was a natural gentleman. As they had walked deeper and deeper into the earth, when claustrophobia might have gripped her, he had kept her fascinated with his talk of the moorland plants and the geology they reveal; and now, just when she needed that pause between first and second wind, he had dressed it up in a little guessing game.

But talk and games both finished the moment they left the bridge and entered the level. Here, for the first time, they encountered other miners – or rescuers as they had now become. The first sign of them was the rumbling of a tram wagon along the rails that now ran beneath their feet. In a moment they saw the man pushing it, a pale speck of movement where the perspective of the tunnel pinched out into darkness.

"Whoozat?" the fellow called out.

"Streamer!" Chigwidden shouted back. The walls of the level distorted every sound; conversation at that distance was impossible. When the gap between them had halved, 'Streamer' Chigwidden added, "Is all decent? I got Mrs. Troy here."

The other clearly did not trust his ears for he waited until they were almost met before he said, incredulously, "Who?" He was naked to the waist.

"He's right," Elizabeth said, envying the cool skin the fellow must be enjoying.

"Why . . . missis . . . he in't safe for'ee down here." To Chigwidden he added, "How did'ee go and bring she down here then?"

"I'm a nurse," Elizabeth answered. "Are there any wounded men at this level?"

He nodded grimly. "Burr and many."

"Then we're wasting time. Come on, you can pass us here."

She drew herself into a niche; Chigwidden scrambled nimbly over the tram and each party resumed its errand. As they walked, Elizabeth struggled out of her oilskin jacket. Fortunately it had been a warm summer evening and she was but lightly clad above the waist. Every stitch clung to her as if she had just stepped from a lake.

They arrived at the man-engine shaft as the first of the victims was being extracted from the debris. He was dead, a young man in his twenties, horribly mangled. There was an argument about his identity until the consensus agreed on Billy Moyle.

Henry Moyle, the lad's uncle, lifted him impassively and carried him away into a drift at right angles to the lode.

His removal started a small fall of rock. They all froze, wondering would it swell to a landslide. Elizabeth realized what tenuous chances now separated them all from the fate that had claimed young Moyle.

The debris settled again. Everyone was coughing. Elizabeth could hardly see, her eyes were so crammed with grit and water – some of it tears, some of its sweat.

The air slowly cleared to reveal a small pocket, a space, beneath two canted beams of pine, wreckage of the man-engine. From that space came a piteous moan. The rescuers were suddenly oblivious of their own danger, immune to dust. They burrowed like moles to enlarge the space. The trapped man, they soon discovered, was Nevill Kernick. His right arm seemed to have two elbows.

"He's gwin to lose that," one miner said. "We shan't get he out with that."

"Let me see." Elizabeth nudged him aside.

The limb below the break was warm; there was little blood to be seen, externally, anyway. It was worth trying to save.

Chigwidden put the splints and bandages into her hands even as she turned to ask him. Moments later the broken arm was splinted, not good enough for healing but it would let them move him.

From that moment on no man there questioned her presence; indeed, as each new victim was found, she was the first to be called to his side.

The next fifty hours blended to one long purgatory for Elizabeth. Thanks to the temperature and humidity – both near the hundreds – no trapped victim was going to die of exposure, but to work in such conditions was appalling – especially for her, unused to it as she was, and dressed moreover from neck to toe. Yet she worked right through, taking brief catnaps whenever she could.

There were more survivors than anyone had dared hope, but many of them had dreadful injuries. The sheer tenacity of the spark of human life astounded her, as did the courage and strength it evoked in the rescuers. She saw men lift weights at which a horse might have baulked. They picked and hacked and hammered until hands that had been hardened by a lifetime of such work became one mass of weals and blisters – until those wounds, in turn, oozed blood. And still they laboured on. She thought herself no heroine.

But others did. In later years, to judge by the legends that grew around the Deepwork Man-Engine Disaster, she had found some trick of dividing herself into half a dozen Elizabeths, each capable of ministering simultaneously to as many wounded men. Yet it was true that she managed to reach every level where survivors might be found. No drift was too narrow or too steep for her, no ladder too insecure, no climb too arduous. Before the first day was done, in those infernal depths where day and night had long been banished, the levels and drifts and winzes of Deepwork coalesced in the fever of her tired brain into one nightmarish blur of rock and dripping water. Finally even the wounded themselves became, as it were, multiple copies of one eternally tortured and broken human frame.

Streamer Chigwidden never left her side, guarding her when she slept, waking her gently, reluctantly, when she was needed again. A brother could not have been closer.

Four doctors attended the accident. In the beginning, when the survivors were managing to bring out some of the more lightly wounded, they stayed above ground. But when Doctor Reeves heard she was below, he went at once to join her, old as he was. Later Doctor Thomas, a much younger man, came below, too. The emergency aid underground, coupled with the more intensive care above, saved many a man who would either have bled to death or would never have survived the sheer pain of a journey to the surface. Eventually, when hopes of finding more survivors were slim, it was Doctor Reeves who turned to Elizabeth and barked, "To grass now, woman!"

She began to protest.

"If you don't go voluntarily," he told her, "I'll truss you in that sack and ring you up in the kibble."

Her exhaustion had produced that paradoxical state where, though monstrous sights and heartrending cries made no impression, the smallest acts and words could assume a ridiculous importance. She knew his threat was jocular; that is, in those remote corners of her mind where lurked the last shreds of everyday standards, there was a passing recognition of it. But to the rest of her, a dumb, washed-out animal trained only to stem blood and splint bones, his words seemed more like a sentence of banishment. She burst into tears and collapsed.

Strong hands encircled her. Strong muscles raised her and set her feet on the path toward the day. A strong arm stayed her each step of that last and worst of her wanderings in hell. At first she assumed it was Streamer again; yet his walk was . . . changed, the grip when she faltered had none of his kindly deference. She stumbled onward, upward, not really caring who her companion might be.

But when they stepped out into the dawn she looked up and saw his face and smiled. To discover Bill at her side, still holding her and staring deep into her eyes, was then the most natural thing in all the world.

She slept the clock round, first in Captain Body's office, then at home in Wheal Lavender; she did not wake when they moved her – indeed, she hardly stirred. Doctor Reeves, himself in a fair state of exhaustion, called by on his way back to Helston from Deepwork; he said only that she was to sleep all she needed.

Courtenay had been at the scene of the disaster, of course, not merely to help where he could but to report for the *Vindicator*. When he heard that Elizabeth was underground he had to be restrained from going below to join her. Twice he tried to sneak down; the captain threatened to throw him off the site if he was caught at it once again. David Troy had better luck. Being less impetuous than Courtenay, he waited his chance and then simply walked in by the Mellangoose adit and down the Long Stope. Of course it had been he who helped her back to the surface when exhaustion finally claimed her, he who carried her in his arms across the moor, he who slept like a watchman in the captain's outer office until they came to take her home. And even then he followed.

Oenone's instinct was to refuse him admission but there was something about the young fellow, an intensity of purpose that shone from his coal-black eyes and would not be denied. Surprised at herself, fearful of the wrath to come, she nevertheless let him in and brought him up to sit at her mistress's bedside. His reserve of wakefulness was a miracle. Elizabeth never stirred but his hand was there to smooth away a wisp of fallen hair, to straighten a rumpled pillow, to pull the creases from the turnover of her sheet. Oenone knew he had no business there, but his solemn earnestness overcame all her doubts; somehow he conferred a *rightness* upon his presence that waived all convention. And when she saw how serenely her mistress slept, she could almost believe that, by mysterious and marvellous means, some balm of comfort passed continually from him to her.

The first rays of the following dawn crept over the Pallas woods, reaching in through her pale curtains, resting softly on her eyelids; they stirred her to awaken.

She blinked. The world took some moments to resolve. Its two swimming images flew about her in separate realities; Bill was in both of them.

The images settled. It was not Bill but that other fellow . . . the name would not come . . . the stranger with the halo of light trapped in his hair. The fanatic. The preacher-man . . .

David Troy!

She closed her eyes again, hoping he would vanish.

"You will be hungry," he said.

She opened her eyes; of course he was still there.

"Was it you?" she asked.

"Yes."

Her disappointment was acute though her flesh was still too tired to show it.

"Watching you," he said, "at work in the mine and here, asleep, I have felt closer to God than at any other time in my life."

A vague memory of his earlier ranting came back to her, but his actual words were beyond recall.

"I will bring you a tray." He rose and left the room.

She got up, too, intending to go along to the water closet, but first she tidied her hair and put a little discreet powder on her cheeks; later it seemed an odd ranking of her priorities, out of line with her usual character. But at the time she accepted it as natural. Only her instincts had fully awakened.

He was a long while fetching her breakfast. When he finally appeared she saw why, for the tray had been laid out with an exquisite care that was certainly not Oenone's. There was even a small bowl of pansies, picked from the little bed beside the front door – something that would not even have crossed Oenone's mind.

She touched them delicately. "Did you pick these?"

"Yes."

"Why?"

He looked at them at her, and smiled. "I can't rightly say."

He had even taken time to polish his boots, she saw.

His gentleness, his uncertainty were quite unlike Bill's. The two men, she now realized, were actually very different. Their likeness was no more than you might find in any run of family portraits.

Memories of his behaviour up at Pallas Consols began to revive. "Didn't you say . . .? You said something about sin . . . the sins of the Troys?"

"I was lost in Error." He spoke in the same matter-of-fact tones in which another might say, "I was lost in Penzance market." *Error* was an actual location, like the Slough of Despond, in his Bunyanesque map of the world. "Will you not eat?" he added.

"Not if you're just going to sit and watch."

He shook his head.

"Go on. I can't face this mound of bacon and eggs. You have them and I'll eat the toast and marmalade."

"Are you sure?"

She passed him the plate with the cutlery pinned beneath her thumb. His hand closed over it, to prevent them from sliding off. His touch was warm, a part of her revival.

She spread her toast. "Well," she mused. "So you are David Troy."

He was wolfing down the food. She herself was famished beyond all the degrees of hunger but the sight of him made her realize how long she must have been underground. With his mouth full, he could only smile and nod. It struck her that he, too, was behaving somewhat out of character.

"Your late husband's cousin," he said at the first opportunity.

"Did you know him? You are somewhat alike. I don't know if anyone's ever pointed it out?"

"We moved in very different spheres. Morwenna must have told you of the 'Poor Troys'? One of them now sits before you."

"Facing another!" she said.

He looked around at all the fine furniture. The expression in his eyes was complex. She expected to see envy and derision, and was not disappointed; yet it was overlaid with appreciation and even – though it surprised her – an odd sort of approval.

But she knew what he was thinking. "There's not a stick of it I could afford to replace, Mr. Troy." she told him. "And if we're to play that game, then I must add that your boots are a great deal newer than even my newest pair of shoes."

He tried to tuck them farther beneath his chair. "A walking preacher needs good boots," he said defensively.

"Is that how you make your living? Walking around and preaching?"

His eyebrows rose. "Have they really told you nothing about me?" It seemed to surprise him that he had not been at least a weekly topic among them.

"Well, how do you make your living then?"

"I'm a solicitor. I'm sorry – I thought you knew."

"Where d'you live?"

"Penzance."

"Oh. I go there quite often. Funny I've never seen you."

He smiled. "I don't actually practise up and down the pavements. I do have an office, you know."

With a playful, inverted grin she accepted the rebuke. Then she grew solemn again. "Oh, we shouldn't be smiling and talking like this!" She closed her eyes.

She was the most beautiful woman he had ever seen.

"What is the news?" she asked. "How long have I slept?"

"We came out of the mine about twenty-five hours ago."

"And the latest news?"

"It is dismal,"he warned her.

"I must know it."

"Without you the toll of the dead would have been double what it is. I have never witnessed . . ."

"How many?" she insisted.

He sighed and put down his plate, which was now empty; not even the rind of the bacon was left. "When Doctor Reeves came up – in other words, when active rescue work came to an end – about fifteen hours ago, there were forty-seven men still unaccounted for. But . . ."

"Forty-seven!" she cried in anguish.

"Yes but some of them might not have been down there at all. They might be in gaol in Penzance . . . or sleeping off their drunkenness in some ditch on Goonhilly . . . cutting stone over to Manaccan . . . or fishing out of Porthleven. There are a hundred places they might be. You know what wretched lives they lead."

She was only slightly comforted. "I do now." She shook her head. "I had no idea . . . no idea."

"The Almighty works in mysterious ways," he said, seeking instinctive preacher-words to comfort her.

The vague implication that God might have engineered the entire disaster merely to open her eyes to the conditions under which the miners worked appalled her. He saw her disappointment without understanding it; and yet perhaps some less committed streak of his character – what he would call 'an unswept corner of his soul' – dimly grasped its origins, for he quickly generalized the comment: "I mean, we cannot possibly know the reasons for this visitation of His chastisement. Even the word 'reason'. . . ."

"Please!" Impatiently, she waved him to silence. After a while she went on, "Now that I do know, I have no idea what to do about it."

"There is a better way," he said quietly. "The entire system of ownership is wrong. God gave dominion over the earth and all its fruits to mankind, not to certain privileged families."

She gave a weary groan. "No doubt, no doubt. But that's very little help to me. I shall be up and about in an hour. I have to return to the Pallas workings and I have to do something. Are you suggesting I should give it all away to the tributers and bal-maidens? I don't see what that would achieve, frankly."

He did not answer her directly. After a pause (and no one knew better how to make a pause compelling) he said, "Mrs. Troy, I believe you may have been chosen, especially chosen, to make the most far-reaching changes here. Please hear me out! I know you will laugh at these notions. You probably set at naught all you did at Deepwork for those wretched men, but . . ."

"It was little enough, Mr. Troy. Exhausting, I grant you, but not in the least heroic. I ran no risks. Believe me, I saw true heroism down there."

He shrugged. "I would argue that point with you until the end of time, but it's beside my present purpose. Let me put it another way. The system of ownership which may have served mankind well enough in simpler times is now our winding sheet. Matters were very different in the past. A Tudor king endured the same fleas as plagued his lowliest peasant. He suffered the same bad teeth, died of the same ignorant quackery. The same bitter winds roared indifferently through palace and hovel, alike. The same woodsmoke choked all. But think how it is now. Think of life at the present court and contrast it with your . . ."

"But my dear Mr. Troy, I have no idea of life at court – neither Henry Tudor's nor Queen Victoria's! Hasn't Morwenna told you – I'm no more than a horse-doctor's daughter!" She remembered some medical gossip she'd overheard at Guy's. "Anyway, I once overheard an eminent physician say that if Prince Albert had been an ordinary member of the middle classes, he'd be alive today. He died of *too much* medical attention. A dose of benign neglect, three times daily, was all he needed."

Troy fought to master his anger; he was unused to having his finest flowers of metaphor trampled underfoot like this. "As you wish," he said curtly.

She relented. There was something most endearing about his intensity; and it certainly made a change from Courtenay's bland, immature, over-confident, secretive . . . no – she must not talk Courtenay down, either.

But what was she to do now? Say goodbye? Hope we meet again? The thought that they might *not* meet again suddenly struck her, bringing a moment of panic. She wanted to see him again, to talk with him about serious things, to share some of his answers to the great questions of life.

"I'm sorry," she said. "I don't suppose either of us is going to make much sense at the moment. I can only think of those poor families who've lost a husband, a son, a brother . . . Something must be done for them."

"How right you are, Mrs. Troy. I stand rebuked. As to the bereaved, I heard Mr. Rodda mention something about organizing a national appeal through the popular press."

"Oh, he's a good man."

"Your partner, I understand?"

"I beg your pardon!"

"In the *Vindicator*. Surely you and he own it jointly?"

"Oh yes. It was your use of the word 'partner.' No one can be a partner to Mr. Rodda."

The opinion made him smile.

"I must get up," she said. "And you must go. Next time I'm in Penzance, let's meet, eh?"

Her directness left him flustered. It pleased her to see him off his high horse. She felt a desire to tease him, to keep him down there, dismounted. "Now I've embarrassed you! I know! You're probably one of those poor, noble lawyers who's always defending people for nothing. While I – as you so forcefully and eloquently made clear the other night – am a bloated capitalist. So let me be the one to invite you to dinner at the St. Michael. We'll share a rack of lamb and a bottle of claret. We'll see which of us can corrupt the other first!"

The suggestion shocked him. All the way to the door he made negative-sounding noises.

But, she noticed, he could not *quite* bring himself to reject the invitation out of hand.

CHAPTER TWENTY-SIX

COURTENAY HAD NEVER WORKED so hard – or at least so consistently – at anything as he now did at the Deepwork Disaster Appeal. His byline appeared above dozens of accounts in all sorts of likely and unlikely journals, from the augustan *Times* to the most obscure provincial rag. Branches of the appeal were opened all over the world, wherever the exiled Cornish miner, the "Cousin Jack," had taken his trade. The whole campaign climaxed toward the end of summer with a grand meeting of appeal organizers and the larger patrons at the Westminster Central Hall. The star attraction was to be the heroine of the hour, Elizabeth Troy. Courtenay managed to keep the news from her until she was safely up in London, at what she now called her "usual" hotel in Paddington, though she had stayed there only once before, at the time of the High Court hearing.

"Oh but I *couldn't!*" she protested when at last he showed her the handbill. "I've never spoken to a crowd larger than half-a-dozen in my life. I couldn't possibly talk to a gathering like that."

"It would mean everything to the fund, you know."

"But the Central Hall, Westminster! It's *vast!* And I've got no speaking voice at all."

"All those people – they've worked so hard to make a success of it. I'm sorry I volunteered you like that, but it never occurred to me you'd refuse. I suppose I shall just have to . . ."

"Oh, Courtenay! To call it refusing is a bit hard. All I'm saying is that

I shall be petrified and . . . and just dreadful. I *know* it."

"But you're the centre of the whole thing. Don't you realize that? The name of Elizabeth Troy is spoken in every drawing room between . . ."

"Oh, I know! I think it's utter nonsense. I'm supposed to be the Grace Darling of Cornwall. Suddenly every hostess in the county wants to entertain me, and I've been pestered by reporters and lady journalists ever since I stepped off the train at Paddington."

He smiled. "And you still think people won't flock to hear you?"

She said nothing.

"Very well." He turned to leave her. "I'll tell them . . . oh . . . that you're indisposed . . . or something."

"And you'll deliberately make it sound even less convincing than that! I know you." She held herself stiffly. The air rushed in and out of her nostrils as if she were having to pump herself up. "Tell them I'll just say a few words. When is it?"

"Tonight. At nine o'clock."

"Oh God!"

"It'll be over and done with all the sooner."

"I'm supposed to be up here in London to rest and get over it all. Doctor's orders."

He laughed. "Go on – you thrive on it." He sat down again. Or, rather, he lay stiffly to attention in one of the chairs. His smile was lazy, all-knowing. "And afterwards . . ."

"We'll have to see about that," she said.

"We've hardly had a minute together for months."

She didn't want to talk about it; she just wanted it to happen. To change the subject she asked whether he knew David Troy.

Her brusqueness amused him. "Actually, he was there at Deepwork during most of the rescue," he told her.

"Yes that's where I saw him. I didn't know him at all, of course, but as soon as he knew who I was he started ranting wildly about the sins of ownership and property."

"So I heard."

"What d'you think of him?"

It was several seconds before he answered, "He's a lot shrewder than you'd suppose at first meeting. For all his ranting, I don't believe his religion is anything like so deep as he makes it appear. I could be wrong but I fancy he'll soon grow dissatisfied with the role of itinerant preacher."

"Everything's a *role* to you, isn't it!"

"The world is a cast of thousands, yes. I think friend David may very soon get bitten by the bug of politics – if, indeed, it hasn't bitten him already. He's on the county council, you know. 'Tis pity he's so poor."

"Why?"

"Otherwise he'd soon be up here in London, as an MP. He's the sort who'd be a cabinet minister before he's forty – *if* he had the money." He shrugged.

"I only met him those few seconds," she said.

"We're straying from the point." He grinned "You don't find you're lonely here?"

"I have Oenone."

"I mean after lights-out."

Elizabeth laughed. "We share the one room. In fact, we share the one bed. I see no reason to splash money around on . . ."

"But she's your *maid!* How could you?"

"That's only one of her roles – to put it in your terms. She's also a good, loyal friend. A simple friend who doesn't involve me in . . . complications."

"But . . . the same bed!"

She said tartly, "There have been times in the past when you've not considered yourself too grand."

His jaw dropped. "She told you about that?"

"Not in so many words. Her anger at you is enough of a hint."

"It's long past," he insisted.

"Oh, I don't doubt that."

He rose again and began to pace about. "And I'll tell you what it was – madness – a fever – a raging in the blood. I was an insatiable . . . a beast. I just didn't know how to cope. Not then. I became a sort of glutton. But I bitterly regret it now. If you could help her to believe that, Beth – you'd be doing her a service, not me. It's wrong for a warm-hearted, good-looking woman like that to isolate herself just because of what I did."

She had never seen him so distressed, or at least so *genuinely* distressed. She stood and went to him, putting a hand on his sleeve.

He folded her in his arms. Suddenly she wanted him, with an intensity that almost overpowered her. "I'm not in love with you, you know," she felt compelled to say.

"That's what makes it so easy for us. We're neither of us *goaded* by that dreadful, all-consuming, won't-let-you-eat-sleep-rest obsession."

"You'll be on the platform tonight, too, I hope?"

"Right beside you. And you'll be splendid."

She was, too – much to her surprise. She had prepared a somewhat flowery oration but when she found herself standing on the platform and staring into that ocean of indistinguishable faces, she felt too small to carry the weight of it. The words fled and all she could do was describe the disaster as she remembered it. She wanted them to understand that what they called heroism was really no more than the instinctive behaviour of ordinary people; she had seen too much "heroism" during those dreadful hours to suppose it was rare or special. If her name was largest on the handbill, that was only because she had been privileged to move throughout the mine, wherever a victim was discovered alive. She had seen more than any other and she wanted them to share her witness – and to share, too, the privilege of knowing what fine people they had been working for during these past weeks.

It was not the speech anyone had expected but, once the initial surprise was over, they warmed to her and, at the end, gave her a standing ovation that lasted several minutes. It took a further hour for the hall to clear; everyone wanted to speak to her, to shake her hand. But at last she and Courtenay were able to leave.

"Didn't I tell you!" he crowed. "Throwing a challenge to you is like throwing fish to a sealion."

She began to relax. "What you call a challenge is actually the threat of chaos . . . the Lord of Misrule knocking at the door. It's a kind of panic, like when the ward's in a mess and matron's coming up the corridor. I wish I could find a calmer way to live."

They hailed a hansom in Birdcage Walk and Courtenay gave the name of a restaurant in Holborn. As they set off he told her, "There was one person there who hung upon your lips and drank in everything you said."

"Who?"

"David Troy. I wondered if you'd noticed."

"Good heavens, Courtenay – why didn't you tell me? I didn't see him."

"He slipped away pretty smartly at the end. He must be feeling utterly caddish now."

"Why?"

"For making use of a tragedy like Deepwork to shout his dogmas at you."

She stared at the haunches of the trotting horse in front of them. Its hip bones, deformed by the years in harness, seemed almost to break out of its skin – left, right, left, right, left, right . . .

"If a belief is sincerely held," she said, "does it really matter if it's wrong?"

"I've thought quite enough about David Troy for one day," he answered.

The trotting hooves said, yes, no, yes, no . . .

They had come up through Victoria, skirting the back of Buckingham Palace; soon they reached Hyde Park, where they turned along Piccadilly.

Elizabeth stared out at the crowds with great curiosity. "The fashion now seems to be to show one's ankles," she remarked. "Especially among the young. I wonder who'll be first to try it in Cornwall. Lilian, I expect."

He laughed awkwardly. "Dear God – I hope not!"

"It's only a few inches, gap," she went on, "yet it completely alters the character of a woman."

Again that laugh, hesitant, unsure. "Are you being serious, Beth?"

"Can't you see what I mean? With *our* dresses, the way we sweep the foot pavements as we walk . . . we might just as well be on castors. I mean, we seem to glide along. But with this new fashion, well, the shoes look like little black rabbits taking it in turns to go darting forward. Women aren't on castors any more."

"Ah! The secret is out! You all have" – he lowered his voice and almost whispered the word – *"limbs!"*

She gave him a playful push. "I wonder if I'm every going to live in London," she mused.

"I thought you did your training here?"

"Not the West End. The London I know is a couple of miles east of all this."

"Surely you couldn't leave Cornwall now?"

"That first day, when I got off at Pallas Halt and walked around the lanes until I was lost, I wondered if I might stay down in Cornwall, so I looked at each tree and house and every little side-road and asked myself, 'What are you going to mean to me one day?' Don't you ever do that, Courtenay? What I'm saying is if I ever do live in London then all these streets, all these buildings, they'll all *mean* something, won't they?"

"Yes."

"Then don't you think that at least some little hint of all that meaning ought to sort of cling to them already?"

"You do get some strange notions, Beth. I blame Hamill's influence. He . . ."

"For instance," she interrupted in her eagerness to make him agree, "take this building here with these beautiful iron gates. I have no idea what it is, but . . ."

"The Royal Academy."

"And I can't even imagine what's behind it."

He joined the game. "Try."

She closed her eyes and smiled. "I get the feeling of a wide street . . . theatres . . . big, new hotels . . . fashionable restaurants . . . a square with a lake and fountains?" She opened her eyes and looked at him. "Am I right?"

He shook his head. "Not even close. It's all private apartments. Some shops – quite chic but not *the* places, you know. And The Albany's there, too, where all the swell and idle bachelors have their sets of rooms – so you can probably imagine what else you might find in this neighbourhood."

Something in his tone made her look again at what she had supposed were fashionable young ladies; she clutched his arm and laughed at herself. "For heaven's sake don't tell Lilian what I said!" But after a while she returned to her theme: "The minute I saw Wheal Lavender, I knew."

"Knew what?"

"I knew that house was somehow already a part of me, of my life."

He cleared his throat. "And the minute you walked around into the back yard? What then?"

She looked away, across the street. "It's so hard to talk about. Why d'you *need* to keep talking about it?"

"If you keep it festering in silence, then it exercises the most dreadful hold on you. It has poisoned us all, the whole of Society, but we *are* just beginning to recover from it."

She said nothing.

"Don't you agree?" he pressed.

"Perhaps."

"Well then . . ."

After a pause she said, "What if you don't *want* to be free? What if you find you rather like that secret power of it? If there's a kind of . . . I don't know – a primitive . . . terror in being possessed by it? Something you don't want to debate and talk about – no matter how earnestly or high-mindedly. What if you don't want the idea of it to become so commonplace we'd be discussing it between the porridge and the marmalade?"

He was reluctant to answer. She went on, "I need half-glimpsed things in my life, half-understood, half-expressed, half-formed . . ."

"Half-truths?" he suggested with a laugh.

"Yes, even half-truths. They protect me. They leave many avenues open."

Should she tell him such things? He might grow up too soon, pass beyond her, leave her stranded among all those enticing avenues and no one to help her explore them.

He said, "Sometimes I feel such a . . . such . . . so *tender* toward you, Beth. And my physical desire just fades. I wish it could always be like that."

"Don't you think desire is a kind of tenderness, too?"

"Not for me."

She waited for more but he fell silent. Later, as if it were a belated continuation, he said, "We can never hurt each other because we will never really be in love. Because we aren't opposites. We're only different."

She did not welcome these new insights in him; his earlier immaturity was more comfortable because is posed no challenges.

But when they had finished their supper, safely locked in their *chambre privée*, they shed all their delicate insights along with their clothes. It was two o'clock before he brought her back to Paddington.

The following morning she awoke early, as she always did on those "mornings-after." Oenone was snoring.

"Not bad looking," Courtenay had said.

She tried to imagine him lying beside Oenone, his lips on hers, his hands straying over her body. Had Oenone, too, bruised that firm, supple, sinewy flesh with her bites? Had she threshed beneath him, uttering those same primitive, formless cries, hating herself but loving the torment? Had that same astonishing blend of loathing and adoration made her want to kill him, crush him to nothing, pull the remnant of him into her, lose him, own him, imprison him, possess him . . .?

And when the force of that desire was denied, did it turn into the eternal and implacable hatred Oenone now displayed for Courtenay and all his works?

Oenone turned over; the snoring stopped. Last night, the buildings and streets of London had yielded no clue as to Elizabeth's future; so, too, there was nothing in Oenone's outward bearing to say whether or not Elizabeth was treading that identical barren path, just five or six years behind.

When she was dressed she went out for an early walk along Grand Junction Road toward Hyde Park. The milkmen were all out, ladling their adulterated product into jugs and billycans brought out by the scullery-maids. There was a lot of crude joking going on. One of the men offered her a cup but she had brought out no money.

"A smile will do, my dove," he said. "There's not many as cheery as you at this hour. Sweet dreams, was it?"

She accepted the offer and thanked him gratefully, though the milk was undoubtedly watered.

Other maidservants passed her on their way back from the bakery. The hot, yeasty smell of oven-fresh rolls and bread assailed her. She decided she would only go a short walk.

Rain had fallen in the small hours. The dust had been washed away; the tarred wooden setts of the roadway gleamed. Puddles lurked in the timeworn hollows of the paving. The hem of her dress – fortunately detachable – became soaked and heavy. It made her remember the "fashionable" young ladies she had seen last night in Piccadilly. What a mistake! She cringed at her own naivety.

As she neared the end of the street, she heared a door slam. She turned and saw, tripping down the front steps, pulling on his gloves, arranging his bowler hat – David Troy.

"Good morning, Mrs. Troy," he called out.

As she waited for him it struck her that he must have been doing the same – waiting for her – at one of the front windows. How long had that vigil endured? Had he been there last night when she returned in the cab with Courtenay?

On his way down the garden path he removed one glove and plucked a small, red bourbon rose that rambled up a decaying trellis. With deft fingernails he nipped off the thorns; then he replaced his glove. She thought it was for a buttonhole but he presented it directly to her.

" 'Not of itself but of thee!' " he said.

She flushed with pleasure. "Thank you kind sir. I hope the owners of the house won't mind? Are they friends of yours?" She looked up at the windows, all blank.

"I didn't even think of them. Anyway, there's no one up and about."

"Ah! Sin is only sin if you're caught out, eh?"

He blushed. "I assure you — the very idea of theft never even entered . . ."

"I'm only joking, Mr. Troy. I'm going for a walk in the park. D'you want to come too?"

"I'd welcome the chance to talk to you."

"As long as it's not talking *at* me."

"I hope you'll forget that soon. I've already told you how much I regret it. Here, let me do that."

He took the rose from her and began to work it behind the feather in her bonnet.

She looked up into his face; the more she knew of him, the less she sought comparisons with Bill, despite the superficial resemblance. It was a good face, full of strength and character without being rugged; indeed, there was a fine sensitivity in every line of it. You'd trust him just to look at him. "What d'you want to talk about then?" she asked as she resumed her stroll.

He crossed behind her to walk at her outside. "I thought you were wonderful yesterday evening, by the way."

"I'm sorry I didn't notice you were there. Somehow one doesn't see individual faces from the platform, you know. Mr. Rodda told me he saw you, but only much later. I mean, it was too late . . ."

"You needn't explain," he said.

Actually, that's right, she thought.

He went on, "I wouldn't have expected you to seek me out, anyway."

"Why did you give me this rose just now?" She turned to him encouragingly.

He studiously avoided her eyes. Many answers flitted across his face before he said, "Impulse. No real reason at all."

"What did you want to talk about?"

"I wondered if you'd thought any further about our last conversation?"

"My memory's rather vague. We discussed whether your boots were newer than my shoes, didn't we?"

He laughed. "Hint taken."

"Not easy when it weighs a half-ton. Let's talk about you. Tell me about yourself. What sort of people to you represent? Where d'you live? What are your recreations . . . you know the sort of thing."

Bill had always been reluctant to talk about himself. But David leaped in at once: "I do less and less actual court work these days — unless there's something that absolutely cries out for it."

"Is it the person who cries out — or the principle?"

He looked at her sharply. "*You'd* make a lawyer!"

"I doubt it. I'd find it hard to separate the two – the person and the principle."

"Well, in my case it's usually the person. I leave the discussion of principles to the county council – I have a seat there, as perhaps you know. That takes up a lot of time."

"It's not paid though, is it?"

"Fellow Liberals steer bits of work my way . . . wills . . . conveyancing – that sort of thing. Incidentally, talking of wills . . ."

"Yes, I thought we were going to!" When he did not share her laughter, she gave him a playful nudge. "Come on, now! Why shouldn't you be interested? After all, your family might very well have inherited Pallas."

"Ah, you know the story, do you?"

"Your father was a younger brother to Bill's father, wasn't he?"

"Oh – but we came much closer than that! Don't you know?"

She shook her head.

"Shall I tell you?"

"Please."

They crossed the Bayswater Road and entered the park by the Victoria Gate. Apart from a few grooms, out exercising their horses, no one else was about. The sun was above the trees, though, and the night's chill had gone.

"I take it you understand," he said, "that in English law, land cannot be passed on like money or goods?"

"Yes, I know about that. Real estate and personal estate."

"And you know why?"

"George Ivey says it's because in each century the law gets rewritten to allow the ruling classes to do legally what they did illegally in the previous century. And back in the days of chivalry, what they wanted was to be able to borrow money off the Jews without allowing the Jews to seize their lands in default of payment. So they invented a legal fiction whereby all land 'really' belonged to the crown. Every landowner was 'really' just a tenant of the king."

Troy laughed. "He sounds like a good fellow, your Mr. Ivey. I must start cultivating his company."

"It's a matter of taste. How does all this affect you and me and Pallas?"

"Well, to continue in Ivey's vein – it meant that the original owner of land could leave it to his son – or his daughter, come to that – but only in a sort of trust for future generations. In theory they were still all tenants of the king, of course. The original owner was called the tenant-in-chief, the son was the tenant-for-life, and later generations were tenants-in-tail. In other words, the ownership of the land was *entailed*."

She shook her head in bewilderment. "What *is* it about humans? If there's a choice between an easy way and a complicated way . . ."

"Look at it from, say, an Elizabethan nobleman's point of view. It didn't matter how rich you were in those days, if you owned no land, you were a nobody. Land was everything. You couldn't vote without land – not even in the parish. You couldn't sit in parliament – in fact, that was the case until very recently. In short, without land you had no status whatever in Society. In our time, now that money has become far more important than land, it's hard for us to imagine *their* frame of mind – when there were no canals, no railways, no industry, no other large source of wealth apart from land. No wonder we frame our laws so as to make ownership of a factory far more imortant than merely working in it. And no wonder they framed their laws so as to exclude the city merchants and Jews!"

"But it must have been a great nuisance – to find that the land was virtually untouchable."

"Precisely!" He smiled. "So the ruling classes (being, after all, the *ruling* classes) not surprisingly bent the rules. It was cumbersome and capricious, but it did allow for the legal transfer of entailed land. Funnily enough the process was mostly used in order to *preserve* the entail! Isn't that typically English – to bar the entail in order to preserve it!"

"I can't follow that."

"English law hates perpetuities – open-ended commitments. And an entail is a kind of perpetuity. So the best way to preserve it is to bar it after it's run three or four generations and then start a new one. That's what happened with Pallas. And it concerned Bill's father and grandfather. And" – he looked meaningfully at her – "my father, too."

"Ah!"

"Yes. The *old* system for barring an entail was among the most ludicrous ever devised. It was called Fine and Recovery and it worked like this. Suppose I owned some entailed land and I wanted to sell it to you. We'd have to act in collusion to bring a fictitious lawsuit to achieve the transfer. You would sue me, saying that you were the rightful owner of the land. I would bring a friend to court, a man-of-straw, and I'd swear it was he who told me I owned the land – so let him now justify that assertion. My friend would refuse to do so and the court would then award the land to you as its 'rightful' owner! You, of course, would privately have paid me the agreed sun, held in trust by our lawyers pending the court's ruling."

"And did no judge ever question what this man-of-straw was supposed to have said?"

"But it was a legal fiction."

"Exactly. Didn't any judge question it?"

"No, no, no," he laughed. "A legal fiction is something a court is not *allowed* to inquire into. If the parties themselves don't raise a point of law (and of course they're careful not to), then the court will do nothing of its own motion."

"Oh, isn't that wonderful! When Ivey says the law will always aid the ruling class, he's not far wrong, is he!"

"It's a bullseye. The process of Fine and Recovery was mainly used by father and son to break an existing entail and create a new one."

"Does it still go on?"

"Not in that form. Fine and Recovery was abolished in the great reforms of 1833. However, the honest, open system that replaced it achieves exactly the same thing. But – and this is why I've explained it in such detail – guess who earned a footnote in legal history by being the very last pair, father-and-son, to make use of the old procedure?"

"Don't tell me!"

He nodded. "Robert and Samuel Troy – my grandfather and uncle – Bill's grandfather and father. In fact, they started the process in 1832. The action was successful and the Fine was granted. But then my father, George Troy, entered his own claim at the foot of the Fine – not unnaturally, since the Fine would effectively disinherit our line of the family."

"Did your father win?"

David's smile was ambiguous. "It was never tested because, when the new system was introduced the following year, Robert and Samuel abandoned their pursuit of the Fine and went through the whole process again in the new, 'honest' way."

"And your father didn't challenge that?"

"Couldn't afford to." He stopped and faced her. "So you see, Mrs. Troy, for the want of a few guineas, I might now be the owner of Pallas."

"Oh Mr. Troy – I'm so sorry."

"Oh, I wouldn't have wanted my own life any other way. I was always sorry for my father though."

"I mustn't stay out too long." She turned and they began to retrace their steps. "Perhaps it would have been better if you had inherited the estate," she told him.

"You don't mean that."

"You could have given it all away. You could have given the mines to the miners so that they could bankrupt themselves instead of you. And you could have given the land to the smallholders, so that they could go on merely subsisting and never contributing a penny to the general wealth of the county. And you could give Pallas House and all its treasures to Polglaze and his merry staff of wreckers, so that they could neglect it and smash it bit by bit on their own behalf instead of on yours. And I could retire to my little lodge and do my garden and play the piano and go a-picnicking and see my friends and never have another troubled hour!"

His answer astonished her. She expected protests, argument, a political lecture, a sermon . . . but all he said was: "Have you been talking to Morwenna?"

"Certainly not! We're hardly on speaking terms. She goes about telling people I drink and that I'm a socialist. Have *you* been talking to her? I thought she always cut your side of the family dead." .

"So she did. All her life. But then suddenly, a couple of months ago, just before the Deepwork Disaster, she met me upon the road and . . ." He went on to describe their meeting. "She was playing some devious game, of course, but I still can't imagine what."

"Its only aim would be to get me out and herself back in. You'd be cast aside as soon as you'd played whatever part she'd planned for you."

"Yes, but what part? I've puzzled over it scores of times and I can't see it."

They walked on in thoughtful silence, back out of the park. Elizabeth said, "Could it be . . . you say your father 'barred the Fine' — is that the right term?"

"You could put it that way."

"But he didn't proceed with his case, so presumably the Fine was valid?"

He stopped in the middle of the Bayswater Road. "By Jove, you should be a lawyer! I'd never thought of that. To me it was just so much ancient history. What you mean is that if the Fine was valid then Samuel, Bill's father, *was already the outright owner* of Pallas when he and his father started the action under the new system."

"But where does that lead?"

He shrugged and they resumed their homeward stroll. "Some interesting byway, I'm sure. But as to Morwenna working that out — I'm afraid not. It would need a mind like yours and she simply hasn't got it. No, she just wanted to stir something up. She was trying to encourage me to meet you (while seeming to *dis*courage me, to be sure). I don't know what she supposed might . . ."

"Is that why you came to Deepwork that night?"

"No. That was chance. I was on legal business in Carleen."

They were drawing near his gate. Ten yards short of it she paused. "Whatever the reason, Mr. Troy — and whatever the Dragon's purpose — I at least am glad we've met. I hope it won't be another two months before we meet again."

They resumed their walk. "I'm still waiting for that rack of lamb, Mrs. Troy."

"And the claret."

He laughed and wagged a finger at her.

He watched her all the way back up the street. How futile it was to seek to plan one's life, he thought. Encouraged by Morwenna, he had (though for his own reasons) planned that Elizabeth should fall in love with him.

The one thing he had never envisaged was that he might fall in love with her.

CHAPTER TWENTY-SEVEN

ON THE TWO OCCASIONS Elizabeth had been in David Troy's company, she had no doubts about him at all; but as soon as the magnetism of his presence was removed she felt somewhat less sure. From time to time it crossed her mind to go into Penzance and take up that invitation, yet something always held her back. She could never put her finger on it, but it was there, a disquiet that refused to settle on any particularity of his.

He was interested in her – no one could doubt that. And in himself he was an interesting man. A little intense, perhaps; a little too solemn at times. But surely that was better than George Ivey's jovial brand of cynicism? He was ambitious, too, but in a high-minded way; it would be most unfair to say he was out only for himself. Above all, he had been admirably frank about Morwenna's approach to him.

Yet, for all that she wanted to believe in him, for all that she longed to know him better, something fanned her caution.

She could hardly discuss him with Courtenay. And Hamill had no time for either lawyers or nonconformists, let alone for a man who was both – and a Poor Troy to boot. Oenone was, for some strange reason, in awe of David, ever since his bedside vigil after the disaster. The only person Elizabeth could possibly discuss him with was Lilian. But how to open the subject lightly, innocently?

In the end it was Lilian herself who furnished the opening. "What d'you think of George?" she asked one day.

"Are you having second thoughts?" Elizabeth countered.

"*Hundred*-and-second thoughts, I should think. I just can't make up my mind."

"He's a good lawyer."

Lilian sighed. "You know how they say men are all deceivers . . ."

Elizabeth was alarmed. "He hasn't . . . you haven't . . ."

"No, not that! Although that's what people mean – men are only out for that one thing and if you give it them, they'll thank you, leave you, and forget you. But I think men are deceivers in far worse ways than that."

"For example?"

"No matter how well you know one, you'll never know what he's really thinking. There are some parts of their minds you'll never reach."

"It's the same with women, surely?"

"Perhaps, but in a different way. Women can share their thoughts with other women. Even if they don't actually come out with everything in words, we always *know*, don't we? But men aren't like that, not even among themselves. When they get together in their clubs or down at the local, they still keep that secret self hidden. There's a sort of Flying Dutchman in each of them. I'm not putting it very well but d'you know what I mean? Has any man ever been completely frank with you?"

"No, but to be fair the reverse is true, too, Lilian."

She sighed. "It's different. I can't tell you how, but I just know it is."

"Anyway, how does all this refer to George?"

"I told him once — I was being flattering, of course, and trying to make him think I was terribly profound and interesting. He began it by saying that if he had set up practice in London, his life would be dull by contrast with life in Helston. So I told him that London, or any big city, would just tear him apart — because he's almost two people, you know. I said he'd have made a great success in London, become a grand commercial lawyer, steering great enterprises through legal shoals and narrows. But outside his working hours he'd have become that other person. He'd've courted the society of raffish, artistic boulevardiers and told himself this was the *real* life. I even made a joke of it. I said that his divided corpse would have given them all a problem. His bohemian friends would have said, 'This corpse is for the lawyers to bury,' and his legal partners would have answered, 'No, no — he is for you; he was never one of us.' I was only joking — well, half-joking — but he looked at me in such a strange way! I'll swear he was on the point of telling me something about himself — something very important. And then" — she sighed again — "it was like doors slamming shut all over his face."

Elizabeth thought awhile and then said, "You couldn't call that deception though."

"I can — and I do. He's courting me very hard at the moment, but there's that important bit of him that he won't talk about. It's between us like a wall — no, like a knife."

Elizabeth saw she'd never get a better opening into a discussion of her own problem. She echoed Lilian's sigh and said, "I'm in the same sort of quandary myself, to be quite honest."

Lilian was agog. "Over Courtenay? Don't worry. I can tell you *everything* about him."

"It's David Troy."

Lilian was baffled. "The fellow who ranted at you on the night of . . . I didn't even know you knew him."

"We've met a couple of times since, actually. He's quite different when you get to know him."

"Ah ha!" Lilian licked her lips and raised her eyebrows encouragingly. "There's something very . . ." Elizabeth faltered. The words did not come easily – or they came too easily and were immediately qualified in her mind before she could speak them. "In fact," she said at last, "I oughtn't to tell you anything. Let's go to Penzance one day next week and you can meet him and make up your own mind. And then you can tell me what you think."

And so it was left. "Next week" with Elizabeth was a very moveable feast.

Meanwhile, her rather less complicated involvement with Courtenay continued. As her feelings concerning David Troy intensified, both for and against him, it had the strange effect of removing all doubt, all scruple, over her relationship with Courtenay. They became quite reckless. Soon their assignations needed no more arranging than the lift of an eyebrow. Then, in the bat-haunted dark of the Wheal Pallas tunnels, in seedy haylofts, in unkempt coppices . . . in a dozen lunatic, dangerous places, they would meet and enjoy that most primal dance of the flesh.

Once, on a wild wet foreshore at Trequean Zawn, sprawled and gasping among the seaweed and the banded agate rock, she had opened her eyes to see, on the clifftop far above, the undoubted silhouette of a man. He was staring down at them through a pair of binoculars. She rolled over at once, thrusting Courtenay with her, beneath a rocky overhang (and almost spoiling his unfailing determination to finish like a gentleman).

"What?" he asked furiously.

"There's someone up there, a man with binoculars."

Shaking now with fright he crawled a dozen yards away, all beneath the protective shelf. There he masked his head and face with strands of seaweed, and peeped out. "No one," he said after a long inspection.

She risked peeping out herself.

Only the sentinel finger of the abandoned Trewarvas mine chimney, right on the cliff's edge, broke the sheep-nibbled, gull-dappled skyline; a circumcised spire.

She felt violated. Some prurient stranger had thrust his curiosity into her own sweet, intimate world. It was like a rape.

Which of her neighbours might it be? With such large binoculars he must have recognized them. Her best hope was that he should turn out to be no neighbour at all, but some kind of rare autumn visitor, a seabird enthusiast perhaps, down here for an ornithological adventure. Otherwise, how long would it be before one friend-in-the-know became two, then four, then eight . . . and what when the ripples widened to include Morwenna?

The Dragon would especially have welcomed such news at that moment. Elizabeth's work during the disaster, and her later involvement with the relief fund, had made her quite a social catch – not to mention the fact that Morwenna's abandonment of the case seemed to confirm her as the heiress of Pallas, with all the advantages *that* position conferred. There was hardly an evening when Elizabeth was at home these days.

Nightly at her neighbours' dinner tables she scanned their faces for cold looks, listened for whispers, awaited the first of their snubs. None came. She told Oenone she expected the Dragon to begin spreading some especially vile stories about her – far worse than just saying she was a drunkard. The Beckerlegs and all their below-stairs spies listened hard but heard not a whisper. She waited, too, for an extortioner's note to drop through her letterbox; none arrived. In the end she almost began to doubt she had seen the man at all.

On top of everything came depressing news from Pallas Consols, where work had resumed as soon as the dead and the debris were cleared: Yet another exploratory drift had failed to locate the Great Wheal Vor lode. They had now dug and abandoned four such passages. The cost was climbing toward two thousand. It curdled her stomach even to think of it.

In the end, these pressures drove her – still against that last ounce of her best judgement – to seek out the company of David Troy. A few weeks after her conversation with Lilian, the two young women went into Penzance and took him out to dinner.

He twigged at once that Lilian had been brought along for an impartial opinion. He was attentive to her without being blatant about it. She, too, Elizabeth noticed, felt the magnetism of his personality.

"By the way," he said to Elizabeth when the introductions were over, "I went to Somerset House when I was in London. Our little chat about the descent of Pallas got me curious to see old Sir William's original will. You know that all wills are kept at Somerset House after probate."

She nodded. "And?"

He glanced at Lilian. "I hope the future wife of your attorney won't think I've done anything unethical."

Lilian gaped. "But I am not engaged, Mr. Troy."

He laughed. "You Helston people imagine there's some thick crystal wall between you and the rest of the country. But when lawyers meet, let me assure you, their gossip would put the Chapel Women's Committee to shame. We get to hear, or see, *everything* that goes on." He smiled at Elizabeth to recruit her laughter, which she gave without truly wishing to; then he did the same to Lilian.

"Tell us about the will," Elizabeth coaxed. "Ethics don't enter into it. After all, he was your great-something uncle, too."

"Well, that document did have one unusual feature. Most estates are left 'in tail-male' – in other words, to the male heirs. There was one, I believe, left 'in tail-female' by some old eccentric who fell out with his sons. And there were once quite a few estates left 'in tail-general' – to the males if any, otherwise to the eldest female. Descent 'in tail-general' rather went out of fashion in the seventeenth century, but it's there in Sir William's will."

"How strange. Does it have any practical consequences?"

He smiled, as if he could say a great deal, but he spoke only one word: "Remote."

"Oh, do tell us!" Lilian begged. "I adore these remote legal possibilities. They always come to pass."

"Not this one."

"Never mind that. What is it?"

"Well, if one could show the barring of the original entail to be fraudulent — not just invalid on some technicality, you understand, but with malice aforethought . . ."

"Oh stop this legal pettifogging! What would it mean?"

"It means I might now be the heir to the estate."

The women laughed delightedly. "Oh, let's try!" Elizabeth urged. "You can inherit every last debt and I can retire gracefully."

"There is a more sobering possibility," he went on. "It's equally remote, fortunately, but a bit of a spine-chiller nonetheless."

"What?"

"If the original barring of the entail was simply defective rather than fraudulent, then the estate could conceivably descend in tail-general to Morwenna."

Elizabeth felt the blood draining from her face — from her entire body, it seemed. David watched the effect closely. When he was sure of it, he chuckled and said it was only a lawyer's joke. In reality it was quite impossible. "If it could go to her, it could even go to the American Troys," he said, as if that were the ultimate absurdity.

Elizabeth was determined not to let him go. "You said all that just to test me," she accused.

He thought of denying it, she could see the hesitation behind his eyes. Then he nodded ruefully, allowing by his gesture that he had been foolish to try.

"Why?" she pressed.

"Because the last time we spoke about Pallas you implied that you were heartily sick of it and only wanted an honourable end to your servitude." He turned to Lilian. "Does she imply the same to you."

Lilian looked at Elizabeth. "You do," she said.

He nodded. "But I believe that, as with Morwenna before you, it's found its way into your blood. To deprive you of it now would be like tearing out your heart." He was utterly serious now. He turned to Lilian and said, "We must never let it happen."

"No!" she said fervently, wondering why he included her — and why she suddenly felt it was an important aim in her life.

"I'm going to pour you a glass of claret," Elizabeth told him briskly, to change the mood.

"It would be a waste," he said. "I shan't drink it." His dark eyes quartered the room, noticing everything, weighing it, judging it. He was determined to keep their mood solemn now, for some reason. "Also while I was in London," he went on, "I bought a copy of *In Darkest England*, by General Booth, the man who founded the Salvation Army." He turned to Elizabeth. "It asks the same question you asked me immediately after the disaster: 'What can I *do* about all this poverty, this denial of human dignity?' You disturbed me profoundly when you asked that question. In trying to answer it – to find an answer that was applicable to *you*, the owner of the mine – putting myself in your place, as it were – I began to see that until now I have been seduced by Utopian dreams. And Booth confirms it. He calls the socialist answers a 'promissory note cashable on the Bank of Hope' – no real answer at all."

"What is the answer then?" Elizabeth asked.

He shook his head. "I don't know. I keep hoping you'll find it. And meanwhile . . . meanwhile . . ."

"What?"

A hopeless look darkened his face. "It just goes on and on. May I tell you a story – something that happened this very morning?"

They both nodded their assent and hung on his words.

"It isn't pleasant, I warn you. But it may explain why I'm perhaps none too jolly company this evening. I defended a woman in the police court today. She was once a member of our chapel – not that those fine gentlemen would have anything to do with her now."

"What was she charged with?"

"I'll come to that. Her story is as bad as anything in Booth's book. Worse – because it didn't happen in some vast, teeming city rookery where the scum of the earth inevitably floats. This happened *here* – in dear little Penzance, where you can walk from one edge of the town to the other in fifteen minutes . . . where one caring parson and one conscientious curate could, between them, know every family."

"What was it? What happened?" they pressed.

"They plucked her, nine-tenths dead, from the sea off the Battery Point. They thumped and squeezed the water from her. They galloped her to the hospital. They gave her a few spoons of gruel. And then, before she was warm again, they marched her down to the police station – though she could barely walk – paraded her before the sergeant – though she could barely stand – and there they branded her a criminal."

"But how?"

"They charged her, among other things, with the offence of seeking to end her life, a life that had grown more intolerable than any man – and certainly no bunch of beefy, overfed bullies in blue – has any right to ask another human soul to endure."

"Attempted suicide?"

He nodded. "There were offences of soliciting and drunkenness to be 'taken into consideration'! *Consideration*, dear heaven!"

"What happened."

"Oh . . . this caring and Christian civilization, which had managed to ignore her every long year of her life, all at once summoned up enough *consideration* to dispose of her in nine minutes. She is now at hard labour somewhere. Bodmin or Exeter, I suppose." He stared at them, tears of anger, tears of pity, trembling on his eyelids. "Oh . . . my dears!" he said bitterly. "Life is foul. Life is foul."

Elizabeth reached a hand forward and touched his cheek. A tear began its erratic passage down her own. "Oh David!" When she had command of her voice again she asked, "What'll you do?"

"Speak out. What else am I trained for?"

"Here, in Penzance?"

He nodded. "This coming Sunday, down by the dock. I'm sending round handbills now. Will you come?"

"Of course I will."

"And you, Miss Rodda?"

"Nothing would keep me away, Mr. Troy."

On their way home that night Elizabeth said, "Well?"

"He certainly is an extraordinary man," Lilian agreed.

"Sincere?"

"Yes. Even noble. You feel . . . I don't know – you feel you're in the presence of someone quite out of the ordinary. In a way, you feel that everyday judgements aren't . . . well, just aren't big enough to fit him. And yet I feel I know exactly why you hesitate."

CHAPTER TWENTY-EIGHT

IT RAINED FAT NEEDLES all that Sunday morning; Elizabeth and Lilian felt sure the meeting would have to be called off. But as the churches began to empty, the first bands of light appeared on the southwestern horizon. By one o'clock half the sky was blue, though a vast gray vault still roofed Penzance. At two, when the meeting began, it was bright sunshine, everything washed and gleaming, a memory of summer. The walls and pavements were wreathed in steam.

The event was held on the broad quay at the inner end of the floating dock. Spare Trinity House buoys, intended for marking shoals and wrecks, lined one side of the open space; the two constables on duty were kept busy hauling lads and adventurous young men down from them. The landward side of the open space was hedged around with port buildings, including the Harbour Office and the Customs House, all closed and shuttered. The large habour beyond the floating dock was one mass of fishing boats, so tightly packed that a man could walk from the wharf to the end of Albert Pier over their decks; no Cornish fisherman would go to sea upon the sabbath. One of the skippers had lent his trawl-net cart for David to use as a platform.

As the clock on St. Mary's struck two, people were still pouring down Quay Street and coming around the corner from the new Esplanade. None of the Penzance clergy were there but the Reverend Thomas Tregeagle, a deacon of the church and a beacon of the Liberal Party, had come over from Hayle to conduct the meeting. He began with prayers. The late arrivals sidled in on tiptoe, trying to suggest that their continued movement was an illusion. There were at least four hundred people assembled by the time he finished. Elizabeth and Lilian, though offered a place among the committee members on the cart, had elected to stand at the top of the short flight of stairs by the Harbour Office, out of the public gaze.

Tregeagle began his speech by saying that David Troy needed no introduction. Ten minutes later, when he was still speaking, Elizabeth — and most of the others — began to feel he had been right first time. But he finished his eulogy at last and announced, with a twinkle in his eye, that the subject Mr. Troy had chosen was "The Work of a Missionary."

A murmur of disappointment ran through the crowd. "I already heard he do that one," Elizabeth heard one woman say morosely, "when he did preach up Ludgvan." The handbill had promised a local scandal of great importance.

As soon as David stepped forward, however, they fell to silence — not just the absence of coughing and whispering, but the sort of silence you can touch. Elizabeth's heart was pounding far more strongly than when she had braved the audience at the Central Hall. She looked about her, certain that Lilian must hear it; but she, like everyone else, was transfixed by the still, silent figure on the platform. He had them all in his hand before he'd uttered a word. Partly it was his reputation, of course, but there was something in his very presence, a golden aura of extra reality that seemed to envelop him and compel their silence.

"I see many old friends among you," he began. "The last time I spoke to you it was about the work of our brethren in Africa – the Dark Continent. I told you of Mr. Stanley's Zanzibaris, how they lost faith and merely went through the motions of their toil in plodding, brooding, sullen despair. I described the ivory raiders and their sinister human plunder in forest glades that stretch far beyond the running power of one pair of legs. I dwelt with you upon the lot of the poor Negress, who, the more Providence has endowed her with charms, the more miserable does her plight become. You were shocked. And why not – it was a shocking tale. You were moved to pity, which is that spark of tenderness God ignited in you at your birth. To pity, aye, and more. You dug deep into your purses and between us we endowed a missioner to travel far and wide among those wretched children of the Lord and alleviate their miseries."

He paused, challenging them to guess what was coming next. They knew his style well enough by now to suspect that all this talk of missionaries was a blind. He smiled grimly. "Today I shall shock you, too. If there be any among you, faint of heart, delicate in your susceptibilities, look to your smelling salts – or take to your heels – for, oh yes, I shall shock you! And I shall move you to pity, too. But if you have your purses about you . . . why, keep them shut! It's not your money God seeks today. He wants more of you than that." That smile again. "You shall see!"

So far he had spoken with his arms folded, standing above them with his heels well apart. Now he revived his hands, began to use them; between them he moulded his words and invoiced them to his hearers. "Today I come with news not of the Dark Continent but of one Dark Parish. Today you will hear nothing of black skins – but plenty of black souls and blacker despair. For today I tell you the life story of . . . well, I need not name her. You all know her name. To you" – he began pointing at random among the crowd – "she may have been Mary. To you, Tamsin. To you, Johannah. You, brother, may have called her Curnow. You . . . Trevenen. You, sister . . . Pascoe. But you all know her name for she has a thousand.

"She's a Cornish maid – or was. She was born not a mile from here: in Wherrytown, in Madron Road, beyond Chyandour, in a cellar in Alma Terrace – why, I believe you know better than I where she was born. You've walked past it scores of times. You passed it on your way here today. You passed it *on the other side."* He let that sink in before he continued. "Her father had work in those days, in the old Wherry mine, building the Great Western Railway embankment, paving Market Jew Street . . . he caught what he could, and lived by it – until he caught pneumonia and died of it. And then little Mary's life plunged from mere poverty to . . . to a condition we cannot name. For to name it would be to confront it. And to confront it would be to *do* something about it."

The heard the tremor in his voice; their silence, if that were possible, grew even more profound. "For a while the neighbours rallied around, as neighbours always do. Not *you and I*, of course. We were not her neighbours. We were far away *on the other side* of the town. But charity cannot last for ever. More deserving cases arose – or ones more recent in memory, anyway. Mary's mother, who never begged so much as a twist of sugar that she did not swiftly repay, was forced out to beg for her very survival and that of her little family. A kindly gentleman gave her a leaflet on the virtues of

Thrift! Thrift? The week's income of that fatherless household was eighteen pence. Oh, indeed they were a thriftless lot, that family!

"But all was not dark. This is not London or some other teeming city where such creatures are damned from the hour of their misfortune. This is Penzance! We look after our own – proper job. Here there are no *un*deserving poor. It was our turn to remember we were her neighbours, to rally round and find her some work. And my – didn't we just! The kindly owners of that alehouse down the road gave her work scrubbing out the bars at half-past-four each morning. I remember once I had occasion to pass the place at that hour and I saw little Mary Curnow (let us call her that). She would then have been about ten, a pretty child. She was leaping up and down on the pavements outside, peering through the windows at the summit of each leap, seeking glimpses of her mother. I remember as if it were yesterday saying to her, 'Be careful, little one! The frost is so thick upon the flagstones you might slip and hurt yourself.' And I gave her threepence. But I could not pass that way each day. Nor could you. And nor was my purse bottomless.

"By mid-morning . . . well, I hardly need go through each hour of her day. You know how it was – you met her about the town as often as I. So you can guess that by eleven each evening poor, exhausted Mrs. Curnow was" – he paused and smiled his foregiveness – "straining her eyes by the light of one small candle to sew the buttonholes into, what was it? – the fourth shirt of the evening? And only two more to go! Those shirts were left in for her by kindly folk like you and me, determined above all that she should not want for work, however ill it might pay." He smiled wanly. "Beautiful buttonholes they were! She made fine art of her sweated labour. Yet the best we could do was to turn sweated labour into a fine art!"

His shoulders slumped; his voice prepared them for bad tidings. "When Mary was fifteen you'd have thought her no more than twelve – care and deprivation had made of her a twelve-year-old girl with the sad, all-knowing eyes of an old woman . . . ah, I see you remember her now! When she was fifteen, as I say, her little brother and sister died. I forget the exact year – it was the one whose winter went so hard with the poor. Poor Mrs. Curnow, beside herself with grief, was tempted to the alehouse to drown her sorrow. Soon she was more often in the place than out of it. Let us pause a moment to condemn her roundly for her sin. Why not! We did so at the time. And oh, we have had so much practice since!"

A stir went among them. They did not resent his criticism of them, that was standard fare. But this was new – this note of attack upon religion. The Reverend Tregeagle and the personages of the committee exchanged glances and then tried to look as if they hadn't. David continued: "A charitable family whose name is well known to you all – indeed, some of you know it as well as your own – took in little Mary and paid her five shillings a week to sleep in the cupboard under the stairs and do the work of scullery

maid, gardener's boy, laundress, boot black . . . yes, five shillings a week.
It would have been sinful to pay her more. She would only have used it to
support her mother – that evil, addicted, drunken slut. In any case, Mary
was very soon an orphan.

"But didn't she look well on it! Wasn't she filling out into a bonny,
buxom little lass! If you didn't notice it, let me tell you – the son of the
house did. Oh he was a scamp – a real scallywag! She saved her honour, and
shielded his, when she gave in her notice. Naturally her mystified
employers wrote her a most indifferent character. The ingratitude of the
girl! After all they'd done for her!

"We profess to shudder when we read of the barbarities of the Dark
Ages, of the shameful rights of a feudal master over the bodies of his vassals.
But oh my friends I say to you, may God help the pretty and penniless
orphan girl in any town in this Christian land! Hunted from dawn to dusk,
from pillar to post, she is endlessly put to that monstrous choice: Starve or
Sin. For your own soul's sake, my dear friends, I hope you cannot name the
house, public or private, where poor Mary was finally driven to buy the
right to live – by sacrificing the very virtue that alone gives life its value.

"I hope you did not know the men who badgered her so, who pleaded
with her, threatened her, cajoled, bullied, whipped her until *she* . . .
sinned. Perhaps I am too hard upon those men. They were not all bad. At
least, once the deed was done, they had enough religion in them to
recognize the sinner for the vile, wanton harlot she was. Upon the instant
they cast her out – for fear such a degraded creature might pollute their own
fair ones. So let's give them their due – they remembered their religion at
the last.

"And when in weeks to come they saw her, a drab outcast on the
streets to which their banishment had led her, ruined, her word believed by
none, her life one long, ignominious slavery . . . as they watched her swept
downward, ever downward, into that bottomless perdition . . . they
remembered an art they knew from long ago, from her childhood: They
passed her by *on the other side!*"

A strange collective sigh, almost a groan, went up from the crowd.
David was shivering now with passion; if the Last Trump had sounded he
would have finished his tale – and they would have heard him out. "And
what of Mary?" he asked. "Poor child, poor child – no one was there to tell
her that even in the depths of her despair, ogled and leered at, scorned and
spat upon, even there she was far nearer than her persecutors to the pitying
heart of One who, in His time also, had been despised and rejected of men,
One who knows only too well what it is to endure scourge and spitting.

"So it will not surprise you to hear that, just ten days ago, the same
despair drove her weary frame, despoiled and ruined, to . . . *here!*" He
turned and stabbed a finger at the battery wall to his right. His eyes were so
fixed upon the spot he seemed to see the action unfolding as he described it.

And they saw it, too, through his eyes, his words. "She stood upon that wall with this whole uncaring town at her back, and she hurled herself into the sea."

One great sound went up from them, something between a sigh and a moan.

"Ah! I know – I know. To you and me it is a dreadful thing, an abomination before God. And in any case . . . the sea! So cold, so indifferent. Just think, my friends, how deep a soul must sink in the scale of human misery before such a death is welcomed as a joy and mercy."

All around her now Elizabeth saw people weeping openly, men and women alike. David was pitiless: "Yes, you wish it were happening now. I feel it in your tears. Oh, good people, I wish it, too. How we would dash forward to save her, eh? With what jubilation would we carry that lost sheep home and do as Our Lord would have done – feed her, clothe her. . . . We would not rest, would we, until we had heard that marvellous laughter in paradise, the laughter that greets the return of the one erring lamb into the fold from which we virtuous ninety-nine have never strayed. Oh, if only she were alive now – how we should cherish her!"

His accusing finger released its vigil upon the battery wall and returned to them. He smiled their deliverance. "Then take heart, my friends, for indeed she did not die. And, in a way, you could say it was *we* who rescued her, for at least it is we who pay the taxes that employ the men who did the brave and noble deed. They rescued her in our name. But that was not the end of it. They had more wonders to perform – also in our name. They fed her? Clothed her? Cherished her? May we now hear that laughter in heaven? I fear not, for that is not how we, in our earthly wisdom, have asked our law to deal with such wretched people. No – let me tell you what we did instead. Last week, in clothes still damp and reeking of the sea, we dragged her to the court. And there we, who had ignored her desperation for nineteen long years, bestirred ourselves and remembered our duty at last. In the space of nine minutes we sentenced her to three years at hard labour. At last, at last, poor little Mary knows how tenderly we care for her. Listen!"

The weeping stopped. Everyone stared at him expectantly. His eyes rose heavenwards; theirs followed. He put his head on one side, as if straining to catch some faint sound; they understood. He almost whispered his next words, as if fear had chilled him: "I hear something, but it is not laughter. There is no joy in Heaven at what we have done."

Eyes met eyes and were glumly averted.

Into their misery David threw a lifeline: "Yet nor, I think, is there condemnation. Not *utter* condemnation."

His smile began yet again to proffer hope; they held their breath to catch the very crumbs of it. "Of course not." He spoke as if they knew it very well already: "Condemnation is one kind of judgement. And Judgement, as you learned in your earliest catechism, is suspended until after we are dead. That is God's first mercy to us. We are yet alive: Judgement on us is suspended. There is time, there is yet time. How much? Only God knows that. You may die this very night,yet you still have these few hours left in which to make amends. You may still leave some legacy of good behind to help wash out this monstrous stain upon us all."

They were so uplifted now, Elizabeth thought one puff of wind would carry them off.

"How? Do you need to ask? Do I need to tell you? Well, I shall: You have missed one tide; see you catch the next. In your own private lives, no longer pass by on the other side. Do unto the least of His brethren what you would certainly do unto Him. These are private powers for good. You all possess them, rich or poor. No law may stop you from exercising them. But today many of you – most of you, I dare to guess – have public power, too. For too long the law denied you that power, but now it has yielded. Now you may use it, too. You may elect those who will remould society until its public face is *your* private face . . . until it cares for the downtrodden widow, the destitute family, the outcast orphan no less than *you* care . . . until, in the law no less than in your heart, we are all we one Body, every man and woman on Earth your brother and sister. Hark!"

He reached his ear heavenward again; this time they all watched him. A sadness filled his eyes. "Not yet," he reported. "But there *is* still time!"

CHAPTER TWENTY-NINE

THE HOLE IN THE WEATHER that Sunday afternoon was brief. The rains began again the following day, heavier than ever. The wind dropped and the rainclouds just sat over west Cornwall, emptying themselves in one ceaseless downpour.

During Wednesday night Deepwork flooded up to the 140 Level. Fortunately, the rebuilt man-engine had been linked through a set-off coupling to a massive bucket lift that "shammelled" or raised water to a series of bucket lifts, each off-set from the main rod of the man-engine. In normal times, therefore, the 36-inch flat-rod engine could power the man-engine *and* keep the mine in fork. Now, by recoupling the 54-inch to its old pumps, they were able at least to prevent the floods from rising further. But the latest exploratory drift at the 180 Level, in the still-unrewarded search for the Great Lode, had to be abandoned for the moment.

The two pumps added an extra forty-thousand gallons an hour to the Pallas stream, which, in turn, went to swell the larger Cober. It was the same with all the other small tributaries. By Thursday the rivulets that normally kept to their orderly stone kennels on each side of Coinagehall Street were flowing in sheets down the gutters and pavements. The swollen Cober overran its banks down in St. Johns so that the Loe Pool, which normally began a mile or so from Helston, now lapped at the very feet of the town. Even Elizabeth's new glasshouses, which she had thought safe enough on the hillside, were threatened.

When the rising waters endangered the ovens at the gasworks, it was time to enact the centuries-old ritual in which the mayor and corporation called upon the squire of Penrose, presented him with a leather purse containing the once-princely sum of three-halfpence, and craved his leave to cut a channel in Loe Bar. Nowadays it was such a formality that, before Squire Rogers heard the knock at his door, an entire rural army — men with shovels and farmers with horses and carts — was already making its way along the coast roads, from Porthleven in the west and Gunwalloe in the east, all converging on that mighty bank of sand and shingle.

Courtenay, who went out to report on the event for the *Vindicator*, sent word to Elizabeth that it was a sight she should not miss. She put up her oilskins and returned with the messenger in his pony and trap; Oenone, hearing that Courtenay was there, said she had seen it twice before and wasn't really interested. The converging crowds were so thick that the trap could go no farther than Wheal Unity, just above Tye Rocks at the eastern edge of Porthleven, more than a mile short of the Bar.

The rain had lightened to that maddening sort of Cornish drizzle which floats as much as it falls, dancing inward beneath the brim of a sou'wester hat, wetting everything not actually tucked inside the oilcloth. Rivulets of it ran down her face and neck, soaking her collar no matter how tightly she pulled the drawstring in her oilcloth jacket.

The sea was slick and almost waveless. Its huge, rain-mottled face heaved and shivered like some great, slow creature in its death throes. The coast road, which followed the shoreline but ran halfway up the sloping, grassy cliff, was a quagmire.

It was a strange procession — dozens of people, almost all of them in oilskins, trudging and splashing in unison with hardly a word among them. The swishing of the stiff cloth would have drowned most conversation, anyway. At the point where Wheal Unity gave way to Wheal Penrose — both mines being abandoned — the road climbed a few feet and found harder ground, bare sheets of rock in places.

The twists of the road obscure any view of the Bar until the walker is almost upon it. When Elizabeth reached the Penrose gatelodge, which stands immediately above the western end of the Bar, the panorama suddenly before her was impressive indeed. Immediately below her, at the high-water level, was the mouth of the Wheal Penrose adit, from which an angry torrent of water was roaring down over the steeply shelving rock, turning the sea pale. It was hard to believe such an outpouring had no effect on the Loe, whose level had risen several feet a day since Monday.

The vast sandbank stretched away until its farther end was obscured in the drizzle. The Loe is always above high-water, even in a summer drought. But today it was all of twenty feet higher, a difference that grew with every hour of the falling tide. The receding waters of the bay now exposed a shelving expanse of glistening sand and shingle. And it was there that the rural army were now working like demons to open a channel.

"It'll be an hour or two yet, Mrs. Troy."

She turned to find the bank agent, Mr. Vivyan, at her side. She had a brief mental image of the bank doors left open, the tables unattended, piles of cash and notes lying around.

"It's obviously going to be quite a sight," she replied. "I've never seen the Loe so high."

"I expect you were worried for your glasshouses?"

"Five more feet and I would have been."

"It's miserable weather, all right. Wouldn't you want to go indoors with the gentry?" he nodded toward the gatelodge.

She followed his gesture, looked at the upper windows, and turned swiftly away again. Among the people – the gentry – pressing their noses to the small panes she had seen Morwenna.

"It's a far better view from here," she said. "You haven't seen Courtenay Rodda, have you? He's supposed to be here somewhere."

"I expect he's down there where all the work's going on. Want to borrow my binoculars, do you?"

She froze. There was nothing strange about the binoculars themselves; indeed, she could count half a dozen others without turning her head. But there was something in his manner – a knowing little smile, a deliberate speed as he thrust them toward her.

"They look powerful," she said. Her throat was dry.

"One can see everything with them!"

Did he lay a particular stress on that *everything*?

She thanked him and put them to her eyes. "It's not something a rose grower would need too often," she said casually as she adjusted the focus.

"Life isn't all growing roses!" he laughed.

Her search revealed Courtenay, deep in discussion with Dan Merrick, the council's clerk-of-the-works and the commander of today's battle with the elements.

"It's not a very big channel," she said.

"You wait!" Vivyan told her. "It starts so small you wouldn't look at it twice," he said. "But before you know it, there's a torrent nothing can halt."

She handed him back the binoculars.

"Like a lot of other things in life, I suppose," he added.

Her heart sank. His comment could be a perfectly ordinary bit of parlour philosophy, or it could just as easily be a heavy hint. Nothing in his manner suggested this second possibility, but that could very well be part of a cat-and-mouse game, if that were what he was now playing.

"I think I'll go down on the Bar," she said.

"I'll . . . er, see you again then, Mrs. Troy."

Even the standard Cornish phrase for casual partings had an ambiguous ring to it now. Heavy-hearted, she descended to the shingled top of the Bar and set out to tramp the quarter-mile between herself and Courtenay. On the way she passed several farmers struggling with carts no more than a quarter full of sand. A mongrel spaniel bitch with a touch of red setter in her was having great games at the edge of the Loe, racing down the shingle, putting up the waterfowl near the fringe.

"Hello!" Courtenay came out of the drizzle toward her. "I could do with some of the brandy your David Troy was so eagerly spilling at Praa in the spring."

"I don't know why you say my David Troy."

He laughed.

Impatiently she told him, "I think I may know who our spy was – the man who saw us near Trewarvas that afternoon."

He became serious at once. "Who?"

"Vivyan, the bank agent."

He relaxed and chuckled. "Never. On my life, never."

"He has a pair of binoculars."

"Oh, why didn't you say so at once?" He looked up at the crowd around the gatelodge and added, in the same ironic tone, "He's well disguised today then."

"It wasn't just that. It was something in the way he asked me if I'd like to borrow them. And certain things he said after."

"Such as?"

In her mind she rehearsed telling him what Vivyan had said about things in life starting small and growing into a torrent no one could stop . . . and that final 'see you again!' It sounded so thin she hadn't the courage to actually come out with it. "Not what he said, just the way he said it."

Courtenay still thought she was being ridiculous. "It could just as easily have been David Troy."

She started. 'Why d'you say that?'

He nodded toward the crowd. "He's up there, too. Didn't you see him?"

"No – are you sure?"

"Anyway, he's also got a pair of binoculars. *And*, just like old Vivyan, he's not exactly noted for tramping our remote clifftop paths, either. Doesn't that make him another prime suspect?"

She sighed. "I suppose I am letting my imagination run away with me."

Courtenay led her to the edge of the channel the men were digging. "Will you be finished before dark?" she asked Dan Merrick.

He looked at the sky and nodded confidently. "I reckon so. Well before."

"Whose setter is that?" she asked.

"Mine I'm afraid, Mrs. Troy," he replied. "I'll catch her and tie her up when I've a minute to spare."

"I brought some lunch," Courtenay told her as they withdrew. "A loaf of bread, a glass of wine . . . and thou?"

She chuckled. "No singing in the wilderness?"

"In *this* epidemic of binoculars?"

As they walked back across the Bar he went on, "Talking of the great and good David Troy, that was quite a performance last Sunday."

His flippancy angered her. "It was not 'a performance.' "

He ignored her tone. "It still needs a bit of polishing, mind. The climax is ambiguously divided between the two messages – religious and political."

"It was *not* a performance!"

"I suppose the same is true of Our Dave himself, though."

"I'm not prepared to discuss it like this, Courtenay. Mr. Troy . . ."

"You don't mean 'prepared,' you mean 'ready.' You're not *ready* to discuss him yet. You're still mesmerized by the man. But one day you . . ."

"Mesmerized?" she shouted scornfully.

"Do you believe in poor little 'Mary Curnow'? D'you think she actually exists?"

"Not under that name. Anyway, he made it clear he was talking about a whole class of people like her."

" 'Clear' is not the word I'd choose."

"Oh come now – no one could have imagined it was the literal biography of just one . . . anyway, what does it matter? Such things happen every day."

"Do they? You know that, do you?"

"As a matter of fact, I do. It just so happens that Lilian and I were in Penzance last week and we dined with Mr. Troy, and . . ."

"Yes, she's told me of these assignations."

"Don't be absurd. He'd just come from the police court, where he'd defended that poor girl – or one very like her. So there!"

"And what was the sentence?"

"Gaol, just as he said . . ."

"How long?"

"I don't know. He didn't say."

"Ah!"

His tone was so smug she had to ask him what *he* knew about it anyway.

His recitation was matter of fact. "I know the woman's name: Henrietta Winsor. I know her age: thirty-four. I know she has twenty-three previous convictions, two of them for keeping a disorderly house, four for threatening behaviour, the rest for soliciting and drunkenness. And I also know that her sentence last Friday was one month – just long enough, I would think, to disintoxicate her and dry out her clothes. Oh, and the sentence was for being drunk and disorderly – yet again."

"And attempted suicide. She did throw herself off Battery Point."

"The attempted-suicide charge was dropped."

Elizabeth laughed uncomfortably. "It can't be the same woman, Courtenay."

"That's what I kept thinking, all last Sunday afternoon, while I listened to his impassioned oratory."

"I didn't see you there."

"I'm well aware of that."

"Anyway, how d'you know all this?"

"It's amazing the things one picks up working on a newspaper, Beth. We have a very effective young stringer in Penzance. My last little chore on Saturday evening was to sub his police-court report."

"Oh, you're sharp enough to cut yourself, I'm sure. Anyway, all this just bears out what I said in the beginning. It wasn't a single girl's biography, it was a portrait of . . . well, of Penzance itself as much as anything."

He gave her a sad little smile and said, "Now *that's* what I mean by 'mesmerized.' Anyone would be willing to grant an orator a bit of licence, but most people would feel just a *leeetle* bit let down at the yawning gulf between the fallen angel who so wrung our hearts and withers and the boozy slattern on whom she was modelled. Unless they were mesmerized, as I say."

His tone was a sight too lofty. "You're jealous!" she laughed.

He forced a laugh, too, but the lobes of his ears went scarlet – something she had never seen before. "Mesmerized!" he assured the sea and sky, with a tendentious, dying fall upon the word.

"Jealous!" she crowed.

"I'll tell you something else that's come my way. Did you wonder why none of the local clergy were there? Troy's not on bad terms with any of them, so why d'you think old Tregeagle came over from Hayle to chair the meeting, eh?"

"You're going to tell me, whatever I may think."

"No — go on, go on. You say!"

"Don't be such a child, Courtenay."

"You must at least know that Tregeagle's a big cog in the local Liberal machinery? Well, David Troy is being groomed as Liberal parliamentary candidate for the St. Ives Division. In his forthcoming orations — see if I'm not right — the religious exhortations will slip down into second place. After that, they'll disappear altogether. He won't be selling Heavenly Mansions then — no, it'll be Paradise-on-Earth. It was all there in Sunday's trial outing."

"It must be awful to have such little faith in anything, Courtenay."

"Like everyone else, I blame the newspapers. But what makes you suppose your state of delusion is any better in the end?"

"Up in London, when you told me your opinion of David Troy, about his being poised between religion and politics, and going to Westminster and so on — did you already know all this, the Liberals grooming him, etcetera?"

"Whispers, yes."

She gave a sort, disappointed laugh. "And I thought that, for once, you were being really perceptive! You were just retailing whispers."

"When you say I'm jealous, you're right. I'm jealous of someone who can pour forth lies as huge as Olympus and yet retain your respect, while I, who merely whisper half-truths that turn out to be wholly true, I forfeit it."

She stopped in her tracks, compelling him to stop, too, and face her. Then she gave him a jocular push, which he rode easily. "You're far too robust to play the injured junior, my dear," she said.

Her face softened. He began walking again; they were almost at the foot of the slope up to the gatelodge by now. He said, "For all our quarrels, Beth, and despite the fact that we'll probably murder each other one of these days, I'm actually very fond of you. I don't want to see you hurt."

Casually she took his arm. Anyone watching — with or without binoculars — would think it was for assistance with the gradient. "I know, Courtenay. Pay no heed. I am grateful."

They arrived among the crowd of onlookers at the crest of the little slope.

"Well, well! And who's minding the shop?" It was the unmistakable voice of David Troy.

They both looked up and saw him standing before them, arms wide, and the warmest smile of welcome on his face. Elizabeth's immediate thought was that she had never seen a man less troubled by the cares of the downtrodden poor.

CHAPTER THIRTY

FROM THE GATELODGE a pretty little scenic drive winds a mile or two through the Penrose Estate, along the side of the hill that forms the western rim of the lake. The three picknickers followed it and, after a few hundred yards, came to a rhododendron grove, sloping down from the road. "We'll not find better shelter than that," David said.

"Nor a better view," Elizabeth added when they reached the heart of the grove, which they found to be horseshoe-shaped, opening out over the swollen Loe. They could watch the progress of the cut in perfect seclusion and comfort.

The drizzle had eased; they could at last shed their oilskins and begin to dry out again. They spread them on the soft, damp rhododendron litter and used them for groundsheets. Courtenay opened his hamper.

"You brought enough," David commented.

"I thought the photographer was staying on but he had a wedding."

"Oh, whose?" Elizabeth asked.

"No one important – except to Mr. Troy."

"Why to me?"

"You owe them your lunch, of course."

There was roast capon and sliced ham, potted shrimps and Melton Mowbray pie; for vegetables there were cold bubble-and-squeak and a leek-and-mangold pie; and for pudding, the most scrumptious-looking chocolate cake Elizabeth had seen in years. But there was nothing to drink except two bottles of wine – a hock and a burgundy.

"Looks like a trip down to the pool for you, boy," Courtenay told David as he poured some hock for Elizabeth.

David smiled and held forth his glass.

Courtenay parodied surprise. "Are you sure?"

Elizabeth was horrified. "No," she told him, "you stick to your principles."

Troy laughed. "It's a matter of indifference to me."

"That's not what you told the Band of Hope last year," Courtenay reminded him.

"A preacher tries to match the sin to the sinner. Preach on avarice to bankers, on pride to civic dignitaries, on envy to schoolgirls, lust to schoolboys . . ."

"And to newspaper owners?"

"Oh, preach on every sin in the calendar," he said without a moment's hesitation. "Not that it would do any good!" He clinked his glass against the neck of the bottle, as a calf might nudge its mother's teat.

Elizabeth felt oddly betrayed as she watched the wine come bubbling out. Perhaps he sensed her disapproval for he turned to her and said, "I'm sure this pleases you greatly."

"But why?"

"Didn't you once tell me your vocation was to modify my . . ."

"Oh that!" she interrupted, annoyed that he should bring it up now. "That was just a joke."

"I missed it," Courtenay said.

David looked at him uncertainly. She realized she had never before seen him in the society of another man. He was quite a different David. If *she* had said something about his having to drink wine, he'd have gone down to the lake for water – just to show her. But because the challenge had come from Courtenay, he had accepted it – just to show him! She watched them in fascination.

"If she makes as good a job of reforming me," David went on, "as she has of the *Vindicator*, I'll have little to grumble at."

She interrupted. "You are misinformed if you think *I* reformed the *Vindicator*, Mr. Troy. In any case, I'm surprised you admire our paper. I wouldn't think it nearly Liberal enough for you."

He turned to her, smiling as if she had said something most clever. "Shall we talk about that?"

He was so unlike the David she knew that she was at a loss to explain the change. If he were another woman, she might almost imagine they were competing for Courtenay's affection; but that could hardly be it. Yet the change must have something to do with Courtenay's presence. In the end she decided it was because Courtenay was so flippant and would-be wordly. David would never show his true self to him but would rather hide behind this mask of amused tolerance, drinking wine and pretending he could be as cynical as the rest.

Courtenay took his chance. "We'll talk about it if you wish, Troy. The word is going around that you'll be the next Liberal candidate for St. Ives."

David gave a noncommittal shrug. "It would be a natural step from the county council."

Elizabeth divided out the pie. "But is it true?"

David took the smallest slice. "Salisbury's still riding high. I doubt if there'll be an election this year or next – though Gladstone would win it easily. The party would be ill-advised to pick a new candidate – especially an untried candidate – so early."

It sounded like the speech that had won him the selection.

Courtenay chewed thoughtfully, staring across the water. "Gladstone . . ." he mused. "No one knows better than that man how the vine of religion can yield the grape of office. An industrious toiler in that vineyard could prepare a great deal of fertile ground in one or two years."

This almost open sneer took Elizabeth's breath away. She prepared to rush in as peacemaker. But David was as mild as milk. "That might have been true once," he replied.

Even Courtenay was startled. "Go on – it still is," was all he could say.

"Not if he has the Press against him."

"But practically every paper west of Plymouth is pro-Liberal."

David laughed. "This is excellent pie, you know. Will our host carve the chicken or shall I?"

"You do it," Courtenay replied. "It'll be good experience for you – carving things up." He took a bite of the vegetable pie and asked, "Which paper d'you think would be against you?"

"All of them, curiously enough. They're not so much Liberal as old-fashioned Whig. They're in favour of Liberal principles as long as the old ascendancy is firmly at the helm. They shudder at us, the new, nonconformist, lower-middle-class upstarts who are claiming the party as their birthright. We shock the old guard on both sides with our demands for Irish Home Rule, abolition of double voting, extension of the franchise, local discretion in the regulation of alcohol . . . good heavens! – we're worse than socialists!"

"What you new upstarts need," Courtenay said, as if the notion had just occurred to him, "is new, upstart papers of your own."

"Oh, one would be enough, you know." David grinned. "We need a paper that is Liberal out of a passionate conviction – not because that's where all the family money is and always has been."

"There would be risks in it," Courtenay went on. "Practical risks."

"And moral ones," Elizabeth interrupted.

David turned to her with interest. "In particular?"

"For example," she said, looking him directly in the eye, "what would such a paper do if it discovered that the preferred candidate was not quite all he seemed?"

He held her gaze. "That's why it's so important not to rush into these matters, Mrs. Troy. The examination must be thorough; the choice, deliberate and careful." He turned to Courtenay again. "What practical difficulties do you foresee?"

"The most obvious one is the matter of offending certain existing advertisers and readers."

David nodded understandingly. "That would have to be balanced – *more than* balanced – by attracting new ones. Of course, if the change came about so slowly as to be almost imperceptible, the losses you speak of need not occur. Or they would be masked by the general growth and attrition of any such enterprise."

"Hmmm." Courtenay drained his glass and turned to refill it. Smiling he poked the bottle toward David – who shook his head and then sipped his first little mouthful of the wine. His grimace softened from suspicion to mild satisfaction.

"The heavens do not open," Courtenay pointed out. "Clouds do not roll. No lightning flashes, no thunderbolts descend."

"A couple of years, then," David said, apropos nothing. Turning to Elizabeth, he asked, "How are they getting on with cutting the Bar?" He unhooked his binoculars and offered them to her. She held up her greasy fingers and shook her head. He put them to his own eyes. "Pretty soon now," he told them.

"What news of Mary Curnow?" Elizabeth asked.

He heard her; she knew it by the sudden rigidity of his arms, which were still holding the binoculars to his eyes. "That dog of Merrick's never gives up," he said. "It's having the time of its life with those ducks." Then he looked at Elizabeth, quickly, as if her question had only just registered. "Mary Curnow? Now her story could win a great many new readers. And it could be used as a method of advancing Liberal ideas in a practical, living-and-breathing sort of way." He turned to Courtenay. "When I saw you at the meeting, you know, I half thought that's what you had in mind."

Elizabeth answered him. "He traced her as far as Henrietta Winsor and gave up in disgust."

David shook his head sadly. "I can well understand that. It's many years since poor Henny qualified as one of the Mary Curnows of the world. Yet in a way her story is far more heartrending. She was a mere seventeen when she went out to Long Rock and flung herself beneath a train – and she survived it. *That's* when they gave her three years at hard labour – during which time, of course, she learned all the other criminal arts that have since made her life tolerable. Crime is now the only level at which we allow her to live."

Elizabeth now felt completely adrift.

David continued: "That's where a newspaper would be such a valuable ally. I'm rather glad you raised this matter, Mrs. Troy. In a public oration like the one you heard me give, one has to simplify the truth. One must chip it away, like a sculptor with his block of marble, until a grander Truth is revealed. The maturity of a large crowd is no greater than that of a twelve-year-old, you know. But the readers of a newspaper can be treated as maturely as I treat you or you treat me. You" – he turned to Courtenay – "could tell the full story of the life of Mary Curnow (as we would have to go on calling the unfortunate Henrietta). You could make them see the full iniquity of it in a way that simple oratory never could."

Courtenay chuckled and patted him on the knee. "By heaven, you'll do," he said.

Elizabeth began to repack the hamper. On their way back to the lodge, Courtenay, out of David's hearing, murmured to her, "Well? Solid silver – or electroplate?"

"You were trying to show him up," she protested.

"I wondered if you'd notice."

A murmur went up from the crowd. The first small trickle of water had begun. The three of them hastened forward, but then David stopped to buttonhole an acquaintance.

"There's still a lot of truth in what he says," Elizabeth pointed out, as she and Courtenay pressed on. "And his political programme is absolutely . . ."

"I agree with every point in his programme – except for the first three."

"What were they – I've forgotten?"

"They were: David Troy, David Troy, and David Troy."

She walked away from him angrily.

Among the crowd she espied Uncle Hamill.

"Didn't I see you with David Troy?" he asked as she drew near.

"And Courtenay Rodda. I'm as out-of-concert with those two men as I've ever been with anyone."

"Save it for later," he told her. "Just watch this. You can keep your Niagara and your Victoria Falls. You'll never see anything like this again in all your life."

Nothing seemed to be happening. At the end of the gash in the Bar a sluggish trickle of water pushed a muddy finger out to sea. For a while, the only sign of its growing strength was the increasing violence of that meeting of the waters. The churned-up ocean gleamed ochre and green. Soon a long freshwater fist rammed its way out into the bay. Then, to cries of "Look! Look!" the Bar itself began to crumble visibly. Long cracks developed in the sand. The walls heaved over or subsided into the rushing torrent, which instantly picked up the burden – a thousand tons at a time – and hurtled it down to the sea. The tide was flowing again but the difference of level was still over thirty feet.

By now the bay could no longer accept the inflow. The sea itself began to erupt in white, churning anger. As far as the eye could follow in the gathering dusk, the turbid freshwater river pushed out into the bay. Two great whirlpools had formed, one each side of it. Soon it seemed that the entire bay was being stirred in one vast cauldron. The force of the whirlpools began to nibble at the foot of the Bar, which was now crumbling along more than half its length. The sound of it was like the settling of a million starlings, far, far away.

Before long, the escaping water had dug its way down to the bedrock, whose uneven surface was causing great pale spines of turbulence of become fixed in the rushing surface, like the tail of some prehistoric monster. When more sand fell into it from the edges of the channel, it seemed that the monstrous tail threshed from side to side, as if it were sweeping the Bar away.

Elizabeth glanced at the Loe. "But the level hasn't fallen an inch!" she told Hamill.

"Of course not. It's hardly started yet!"

On and on it went, scouring wider where the rock prevented its scouring any deeper. The whirlpools quickened. Now the entire Bar was being nibbled into the sea. Its destruction would be a race between the widening channel at the middle and the crumbling away along its edge. The birdlike noise of the water had deepened to a roar.

"Oh no!" someone called out. "Stop her! Come back, sir!"

Dan Merrick's setter had triumphed at last. Instead of dashing into the water and frightening the wildfowl, she had wormed her way to the margin, hiding herself in ruts left by men and horses. And in this way she had at last been rewarded by the capture of a duck too young, too old, or too ill to escape. In her ecstasy she set off on a short lap of honour in the water; unfortunately she was right by the winding inner maw of what was now the shortest, fastest, most destructive river in the world.

Merrick himself ran back onto the Bar. He whistled and shouted and waved his arms but the dog gave no sign of hearing him. Then it appeared that the creature might, miraculously, escape the pluck of the water and complete the circuit back to land. The onlookers dared to hope. Every eye was rivetted on that bobbing little head, a reddish-black hole in the reflection of the evening sky.

It became apparent that the dog, though swimming vigorously, was making little headway.

Then she made none at all.

Merrick shouted and whistled like a demon; he ran forward still farther, jumping up and down and waving his arms. Perhaps she heard him then, or perhaps that was when she became aware that for all her exertions she was actually moving backwards with respect to the shore. Her swimming became frantic, but within moments she was sucked over that smooth and sinister dip in the surface. The duck was still between her jaws.

A dread silence fell upon the crowd.

"No," Elizabeth whispered. "Please God, no!"

Two men ran down to prevent Merrick from attempting anything more foolish than he had already ventured. But they all knew it was over. They just stood and watched the inevitable happen.

One could imagine that some mighty underwater claw had the poor little wretch in its grip. It plucked her down into the race faster than the water itself seemed to flow. Then it dashed her into the first white cauldron of boiling fury. The creature must have released the duck, for one piteous yelp carried clearly to the watchers from out of that raging torrent.

Elizabeth could not take her eyes away. Awful as it might be, there yet was something grand in such a death. The gargantuan forces pitted against that tiny spark of life, the defiance in that single yelp, which had conveyed neither terror nor surprise but had rather been a simple assertion: *Still here! Still here!* . . . there was something barbaric, ancient, almost noble in the contest.

Once more, for the merest instant, she saw its head again, in the muddied gray fury where the long arm of outgoing water punched down the face of the sea. It was impossible to imagine that even a fish might survive that five-second voyage. As if to underline the point, an uprooted tree that had been floating just beyond the dog, now followed her down the channel. It broke in two with a tremendous crack as it passed through the first turbulence. Minutes later the fragments of it were still surfacing, far out to sea.

In the silence Elizabeth became aware that the roaring of the water had deepened beneath the range of human hearing; its note was now to be heard through the soles of the feet, or in the pit of the lungs. Long after that they sought the little dark-red speck in the broad, pale, muddy street of fresh water that now flowed far out into the bay – to the horizon for all they could tell; but the gathering dusk turned every bit of flotsam into a canine head. Dan Merrick was back among them, smiling wanly, trying not to weep, only just succeeding.

If the creature's life had been a sacrifice to some local Triton, that water god now showed his appeasement. The channel was so wide that the outflow grew calm and streamlined. The edges began to be eaten away as smoothly and as gracefully as in those first few moments – but swiftly. A man down there would now need to run to keep up with the appetite of the river. Within two minutes, clear, slick water was pouring out over the entire length of the Bar. Only the remnants of its former turbulence persisted along the line where the sand was scoured down to the rock.

And now, too, for the first time, one could see that the level was falling. It was only a foot or two as yet, and by far the greater bulk of water still lay penned behind the submarine remnant of the Bar, but it was going down.

For fifteen minutes more they watched it pour out, saw it change from millrace to stately river to sluggish stream . . . until at last its behaviour was no different from the hithering-thithering flow of any other tidal estuary. Banks of reeds, drowned two weeks ago, now stood forlorn, marooned on mudflats that were many feet above low-water. By then the crowds had thinned to a handful. Courtenay and David had both gone. So, too, had Morwenna.

Hamill and Elizabeth stayed until, in the last glimmer of the day, they saw the flow reverse and the Loe felt the unaccustomed pressure of an incoming tide.

The sodden banks, newly exposed, made strange lipsmacking noises as they continued to drain. Sounds of joy, she wondered? Did the earth rejoice that the eternal pressure had at last been relieved?

"It'll be sealed off again within a week," Hamill said briskly. "And come the next gales, it'll be rebuilt as high as ever."

They started for home. "Oh, I meant to tell you about David Troy," he added.

"Yes?"

"He's had quite a few meetings with Morwenna lately. They're up to something, I know. I wouldn't mention it, except that I hear you've been seen with him a time or two yourself."

"He's under no illusions about Morwenna," Elizabeth assured him.

"Nor you about him, I hope?"

"He's nothing to me."

"Good. I know what a terrier you are once you've set your hand to the plough."

Hamill was wrong when he said the Bar would take weeks to rebuild. The gales came the very next night. The huge waves and violent currents, which over the years had claimed so many lives along that deceptively soft and sandy shore, lifted and redeposited every particle, every half-polished pebble — as if the salt water wished to show the fresh what *real* power is.

By Sunday, only those who had witnessed it could believe it had ever been cut.

CHAPTER THIRTY-ONE

THAT AUTUMN CAPTAIN BODY reluctantly advised the abandoning of the latest exploratory drift, which alone had cost nearly a thousand pounds, for it had gone to the boundary of the Pallas Consols sett without sight or smell of the Great Lode. What it had revealed instead was a heave in the strata.

"What he do mean, see," the captain explained, "is that the lode we'm seeking here, at one-eighty on the edge of the sett, is really at one-eight-five here in the middle."

"If you know that, why don't you dig there?" she asked.

"Well, that's only an example, like. I aren't saying he *is* there."

"What you *are* saying is that it could be anywhere."

"I reckon so."

"So what do we do – dig wildly in all directions? And, come to think of it, how would that be any different from what we've been doing all along?"

He looked uncomfortably at this model of the mines. "I calculate if we was to sink a winze here" – he indicated a spot near the bottom of the Wheal Tor whimshaft – "we might catch 'un."

"How deep?"

He shrugged. "We should have a good idea by one-ninety, missis."

"Which means another ten fathoms to fork out – and maintain in fork – throughout the entire mine."

He chuckled. "Well now – if we was to open up the Wheal Fortune adit, he'd be five fathoms *less* than what we're forking now."

"I walked straight into that, didn't I! Oh, very well! I suppose you'd better open it up. What is it – half a mile? Four-fifty fathoms of drift? Five to six hundred pounds? A whole year's profits! We'd have to keep the mine in fork continuously for nearly three years before that will pay."

The captain waited in silence.

"Very well," she said hopelessly. "Every day's a gamble, I suppose."

"Lowering the adit's never a gamble, missis."

"Oh yes it is – we're gambling that the drifts and levels in Carnmeal, Wheal Metal, and Wheal Fortune don't collapse once we start forking out Pallas Consols through them. Lord – how do I manage to sleep o' nights!"

On the brighter side, the changes she and Pascoe had made about the estate began to prove their worth during that season. The "Archipelago" was a most inconvenient farm, of course; had it not been so scattered, they would have employed only six labourers instead of seven. The extra man, Joel Bose, was needed to go around with a donkey and cart, carrying materials and machinery from field to field and bringing the produce to a central point for washing and packing. That point was the old mill house in St. Johns at the foot of Helston, where she kept half a dozen girls in more-or-less full-time work. When Joel Bose was carrying vegetables, one or two of them would go out and meet him by the water meadow below the glasshouses and there they would wash the produce in the little meandering Cober, now safely confined between its banks once more.

All that winter they sent violets up to Covent Garden. They were a perfect crop for planting up any little corner of a field or under-used back garden. The men would pick them twice a week; they hated it – the stems were too fine and delicate for their clumsy great fingers, and the work had to go on whatever the weather. The task became even more odious when the new stinging-nettle seedlings began to germinate; no plant has a sting so hot as a baby nettle on a raw, wet February day.

Each evening the girls would bunch the cut flowers and leave them to stand in water overnight. They adored the work, of course. They were indoors, safe from the weather. They carried a beautiful scent back home with them. And the task itself was so mindless, they could all chatter away to their hearts' content. The only drawback was that two of them had to come back at half-past four next morning to take the bunches out of water, pack them into cardboard boxes, and carry them up to the station on a handcart in time to catch the six o'clock train.

The income from violets was fair in its own right, but the system was really just a practice run for what they hoped would be their big floral money-maker of the year, the spring bulbs – jonquils, paperwhites, narcissi, and daffodils – the first of which began to bloom in early March. Before then Elizabeth had been sending hothouse lettuce up to London, not because it was an especially profitable crop but because it was easy to germinate, quick-growing, and needed no special skill or equipment. By March, the last of the lettuce had gone and all three houses were planted out with tomato seedlings, which she and Oenone had raised, fussing like a pair of broody hens at Wheal Lavender. Oenone's brother Henry had been especially scornful.

A week after setting out, the leaves were all mottled yellow and the plants looked set to die. Disaster threatened, for no reserve crop had been planned. Mr. Vivyan, who was a scientific gardener, told them to water the plants with manganese sulphate, but Elizabeth got muddled and bought magnesium sulphate instead – three pounds of it, which raised the pharmacist's eyebrows more than somewhat, since a single teaspoonful is usually enough to cure the worst constipation. Fortunately, the chemical (otherwise known as Epsom salts) did not have the effect on tomato plants that it has on the human frame – indeed, it had no observable effect at all. Meanwhile, Elizabeth had noticed how the wild volunteer tomatoes seemed to thrive down at the sewage farm, so she got the men to mulch the tomato beds with treated sewage solids, and the mottled leaves coloured up again in no time.

February was dry enough to let them break some of the larger fields ready to set the early-crop potatoes. The girls were given the job of cutting the seed, leaving just one eye to sprout on each bit of tuber. The juice combined in some strange fashion with the remnants of soil on the potatoes to turn the skin of their hands black. They tried every kind of bleach and soap, until Elizabeth brought in a tub of her favourite goose grease, and that was the answer to it.

Pascoe had three railway trucks full of sand brought over from Hayle Towans; it was actually not sand at all but, like Loe Bar, ground-up seashell and therefore almost pure lime. But the Hayle sand was much finer than that of Loe Bar, which, if spread over the land, would need generations of farming before it yielded its calcium. He also reached an agreement with the sewage farm to take all their solid waste after treatment; he'd noticed what a century of carrying the night-soil of Penzance out to Gulval had done for the fertility of their fields. What they had achieved bucket by bucket, Pallas would now win by the cartload.

Elizabeth continued to meet David Troy from time to time. In his strange fashion, it could still be said that he was courting her; but his political work gave him as little time as the farm allowed her. Much to her surprise, he did not at all approve of what she was doing.

"You should give out the orders at seven each morning," he advised. "Walk round at noon, and again last thing at night. I hate to see you working away like a labourer."

"Then it's as well you visit me so rarely," she replied. "I've explained to you why it must be me and not Pascoe who manages the farm."

She asked him whether he saw much of Morwenna.

He chuckled and said, "Enough."

"What d'you find to talk about?"

"You, mostly. Don't worry – she's becoming a rather pathetic figure."

By the beginning of March they had a fair idea of how much profit a few square roods of violets could bring in, and they could make a conservative guess at the income from bulbs.

"How do we communicate this good news to our tenantry?" Elizabeth asked Pascoe.

"Put up the rents," he said laconically. "Then wait for the sky to fall in."

She asked David if he thought that was the right way.

"What other ways might there be?" he asked cautiously.

She showed him her own preferred draft of the letter announcing the rent increases. It explained in great detail to each tenant how he could modify his farming practice in such a way as to meet the new rent and still have extra in the bank (or, more likely, under the mattress) at the end of the year.

He handed it back to her with a single word: "Terrible."

She began to wish she had not involved him. "I'm not asking for a political argument . . ."

He grinned and shook his head. "And I'm not giving you one. I'm talking tactics. This letter is dreadful tactics. Look – you're trying to change these people's whole way of thinking. It's not like saying plough with my new steel-tip ploughshare instead of that silly thing your grandfather got from the blacksmith. (Mind you, even that much change would be hard enough for some of them to contemplate!) But you're trying to change their most fundamental attitudes and practices. Take the advice of a seasoned preacher – you can't do that sort of thing with mere reason." He smiled disarmingly. "At least, I hope you can't, or I've been wasting my time all these years."

"I'm not really appealing to reason," she pointed out. "On the one hand I'm hitting at their purses; and on the other I'm saying they could be richer next year. That's what Pascoe calls the stick and the carrot."

"It's still just reason. Stick reason . . . carrot reason."

"What then?"

He winked. "Hellfire! Give 'em hellfire. Scare them witless. And only *then* hold out salvation."

"Yes but in practical terms . . ."

"In practical terms just send out the letter. Dear Farmer Jones, This is to notify you that your rent will go up five shillings an acre from next Quarter Day. If you can't pay it, prepare to move on. Sealed with a Loving Kiss, Mrs. Troy."

"But there'll be a riot!"

"I doubt it. Anyway, that's where you have to take command. Keep the initiative. Hold out salvation. Mind you, you must never make it sound easy. They must see it as a challenge that lies *just* within their grasp."

So they sent out a letter. And the sky did fall in.

Angry farmers and smallholders were at the gates of Wheal Lavender within hours of the first postal delivery. Soon they clogged the lane. Elizabeth had deliberately spent the morning out with the Fourborough, which she had joined the previous autumn. By the time she rode around the corner, in sight of home, her angry tenants had had the chance to do a great deal of talking among themselves. That was another piece of David's advice – get them feeling and thinking as a group. A group is always more stupid and more malleable than a gathering of individuals.

But her heart was in her mouth at the sight of them all. It was one thing to work out the tactics in the comfort of David's office, and then to rehearse them at Pascoe's fireside with a rum toddy in her hand; it was quite another to see the crowds all standing there in the lane, red-faced and in their best Sunday black, on a raw March morning. However, they fell back respectfully and looked to their "committee' – John Trenoweth, Harry Tiddy, Willy Kemp, and Jimmy Blythe – the ones who had made the loudest noise and the most aggressive suggestions while they had all been cooling their heels.

She pretended to be greatly surprised at their anger. She pointed out that they could hardly stand out there and discuss it in the lane; so instead she proposed a gathering in two days' time, at eight in the evening, in the covered market in Helston, when she would have one or two suggestions to lay before them. She invited them to bring their wives as the Pallas Estate would be providing a supper afterwards. She hoped it would be an amicable occasion – "But if any of you have a notion you'll be able to talk me into abating these new rents, you may forget it now. Those days are gone for ever."

She left them angry, bewildered, fearful . . . and also a little curious; which was exactly what David's strategy called for.

That evening he came out to see her, to ask if it had worked.

"So far as I can tell. The worst bit is yet to come. I don't suppose you'd escort me to the meeting, David?"

He looked at her in alarm. "I hardly think I could."

"Not to speak, just to lend your moral support."

"For a rise in the rents? I'm a prospective Liberal candidate, my dear!"

"Also," she said carefully, "it would be nailing your colours to the mast. You'd be letting Morwenna know where your loyalties lie."

But he shook his head and said, "Not yet."

At half-past seven that evening, she set off for the covered market. Pascoe had been there since six, making sure of the arrangements, so she knew she would have a lone drive into town. But at Pallas gates — the splendid, new gates and gatelodge "given" to her by Zakky Gilbert — she was flagged down by a man waving a lantern.

It was Hamill.

"Is something the matter?" she asked.

"Let me come with you?" he almost pleaded.

"Of course! Climb up — d'you want me to help you? Put out the lantern. You can leave it by the gatelodge door."

He needed no assistance in climbing up. She could feel the agitation in him. "Something *is* the matter," she said.

"Prepare yourself for an unpleasant shock, Beth. I don't think this evening will go at all the way you've planned it."

"Why not?"

"You forgot Morwenna."

CHAPTER THIRTY-TWO

MORWENNA ARRIVED AT THE MARKET around a quarter to the hour, while Elizabeth and Hamill were still driving furiously through Lowertown, a steep and uphill mile away. Pascoe did not notice her entry among so many. Naturally he tried to prevent her from speaking but was himself shouted down — in most cases by men who had never had a good word to say for Miss Morwenna in the old days.

"My friends!" she began as she meant to go on. "My dear old friends and neighbours, we have known one another all our lives. It would be pointless for any of us to tell falsehoods among ourselves. I certainly don't intend to try it. You'd see through me at once. But the truth is hard. Harsh — especially for me. It is bitterness to me that I have to begin with an admission that my dear brother — may his soul rest in peace" — there was a catch in her voice — "my dear brother, whom you all knew, and who was such a good friend to you . . . did there ever live a kindlier man? Or one more ready to listen to a neighbour's tale of woe? If there was, I don't know him, and I don't suppose you do, either."

A murmur of assent went up at that.

"Many a winter would have gone hard with you if he had not heard your reasonable pleas for mitigation of your rents. But now I have to confess that this same brother, in the closing weeks of a life cut tragically short, was so ill-advised . . . or" — she shrugged, hesitated, forced the words out of her reluctant lips — "*influenced* in some way to make a new will. His earlier will, made when he still had all his wits about him, had enshrined a tradition that went back over a hundred years, to the great founder of our estate. Since then the lands have passed down in the time-hallowed manner to the eldest male heir. Well, you know how my brother revered the family tradition. There can be not the slightest doubt that he intended resigning his military commission (indeed, he had already done so) and returning here with his new young wife to take up the burdens I had so reluctantly, but I trust ungrudgingly, shouldered since our parents' untimely deaths. And I equally have no doubt that, under his firm hand, with his loving guidance, his new young wife would, over the years, have learned sufficient of the business of so large an estate to enable her to become its trustee for a few short years if history were sadly to repeat itself and the true master were to pass on before the true heir were mature enough to put up his rightful mantle."

She stabbed the air with her finger to emphasize this next point: "But I cannot possibly believe, and nor I'm sure, can you — nor could anyone who knew him *in the days before that stroke so cruelly afflicted his mind* — no one can believe that he intended the estate to pass for life into the hands of a young woman, barely out of school, whose rural skills never went beyond handing her father a tub of liniment when she occasionally accompanied him on his veterinary rounds — or dashing out into the herb garden to pluck a sprig of thyme to garnish the Sunday roast."

Laughter and vigorous nods of affirmation.

"How could Bill Troy intend to saddle you with such a burden? D'you suppose that in his wildest dreams he ever envisaged such a situation as we face tonight? Of course not. I beg you — on my knees I *beg* you — deal kindly with his memory. Think not that your present afflictions are of his wilful making. But just see what mischief may follow when a man's head is turned and he is induced to throw aside the carefully nurtured tradition of his family! Just look at the result! Our beloved Pallas has passed into the careless hands of an untutored foreigner. She has not the first notion of rural economy. She does not understand that investment in the soil may take years to show its dividend. No, she must have it now! She has thrown good money after bad – your money – she has thrown it into mining ventures that will never pay *you* a penny. And now she wants more. Your income falls, but hers must rise. Her husband is hardly cold in Helston churchyard, and already this insatiable young townswoman is fattening her appetite with peremptory demands for yet more of your hard-won income. The most despotic and avaricious government in history has never dared send out a demand so impertinent as this."

She flourished aloft a copy of Elizabeth's letter of notice.

"And where will it end, eh? Another five shillings next year? And another . . . and another? Oh, I know what's going on in her mind! She's read a book or two on vegetable gardening. She's spent long hours in conversation with her bailiff – a landowner who couldn't even manage his own estate wisely . . ."

"Have a care, Miss Troy!" Pascoe shouted furiously.

"Oh I do, Mr. Pascoe. I have a care for these good people. I am a *real* Troy. I've had a care for them since the hour of my birth!"

Elizabeth and Hamill were at that moment entering the outer porch. She heard the last exchange and from it guessed the tenor of what had gone before. Her plan for the evening – David's plan – was clearly in shreds. She drew a deep breath and walked in.

They saw her. All eyes turned her way. Someone began to hiss. It was briefly taken up by others; but there were some there who had not quite lost all sense of propriety; the *ssss!* was finally drowned out in the *sshhhh!*

Morwenna's eye was roving over the crowd; she was wondering whether she had said enough. She had seen many a preacher spoil his sermon by tedious repetition of a point already perfectly grasped by his hearers.

"But she's our landlord," a voice called out. "If she do insist, there in't nothing we can do about it. We aren't left to say no to she."

"If you *all* refuse her this blood money," Morwenna said, "what can she do? Evict the lot of you?"

Laughter and cheers. Good old Miss Troy had hit upon the answer!

She spoke again: "And bear this in mind – a life tenant who so grossly mismanages an estate can be replaced by a board of trustees." Her eyes patrolled the gathering; she smiled grimly. "In short, before many months have passed, your rightful landlord may be back in her rightful seat."

"And what then?"

"This!" Morwenna held Elizabeth's letter above her head and tore it in two.

The cheering shook the rafters.

Elizabeth saw that only something equally dramatic would now serve her purpose. With Hamill at her side she strode through the racket, the jeering, the grinning faces. Torn up demands were fluttered in her way but she brushed them all aside. When they reached the platform, Pascoe, who was still on the floor of the hall, joined Hamill in helping her ascend.

"I couldn't have stopped her without force," he said.

"Don't worry. She'll make no difference in the end. You stand over to one side. You, too, please, Uncle Hamill. Slip out and fetch the police if it gets too rough." When Hamill squared himself up for an argument she added, "And please remember — however it may seem to the contrary — I know exactly what I'm doing here. Don't feel you have to join in."

As she straightened herself, Morwenna came to her side. "Don't try, if you've any sense," she said vehemently. "You've lost already."

Elizabeth ignored her, waited for the cheering to subside. She let a silence grow.

She knew exactly what to say. The whole shape of her argument was suddenly there in her mind. But then she saw something that entirely blotted it out.

At the back of the market, as far from the speakers' platform as it was possible to get, half-shaded by one of the pillars, she saw David Troy.

He realized he had been spotted, too, for he at once withdrew into the full shadow.

Now a dreadful indecision gripped her. She would never be given a better opportunity than this to force him to declare his loyalties openly; but dare she take it? If she lost, she would lose the battle with her tenants, too; she'd become the laughing stock of the district; she'd never regain full control of Pallas

She decided it would be madness to take such risks. Reluctantly she turned to face her tenants and do the job herself. Almost conversationally, she said, "Correct me if I'm wrong, but it would seem that some of you actually do not *wish* to meet this increase in your rents?"

There was an astonished outrush of breath; some shouted abuse, others laughed at her affrontery. And then she found that she could not go on.

It was no use telling herself what risks she was running, part of her simply refused to cooperate — was so desperate to know whether David were truly on her side or no that it would hazard everything to learn it.

"Well . . ." she stammered, "then . . . that is . . ."

The meeting, all those faces, the shadows — it all began to dissolve and swim around her. Only one point remained fixed — the pillar behind which David was still in hiding.

"If you all refuse . . . why, I suppose . . ."

Would he never show himself?

Someone began to laugh. It spread until everyone was at it. And still David would not budge.

So there is was. He had, after all, declared his loyalty. Despite all his fine words, he was not her true supporter.

A great calm overcame her. In a way it was a relief to have the truth at last, after so many months of doubt. She turned again to the crowd, raised her hand until they were silent once more, and said in that same almost-conversational tone, "Then you needn't pay!"

In the stunned silence that followed this apparent surrender David leaped from his concealment and began striding toward the platform. " 'Tis David Troy . . . David Troy . . . David Troy . . ." The murmur ran around the hall. The crowds parted before him only to close eagerly behind – and press forward. This was unexpected excitement indeed.

Elizabeth glanced at Morwenna and found her smiling as if victory were already sealed.

"Are you mad?" David hissed at Elizabeth as he leaped up beside her.

"For a while I began to think so," she said.

Her smile made him pause. Understanding dawned. "By heaven – you did it on purpose!"

"You still have a choice," she answered quietly. "I'm quite ready to fight my own corner. You may pretend you came up here to chair the meeting and prevent disorder."

But he shook his head. To give him his due, he did not even hesitate. Morwenna joined them at that moment, ostentatiously taking David's arm. She turned him to face the meeting. "Here's another proper Troy," she said. "Let him tell you, too."

David politely disengaged himself and, folding his arms – his favourite posture, it seemed, from which to launch an oration – began to speak. "I believe you know me. I'm from the branch of the Troy family that did *not* inherit the terrible burdens of property."

Laughter.

"Like you, I've had to work for every penny I've got. And like you, I deeply resent it when people who've never done a hand's turn in their lives want to take some of it off me – merely because they happen to own something I'm still too poor to buy." His look challenged them. "Isn't that the heart of it now, my friends? You slave all the hours the Good Lord sends, and for precious little reward, and then some foreigner posts you a letter demanding more! And what makes it so galling in this case is that the foreigner hasn't been in the county two years, and her ownership of the land into which you put your sweat and lifeblood derives from a marriage that didn't even last a day."

There was a great roar of approval at this. Morwenna gave a triumphant laugh and began to clap. David had to raise his hands to quell the applause.

"But worse even than that – worst of all," he said, "is that you know in your hearts, if you worked till you dropped, and even if the rents were to remain as they are until the crack of doom, you'd still never be able to save the price of your own land. Aren't I right?"

A growl of assent confirmed it.

"So when Mrs. Troy said just now that if you don't wish to pay the increase, then you don't need to – why, I'm sure she meant is sincerely."

Everyone turned to Elizabeth. She gave no sign of noticing it, but continued to stare at David; no emotion whatever showed on her face.

"But that's not the end of it." David reclaimed their attention. "Not for you, and not for me. One of my interests – one of the things I feel most passionately about in this life – is the open sore of rural poverty. If I had a penny for every hour I've spent wrestling with that problem, I tell you – I'd have a purse big enough to solve it on my own! There are those who'll tell you that the government ought to take money off the rich and give it to the poor."

"Hear hear!" came the cry from several quarters.

"I don't agree with that," David argued. "If you confiscated every income above a thousand pounds in this country, you'd put less than six months' wages, and I'm talking about the present miserable wages, into each poor man's pocket in the kingdom. Less than six months! So that's no answer. Others say confiscate the money and invest it in new businesses run by the government. Well, if any man amongst you wishes to work for a man in a top hat and starched collar who lives in a palace up London, who never saw a blade of grass that didn't grow in Parliament Square nor get mud on his patent-leather shoes that didn't lie in the gutters of Whitehall, all I can say, boys, is good luck to him!"

They thought that a great joke.

"So what is the answer, eh? I'll be quite candid, my friends: I just don't know. But" – he held up a finger and his smile was full of sudden promise – "I believe I saw the first glimmer of an answer a week or two back." He turned to the side of the hall. "Mr. Pascoe, you have a piece of paper there, I believe?"

Pascoe looked inquiringly at Elizabeth. She gave a wary, noncommittal shrug, as if to say, 'It's out of my hands now.' Pascoe came forward to the platform and handed over the document.

"It's a farm account," David told them, holding it up. "And a strange sort of farm it is, too," he mused. "An acre here. Half-acre there . . . spread all over the parishes. But taking all those little parcels of land together, there's forty-seven acres arable. Well now, the average rent brought in by all the arable lands of Pallas is . . . what?" He turned equally to Morwenna and Elizabeth.

"Thirty-five shillings an acre," Elizabeth said clearly.

"Thirty-five shillings an acre," he repeated. "So if Pallas was landlord to this scattered farm, its rent would be . . . about eighty-two pounds." He turned to read from the document. "The rest of these figures now are for the half year. Wages, I see, come to two-hundred-and-forty-five pounds, fourteen shillings. Runnings costs, and they are mainly charges for railway carriage to the markets, they come to one-hundred-and-eighty. Capital expenditure not represented in the rent is amortised at one-hundred-and-fourteen pounds, nine and tenpence. Adding that all together with six months' rent makes a grand total of five-hundred-and-seventy pounds odd." He looked up and smiled. "My dear soul – that's a lot of money, isn't it!"

Another rumble of assent.

"But here's the bit that caught my eye: The *income* for that same period has been over seven hundred and forty pounds."

There was a gasp of disbelief but he spoke loudly into it. "Perhaps now you know which farm I'm talking about! The owner of this farm could slap another twenty pounds on her own rent – what? she could *double* it – and she'd still be smiling." He turned to Elizabeth. "Isn't that so, Mrs. Troy?"

She looked out over those expectant faces and said, "The income of my little farm will be over thirty pounds an acre before the year is out."

"Judas!" Morwenna cried, advancing upon him.

"I haven't done yet!" he told her, brandishing the paper like a talisman to ward her off. He swung round to include the whole meeting. "I haven't done yet!" Silence fell again. "When Mrs. Troy, who, as you all know, is an ignorant foreigner, a townswoman who never tended more than a few flowerpots in her life – when she says you need not pay the increase, she means that if you . . . if any man present is willing to stand up this minute and swear to the rest of us that he could never achieve in a year what she has achieved in six months – then he may continue to pay the old rent!" He turned to her. "Am I not right?"

They all waited for her reply. She looked them over slowly before she said, "Mr. Troy has caught my meaning exactly." Over a small but rising hubbub of protest she persisted: "But before any of you volunteer to go on paying the old rent, understand this: I firmly believe there are men among you who *want* to see a finer dress on their wife's back, and a better coat on their own . . . men who *want* to see their children better shod and schooled . . . men whose backache would be cured by a little bit of gold beneath the mattress. They are the men who will see that where I've scraped ten pounds they'll clear forty. They're the men who are going to laugh at a *further* five-shilling increase next year, because . . ."

A gasp went up at that.

"Oh yes! Please understand that. The Pallas Estate is now on its way back to prosperity. Not just for the *men* among you, but for its poor ignorant townswoman-owner, too. Tonight we turn the corner. All of us. You and me. And those who are too faint of heart to begin the journey with us now will have double the road to run next year – and treble the year after. So think carefully before you volunteer for the easy way out!"

"This is a trick!" Morwenna shouted. "Anyone can pluck figures out of a hat . . ."

"The accounts have been audited," Elizabeth answered. "Mr. Pascoe has the books over there. Anyone who wishes may see them – he'll find Mr. Collins's signature at the foot of it."

They all looked at one another. There was a general feeling that they had been tricked but none dared voice it.

" 'Tis well enough for you, Mrs. Troy," one farmer grumbled, "but how's the likes of we to afford hothouses and that?"

"It's no different from the cost of a new cowshouse or a haybarn. The estate will bear the capital cost. But how can we do that if we never achieve any surplus income?"

"And how are we going to afford seed and that? They daffodilly bulbs isn't . . ."

"That's a fair point." She felt it was time for a concession. "I'll tell you what I'll do – I'll supply you all the bulbs you want – *and* I'll allow you one season's credit. But that's only to start you up. After the first season I'd expect you to pay for your own. And again I must make this point: How can I afford to do that if I never have any surplus?"

"But we don't know nothing about they old bulbs."

"Then aren't you lucky to have a neighbour who's six months ahead of you, Mr. Carey! If I wished to know the trick of raising thistles, I'd surely come to *you*." Against their will they laughed, for all Cornish humour is at someone's expense. "So I give you leave now," she went on, "every one of you – you may walk my fields any day you wish. See how we manage. I'm sure that before the year's out you'll have found ways that are ten times better than mine. I'm not that sort of farmer who discovers something good and then keeps it jealously to himself." She joined their renewed laughter as she concluded: "I *want* you to be rich. I want you to be so rich this time next year that you, not me, will arrange this meeting – and you'll be begging me to make it *only* five shillings on the rent."

There was a roar of disbelieving laughter at that; but the mood of the meeting had swung her way. People were beginning to glimpse that the impossible might after all be within their grasp.

"I only got a acre-and-half," one man, a miner, complained. "What's the good o' that?"

"For a start – Mr. Weeks, isn't it? – for a start, Mr. Weeks, you can turn that useless old donkey out to graze the Flow. You're never going to win a race with that old thing."

More laughter.

"But there are things you can win. For instance, you can win your own family's vegetables out of half an acre. And on the remaining acre you can plant daffodils and violets. I'll supply the bulbs and the seedlings. You'll easily clear another twenty-five pounds a year."

"Yes, but he's going to be a lot more work, missis."

"If you want prosperity without toil, Mr. Weeks, you joined the wrong planet in the wrong century."

Morwenna at last realized that the prize of which she had been so sure only fifteen minutes earlier was now as far from her as ever. "You'll regret this!" she cried out in her fury. "Mark my words. All of you. You'll regret this! A farm is not a factory — and only an ignorant townswoman, or a miserable turncoat of a politician, would try to turn it into one."

Elizabeth nudged David, who, now that the eyes of the crowd were no longer upon him, was allowing his anger to show. "Together at last," she cajoled.

CHAPTER THIRTY-THREE

ELIZABETH HAD BEEN TOO NERVOUS to dine earlier that evening. Now she took David, Hamill, and Pascoe out to a celebration supper at The Angel. They sat in one of the private rooms upstairs.

"On the whole I'm glad Morwenna intervened," she told them. "If any tenant of mine had lingering hopes that the Old Order might one day return . . . well, he now knows better."

"You saved the day," Pascoe told David.

"More than the day," Elizabeth added with a meaningful look.

David withheld his smile. "It was an underhand trick," he replied with jocular aggression.

They all laughed — but she knew he resented what she had done.

Or, she wondered, did he? Could it be a politician's instinct always to preserve a small toehold on whatever platform was opposite to the one he was currently occupying? With David one could never be sure.

Hamill patted him on the back. "You must be the only Liberal in the land to march beneath a banner that reads: *Forward to Prosperity — Raise the Rents!*"

"But was I wrong?" David challenged.

"You're preaching to the converted here, old fellow," Pascoe told him.

At the height of their celebrations they were interrupted by a knock at the door. It was the hotel's maid-of-all-work. "If you please, mum, there's a Mrs. Mitchell below, says she's your mother, and may you kindly step down and see her?"

Everything in the room seemed to shift. Elizabeth rose and then sat down again. "My mother?"

"So she says."

"But she's supposed to be in Italy. Describe her to me." She knew she was merely buying time.

"Why, she'd be about your size and colouring, mum. I dunno – she got her done hair up in a bun, like. Got little, round ears, she has. And her lips would be a mite thinner than what yours is. I dunno."

Elizabeth nodded. "It sounds like her. Tell her I'll be down directly." When the woman had gone she looked about her and said, "I must gather my wits. My dear soul! Of all the ways I imagined today might end . . ."

"Shall I come down with you?" Hamill asked. "Or . . ." He glanced at David.

"No!" Elizabeth insisted quickly. "She'd only . . . she's an out-and-out . . . well, never mind – I'll see her on my own first."

She rose and gave herself a critical survey in the looking glass before she left them. "Of all things!" she said to no one in particular as she went downstairs. "And today of all days!"

The woman standing alone in the hotel lounge, surveying herself in the looking glass, exactly as Elizabeth had done above, was indeed Mrs. Mitchell.

In mid-appraisal their eyes met. Elizabeth expected her mother to turn but she stood as she was, suggesting that the magnificence of the moment had paralyzed her. Tears brimmed in her eyes. Slowly she opened her arms toward the reflection of her daughter. "My lamb!" she quavered.

Elizabeth ignored the invitation. "No need for all that, Mother. It's only you and me."

The woman lowered her arms and turned, only to raise them again. "My poor child! I had no idea. I had no idea, until I read the newspapers last week. And then, of course, I came immediately."

Elizabeth winced at her embrace. "Had no idea of what? And what newspapers?"

"We get everything so late in Italy. I know I'm months out of date. I mean this beastly court case."

"You're more than a year out of date."

"I know, I know – but as soon as I saw what trouble you were in, I realized that a mother's place is . . ."

A thought occurred to Elizabeth. "You haven't read any of my letters!" she said.

"Indeed I have."

"No – you threw them away unopened, I'll bet! Then you happened to be lining a drawer, or something like that, with some ancient copy of *The Times*, and you came across the court report! You suddenly realized I didn't just marry some insignificant army captain but . . ."

"Elizabeth!" The tears were ready.

"Your last words to me, Mother, were to the effect that we could never live beneath the same roof, that you had never loved me . . ."

"But my darling! That was . . ."

". . . and you never wanted to see me again, and if I was hoping for a farthing of Dad's estate, I could bay the moon. What's wrong with Italy, Mother?"

"Oh you're such an unforgiving child!" She looked at her own reflection as if she might recruit a little support there.

"What's wrong with Italy?" Elizabeth pressed.

"*That* odious country! You'll oblige me by never mentioning its name again."

"You said father's legacy would last much longer in Italy. For ever, in fact. What's gone wrong?"

"I begged you never to mention it again."

"You've spent it all, haven't you."

"Not quite." She burst into tears.

Elizabeth stood in acute embarrassment and watched her mother sob. In the end, much against her will, she reached out and gave her arm a squeeze. Mrs. Mitchell rallied immediately. "Thank you, dear. I'm in a slight hole, as a matter of fact. I wonder if you could just send someone out to pay off my cabbie?" She turned to the mirror-Elizabeth and explained. "I came directly from Victoria to Paddington to Cornwall, you see, and have had no chance to change my . . ."

"How did you know I was here? Oh, I suppose that was in the papers."

"No!" Her mother was all excitement again. "That was the most astonishing thing of all. I was talking to the cabbie at Victoria and your name rang a bell with him, and then another cabbie said you were the heroine of the something mine disaster and last time you were in London you stayed at an hotel in Paddington. So we went there and the hotel gave me your address."

"The same address, funnily enough, that was at the top of all those letters of mine which you claim to have read! Give that bell-sash a pull." She sat down and tried to think what to do next.

"The cabbie in London wouldn't take a penny – because of my wonderful daughter."

"Your wonderful daughter was almost lynched by her own tenantry this evening. You'll get no free rides down here."

Her mother came over and stood behind her chair, putting her hands on her daughter's shoulders. "It's so lovely to see you again, darling. I can't tell you how much I've missed you."

"I'll bet you can't."

A waiter answered the summons. Elizabeth asked him to take care of the cabfare.

"It's all the way from Penzance," her mother confessed shyly. "I was so comfortable in the train, you see, and that horrid little branch-line looked so uninviting. I'm sure everything will seem quite different by daylight."

Elizabeth nodded at the waiter. When he had gone she asked her mother how she had managed the train fare. "I gave them my name and address – care of you at Pallas House. I hope that was all right?"

"Pallas House, eh?" Elizabeth gave a grim laugh. "I'm almost tempted to inflict you upon Morwenna."

"Upon *whom*, dear?"

"Never mind. You'd better stop here at the Angel for a day or two, until we can ready a room for you at Wheal Lavender – that's my home, by the way, not Pallas House." She rose. "I have guests to whom I must return. Now listen, Mother – I don't know what fancies you've indulged since reading of my apparent fortune, but understand this: *I am poor*. Pallas Estate is on the verge of bankruptcy. Every penny we can spare must go toward new investment. So there is nothing – not one brass farthing – to splash about. While you're at the hotel here you'll eat table d'hôte – and you may have half a bottle of wine a day. And . . ."

"*Half!*" Her mother was scandalized.

"That's half more than I allow myself." She fished in her purse and counted out five sovereigns. "That should last you a day or two," she said, handing them over. "You're to open no accounts at any of the shops. If you do, I shall publish a disclaimer of any debts you may run up."

Through all this her mother went on smiling seraphically. "Your bitterness is so understandable, my darling. I know I was a poor mother to you, and I said and did things that were *almost* unforgivable. But I've made my peace with myself and now I intend to make it with you, as well. Revile me all you like – I shall understand and forgive. As long as I can be near my lamb again and help to make her happy . . ."

Elizabeth rose and went from the room.

CHAPTER THIRTY-FOUR

THE ST. AUBYNS were at home – indeed, they were At Home, for the carriages of the local gentry were lined up in the courtyard. David and Elizabeth were disappointed. They had come over the causeway to St. Michael's Mount, officially to deliver some legal papers to Lord St. Levan's agent. Privately, they had hoped to look over the Abbey, the home of the St. Aubyns; but it was closed to the public whenever the family were in residence.

"I thought you knew them," David grumbled as they went back down the lane.

"Of course I do, but I couldn't just take you in, not without first asking their leave. D'you *want* to know them?"

He looked back at the Abbey walls, a stubborn glint in his eye. "When I'm the officially adopted candidate, it won't be a question of what I want — or what they want."

"First catch your hare!"

"Don't you worry about that." They had reached the village that nestles at the foot of the rock. "What now?" he asked.

"Let's walk around the shore instead. Is it too early in the season for a cream tea?"

"We mustn't be caught."

She was puzzled.

"By the tide."

There was no easy path around the island so they wandered aimlessly about a bit of the shore, a bedraggled space of rock, seaweed, and weeping sand. Above them towered the Abbey; from this angle its true character as a fortified castle became clear. From Penzance, or even from Marazion, just a quarter of a mile away across the causeway, the romantic spires and turrets that have made the island such a favourite subject for artists down the years, turned it into a fairy palace.

As they walked they returned to the topic that had vexed Elizabeth ever since the night of the tenants' meeting.

"My mother can't stay down here for the rest of my life," she said. "I have worries enough as it is."

"Then you shouldn't have accepted the responsibility," he told her. His manner was restless, even brusque.

"What else could I have done?"

"Make her an allowance on condition she goes back to Italy. Or France."

"You don't really mean that, David."

"If you say so." He threw a flat pebble, trying to make it skip, but the water was not calm enough.

She ignored his tone. "I have no idea what my father's estate came to but . . ."

"That's easily discovered."

"No, no. It's all water under the bridge now. I don't *want* to know. I'd only get angry to no purpose. The point is that even if I somehow arranged an income for her — wherever she lived — she'd only run through it again in the same short order."

He was silent. "Talk," she told him.

"You're starting to think like *them*." He looked up at the Abbey.

She followed his gaze. "The St. Aubyns?"

"Their class. You're starting to think like their class — portions, annuities, dowries, investments . . . what would be wrong with making your mother work for her living?"

Elizabeth laughed.

"I'm serious," he told her. "What better way is there to teach someone the value of money?"

She stopped laughing. "But what could she do? She'll be fifty soon. She's never earned so much as a crust. All she's good at is spending the stuff."

"You could settle her in a little seaside cottage in Falmouth, or across the bay in St. Mawes, and she could do teas and sell curios."

"And in winter?"

He grinned. "Even from Falmouth it's a dreadful road up over the downs to Helston — and a long way around by train. From St. Mawes it's just about impossible."

She chuckled. "It's *almost* an idea, David. A little curio shop . . . she might accept it. But cream teas is something she'd have to hit upon herself. It'd be fatal if I suggested it."

There was still that impatience in him. Their conversation drifted aimlessly until she said, "Let's go and see if anyone's doing teas yet."

"I'm not especially hungry," he replied. "However . . ."

She laughed. "Now how did I just *know* you'd say that!"

Her feet welcomed and surer footing of the granite setts that paved the road leading through the village and up to the Abbey. They found a cottager, a fisherman's wife, willing to provide tea and saffron cake. She showed them into a parlour that was like a museum of popular curios — china dogs, teapots, porcelain biscuit barrels, ships in bottles — most of them from the earlier half of the century. "Anything you see and want to buy, my lovers," she told them, "they'm all for sale."

When they were alone again Elizabeth said, "You're still angry with me."

"I was never angry with you."

"You were. I can tell. You can't hide something like that from me."

"You've no idea what I hide from you." He glanced out of the window. "We mustn't forget the tide."

She began a minute inspection of the proffered ornaments. Casually she said, "Can I ask you a serious question, David?"

"Of course."

"D'you think you're really suited for parliament?"

He gave a little laugh of astonishment. "What ever makes you ask?"

"Your behaviour at the meeting the other night."

"*My* behaviour! I like that!"

"No — listen! Until then I'd have said you had every quality needed. You have passionate ideals, you're a brilliant speaker, a superb organizer, and you've a mind as sharp as a scalpel. And above all, you've got patience."

"Poverty teachers patience."

"But the one thing I doubt is your ability to lose a skirmish gracefully."

"Oh, I see!"

The woman came with their tea. "Spotted anything you might fancy, my lovers?" she asked.

Elizabeth, who was still pretending to look at the bric-a-brac, answered, "You have some lovely things, missis. Unfortunately, my own house is already rather cluttered, you know."

David smiled at this equation between peasant china and the Rembrandts. But when the woman had gone Elizabeth pressed her point. "You know what I'm talking about, David. We had a skirmish, you and I, and I forced you to declare your loyalties when you would rather not have done so. And you haven't taken it at all well. Life in parliament will be full of such petty defeats."

He shrugged. "Before I take that up, may I ask *you* a serious question?"

She sat down opposite him, smiling ruefully. "In the circumstances I can hardly say no – but trust you to see it and take full advantage!" She began to pour out the tea. "The St. Aubyns would raise a delicate eyebrow if they could just see this. She's a milk-in-last person."

"If you had an absolutely free choice in life, Beth – or let me put it another way. Suppose the trustees suddenly decided to put the estate on the market, and . . ."

"But Morwenna will never, never . . ."

"I know that. But just supposing! I'm trying to discover what you really want in life. Suppose you found the Great Lode and could buy the estate out of petty cash. The question is: Would you?"

After only a moment's thought she realized, to her own surprise, that she would. Rather than admit it, she asked, "Today, you mean? If all this happened today?"

"Does it matter?"

"Of course it does. If they sold off the estate before I'd had a chance to see my plans bear fruit, then naturally I'd buy it and finish the job myself."

"But you'd still have the life tenancy, whoever owned it. You wouldn't need to buy it in order to carry out your ideas. Possession is nine points of the law."

She grinned, as if the idea were slightly naughty. "But *ownership* is all ten of them!"

He laughed unwillingly.

"What was your point in asking?" she pressed.

"Surely you see? We must hope that Morwenna doesn't take it into her mind to sell before you've found the Great Lode."

"But she'll never sell, not in any . . ."

"She would if someone pointed out to her that the more your reforms raise the value of Pallas, the more you stand to inherit from the proceeds of the sale. There would come a point where her loathing of you would outweigh her love of an estate that is, in any case, completely outside her influence. Her attachment to Pallas is now sentimental, historical − nothing more than that. It will fade."

Elizabeth did not want to dwell on these possibilities. "I shall need to find the Great Lode anyway," she said, "just to pay the lawyers. D'you know what the fees for my two days in court came to? They've presented the bills at last. Two hundred guineas! A hundred a day! I just wish I could earn . . ."

"Montague? A hundred?"

"No − he's *only* twenty guineas a day. I nearly had a fit when I heard that. I think George Ivey is hoping to fund his new solo practice entirely on the proceeds of my case."

"Is George going into solo practice?" He was interested.

"I'm only guessing," she warned. "I imagine he'll make the move after he's married. Don't tell anyone, by the way, but he and Lilian will be announcing their engagement next week."

"They'll suit each other," he said ambiguously.

"You still haven't answered my first question."

His face hardened. "I've been answering it − if only you weren't so stupid and emotional − and blind to your own best interests. My whole point is that now you've succeeded in exposing me, you have no one close to Morwenna. You'll have no idea what's going on in her mind."

Elizabeth thumped the table, almost upsetting her teacup. "It was more important to me to be sure of your loyalties."

The answer infuriated him but he clamped his jaw tight against any further outburst. "You make the point for me," he said coldly. "You are stupid, emotional, and blind."

She rose. "Perhaps we'd better leave then." She put a shilling and a few coppers on the table.

At that moment they heard the rumble of carriage wheels outside.

"Too late," he said bitterly.

"What's too late?"

"We are now cut off by the tide."

"But the gentry are only just going."

He spoke as if she must be feebleminded to require the explanation: "Horses and carriages can still get back over the causeway when it's drowned under eighteen inches of tideway. People can't."

They ran down to the little breakwater behind whose shelter the causeway rose to become the village's one street. They were, indeed, too late. At least a foot of water was now swilling over the weed-encrusted stone that wound its serpentine way to the mainland. "This is your fault," he said quietly. "Wanting to rub my nose in your petty little victory."

"David! For the love of . . ."

He raised his voice and asked furiously: "You think I don't see through you? I know you far better than you know yourself."

"You know nothing!" She heard her tone becoming querulous. "Well, I'm not going to stand here like a fishwife!" She looked at the line of submerged stone, dark against the paler sand of the natural causeway. "It's only a foot of water anyway."

She stepped out boldly – far more boldly than she felt – toward the drowned causeway. The water looked cold and slick. Still, it would only be up to her knees.

She was just about to let her feet take the plunge when something heavy fell around her neck. For a second she thought David had struck her, then, looking down, she saw that his boots, tied together by their laces, were now hanging on her chest. As she turned to protest he swept her up into his arms. "No sense in our both getting wet," he muttered grudgingly.

His strength surprised her – or added to her surprise. She looked up at him. He was so angry still – so solemn, striding out like that, swirling through the water. When they were nearing the landward end of the causeway, she could bear the silence no longer. She giggled.

"I'm glad you think it's funny," he said.

"My hero!" she murmured. "Actually, with those fantastic pinnacles and the sun and those glorious Turneresque clouds and your hair all wild, there *is* something wonderfully heroic about you."

"Don't think you can wheedle your way around me," he responded. "I'm in the right."

"Don't you want to be a hero?" she teased.

"If you ever dare force my hand again like that . . ."

"So strong!" she cooed. "So masterful!"

"If you refuse to take me seriously, Beth, I shall let you go."

She laughed; the boots around her neck shifted perilously.

He paused. "Better put them round my neck now, before they fall off altogether."

She complied. Their eyes met. For a moment she felt sure he saw the humour of the situation. The living moment teetered between his mood and hers. Then, his lips clamped firmly together, he stepped out again. "You are the most maddening, cantankerous, stubborn . . ." At that moment he trod into a thicket of seaweed and missed his footing. There was a brief, desperate struggle to recover his balance, with Elizabeth screaming and clinging ever tighter to him; and then they both fell sidelong off the causeway.

The sudden cold was so intense it winded Elizabeth. She opened her mouth to scream again – and found herself voiceless; indeed, she was hardly able to breathe. But as the shock passed its peak, a strange paradox overtook her senses: The sea now felt almost too hot to bear. They were close to shore and the water was shallow. She was sitting on soft sand, being gently pushed and plucked by the tiny waves.

David was sitting a little way off, staring at himself, at her, at the sea, in disbelief.

She splashed him. And at last his dignity collapsed. He gave out a great boyish roar and splashed her in revenge.

Then it was pure childhood. They laughed and roared and thrashed the water at each other and hooted . . . until, in the end, the cold and their exhaustion defeated them. He sidled over toward her and, reaching forth his hands, pinned hers and stopped their horseplay.

She sat there, breathing heavily, soaked, bedraggled – and yet happier than she had felt in years.

"We're ridiculous," she said.

Their heads were close together. His eyes stared deep into hers; behind them lurked a strange reluctance.

"Two grown-up people . . ."

The space between them narrowed.

". . . pillars of respectability . . ."

He swallowed audibly. She could see the pulse in his neck.

". . . playing like . . ."

Their lips met.

". . . mmmmmm!"

The myriad-eyed town behind them, the unsheltering sea around . . . all ceased to exist. Every part of her came alive, warming to the tenderness of his touch. How long it endured she had no idea; there came at last a moment when nothing but the damp April air brushed her lips. The chill water reaffirmed its embrace . . . and he was standing above her, stretching forward both his hands.

She reached up and clasped them. He raised her. She prepared for another embrace but he let go with one hand and turned half away. "I'm sorry," he said.

She gave his hand a squeeze. "Liar."

He laughed against his will. "Oh – you're impossible."

"Well, what d'you mean – you're *sorry?*"

He turned completely from her and began to walk toward the beach. "I didn't want this to happen."

"Why not?" She stumbled in her haste to catch him up.

"Not until I could . . . well, until I was able to offer you something."

"Oh David!" She tugged at his jacket. "You're such a . . ."

He turned suddenly. "I've been in love with you, Beth, from the very moment I met you. That night at Deepwork."

She reached forward and took up his hand. They were clear of the water by now. People walking along the Penzance road were watching them curiously. "Kiss me again," she said. "Please?"

END OF PART THREE

PART FOUR

THE SURVIVOR

CHAPTER THIRTY-FIVE

DAVID'S COURTSHIP of Elizabeth was the most reluctant affair. "It's his pride," she explained to Lilian. "It comes of being born poor and achieving everything by his own efforts. Pallas frightens him."

Lilian was noncommittal. She had her own opinion of David, but, knowing how stubborn Elizabeth could be, she hoped that if she said nothing, it might all blow over.

Mrs. Mitchell, who now fancied herself one of the neighbourhood's social queens, was more forthright. She told Elizabeth she could catch something a lot better than an impecunious lawyer with no capital and uncertain prospects. "It's easy to see what *he* wants!" she asserted. "A politician without a private competence!"

The only thing David lacked, in Elizabeth's view, was a degree of physical passion. Whenever they kissed, and she pressed herself against him, the expected response was not there. But what *was* the expected response? He was, after all, a preacher and a man of strong moral principle. Perhaps only marriage could release it in him.

One evening, toward the end of April, she took it into her head to climb Little Tregathennan for a birdseye view of the estate. If David were going to call on her, he'd have arrived by now, so, the weather being fine, she put up her bonnet and set off.

As she passed Zakky Gilbert's, he came to his gate and called out, "I'm coming down your place next week, missis – start that garden wall."

He had said the same words at every one of their encounters since February. "Good," she called back. "I've given instructions to bar the road to Wheal Pallas halvans. I'll only open it for you to carry stone for my wall."

"You're some hard old woman, Mrs. Troy!"

"A bargain's a bargain, Mr. Gilbert."

This time her approach to the hill was from the northwest, across open croft all the way, skirting the fields on the Yeol Parc side. Deep indentations, long since overgrown, scored the earth in regular arrays. They ran roughly east-and-west, obliquely across the face of the hill. They were dug the wrong way for fortifications. Probably they were the remnants of ancient shallow mines, working the lode where it dipped up to the surface. But there were a lot of them; it must have been quite rich country. Had anybody explored deeper since? There was no sign of it now. She wondered who owned the mineral rights. Certainly not Pallas; her sett ended half a mile away on the far side of the hill.

Looking up at the crest she saw silhouetted there the figure of a man. It took only seconds for her to recognize Courtenay.

"You're some fit," he said admiringly when she arrived. "I was quite out of breath from the climb."

"What are you doing here?"

"I was intending to come over to Wheal Lavender, but I thought I ought to check first to see whether a certain brown nag wasn't tethered by the gate."

His tone vexed her. "You needn't bother about that. You can come whether David's there or not."

"David, eh?"

"You needn't behave as if he owns me."

"No one could own you, Beth. Possess you, yes – but not own!"

"Ha ha."

After a silence he asked, "Why did you come up here? I suppose he didn't call on you this evening."

"I wanted to look at the Pallas Estate. D'you remember my first New Year . . ." She broke off, sorry now that she'd recalled the day.

"Do I *remember* it!" He put an arm around her.

She shivered at his touch. He felt it, and his attitude changed subtly. She hated her body for being so vulnerable to him. She should have turned about as soon as she saw him up here.

She pulled herself out of his embrace and stood a little apart. Her eye found it less easy now to pick out the Pallas fields.

"There have been marked improvements," he said. "If that's what you're looking for."

"It's hard to tell in spring. Even the old halvans look green."

"Oh, I come up here quite often. I've noticed it." He closed the gap between them and lightly took her arm. "Why d'you want to denigrate your achievement? Are you afraid of a little self-congratulation? D'you imagine you'd tempt the gods with it?"

"I know how far there is to go still."

"Always so serious."

The sun slipped out beneath the clouds, touching the end of the day with glory. As it rested on Tregonning Hill, he asked, "Are you beginning to feel Cornish yet, Beth? Doesn't this land get into your very blood?"

She nodded contentedly. "Not that I'll ever be accepted as such," she said. "To the end of my days I'll be a 'furriner,' I know that."

"Oh you'll be accepted one day," he promised easily.

After a further silence she said, "Well, I'd better go."

"I'll walk you home. I'm desperately out of condition."

When they reached the cuttings halfway down the hillside she said, "These must be ancient mines – where the lode dipped out to grass."

"I suppose they are. Never thought about it."

"It must have been pretty rich, too – look how close they are together."

He frowned, "Yes, by God!"

"Who owns the mineral rights?"

He tapped his own chest and stared at her in something like amazement. "And it never crossed my mind! Local wisdom has always maintained that the lode was 'just alive' at the edge of the Pallas sett. Here it's supposed to be completely barren."

He leaped down into the nearest of the cuttings and scrabbled in the thin soil with the toe of his boot. "I shall have to come up here with a proper gad – and someone who knows what to look for."

"I can lend you just the man." She felt she owed Clifford Chigwidden that favour. She went down into the cutting and put her arms around him. There were no preliminaries any more, no caresses, no murmured endearments. She was aroused at the first touch of his fingers. She lay beneath him, her back arched, straining to the pressure of him, almost out of her mind at the pleasure of it. One small corner of her conscience remained aloof, telling her that in some obscure way this was all David's fault – for not rousing her . . . for being so *un*passionate . . . for not calling this evening . . . for not being here now to stop her.

Once, at a tribute-day supper at Deepwork, she saw a miner pick up a concertina. He was bantering with his mates, who said he was too drunk to squeeze a note. He was, indeed, pretty drunk, but his hands worked quite automatically, sliding through the leather straps, finding the chord buttons, slipping over them . . . there was no thought behind it, only skill and feeling. His fingers were so sensuous she could not help thinking, *That's how Courtenay handles me.*

After that, whenever she watched men at their work, emptying great sacks, handling stone, starting a draft mare with a click of the tongue, a twitch at the rein, she noticed how the skill was in their very muscles, needing no thought to call it forth – and it always reminded her of that visceral conspiracy between Courtenay and her body. The sack had to spill; the stone was forced to bed just so; the mare could not choose but trot.

When it was over and they lay at peace, cooling their nakedness, she said, "Am I different from other women?"

"In what way?" he asked guardedly.

"In any way that strikes you."

After a pause he said, "I shall be heartbroken when you marry Troy."

She sighed.

"What's love, anyway?" he asked. "Common as dirt. Affection's far more rare. True affection. You'd do better to marry me."

"D'you think what we do is rare? Or do all our friends – everyone we know – are they all at it, too, d'you think?"

"I'm sure they are. The passion itself is universal."

"Everybody?"

Reluctantly he answered, "I suppose there are a few who don't feel it – poor creatures. One in a hundred, perhaps."

"Poor creatures," she echoed.

CHAPTER THIRTY-SIX

DAVID'S SUGGESTION of a curio shop did, in a roundabout way, solve the problem of what to do with Mrs. Mitchell – though it created another, far greater. Elizabeth realized it would be useless to come out baldly with the idea; her mother would have to be induced to it by degrees. As a first stage she took her to see over Pallas House, having chosen an afternoon when Morwenna would be out. Hamill, of course, did the honours.

The old couple got on well from the start. Elizabeth saw a totally new side to her mother; coquetry was the only word for it. From the start she hardly took her eyes off Hamill. Very soon she divined that he wished her to know nothing about art; he wanted to be the one to explain everything to her. All at once (though she had told Elizabeth she had practically *lived* in the Uffizi and the great museums of Rome) she became the world's ignoramus who couldn't tell classical from romantic nor oil paint from water colour. Her rapt attention, her great, dark eyes, utterly captivated the poor old fellow.

Elizabeth took as much as she could bear and then left them to it.

She walked back through Pallas woods, shaken by what she had just witnessed. She remembered how she had once thought of herself as an empty blackboard on which others could chalk up their commands and expectations; now she saw that it was much more true of her mother.

The person whom all the world had known as "Mrs. Mitchell," the frustrated vet's wife, the short-tempered mother, had in a way died with her husband. The blackboard had been wiped clean. She was now a void that craved to be filled with other people's expectations. But the insight brought no sudden rush of sympathy. Ever since Elizabeth could remember, there had been a certain anger between them; perhaps the expectations of a child had been too elementary to satisfy someone so devious, so complicated, so mined through and through with the worm of discontent as her mother.

This was the first time she had been able to view her mother from all sides, as one considers a stranger.

When Mrs. Mitchell returned that evening – rather late that evening – Elizabeth expected the *ingénue* character to be fixed within her. "What did you think of it?" she asked.

"You're a fool," her mother said coldly. "Any single room there must be worth more than the entire estate. Have you had it valued?"

Elizabeth, hiding her surprise, laughed and replied, "I've not even had it catalogued."

"Well, you should. Those servant girls could walk out with a lifetime's wages hidden beneath their skirts any day they wished."

The opportunity was too good for Elizabeth to ignore. "Perhaps you could do it for me?" she suggested.

Her mother leaped at the offer.

"I'll pay you a salary of ninety-two pounds and ten shillings a year," Elizabeth hastened to get in while the flood tide still flowed.

"Salary? But . . ."

"And you may live in the gatelodge free while you're at it."

"But my dear . . ."

"You can't go on living here, mother. You know what we're like, you and I, when we're cooped up together for any length of time. Anyway, it's a dismal walk through the woods from this house to Pallas in winter."

"I should need a maid."

Even Elizabeth was astonished at the speed of her adjustment. 'I'll pay a further twelve pounds a year toward her," she conceded reluctantly.

A feverish eagerness came over Mrs. Mitchell. "And no doubt I should need to consult various authorities from time to time . . . the British Museum, the Victoria and Albert . . . perhaps even the Uffizi . . ."

"We'll cross that bridge when we come to it," her daughter said firmly. "If the work is going to cost *too* much, I shan't undertake it at all – or I'll simply catalogue the principle works."

"People won't think you slightly . . . you know . . . kicking your mother out to live in a gatelodge?"

"They're well used to me by now. Just tell them the truth."

"Which is . . .?"

"Since I had the fabric restored, that little house is the warmest and most comfortable and convenient in the entire neighbourhood."

Her mother was happy enough to move out the following week. An extraordinary number of packing cases containing the relics of her Italian years arrived from a furniture repository in London – together with an equally extraordinary bill for their storage, which, of course, Elizabeth had to pay. Their contents, however, were beyond all reasoning.

To start with, they contained more dresses than any woman in her fifties could wear out in a lifetime. Well, that was to be expected perhaps. But the rest was like the garnering of some demented dealer in curios. There was enough cutlery, crockery, and glass to stock a small hotel – except that each item was a singleton; none of it made up into sets. The same was true of the linen and the ornaments; no guiding mind, no single taste, had brought them together. A crazy woman strolling through a market saying to an army of servants, "I'll take that and that and that . . ." would actually have assembled a more coherent collection. The books and paintings, too, showed no common thread of taste or purpose.

Elizabeth held up the first two frames that came to hand. One was a dreadful oil painting of a Scots terrier, sitting in a crumpled boot, wearing a tam-o'shanter, and pretending to smoke a pipe – entitled *In His Master's Shoes* – and the other held a severe little water colour of the kind that painters themselves appreciate rather more than do the general public.

Her mother, watching her face carefully, said, "What is it, dear?"

"Well – which of them is *you*? Neither, in my opinion."

Mrs. Mitchell gave a naughty smile. "I did rather lose my head. They have such wonderful markets and little curiosity shops in Italy."

Her daughter resisted saying that one could see now where the legacy had gone.

Two weeks later, Mrs. Mitchell began to catalogue the riches of Pallas.

Two *minutes* later Morwenna came storming over to Wheal Lavender. "I absolutely will not tolerate it!" she shouted over the hedge to Elizabeth.

Zakky Gilbert, keeping his promise at last, straightened up and listened with relish – until Elizabeth, who was dead-heading some roses, replied, "Do please come indoors, Miss Troy."

The temperature in the drawing room seemed to plummet the moment Morwenna entered.

"There's little point in my offering you some tea?" Elizabeth asked.

"None whatever. I have just one thing to say to you and then I shall take my leave. You must suppose you're being very clever. But let me . . ."

"I have no idea what you're talking about, Miss Troy, unless this has something to do with the work my mother is undertaking at . . ."

"You know very well that is what I mean."

"Well, I'm truly sorry if she has irritated you. I know what she's like. I don't think there's a more irritating woman in the entire world. I shall tell her to keep as much out of your way as possible."

This response left Morwenna floundering for a moment. But then she remembered her original point. "Your mother? I don't give a jot for her. No – it's what she's doing. That's what I will not tolerate."

"But she is simply producing a catalogue of the contents of the house."

"You must think me utterly simple!"

"And you must think me very devious if you suppose there's any more to it than that. I can't stand the woman and I wanted her out of my house. I suggested she go away and be a matron at a boarding school but she wouldn't even consider it. This was the only other worthwhile and necessary employment I could think of for her."

Elizabeth's frankness unnerved Morwenna. She said, with a most untypical hesitation, "Well . . . if you have any thought of selling . . . if this catalogue has anything to do with some future auction . . ."

"Nothing is further from my intentions," Elizabeth assured her.

"Because they are heirlooms, you realize. They are part and parcel of the realty. Only the trustees may . . ."

"I understand perfectly," she interrupted. Then, to keep up the attack, "Or did you imagine I'd sent my mother in there to spy on you?"

From the discomfort in the other's eyes she saw she was right. A weariness overcame her. "And I had hoped," she said, turning away, "now that the legal processes are so far behind us, and now you can see I haven't bankrupted the estate . . . I had hoped we might begin to mend our relationship."

She turned back and saw that her words had touched something within the older woman. Her spirit sagged. She didn't actually want the Dragon for a friend; she would much prefer the coolness between them to last out their lives. But for the sake of the estate she was ready to build a few bridges. Thinking to hammer home the last nail of her argument she added, "Don't you think it's what Bill would have wished for us – must still be wishing, wherever he is now?"

Morwenna bridled at once. Her nostrils flared, a bitter gleam filled her eyes. "How *dare* you say that!" she thundered. "You have done the very opposite of everything Bill would have wished . . . you grasped the reins from my hands – knowing it was Bill himself who placed them there. I may not have won the legal fight but the moral victory is mine! Ask anyone hereabouts with the slightest respect for the old traditions – they'll tell you! You can't even judge a good Troy from a bad'un! How else could you have turned yourself into the harlot of this . . . this . . ."

Elizabeth clenched her fists. She was closer to killing than at any time in her life. "You had better go, Miss Troy. Your temper and character are every bit as vile as Bill warned me to expect."

Morwenna's hand shot out and fell with a stinging slap across her cheeks. At once tears sprang to Elizabeth's eyes. She came within an ace of blurting out that Bill had put it all in writing to Haskins, but she contained herself in time and said, "Just go, will you."

Halfway down the passage Morwenna turned back and shouted, "And if you believe the legal processes are over – let me tell you, they have hardly begun!"

Such a leaden heaviness now overcame Elizabeth that she could not stir — until Morwenna, by then outside the front door, chose to repeat at the top of her voice the word that had wounded Elizabeth so. "Harlot!" she shrieked.

She roused herself then and hastened to the door; but the Dragon must have made equal haste to her pony and trap, which drove away as Elizabeth came hot-foot outside.

"Harlot!" The cry rang out once more as she passed Zakky Gilbert.

Oenone appeared at that moment. The look on her mistress' face appalled her.

"Thank heavens we keep the shotgun under lock and key," Elizabeth told her.

"There's a way to smother a body in their bed that'd never show."

Elizabeth laughed, though she knew Oenone was, as always, quite serious.

"That brother o' mine, he'll tell'ee. He heard it off of . . . well, a man he once met. He could show'ee."

Elizabeth shook her head and pointed heavenwards. "People like the Dragon are one very good reason for believing in *divine* justice, Oenone."

"Still — fancy 'er shouting *that* word at'ee!"

"I'd better go over and ask Zakky kindly to keep it to himself. He can't have helped overhearing."

But when she approached Zakky he gave her a conspiratorial nod. He almost winked. "I fixed she!" he said.

"You will? Or you already did?"

"Already did. Durn me if that pony don't slip his traces and run off home afore she do reach Pallas gates."

"She won't come to serious harm?"

"Only her pride, missis."

Some ten minutes later a bedraggled Morwenna walked in at Pallas gates to find her pony awaiting her, firmly held by Mrs. Mitchell.

"How lucky that I was here, Miss Troy," she said genially. "I only popped back to get my other spectacles."

Morwenna grunted uncertainly.

"Shall you take him back, the naughty fellow, and bring on the trap?"

"No. The gardener can do that. I'll tie him to the gate."

"We can give each other company back to the house," Mrs. Mitchell said cheerfully.

Morwenna did not trust herself to reply; but the other went on, "I hope my little lamb hasn't been saying things to put you out, Miss Troy." She sighed. "Though I'm her mother, I have to confess . . ."

"She certainly has no love lost for *you*!" Morwenna said.

Mrs. Mitchell was suddenly a monument of female patience and long-suffering. "Why is it? Aiee — why is it? One puts one's very lifeblood into rearing them . . . and little indeed are the thanks one gets."

"That's true," Morwenna said reluctantly.

"I don't know whether she's told you my story?" The question was hesitant.

"Your daughter and I, Mrs. Mitchell, are not on terms – as I'm sure you're very well aware."

"Then let me tell you." The voice was now breezy and full of confidence. "It will shock you, I know. Mr. Mitchell and I lavished every luxury on that ungrateful girl. I should think she had the best education of any woman in England. That is partly why we were left so poor when her dear father passed over. Oh, she had twisted him around her little finger!"

"She has that faculty, I'm sure. That's how she managed . . . well, well, never mind. Do go on."

"You would have thought, would you not, that any daughter with so much as a speck of filial gratitude . . . 'Filial' doesn't sound quite right."

"Never mind that! Go on, go on! I know just what you mean."

Mrs. Mitchell's smile was quite at odds with her tale. "You would have thought she'd have tried to repay her debt to us. But no – not in the tiniest degree. My idea, you see, was that we should start a small infant school with her as teacher and me as its matron. I should have loved that. I have always longed to be a school matron. But no. It was not to be. She upped and left me all alone in the world. There was nothing for it but she *would* be a nurse."

"Nurses meet doctors, of course. Nurses meet military gentlemen. Oh, I see it all now. I'm sorry – am I walking too fast for you, Mrs. Mitchell?"

"Just a little bit, dear. Well I, of course, could not possibly live on the little pittance my husband had left. I had to go to Italy to try to stretch it out, you see. And . . . well, a woman all alone in the world – with no experience of money or management . . . I've no need to tell you what happened. I was *fleeced*! They are such beasts, those foreign men."

"Oh, my dear Mrs. Mitchell – I am so sorry . . ."

"Naturally my desperate letters home were ignored. Not even opened, I should think. Until a kindly nun – an Anglican, I hasten to add – lent me the money to return to my daughter. And even then I had to beg her to let me stay down here. 'I'll do anything, my lamb,' I said. 'Cook for you . . . scrub floors. I've no pride left. My health is broken, my remaining days are few,' I said. 'Only let me stay with you the few years I have left . . .' But – it is not to be. I've been turned out into the servants' quarters, forced to earn my crust. I have no idea what her income may be . . ."

"Five thousand pounds at least," the Dragon said crisply. "And she's just raised it by another five hundred."

Mrs. Mitchell, who had expected to hear some figure in the region of a thousand, was shocked to a standstill – as Morwenna was swift to observe.

"Oh yes, Mrs. Mitchell! She's managed to filch one of the finest estates in Cornwall. For thirty years – and thirty of the leanest years this country's agriculture has ever known – I tended and built up this estate. Not for myself, you understand, but for my brother Bill, who was more of a son to me than anything. I could have married, and married well. I could have rank in my own right by now. But no – I stayed on here – nursed my mother through a long, lingering, and at last fatal illness, and then I brought up Bill as only a mother and sister combined could manage it. I tended Pallas for him. But" – her voice quavered – "he is not here to enjoy it."

"The ingratitude!" Mrs. Mitchell cried out.

Morwenna darted her a surprised glance.

"Well – he did deliberately leave it to *her*, didn't he?"

Morwenna was now in a quandary. It was not her own preferred explanation of Bill's action; but, on the other hand, she did not wish to fall out with someone who might yet turn into a most valued ally. She shrugged noncommittally. "I blame myself," she said. "Bill revered me. Unconsciously, you see, I suppose I must have taught him to trust and revere all women. He could not possibly have known that such . . ." She looked uncertainly at the other woman, who was obviously still smarting at the revelation of the size of Elizabeth's income.

"The self-seeking, avaricious little hussy!" Mrs. Mitchell said bitterly.

Morwenna smiled her triumph. "My poor Bill can have had no idea that such avarice might conceal itself within the sacred outer garments of womanhood."

"Five thousand five hundred pounds! And I must try to live on . . . on eighty! *And* pay a maid!"

Caution prompted Morwenna to warn, "Mind you, it isn't all clear spending money to her. There are small portions to come out of it for Miss Pettitoes, Mr. Oliver, and me – but very small by comparison. And, of course, she has to pay for the odd leaking roof and broken drain here and there about the estate." She gave up when she saw that her companion was barely listening. "I say," she went on, in an altogether more conciliatory tone. "I expect you'll feel lonely from time to time, there in the gatelodge. I do so hope you'll drop up to Pallas for a little chat whenever the mood takes you?"

CHAPTER THIRTY-SEVEN

LATE ONE EVENING, toward the end of August, Elizabeth received an urgent knock at the door. It was George Ivey, with a face as long as a wet week in Pengiggan. She took him through to the drawing room.

He looked all about them, like a conspirator, before he brought out a small object wrapped in tissue. "D'you recognize this?" he asked as he let the paper unroll.

It was a silver teaspoon. "That's the Troy crest," she said. "Yes, I believe there's a service of these over at Pallas. Why?"

"Are you sure it's there? When did you last see it?"

"Where did you get this?"

He closed his eyes, hating what he had to say. "The Chief Constable gave it to me. Poor fellow was crimson with embarrassment."

With sinking heart Elizabeth asked, "When?"

"Half an hour ago. I came straight here."

"Tell me everything you know."

"Have you a brandy? Whisky? Anything."

She poured him a brandy and waited. He sat down on the arm of a chair and passed his hand over his brow. "I can't believe it," he began.

"Well, until you tell me . . ."

"The spoon is part of a complete place setting brought to him by — well, name no names — let's say a respected jeweller and silversmith in Truro. He said it was left for appraisal by a lady in her fifties who gave her name as Mrs. Brown. She said she could let him have the complete service if his price were right. He knew the crest well, of course — and at once asked her how she'd come by something belonging to the Troys. The question plainly shocked her but she covered herself cleverly, saying it wasn't actually her but the Troys themselves who were thinking of selling. She added that they desired no advertisement of the fact. She even gave her true name then."

Elizabeth sat down heavily. "Mrs. Mitchell?" she asked, hoping against hope.

"I'm afraid so, Mrs. Troy. She said *you* are the one who is seeking to sell!"

Leaving him to finish his brandy and find his own way out, she stormed from the house and went directly to her mother – who took one look at her expression and broke into a broad smile, "Hello, dear, how lovely to see you, I was just about to pop over to Wheal Lavender and then I thought no it's rather late, only I think I may have done something just a teeny bit foolish."

"Go on," Elizabeth told her, but she already knew it was useless. Her mother had had hours, if not days, to prepare her explanation. And here it was, pat as butter, seamless as wet paint: "You remember I was saying that any one room at Pallas was worth more than the entire estate?"

"Well?"

"Well, I had a feeling you didn't believe me. So I said to myself, I said, I'll show her. So I took a single place setting to Webber's in Truro. Not one of the best silver settings, you understand – I deliberately took one of the poorer ones, just to show you." She screwed up her face as if in pain. "And d'you know, I spoke to the stupidest man. I don't think he grasped a single word of what I was saying. I think he believes I was trying to steal it and sell it for myself!" She laughed uproariously.

Elizabeth did not join in. "I'll tell you how stupid he was, Mother – he went directly to the Chief Constable, who happens to be an acquaintance of his, and the Chief Constable came directly to George Ivey, who of course came directly to me. And if you are stupid enough to try such a thing ever again, I'll tell you now – and please, please believe this – no one will be stupid enough to credit such a tale twice. Least of all me. Is that understood?"

"I can't think what you mean, dear. What a wicked, wicked man, to go and do a thing like that."

Elizabeth closed her eyes. "Stop this, mother. Just don't say another word, or you might even start believing it." She handed over the spoon. "Go to Truro tomorrow and recover the rest of the setting – and try to be a little more plausible with Mr. Webber than you have been with me."

"Oh, but I couldn't."

"You must. Don't you see? If you don't go back, if we are left to sweep it under the carpet, then the whole county will know for certain."

Mrs. Mitchell still looked dubious but offered no further argument.

"And Mother" – Elizabeth turned to go – "there is honestly no time in my life for incidents like this. One more, just one more, and you are *out!* You may think I don't mean it, but just don't put it to the test."

"Such ingratitude!" Mrs. Mitchell called after her.

Fury almost halted Elizabeth; she paused and drew breath – ready to shout that she'd a good mind to make her go back to Italy and return all the bric-a-brac she'd stolen there, too. But she managed to quell the impulse. Where was the point? She breathed out and continued back down the road to Wheal Lavender.

She was surprised to find George Ivey still in the drawing room. "If there's any brandy left," she said, "you may pour me some." As he obeyed she went on, "Oh, what am I to do with that woman!"

"She's not unique, you know. You'd be surprised if I told you the names of some of the grand ladies of the neighbourhood, who, if they weren't so grand, would be in gaol for pilfering."

"Really? You're not just saying that?"

He passed her brandy. "They have five guineas in their purses and they get caught taking something worth tuppence! However, the shock of being caught is usually enough. You'll probably hear no more about it."

"Well, my thanks to *you* anyway. How are things with you and Lilian?"

He stared into his glass. She wondered if he'd heard. At last he said, "I think I need your advice, actually, Mrs. Troy."

"I find 'Lilian' and 'Mr. Ivey' a bit strange, and it's going to seem even stranger when you're married. I realize we've only known each other a couple of years but, in the circumstances, don't you think we might start using our first names?" She toasted him with her glass. "George?"

He smiled and returned the toast: "Elizabeth. Or Beth – d'you mind?"

She shook her head and waited.

"How much," he asked, "are we obliged to remain that person which our behaviour has always led others to believe we in fact are – even though we may actually be someone quite different?"

She laughed. "It sounds like a nonsense poem from *Alice* – 'They all came back from me to you though they were mine before.'"

"No, I'm serious."

"Could you say it again – or put it another way?"

He pushed his glass from him. "Well, we all have certain patterns of behaviour, right? I go into my office every day. There's a plate outside telling the world I'm a solicitor. People drop in with their legal requirements or troubles and I do my best to satisfy them . . . etcetera, etcetera. To all the world I *am* a solicitor."

"And aren't you? You're not trying to confess you're a fraud, George?"

She thought he would laugh but he looked at her oddly and replied, "I'm not sure."

"You have qualified?"

"Oh yes – if I am a fraud, it's not at that simple level." He touched his forehead. "It's in here. Or" – he lowered his hand to his heart – "here."

"Ah!"

"Don't you ever feel like that?" he asked. "In the middle of fussing about the Pallas Estate and Morwenna and all your other daily preoccupations, don't you ever catch yourself thinking, *What on earth am I doing here?* Isn't there part of you that's convinced you were really meant to be – I don't know – a femme fatale? Or off with the raggle-taggle gipsies-oh?"

Her mind had leaped ahead of him, expecting him to give her the alternative of being a nurse or a wife and mother. The choices he actually offered were so close to the truth, the secret truth she believed no one could guess, that she was thrown into confusion; it was too obvious, and then too late, to deny it. "How did you know?" she asked.

"Thank God!" He relaxed and smiled gratefully. "If you'd denied it, there'd have been no point in talking any further – except the usual platitudes. The gist of my rather clumsy opening question is that I'm not sure how much longer I can go on being a solicitor – and where does that leave me and Lilian?"

"What's your equivalent of a *femme fatale?*"

"The only thing I truly want to do is paint. I feel . . ."

"Heavens – I should have guessed that!"

"You see, Lilian loves me. But the *me* she loves is a solicitor. He has prospects – a fairly assured income – a position in Society. The *me* I want to be has none of those things."

"And you're afraid she might stop loving you?"

He shook his head vehemently. "Exactly the reverse. I'm sure she wouldn't. But what right have I, after courting her as one person, to turn into another?"

"Give her the choice. She can always say no."

After a silence he said, "These things always look so easy from outside."

She decided to risk a confidence. "I don't know whether I ought to tell you this or not, George, but I think you'll find Lilian rather *un*surprised at the news."

He was suddenly all attention. "What has she said?"

"Nothing specific. But – oh, it must be a year ago at least – she said you're like two people. Something about if you died the artists would leave you for the lawyers to bury and the lawyers would say no, you belong among the artists."

"She said that?"

"She told me she'd said it to *you!*"

He shook his head. "She must have tried it out on you and then lost her nerve. I often do that with my court speeches." But the news bucked him up enormously. "Perhaps I will tell her, then."

"If you like – seeing that she's already half-broached the subject with me – I could do a bit of discreet sounding-out?"

"I'd be very grateful."

"Shall we go on a picnic? Next week perhaps?"

"That sounds spiffing. Where?"

"What about Land's End? I've lived here more than two years and never been beyond Newlyn. Isn't that scandalous?"

"I'll clear a day and let you know."

"And could I bring David Troy?"

He looked at her uncertainly.

"What's the matter?" she asked.

"How much does he mean to you, Beth?"

"Quite a lot, actually."

He shrugged.

The gesture annoyed her. "I can't think why people take against him so. You don't know him. He's quite different when you get to know him."

"Different from what?"

"From the public person. Anyway, you can't judge him by ordinary standards. He is a most extraordinary man. What have you got against him?"

George weighed his answer carefully. "Since you speak so highly of him, Beth, I must, of course, suspend judgement until I know him better. I look forward to our picnic on that account, too – now. But I'll tell you this. I know many people who admire the public David Troy, who support him, who will vote for him when the time comes, who will go out of their way to advance his career – and yet I do not know one who likes or admires the *man*. I say no more. Make what you will of that." As an afterthought he asked, "What does Courtenay Rodda think of him?"

"He's the same," she admitted reluctantly. "But you're all wrong."

"Let's hope so."

She saw him to the door. He tilted his head and gave a little smile. "I must say I expected quite different advice from you this evening. I thought you'd tell me I've set my hand to the plough and must now till the furrow to the bitter end."

"Is that the sort of person I seem?"

"Didn't you once tell me – the worst thing about making a choice is all the *other* choices that are then excluded?"

"Obviously I was wrong." She did not want to pursue this line of thought. "Why not start a new life each Monday! Let me know when it's your turn to be parson – I'll burn your ears off with some confessions I've been saving."

He laughed, somewhat dutifully. "Seriously, Beth – this idea that you've got to plough your chosen furrow to the bitter end – it's no basis for a marriage. Not for me. And certainly not for you."

She grasped him by the shoulders and faced him toward the dark beyond the door. "You're turning into a dangerous man, George. You have the spirit of the new artist – and all the subtlety of the old lawyer."

Thinking she could not see his face, he did not even bother to smile as he turned up his collar and set off down the path. When he was a few paces away she called after him.

He paused unwillingly and glanced back over his shoulder.

She added, "I do take what you say seriously."

It pleased him. She went on: "And thank you for your tact *in re* Mitchell."

"It's what friends are for."

"Still – one can't cash cheques on that bank too often. I hope I've made her understand that."

CHAPTER THIRTY-EIGHT

MORWENNA OFTEN PAUSED to admire the thoroughness with which Mrs. Mitchell was working her way through the treasures of Pallas. Most people would have been happy enough to record, for instance, that there was one medium-sized horse picture by Stubbs above the drawing room fire; but Mrs. Mitchell would set down the size, both with frame and without, the medium, and the base. She made a note if a canvas had been relined, or if there were cracks in the underpainting or a bloom upon the glaze. She searched among Sir William's surviving correspondence, and the stewards' books of his day, for the seller's name and the date of acquisition.

It was the same when she catalogued a book. She looked at every page and noted those that were foxed; she recorded defects in the bindings; she made sure every illustration was present and unblemished.

"You'll be at it for years," Morwenna said.

"I expect so," was the happy reply.

Naturally, she had to confer with Hamill a great deal, for he knew the names of every painter, and the history of most of the pieces of furniture. He was delighted, not just to be consulted but to see what an apt pupil she made – considering how little she had known when she first arrived. He never needed to tell her a name twice, or a date, or a style. For instance, there was a little Zuccarelli landscape on one of the upstairs landings, which he identified for her as Picturesque-Pastoral. Weeks later she came across a Vernet in one of the bedrooms and had no hesitation in identifying it, too, as Picturesque-Pastoral. He had never known anyone with a mind so swiftly attentive and absorbent.

She was so interested in all his old Celtic lore, too. He found her quite captivating. In short, she became a new sort of cement in that little community, holding together what had previously been fragmented.

"How I wish Bill were here to see you at work, my dear," Morwenna said on one occasion.

Mrs. Mitchell noticed that she often spoke of Bill; it was as if his memory could not be laid to rest. "Bill would have wished . . ." and "Bill would have approved . . ." were Morwenna's most common justifications for her own desires and actions.

The younger folks' outing to Land's End was fixed for Saturday. George and the two women set off in high spirits, catching the 7.55am train from Helston to the main line at Gwinear Road. There they had a brief wait until the down train to Penzance, where David was to meet them.

"I say, Beth," George exclaimed as they promenaded about, "there's a tale going the rounds in Helston . . . is it true? They say you formed a Black Star Club at school."

"What's a Black Star Club?" Lilian asked.

Elizabeth's vexation answered him. "I suppose my mother has been talking."

"What's a Black Star Club?"

"Just some childish nonsense."

"Oh come on! Don't be a spoilsport."

"Well, when I was at school I was sick of never getting any Gold Stars for good deportment, so I devised a merit scheme of my own for *bad* deportment. It was just a small club to start with but somehow the idea took hold and then the whole school joined, except for a few teachers' pets – who naturally split on us to Old Deathshead, our headmistress."

George laughed and said to Lilian, "Can you believe it – our Beth!"

"How did it work?"

Elizabeth answered wearily. "It doesn't matter now. It was a long-long time ago. My mother was very bitter about it because . . . well, it got me expelled."

Lilian gasped. "Elizabeth Troy – *expelled?*"

"I suppose that's going the rounds, too?"

"Well, I think it's absolutely splendid!" Lilian said. "Do tell us how it worked?"

"I'm not proud of it now." Against her will she grinned. "Actually, my father – years later, mind you – my father told me it was the funniest thing he'd ever heard. Not that he showed it at the time."

"Please, Beth!"

"Oh, it was just the opposite of the Gold Star system. I awarded a Black Star to any girl who was rude or beastly to a teacher, or got caught with dirty fingernails, or . . . Mind you, I didn't give them out for *really* beastly things like cruelty to cats or being unkind to the servants." She sighed. "So now the whole of Helston knows! Oh, what am I to do with my mother?"

George cleared his throat. "That rather depends on how many other skeletons still rattle away in your private cupboard."

The train drew into the station and they climbed aboard. Being a main-line local, it boasted no corridors; they had the compartment to themselves. George and Lilian tried to wheedle more confessions from her but she stared resolutely out of the window and they soon gave up. There was a nervous edge to Lilian's good humour, as if she were determined that today was going to be *fun* even if it killed her.

In the dozen or so miles to Penzance they passed a handful of mine workings, all abandoned, some already derelict. But between Long Rock and the terminus, where the track skirts the seashore, the market gardens on the landward side were bustling with labourers, all busy hoeing, thinning, planting, harvesting. An omen? Elizabeth wondered. A warning to her about the money she was throwing at Pallas Consols – and therefore *not* investing in the farms?

The new adit through the old Wheal Fortune mine was complete and had already helped cut her bill for coals. But the new exploratory shaft below the 180 Level was quickly gobbling up any savings. If they didn't find substantial new reserves of metal soon, she'd have to abandon all new work and concentrate on mining out the already discovered lodes. For his own sake she hoped Courtenay found nothing at Little Tregathennan. As George had once said: "When the gods will destroy a man, they first let him find tin."

The train arrived at Penzance a little late, at a quarter-past nine. David was waiting for them. Elizabeth watched the other two closely for signs of antipathy but saw none. David had already been to the livery stable and collected their transport for the day, an open landau drawn by a matched pair of fine chestnut geldings.

"Very smart!" George ran admiring hands over the lacquered panels. "I wouldn't mind owning that one myself. I bet she'll *go*."

As if he had taken the comment as a challenge, David grasped the reins and set off up Market Jew Street at a cracking pace. At the approach to the Market House they drew level with a young groom, out on some errand in a sleek little fly.

"Bet he makes the far side of the square before us," George murmured.

David's grip tightened on the reins.

"Stop it, George!" Elizabeth said crossly.

George looked at her, all innocence.

Both vehicles had to pause at the edge of the square to let a dray cross in front of them. The fly would be first with a clear way, so George looked set to win his bet. Then David leaned across and said to the groom, "I may be mistaken, young man, but I believe there's a crack in your tyre on this side."

The youngster thanked him profusely – and David was able to saunter across the square and confound George's prophecy.

"Such juveniles," Lilian said.

The two men laughed. Anyone would have thought they were old chums.

The road to Land's End runs ten miles, slightly south of west. To its north are the severe, treeless uplands of the peninsula, so hostile to agriculture that dozens of Ancient British sites – stone circles, burial places, and even the odd village or two – have survived the millennia. To the south the land is lower, more sheltered, deeply scored by lush, fertile valleys. At about the halfway mark the four made a brief detour to Boscawen-un, a circle of nineteen stones, some no higher than a footstool, ranged around a central stone, taller than a man – the Nine Maidens, as they are called.

"Hard to believe they were once flesh and blood," George said with a sidelong glance at David. "As hale and hearty as you and me."

"Fairly tales!" Lilian said scornfully.

"A parable," David offered as a polite correction.

"I don't know the story," Elizabeth said.

George explained, "They say these were nine maidens and a fiddler who went dancing on the sabbath and got turned to stone for their sins – together, it would seem, with at least ten unlucky bystanders. Mr. Troy used to preach a fine sermon on it, if he doesn't mind my saying so."

Elizabeth wanted to ask David if he really believed such nonsense, but that was exactly what George was hoping for, of course.

David smiled at George. "A preacher is God's advocate," he said. "Do *you* believe every tale your clients may tell in court?"

George had to laugh. "You'll do," he said – the exact words that Courtenay had once used, and in circumstances that were not entirely dissimilar.

Lilian skipped a few steps, weaving in and out of the stones. "It must have been a clumsy, clodhopping sort of dance on *this* turf."

George tried another tack: "The connection between sin and being turned to living stone is ancient and universal," he mused. "Think of the Medusa, for instance, or Sleeping Beauty, or Snow White."

Elizabeth, sensing that a disguised skirmish about religion was in the offing, headed them off: "It's always a beautiful maiden," she pointed out. "And she's always woken with a kiss from a handsome prince. Why is it always the women who get frozen?"

"Well . . ." David cleared his throat.

"Ah . . ." George began – and faltered.

Lilian laughed. "Go and kiss one of them, George! Let's see what sort of prince you make."

He danced away in obedience, not to say relief.

Nothing happened of course.

"You're not handsome enough," Elizabeth sneered.

"Or pure enough in spirit," David suggested.

"It didn't work on Lot's wife, either," George reminded him. "So I'm in good company."

As they made their way back to the carriage, David said, "Can you think of a worse punishment than being forced to stand immobile until the end of time, enduring numberless visits by parties of day tourists with their feeble wit and their inane chatter? Imagine wanting to scream out the dire warning that you above all are now most qualified to utter."

George looked up at the sky and said, "The defence changes its plea to guilty, m'lud, and offers no evidence."

"D'you miss preaching, Mr. Troy?" Lilian asked.

They all laughed; even David had to join in.

They made one more short detour before Land's End, through Escoll and along the road to Sennen Cove. They did not go all the way down into the village but stayed up near the clifftop for a view of the aptly named Whitesand Bay – almost two miles long, a gleaming sickle, blinding in the August sun, fringing the dark, disordered mining country around St. Just.

"We could come over here for a swim later," George suggested. "It looks calm enough."

"The mines certainly aren't being knocked here," Elizabeth commented. Every chimney in sight was belching smoke.

"What's that in the water?" Lilian asked, pointing toward the Sennen Cove end of the bay.

There was a blush of deep pink a little way offshore, as if a giant oyster lay open on the seabed.

"Mullet," David told her. "Red mullet. They fatten there all summer and then the Cove fishermen catch them with a seine net and draw them up on the beach. 'Tis some burr and brave old sight, they do say."

"I'd love to see it," Elizabeth told him.

"We'll have to come back at the end of summer then."

"I wonder are those mullet, too?" George was pointing farther out into the bay, where a shimmer of silver played beneath the waves.

"That's pilchard, surely!" David said excitedly. "They could net them today. Let's see what they're going to do about it."

A lane led off to the left, keeping to the ridge all the way along Mayon Cliff to the coastguard station, about a mile north of Lands End itself. Into this lane he now turned the horses, not to seek out the coastguard but to find the huer's hut, from which any seine-netting of the pilchard would be directed. Sure enough, the huer himself was there – together, it seemed, with every fisherman in Sennen Cove and most of their wives and children. A fierce debate was raging.

Elizabeth was by now fairly used to the local dialect – local to Helston, that is. Now she was astonished to find she could grasp only one word in twenty of the Land's End Cornish – and even that with difficulty. David went over to talk to the huer and came back with a report.

"It's a real embarrassment of riches! If they go after the pilchard, they might frighten away the mullet, which are far more valuable. If they do nothing, the pilchard may drive the mullet out anyway. Or the pilchard might go on to some other bay. The Cove would never hear the last of it if Pendeen or Porthgwarra got 'their' shoal of pilchard."

"So what are they going to do?"

"They have to beach the catch at high tide, to get it as far above the water as possible. It'll be high tide in an hour, so they're too late for that. They can do nothing until this evening, except watch and pray."

"But tomorrow's Sunday," Lilian said.

"That's the other difficulty. If the fish aren't beached before midnight . . . one of those fellows is trying to argue that the Lord's Day doesn't begin until sunrise."

"A true Celt," George said. "Old Hamill Oliver would be proud of him."

"I've no patience with it," Elizabeth said.

David looked at her in surprise.

"Well – that shoal could make all the difference between starvation and ease for the entire Cove this winter."

George, in a voice ringing with insincerity, said, "The Lord's Day is the Lord's Day, and a Commandment is a Commandment." As an afterthought, avoiding David's eye, he added, "But voters are voters."

A group of the fishermen approached David, having recognized him as a well-known preacher. They canvassed his opinion.

Elizabeth, pointing at the children, said, "Aren't they beautiful little things."

David smiled fondly at George. "There's no dilemma." He turned to the other two. "What do the ladies say?"

Elizabeth looked out across the bay, at the shimmer of silver beneath the rollers. "What would be the total value?" she asked.

The fishermen stared at the spot hungrily and shook their heads, unwilling to set a price on what they might have to forfeit.

She tried again. "How many barrels?"

"Why . . . four-five hundred, salted and packed."

"And what would the Newlyn merchants pay you per barrel?"

"Thirty-five shilling salted. But he could be forty-two in oil – if we got 'nuff oil, see?"

"So there might be as much as a thousand pounds swimming around out there?"

They wet their lips and looked unhappily to David.

"What does your own minister say?" she asked.

"He's ailing in Penzance infirmary, poor old fellow."

Still David said nothing.

"Well, Mr. Troy?" one man prompted.

David put a hand on the fellow's shoulder. "If you want me to say 'Fish!' or 'Don't fish!' then I cannot answer you. But what I can tell you is this: You must not put barriers between yourselves and God. Don't place me there – nor any other preacher."

But they were not to be put off so easily. "What would you do if you was us?" one asked immediately.

George chuckled.

David said smoothly, "I'd read carefully the Fourth Commandment – Deuteronomy, Four, Twelve. But I'd also study the words of Our Lord in Mark, Two – the sabbath was made for man, not man for the sabbath. Also do not forget Luke, Chapter Five – the miraculous draft of fishes, when, *after* they had caught so many fish that the boat almost sank, Simon Peter fell at Christ's knees and said, 'Depart from me for I am a sinful man.' And Jesus said, 'Come with me and I will make you fishers of men.' Our Lord has not lost the power to teach us through parables. These are the ways He speaks to us still. After a miraculous draft of fishes might not you, sinners all, also become His fishers of men?"

They still wanted some final reassurance, but all he said was, "You asked my opinion. That is the best I can say. Now you must each do as conscience dictates. Never appoint another to stand between you and God. That is the false and easy way of the papists."

They left him and went back to their debate, which raged as furiously as if he had not spoken.

David caught George's eye and said, "It's hard to let go of an absolute."

Whatever George had been about to say, he now thought better of it.

They heard the huer ask one of his mates to prepare torches of rag and pitch, so it looked as if the consensus was drifting in favour of taking the catch.

They turned the carriage about and made their way back to the main road at Sennen village. From there it was a mile – and a long one it seemed – to Land's End itself. Elizabeth was so eager to see the pilchard being netted that night she persuaded the others to stay, too, no matter how late it might go on. They could surely find a room for the night somewhere, and they could manage a bit of sleep during the afternoon or evening.

The first and last cape in England was not as imagination had painted it, nor as any landscape designer with a sense of drama would have arranged it. In fact, were it not for a faded wooden noticeboard picking out the particular headland, they could have argued all afternoon as to which one of half a dozen tongues of land was the most westerly. The neighbouring cliffs are over two-hundred feet high, but Land's End itself rears a scant sixty above the sea – a meagre tongue of grass between two great sheltering wings of cliffs. It denies the visitor any sense of standing on Cornwall's final inch, with the English Channel to the south and the mighty Atlantic all before him.

"The farthest, wildest shore in England," Lilian said.

"It's not very wild today," Elizabeth commented.

They stared across the littered sea to the Longships lighthouse. The water was so calm it was hard to imagine the fury that could imprison the keepers there for weeks on end.

Elizabeth sought the horizon, lost in the heat haze. "Where are the Scillies?" she asked.

"If you can see them, they say it's a sign of bad weather," David told her.

The women found a sheltered spot, out of the sun, and spread their blankets. The men hobbled the horses and left them to graze while they brought down the picnic hamper. There was wine and mineral water. David poured a little of each into his own glass; then he caught Elizabeth watching him and he smiled.

"Half-and-half decisions," she said.

"The worst of both worlds," David said, looking hopefully at George.

But George seemed to have made up his mind to cease his provocations.

Their conversation ranged in a desultory way over a hundred topics, from the myriad colours of the sea to the latest Helston gossip, taking in such peripheral matters as the Irish Problem and Modern French Painting on the way.

After the meal David and George went to check on the horses; then they called down to say they'd just walk along the cliffs to Sennen Cove, to see what the fishermen had decided.

"Shall we see if we can get down to the water?" Lilian asked. "I think there's a way down in the next little cove."

Elizabeth rose and followed her. She wasted no time. "How are things between you and George?" she asked.

CHAPTER THIRTY-NINE

THE WAY DOWN to the ocean led past banks of marine holly and fernfew, wild madder and sea rocket. Where a feeble spring broke out of the sloping grass, dense clumps of bog myrtle sheltered clusters of centaury and pennyroyal. The seeping green water, heated by the sun, filled the air with a spicy languor. Overhead a solitary chough, the "Cornish blackbird," gave out its plaintive mew, spanning the silence by which Lilian chose to answer Elizabeth's question.

"Once when we came down here," Lilian said, "I sat among a whole crowd of seals, sunning themselves on the rocks. They're so tame."

"I don't mean to pry," Elizabeth told her.

Lilian said no more until they had reached the rocks. The smell of rotting seaweed was pungent yet somehow clean. No seals sunned themselves today.

Elizabeth waited.

"What do *you* think of George?" Lilian asked. "I mean, how would you describe him?"

"He's a good lawyer."

"Not that! You know what I mean."

"You described him to me once, Lilian. A solid sort of man to whom you could give a family and then devote yourself to discreet but passionate affairs while he pursued his career."

Lilian sighed.

"Isn't he going to oblige?"

She shook her head uncertainly and then shrugged.

"So, how would you describe him now?" Elizabeth persisted.

"He's impossible. He wants us to go to Paris for our honeymoon."

"How very unconventional!"

"Yes, but he's not interested in the Eiffel Tower and the Bois de Boulogne. He wants to spend all our time in Montmartre, in the cafés, talking to painters, watching them work, listening to their conversations."

"Wouldn't you like that?"

With a vicious tug Lilian plucked a handful of seaweed from the rock. "It's always the way, isn't it? The murderer never looks like the evil, wild-eyed maniac in the penny dreadfuls. In real life he's the sweet, inoffensive little man down on the beach whom you'd ask to keep an eye on your children while you go and buy a magazine."

Elizabeth laughed. "Not that I see any comparison!"

"I do love him, though," Lilian added.

"But not the love-is-blind sort of love."

Lilian stared at her, almost accusingly. "You're a fine one to talk!"

"Me?"

"Oh ho ho – such innocence! You and David Troy."

Elizabeth bridled. "What have you all got against him?"

"I don't know exactly." Lilian shrugged. "But you yourself once said . . ."

"That was a long time ago. I've learned to know him a lot better since then. I don't think people realize what a hard time he's had. I don't just mean the usual struggle for a poor boy with brains and ambition, but . . ."

"He's certainly not short of ambition!"

"Yes – thank heavens. But I mean the struggle to escape from the narrowness of his earlier beliefs. It can't be easy, especially when he's spent so many years preaching them to all the world. Yet he's managed it without becoming cynical or hypocritical."

"Oh, he's quite frank about it!" Lilian agreed heavily.

"Why do so many people despise a poor man who makes a success of things? I should have thought you and Courtenay, above all, would have been more sympathetic – yet you are as beastly about him as I've heard *other* stupid people be beastly about your parents. David is no more successful than they are."

Lilian stared at the ground.

A handful of smooth pebbles littered the rocks where they sat; some were almost polished. Elizabeth stooped to gather a few, then walked a pace or so to the brink of a small creek. The rise and fall of the water was exaggerated by the swirl of the seaweed – long, kelpy strands that beckoned her in. One by one she tossed the stones into the water, watching them shimmer as they fell erratically to the seabed, a fathom or two below. "I'm going to change into my costume," she said.

"We always used to swim bareskin."

They retired beneath an overhanging arch of rock. Despite its shelter Elizabeth looked up from time to time, still half-expecting to see a man with binoculars . . .

"I don't really despise David's success," Lilian said. "Nor his ambition. It's just that – well, as you yourself once said – there's *something* about him one just can't pin down."

"He seems to have won George over."

Lilian's laughter had a strange edge to it. "If David had been a woman, I think I'd have been quite jealous."

Elizabeth distantly remembered having had the same feeling when David had won Courtenay over. She said, "Any good politician must have a touch of the chameleon about him." She turned to face Lilian. "At least the changes in David are all on the surface. You can't say he keeps them to himself."

Lilian knew she was driving at George. She asked, "Has George said anything to you?"

"What about?"

"Me . . . the future . . . anything like that?"

Elizabeth sighed. "As a matter of fact, he has. I don't think I was supposed to tell you, but I caught him in a weak moment after several brandies and, well, out it all came. He's desperately unhappy about hurting you."

"He wants to call it off," Lilian said despondently. "I knew it."

"On the contrary. I think it's going to break his heart, but he believes the only honourable thing is to release you from your vows." And she went on to tell Lilian the whole story.

They walked out into the full sunlight again. Elizabeth piled her hair on top of her head and secured it in one of the picnic napkins.

At last Lilian said, "Call me timid, Beth, but I don't think I have the courage to face that kind of life."

Elizabeth nodded. "I don't think I would, either. George is mad to give up a good career. You should talk him out of it."

"I just feel numb. Do we have to stay and watch this pilchard fishing? I'd rather go home." She sat at the water's edge and tied the drawstrings around her ankles.

"Of course not — we'll go straight home." Elizabeth sat on the opposite side of the little rocky cleft from Lilian and lowered her legs into the sea; it was *freezing*.

"What about you and David?" Lilian asked. "Are you going to marry him?"

The heat of the sun on her black costume only made the cold seem colder.

"I don't know. I shan't know until he asks me."

Lilian gazed at her admiringly. "I wish I could live like that."

"Take the plunge," Elizabeth laughed, and, before she could change her resolve, she slid into the water, turning so as to grip the edge and keep her head from going under. The cold drew forth a scream, which petered out in a series of shivering groans.

"Thank you!" Lilian said. "That's going to make it so easy for me." She submerged her feet and winced.

"You can't just dip your toe into life." Elizabeth grinned. "There are some things you can't do bit by bit." The cold was now beginning to burn every inch of her skin came alive.

"I *know*!" Lilian snarled as she went on slowly immersing herself, catching her breath and whimpering.

"It's lovely, actually," Elizabeth told her.

"Damn you!" Lilian pulled up her legs, which were wet only to her knees.

"Oh, this blissful sun!" She began to rub life back into her toes. "Look — they're blue!"

"I'm going to swim out to that little rock."

"Don't leave me," Lilian pleaded.

"Swim out and join me." When Elizabeth reached the rock she pulled herself up and turned shorewards. Her skin was now glowing with exhilaration. "Do come on!" she cajoled.

But still Lilian havered at the brink. "I need time."

Elizabeth slipped back into the water. "I'll have had just about enough when you're ready to come in."

"I may not go in at all. It's nice enough to have shed all that whalebone."

There was a sudden, explosive sort of groan in the water behind Elizabeth. She looked beyond the rock and saw what she at first took to be a dog's head, in silhouette against the reflected sunlight — a fat, sleek, smooth-haired dog; then she realized it was a seal. It was as surprised as she was terrified. "What do I do, what do I do?" she almost screamed at Lilian — who laughed and, at last, launched herself into the water.

"They're pets," she called out as she swam.

"Is it a he or a she?"

"Which would you prefer?"

The seal vanished so smoothly it left no ripples. There was something devilish in its disappearance; Elizabeth caught a wicked glint in its eye. Pure panic gripped her. She scrabbled wildly at the rock. Tiny barnacles, less than a quarter of an inch across, covered every available inch like a scrofulous disease. They scraped away some skin on her arm. She did not notice the blood until she was out of the water and standing precariously on the minute plateau that the tide had laid bare.

The bright scarlet was like a shout against the black of her costume and the blues and greens and browns of the sea. But it was only a graze, and the flow was swiftly stanched.

The seal broke surface again a hundred yards farther out to sea.

"Whatever it is that attracts them," Lilian said, "we don't seem to have it. Does that arm hurt?"

Elizabeth shook her head. "Too cold." She looked minutely at the roughened skin, so devoid of feeling it seemed not to belong to her.

She glanced once more at the seal, who was now staring out to sea. Relieved, she slipped back into the water. "It's a warning," she said with mock solemnity.

"What?"

"This little graze. One can hurt oneself more by running from one's fears than by facing them."

"You'll make a good preacher's wife, Beth."

Laughing, they began to swim a sedate circuit of the pool roughly defined by the rock and the tapering sides of the inlet. "What d'you actually *feel* about David?" Lilian asked.

"I don't know. Love, I suppose. Friendship. I distrust words. These are just words."

Lilian splashed her. "You're a splendid woman to talk to."

"Well – I feel different things at different times. Sometimes I'm filled with admiration for him . . . his principles. Other times I feel . . . well, that he's betraying them. With those fishermen, for instance, he should have come out and . . ."

"Beth!" Lilian almost yelled.

"What?" She looked around, as if some new danger threatened.

"No!" Lilian said in the same strangled scream. "When I say 'feel,' I'm not asking for a character reference – for heaven's sake. I mean what d'you *feel?* What does he do to your insides? I presume he's kissed you?"

"Of course." Elizabeth chuckled. "The first time was when we fell into the sea, after we were marooned on St. Michael's Mount by the tide and he carried me back over the causeway."

"Well?"

"I liked it. We'd just had a furious argument. I enjoy kissing him."

Lilian counted to ten. "You make it sound like boys and girls playing postman's knock!"

"Well, marriage isn't just kissing, you know. It's money and property and family alliances and . . . There's no doubt about one thing – I'd be a lot more secure in my tenure of Pallas if I were Mrs. David Troy, wife of the local member."

"Say no more! Pallas excuses *everything*, of course!"

"Well, in real life one can't afford to ignore such matters."

There was a sudden flurry of white water. To her horror she saw the seal break the surface a few feet beyond Lilian. It gave a great bark, almost like a laugh.

Then something sleek and cold brushed against her own leg. There must be a whole herd of seals in the little pool. She screamed and lashed out with her foot as hard as she could. Her heel connected with something firm and fleshy; then she was swallowing water and struggling to get back to the surface. She breathed and coughed and retched all at the same time as she dog-paddled furiously toward the edge of the rock.

Laughter, not her own, penetrated her panic. When she reached the shore she pulled herself out and turned – only to find that the "seal" near Lilian was, in fact, David.

"We swam round the point," he shouted. "Where's Ivey?"

She stared at him stupidly.

"He was going to give your toes a tweak."

Horrified, she gazed down into the water – and saw the body of a man – George, of course – drifting near the bottom.

Without thought she plunged in and fought her way down to him. Did she scream as she went? There was a relentless scream in her mind.

The depth was barely three fathoms. She was able to grip his body, get her feet beneath her, and give a mighty thrust on the shingle that carried them both swiftly to the surface.

David and Lilian were waiting, he in the water, she already out on the rocks. He slipped beneath George and gripped his apparently lifeless head in the classic lifesaver position. Elizabeth let go at once and swam to join Lilian, who helped her out.

She hardly had time to turn before David arrived; she was still coughing up salt but she managed to get hold of one arm and, with Lilian clutching the other and David pushing from below, they hoisted George up to the hard, sunbaked rock without grazing his skin on the barnacle crust.

He seemed horribly lifeless – no breath, no apparent pulse. But when she opened an eyelid, his pupil contracted.

"What do we do?" Lilian asked, hysteria beginning to edge into her voice.

"Get the water out of his lungs first," she answered, looking up at David. "Could you somehow hug his legs to your chest and stand up? Hold him upside down? We'll stop his head from hitting the rock."

It seemed like bucketfulls of seawater that poured from his slack mouth and nostrils. Elizabeth crouched behind David's legs and crushed George's chest to them; Lilian tried to join in from the side but Elizabeth shouted "No!"

A few yards away was a narrow strip of sand, so coarse as to be almost shingle, but even so it would be gentler than this barnacled rock. "Over there!" Elizabeth pointed.

Together they manhandled his still unbreathing body to the spot.

"Lie him face-down?" David asked.

"Yes. And then kneel astraddle and push against his ribs as hard as you can. Push and let go." She made sure George's head was in the right position and that his tongue was clear.

"You're just tickling him," she shouted at David. "I said *hard*!"

David looked up at her, uncertainly. "You do it. I'm afraid of breaking a rib."

"Stop arguing!" Lilian began to cry.

Elizabeth changed places and showed David what she meant by 'hard.' Then she stood up and made him continue.

She felt for a pulse but found none; there was still an eye reflex, though.

Lilian was becoming hysterical, babbling that it was all her fault. Desperately, Elizabeth racked her brains for something to occupy her.

"When I push, not much breath seems to come out," David said.

It gave Elizabeth an idea. She told Lilian to kneel down beside George, put her lips to his, and breathe into his mouth when David released the pressure on his ribs. *Better than nothing*, she told herself.

Lilian tried. "It just comes out of his nose," she said.

"Pinch it while you breathe."

After what seemed an age she felt the first huge thump of his reestablished pulse. For a while it was somewhat erratic but then there was no doubting its firmness.

"Stop a moment," she told the others.

He did not breathe spontaneously.

"We'll keep going," she said. "I've known it take quite a time. At least his pulse is regular."

Twice more they paused before George made his first spontaneous intake of breath. Their cheers woke him. He blinked against the daylight. They turned him on his side.

"Headache," he whispered.

Then he began to cough, moaning at the pains in his head.

"Sit him up?" David asked.

But George lurched on all fours, coughing great gouts of thready seawater.

For an hour they stayed there, with George alternately lying and kneeling to cough. There were cramps and fits of shivering – and then quite suddenly he seemed recovered. "Except that I still have the headache of all time," he complained.

Lilian bent and kissed him again. "You'll think us the most unfeeling monsters, darling, but we've never been so glad in our lives to hear anyone say anything so wonderful as that!"

"What happened?"

"You must have hit your head on a rock."

"No," Elizabeth said, and told them what had really happened.

"I remember!" he murmured. "Oh, it was an awful thought. Awful!"

"What was?" Lilian asked.

He shivered.

"We ought to get him up to the clifftop," Elizabeth said.

"I thought I'd die without . . ." He looked uncertainly at Lilian.

"I've been told," she said, gently inclining her head toward Elizabeth. "I suppose I knew it really."

"I have no choice," he said. "Not now that I know what it would be like to die without having tried."

"Could you manage it as far as the bottom of the path up the cliff?" Elizabeth asked.

His eyes did not leave Lilian's face. He said, "I'll manage it to the moon and back if you're with me."

She pulled him to his feet, put her arms about him and hugged him hard. "You're not the only one to be given a glimpse of life without the one thing in all the world that gives it any value," she said.

Elizabeth slipped her hand into David's. He gave her an answering squeeze.

There was a dwelling on the clifftop, the First and Last House, built as an inn though never used as such. The owner was away but the housekeeper, Mrs. Kitto, when she heard what had happened, allowed George to bed down there for the afternoon. Lilian kept vigil at his side.

Elizabeth and David went back to the cliffs, where they sat down on the soft turf. He lay back and almost at once fell asleep.

A great ease filled her. She had never seen such a profusion of wildflowers; within a few feet of where she sat she was able to pick orchids, wild sea carrot, gentian and alkanet, spurge, Cornish lovage, bellflowers, and bindweed, all in blossom. With tamarisk and the leaves of wild asparagus to set them off, she wove a garland for David when he awoke; then she lay down to stare at the heavens, and never again think of Pallas and accounts and rents, and mines and Morwenna and mothers and mortgages . . .

The sun wilted its way down the vault of the sky.

David woke her with a kiss. "Will you marry me?" he asked.

She closed her eyes again and lay there smiling, wanting the moment last for ever.

Gently he placed the garland around her face, framing it. "Will you?" he repeated.

"What happened?" she asked, still not opening her eyes. The sun had scorched her skin; she must look dreadful but somehow it didn't matter.

His voice fell from all around, bathing her. "I thought of death, of life without you. I was sure he was dead, you see."

"And?" she prompted.

"How little I understand, Beth! How I despise myself at times, for pretending to know all the answers. I don't know why you put up with me."

"It's touched us all dearest. I can't imagine life without you, either."

"There's one answer I don't know. Need I ask the question again?"

She shook her head; the blossom caressed her. "You do know. Need I answer you in words?"

"When shall it be?"

"Now," she said. "Today. Tomorrow. As soon as possible."

He removed the garland and replaced its touch with his hands, one each side of her face. "You are so precious to me," he said, his voice choking on the emotion. "I cannot believe it – yet it *is* so. How can it go on and on and on like this – like a voice eternally ascending the scale yet never passing out of range? All the ridiculous, fatuous, overblown things I've ever read about love, things that have filled me with stark disbelief and ridicule . . . they're all true! And yet they're only an infinitesimal part of the truth. Oh Beth!"

Still not opening her eyes, she reached a hand into the blood-coloured dark above her, where his voice was centred, and touched his cheek. "Let him kiss me with the kisses of his mouth," she quoted. "For thy love is better than wine."

It relaxed him at once. He lay beside her and ran his lips all over her cheek, her ear, her lips. "As the lily among thorns," he whispered, "so is my love among the daughters. Behold, thou art fair, my love; behold, thou art fair; thou hast dove's eyes."

"Behold, thou art fair, my beloved, yea, pleasant: also our bed is green."

He pulled himself away – a few inches only. Resting his head on his hand, staring out at the late-afternoon sky, he said, "I never . . . understood . . ."

She opened her eyes and continued, "By night on my bed I sought him whom my soul loveth: I sought him, but I found him not."

For the first time he noticed she had scraped her arm. "Oh my darling!" he said. "How did you do that?"

She put the arm around him, to hide it. "It's nothing."

"How did it happen?"

"Can we be married in your chapel? Perhaps just with George and Lilian as witnesses? Or friends of yours? I don't want a crowd. I don't want a fuss."

"As soon as it can be arranged," he promised. "There'll be certain legal formalities to . . ."

She rolled over as if in pain. "No. Nothing legal! Nothing."

"There must be. We must draw up a deed to reserve all your property to you. I don't want anybody thinking I married you just for the sake of . . ."

"But I'd never think that, David. It wouldn't even enter . . ."

"I didn't mean you. But other people might."

"Do they matter?"

"To a politician they do."

"Well, as far as I'm concerned everything I have is yours – or *ours*." She focussed her eyes on the horizon, now emerging from the heat-haze of the day. "And as for our honeymoon . . ."

He grew tense at the word. "Do we need a honeymoon?"

She pointed far away to the west, where the blue-gray humps of the Scillies were just visible against the brightness of the lowering sun. "There!"

CHAPTER FORTY

MORWENNA AND MRS. MITCHELL wandered aimlessly down the Great Lawn at Pallas House – or the Once-Great Lawn, as it might more truthfully be called – working up an appetite for lunch. Both had endured a trying morning; Morwenna had just heard the first rumours of Elizabeth's impending marriage to David Troy; and Mrs. Mitchell had been trying unsuccessfully to authenticate a small portrait of an unknown youth.

"After your daughter was expelled . . ." Morwenna said hesitantly.

"Yes, dear?"

"Did you not consider sending her to a corrective school? There are some excellent ones in France, or so I'm told. Very severe."

"Her father wouldn't have countenanced that, I'm afraid."

Morwenna sighed. "Yes, I was forgetting. She has that way with men. She can bend them as she wishes."

"Oh, but he wasn't soft with her, Miss Troy. He gave her the soundest caning I've ever heard – on her bare posteriors, too. But that was the end of it. He said the matter was over and done with. She had paid her penalty."

Morwenna pulled her skirts aside to avoid a clump of burrs. "I don't suppose it stopped her wickedness, though?"

Mrs. Mitchell thought hard. "Well, she used to go out quite a few evenings each week – for a walk on the common, she always said. She told me she and a girl-friend used to go up there to skip, and bounce a tennis ball. But since then I've often *wondered*, I must confess. Did she really go out to meet the boys?"

"You never suspected anything at the time?"

"Ah – you know how innocent we all were in our day. No, it never crossed my mind, though she was of nubile age."

"Oh, the hussy! And such angelic features! It's plain to see how she turned Bill's head – she must have had him besotted. I thank God he's been spared the disappointment – that's all I can say."

Mrs. Mitchell glanced carefully around before she murmured, "What makes you think he has been spared, Miss Troy? Don't you think he sees all that goes on here? Don't you feel his presence?" Almost as an afterthought she added, "I'm sure *I* do."

"You!" Morwenna said in astonishment. "But surely you never knew him?"

Mrs. Mitchell was silent.

"Did you?" Morwenna persisted. "Did your daughter introduce . . ."

"Of course not. But" – she smiled knowingly and looked over her shoulder at the house – "I do feel his presence here. Very powerfully. He is *in* that place!"

Morwenna turned to stare at Pallas House.

She put her hand to her heart, as if to calm it, and she stared for a long time.

George and Lilian set their wedding for October, with the honeymoon in Paris; by then he reckoned most of the artists who went out into the country for the summer would be back in their ateliers once more. In September, Elizabeth and David were married quietly in Penzance, at the Wesleyan Chapel in Chapel Street, by the Rev. Thomas Tregeagle; George and Lilian were their witnesses. Courtenay was there, too, of course – being noble and mature and full of wan regret. The *Vindicator* carried the briefest paragraph, announcing the bare fact of the wedding. By the time the social storm broke, the newlyweds were safely lodged in the Hugh House Hotel in Hugh Town on St. Marys, largest of the Scillies.

During the voyage they were the victims of an actual storm, which struck before they were ten miles out of Penzance harbour. It was touch-and-go whether the vessel put about and waited for it to pass, but the captain saw a pale lick of gold upon the horizon and continued the four-hour voyage in high hopes of a moderation. In fact, even at its worst it never blew more than a three-quarter gale; but the effect on the steamer was, in Elizabeth's view, every bit as bad as a full storm.

The *Lyonnesse*, which had seemed so vast when tied up at the extension quay, was now revealed as little larger than a rowing boat, upon which the passengers were mere ants. Mighty ocean rollers, which had met nothing to obstruct their feeding and fattening over three thousand Atlantic miles, now picked them up like a toy. They skittered up the advancing face of each green mountain, sheltering in its lea; but at the peak of it the sea became a grasping fist that held them up to the full force of the autumnal blast. Its sudden hammer-blow made breathing well nigh impossible. And then came the sickening descent down a giddying water-slide, down, down, into the black-mawed cauldron between each swell.

Elizabeth, who, on the strength of one steamer trip from West-minster to Greenwich and back, had considered herself "a good sailor," now learned otherwise. They had the cheaper fore-cabin tickets but she found any sort of enclosure intolerable. Sting though it might, she had to feel the wind on her face – especially after it had carried away her breakfast.

David held his arm tight around her shoulders. "Try to keep your gaze fixed upon the horizon, my darling," he advised.

She grudgingly opened her left eye, only to face a tilting wall of grey-green water with a migraine of ripples scouring its surface. She closed her eye again and tried to shrivel her body away from contact with her cold, wet clothing.

Why had she chosen the Scillies? What idiot, romantic impulse had made her look out over that unruffled summer sea and forget the havoc even a modest wind could bring? No two moods could be further apart than hers as she had lain at ease upon her green bed of wildflowers, that golden August evening – and this blear September gale amid shivering, tilting, heaving cliffs of water.

"If only they were regular!" she moaned.

"Pardon?" he roared almost unintelligibly at her ear.

"I said if only they were regular – I could fit into their rhythm. But they come from all angles."

"That's because of the narrowing of the Channel," he started to explain.

"I'm so glad there are scientific reasons for it, darling, but I honestly don't want to hear them now."

"The other trick is to eat something," he said.

She triced up tighter to the wind and tried not to think about anything – and most especially not about eating.

After a millenium of torment she became aware that they had been joined at the rail by others. She opened her eyes, thinking they must at last be in sight of the islands, but saw only more undulating water, blue-black and silvery gray now – the colours of the deep Atlantic rather than the shallows of the Channel. Silhouetted against it were two rotund forms, one male, one female.

The sky had brightened, the wind was slackening.

"I see your husband is no sailor!" David said in sympathy to the woman.

"A sailor?" she answered in a scandalized voice with a distinct northern ring to it. "I'll have you know, young man, that my husband happens to be Mr. Caleb Rowbotham JP, proprietor of Rowbotham's Mills and Chairman of the Huddersfield Chamber of Commerce. And we are to be the guests of the Lord Proprietor of the Scillies, Mr. Dorrien-Smith, Esquire!" To the skies she added, "*Sailor*, indeed!"

Even in the depths of her misery Elizabeth could see the funny side of the misunderstanding; her laughter, tinged as it was with hysteria, only added to Milady Rowbotham's outrage. From then on Elizabeth felt better – that is, merely dreadful instead of absolutely awful.

"We'll be there in an hour," David told her. "Let's plan what we're going to do this afternoon."

"Sleep the clock round," she told him.

"No — seriously. It'll take your mind off all this."

"I was being serious, actually. Another thing I'd like to do is stand on dry land for three days and simply luxuriate in the fact that it isn't moving. I promise you, darling, if ever I complain of boredom, just point out that at least the land isn't moving beneath me."

The tide being full, the *Lyonnesse* took the northerly passage around St. Marys, off the lee shore. The Scillies, comprising between twenty and a hundred islands (depending on what you care to call an island), spatter the Atlantic in a comma-shaped pattern, ten miles long and half as broad. Only five are now inhabited — by some nineteen-hundred souls; most of them live on St. Marys, whose "capital," Hugh Town, is actually no more than a smallish village.

As soon as the *Lyonnesse* was in the relative calm of The Road, Elizabeth began to improve. A change of clothing, and a cup of weak beef tea before a blazing fire in the hotel lounge, completed her recovery, though she still had no stomach for anything more solid.

"It wasn't *so* bad," she said cheerfully. "A few more hours and I could even have grown used to it, I think."

David laughed. "How turn ye again to the weak and beggarly elements! Let's go out and laugh at the wind."

They donned oilskins and set off around the Garrison.

"Shall we need a map?" she asked.

"It's an island, dear. The longest possible walk is two miles."

Remembering how she'd got lost within half a mile of Pallas Halt, she was not entirely reassured. She also remembered Courtenay under the pump. She gave David's arm an extra-tight hug.

They followed the path at the foot of the old fortifications. With a million tons of living granite beneath her feet, Elizabeth could acknowledge that the sea was magnificent. They stood and watched in awe as majestic ocean combers came rolling up Broad Sound, swamping the Minaltos, and hurling themselves to extinction in long white explosions of spray, clean over the twin peaks of mighty Sampson.

At Garrison Point, where they were no longer side-on to the sea's running, they felt something of its force directly; for even though Annet and Agnes and a host of other small islands took the brunt of the waves, plume after plume soared upward on the wind and peppered their oilskins.

By Woolpack Point the path broke through the ancient defences and led steeply uphill, back toward the town. Here, just beneath the crest, and with a lee sea at their feet, they could nestle in a grassy hollow and stare out over the Atlantic.

"It's like one's imagined picture of a battlefield," she mused.

He said nothing; his eyes ceaselessly patrolled the waters. She leaned over and nudged his pale, cold cheek with the tip of her nose. "Mmmm?"

Wet skin on wet skin was sensuous; for the first time she began to feel for him the sort of longing that Courtenay could so easily awaken — and never truly satisfy.

He leaned his head against hers, but the gesture was ambiguous. "What's really frightening is the fact that if we turn our backs on it and walk away, it won't make any difference. When we're asleep tonight, it'll still be going on. If all mankind . . ."

She risked saying, "What makes you think we'll sleep much tonight?"

He smiled, not at her but at the elements; again the gesture was ambiguous. He continued, "If all mankind were to vanish, it would still go on."

The excitement of his nearness began to shrivel within her. "Talk to me about love," she said. "I've had enough weather for one day."

"What about love?"

She could feel the sudden tension in his arm. She huddled against him. "You know."

"Love," he said awkwardly, "is creation writ small. Love wants to create all the time. That's why it needs two elements — like God and the world."

"And man and wife."

He nodded. "It's a compulsion. Our desires compel us to change each other, don't you think? To recreate each other."

"I don't want to change you, David, only to know you."

It was as if she had not spoken. "Mere appetite," he continued, "is the opposite. Hunger does not desire to change the apple, only to consume it. Hunger seeks nothing but its own gratification."

"It still involves two elements."

He shook his head. "It only appears to. But the second element — the apple — could just as well be a turnip or a stick of barleysugar. All appetites are like that. The second element is immaterial to the gratification of the first. Therefore the appetite between man and woman is not love." He looked directly into her eyes at last. "And it cannot even challenge love."

She hid her unease and laughed. "George once told me that a good lawyer can argue heaven into hell. Let's go back."

The windmill on Buzza Hill was closed down against the storm but the strength of the wind turned its sails merrily anyway.

"Spit in the miller's eye," she said.

He looked at her sharply. "Eh?"

"Spit in the miller's eye."

"D'you know what that means?"

"Put water in the wine, doesn't it?"

"Ah, yes."

But she could see he had some other meaning in mind — probably scurrilous. Had Oenone tricked her? She felt she ought to explain: "In this case, I meant that although the miller tries to close down his mill, the elements spit in his eye and turn the sails anyway."

"Man proposes, God disposes, eh?"

She had the feeling that Hamill's idea of the elements was somehow closer to the truth than David's, but she could never have explained it to him.

Neither ate much at supper. The serving maid removed their half-eaten portions with a knowing smile. As bedtime approached Elizabeth could see him becoming more and more nervous. In a curious way it helped calm her; it yielded to her something of the initiative. She made him carry the lamp, so that he had to light her all the way. At their bedroom door he tried to pass it to her, no doubt with some notion of remaining outside, but she ignored the offer.

Once in their room he put down the lamp and she was astonished to see him take up his book, *Selections among the Letters of John Wesley*.

He almost got away from her. "I'll just . . ." he began, in a nervous voice, quite unlike his usual confident tone. But she reached out a hand, took the book from him, laid it beside the lamp, and, stretching out her arms to him, said, "David!"

"I don't know . . ." He moved awkwardly into her embrace.

"You know I love you – and you love me."

She eased his jacket off his shoulders and down over his arms. But while she turned to hang it over a chairback he fled behind the screen that sheltered the washstand.

"I'll come out when you're in bed," he called. "You disrobe and go to bed."

They both undressed and stood in silence. He, no doubt, was waiting to hear her get into bed. Was he peeping? Did he know her nightdress still lay upon the bedspread?

"Throw me my nightshirt," he asked. "And put out the light."

She turned down the wick until the merest glowworm of yellow trembled upon it; behind the screen it must have seemed as if the light went out. Swiftly she crossed the room to where he stood.

"I said throw . . ."

But she was beside him now, her heart thumping like a mad thing, her body hot and shivery. She felt his nearness by the cocooning of their warmth in the narrowing gap between them.

"Oh David, darling David . . ." She put her arms around the warm dark of him.

He was sideways on to her, moving . . . in the act of turning away? She slithered round and pressed herself to him, face to face, her whole body against his.

His breath was strangled and his whole frame quivered, but the touch of her nakedness had the predictable effect and she felt his flesh harden and rise. He gave out a little whimper.

She ran her fingernails up and down his back, seeking to encourage him, but he just stood there, shivering and making small noises. She took up his hand and put it to her breasts. She slipped her fingers lower down, meaning to ease his entry, but something impacted her palm . . . hot, oozy.

It was throbbing wildly and he was making idiotic, shivery giggles, saying, "No . . . no . . ."

She tried to stop him, clasping that hard flesh tight to hold back the outpouring.

He gave a gasp that was almost a roar, collapsed against her, bit her shoulder. The throbbing ceased and he was limp again.

"Oh, the disgust!" he whispered.

What to do? She tried to comfort him with her free hand, caressing his back and arm. The sweat that bathed him was turning cold and clammy.

Suddenly he wrenched away from her and fled to the bed. The violence with which he raised and then lowered the bedclothes extinguished the lamp completely.

She stooped, picked up his nightshirt, and went across to join him. Between the sheets she snuggled up against him; he had his back to her. He did not respond. She ran her hand up and down the side of him. He was weeping.

"Oh David!" she murmured, turning him on his back.

He offered no resistance.

She began kissing his face, his cheeks, his eyes — kissing away the salt — his brow, his nose, his lips, his throat.

"I'm sorry," he whispered.

"For what!" She went on kissing him.

"For . . . that!"

"Oh David . . ."

"You must be appalled with me."

"But no! No! You fill me with love. You're the most marvellous man ever."

"That can't be true."

She manipulated his arm onto the pillow and then lay on it, her hip against his. "I shouldn't have played such a trick on you," she told him.

After a while he asked, "Where's my nightshirt?"

She didn't reply. When he made a move she pressed her head hard upon his arm, pinning him there. He relaxed again.

"I'll tell you what you could do," she whispered.

"Mmmm?"

"Light the lamp again and leave it very low."

"Can't you sleep in the dark? You do at home."

"How d'you know that, may I ask?" She chuckled.

"Oh — Oenone told me — that time of the Deepwork Disaster." It lacked the ring of truth but she didn't pursue it.

"I can quite easily sleep in the dark but I don't want to. I want — every time I wake up tonight — I want to look at you and just feel happy all over again that for the rest of our lives you'll be there beside me."

At that he rolled on his side, facing her. "Oh Elizabeth . . . Elizabeth!" He began to kiss her as she had just kissed him. "I'm so afraid I shan't be good enough for you."

"Such nonsense!" She was trembling; her heart had gone from standstill to gallop.

"Yes! Yes! The fault is all mine. In my eyes you can do no wrong — you sanctify everything you do."

Her body was about to do what his had done — explode in a solo ecstasy. She half turned to him, arching her back. There was no answering pressure down there. She raised one thigh. A limp hank of softness fell against her; it gave one feeble throb. She closed on it greedily and tried to raise her ecstasy the last few inches to that familiar plateau . . . but it all died on her.

Her disappointment, though intense, was brief. A lassitude overcame her, which she convinced herself was a sort of exhausted contentment. She lay back and pretended to sleep. He lay beside her and slept — unless he was pretending, too.

In the small hours he rose to use the chamberpot. When he slipped back between the sheets she pretended to waken, stretch, "discover" him. With a happy sigh she slithered over his body and settled as if to go back to sleep. After a momentary resistance he relaxed again. She felt his arousal beginning. With slow, sinuous movements she encouraged him until he was firm enough for her to open to him and let him slip in.

He made two or three tentative movements . . . and then died again. He shrivelled inside her until no angle of her body, no subtlety of her movement, could keep him from falling out.

She covered his face with kisses, put her breasts near his lips, but he turned his head aside. She felt unclean. He rose and went to the washstand, where he pretended to wash only his face and hands. She felt more than unclean, more than merely rejected.

But next morning they were happy again. The wind died, the sun came out, the violence of the waves was diminished to mere picturesque effusion. They explored all the lanes and shores of the island, talking of everything under the sun — except what had happened, and not happened, last night. They retired early; and they again failed to consummate their marriage. At their first attempt he was impotent once more; in the small hours he turned to her, firm and ready, touched her breast, and ejaculated at once. This time they said nothing. Nor did he weep.

And that was the pattern of their honeymoon. By day they were the best of companions. Neither mentioned those nightly failures; instead they talked of spiritual love, the future — how splendidly different life was going to be for both of them, the law, his coming career in politics . . . a new vision of heaven and earth. He was brilliant, dynamic, filled with a power that possessed her directly; he was the David who could, at the drop of a hat, gather and hold a crowd with the passion of his oratory. But as night fell, three vampires lighted them to bed – foreboding, dread, despair; they lay together and died their separate, silent deaths.

At the end of the week, unable to face another night in that pit of failure, they moved to the Canteen Inn on Tresco. It made no difference. The threads of their daytime joy grew bare. Through its decaying fabric she glimpsed a mute despair in his eyes – a plea for her to work some miracle. She had nursed dying men who knew their end was near; that hungry plea had burned in their eyes, too. They could not say, "I am dying here," but their eyes could beg for wordless, eloquent miracles.

While that prayer burned, she could feel united with him, strive with all her love and skill to grant it. But as failure succeeded failure, the prayer guttered into darkness. Like a dying candle, it left a cloying scent upon the air between them . . . all the fires that might have been.

Now when he touched her, there was a new fastidiousness in his fingers; it denounced her femaleness in a deaf-and-dumb sermon. She could almost hear it echoing through the dark silence of his mind, but she could not catch the words. And so she could find none of her own, for how can one answer an argument raging miles away in a locked room?

"We are *soul* mates," he said on their last night, laying heavy stress on that word.

It took her by surprise. Later she thought of all the things she might have said. At the time though, she followed a panic-ridden instinct, feminine in a way that did not come easily to her – an instinct to agree with him, humour him, win him by artifice: "I'm beginning to believe you're right," she murmured consolingly.

But his tone was firm. He was stating conclusions, not offering points for discussion: "We did not marry like brute beasts that have no understanding. We have so much to give each other, don't you think? Apart from that?"

"I have never been happier in my life, David. Perhaps, if we're patient, if we don't let it spoil all the wonderful . . ."

"This is our sign from God – we must save ourselves for the higher things. Our dedication is to other people, not each other. I have wrestled with my soul, pondering the meaning of this . . . this . . . whatever one might call it. Not failure. It is most certainly not failure. Oh, my dearest! I have never felt closer to God than during these two weeks. Surely angels' wings have brushed us as we slept! These will always be the most precious hours of our lives. We have come through them with our love purified. We have freed it of fleshly taint, not by *avoiding* it, you see. Not by formal abstention like the papist pharisees, but be meeting it squarely, by exposing ourselves to the temptations of the flesh, and then triumphing over them! We have come through the fires of mere appetite and emerged upon the sunlit uplands of love. Oh, say you feel it, too! Then our happiness will be complete."

After a pause she said, "A child would make my happiness complete, David. Are we not to have children?" The thought that she might never cradle a baby in her arms, hold its dear little head to her breast, was like a prayer to die.

"God will find a way," he promised. "To God all things are possible."

She was almost comforted until he added, "And if not, why – that is a sign, too: that our 'family' is the larger family of mankind, that teeming constituency of the oppressed and downtrodden."

He leaned across the bed and kissed her; he said goodnight with a joyful finality – and with open relief that he need never fail again. She felt that a sharp sword had been laid between them.

"You are beautiful," he told her the moment she awakened next morning. There was a strange, contained excitement in him, a fervour; he could not wait to put these desperate days behind them and embark on their *proper* life together. "You can do no wrong," he said. "Whatever you do, you will sanctify it. Have no fear."

Why do I smile? she wondered. *Why do I fear to destroy these monkish, arid certainties of his?*

Because she loved him still.

Because she could not force him to put that loaded pistol nightly to his temple.

Because he had all the words and she had only feelings.

Because she was now at war with her own desires.

The ferry was to sail at ten-thirty. Before breakfast she went out for a final stroll, alone. She went no farther than Appletree Point, just beneath the Abbey, the home of the Lord Proprietor. She thought briefly of Mr. and Mrs. Rowbotham; were they even now regaling their fellow guests with the blessings of having reached the very summit of the Huddersfield *Haute Monde?*

But the sneer died swiftly within. Unlovely though they were – roly-poly, graceless, smug, snobbish . . . she could yet see them clasped in love, filled with the raptures that cancel out all such petty imperfections.

It was growing into an obsession.

She stared out to sea, unable to address her discontents. The best she could do was wait passively for her mood to lift, as if it were some impersonal wrack.

The man came walking along Appletree Banks from the direction of Crow Point. He was throwing bits of driftwood for his dog to retrieve.

"Morning, my lover!" he said as he drew near.

She laughed. "Morning, me 'ansum! Will it be a fair crossing?"

The dog fretted around her with female, snakelike obeisance, whining, licking her — a frenzy of ingratiation.

"You going Penzance, are'ee?"

She nodded. "We had a very stormy passage out here."

He chuckled. "If you do want to know about stormy passages, you ask she." He gave the dog a gentle poke with his walking stick.

Elizabeth went on petting the creature, more in self-defence than actual fondness. "Why? Has she been on the ferry?"

He sucked his teeth and shook his head, challenging her to guess again.

Suddenly the hair bristled on Elizabeth's neck. She looked more closely at the dog: a mongrel red setter!

"Did she come here out of the sea?" she asked.

The man looked at her in surprise.

She remembered details of the occasion now. "There was a tree. Did she float across in the branches of a tree? Yes, she must have. She could never have survived in the water." She looked down at the bitch, who had settled against her calf and was panting happily in the sun. "Well-well-well, you clever thing!"

"How do'ee know that?" the man asked.

"I was there at the Loe Bar when they cut it. We all saw her get sucked into the outflow. We were absolutely sure she'd drowned."

"But the tree? How'dee know about that?"

"Oh, it must have been floating in the Loe for a week or more. It went out only seconds after . . . what's her name?"

"I do call she Mermaid."

"Of course. Well, Dan Merrick will be delighted to hear she's in such good hands, Mr. . . . ?"

"Gibson. You think I should send she back with 'ee?" The prospect clearly saddened him.

"Not at all! If any creature has earned the Freedom of the Scillies, it's old Mermaid here." She patted the dog, who licked her hand. "Survivor, eh! You're a grand little survivor. Yes, you are!"

Then she added, "What's the secret?"

CHAPTER FORTY-ONE

MORWENNA WAITED UNTIL Hamill had finished reading his latest article aloud to Mrs. Mitchell. What the woman saw in those Celtic bumblings was beyond her comprehension – except that Mrs. Mitchell was the soul of kindness and would do anything to keep the old boy happy. How had Pallas House ever run without her?

She had been quite right to suggest getting rid of old Polglaze and the other servants and engage new ones. They had all been allowed to get dreadfully slack and lazy – *and* they had been carrying tales to that dreadful woman. Why couldn't the daughter have been more like the mother? Morwenna would gladly have handed over the reins then. Mrs. Mitchell understood the *old* values so well. Plainly her marriage to the horse doctor had been very much beneath her. She understood everything, sometimes even before a word was spoken. It was uncanny.

Indeed, it was so uncanny that Morwenna felt she had to talk to her about it.

When Hamill had retired to the library to make one or two small amendments suggested by Mrs. Mitchell, Morwenna opened her mouth to speak. But the other stretched, smiled that bewitching smile which must have broken many hearts in her youth, and said, "Oh, your cousin is so stimulating, Miss Troy, I feel I cannot return immediately to my cataloguing chores. Shall we take a turn around the gardens?"

Uncanny! Morwenna thought.

"My little dove is not happy with her new husband," Mrs. Mitchell said, as soon as they were sure of not being overheard.

"She has told you so?" Morwenna could not disguise her relish.

"A mother does not need to be told such things."

Of course!

"I know the signs all too well, Miss Troy. How often does an impetuous young girl marry the exterior of a man – only to find the interior quite different!"

"How interesting. Tell me more. D'you suppose that David Troy is . . ."

"I say nothing. I'm hardly familiar with the man. And my daughter, as you know to your cost, is determined to manage her life without the benefit of *our* wisdom."

"Manage it? Ruin it, more likely – and this estate. She seems to think of the land as some kind of open-air factory floor!"

"Oh, dear Miss Troy, believe me, I know just how you must feel."

"But do go on about David and . . . what you were saying."

"Not that I've been told anything, mind. But one uses one's experience. One *twigs* these things, as they say. I remember when I was in Italy – ah *bella Italia!* – I spent part of one summer as a guest of the Contessa Favorini. The Count, as you know, is one of the foremost men in the public life of the country. A dynamo of energy. Speaks here, there, and everywhere. Radiates charm as easily as a skylark sings. All the women fall passionately in love with him and envy the poor Contessa quite sinfully."

Morwenna laid a confiding hand on her companion's arm. "Dear Mrs. Mitchell, there is no need to tell me these things. I'm sure we all have our little secrets."

Mrs. Mitchell stared at her with an incomprehension that turned to anger. "No, no! It's nothing like that. The point I'm making is that in private life Favorini is petty-minded, tyrannical, wayward, and . . . no *performer*, if you take my meaning?"

"I see! Yes – I *do* see!" It excited Morwenna to think that Elizabeth might have trapped herself into an empty marriage. "And you suppose that David Troy is . . ."

"Oh, I say nothing as to that. All I *do* say is that the signs are there. The little discontents . . . the unease. A mother notices such things, Miss Troy – as I'm sure you did with dear Bill."

"Of course. Of course!" Morwenna drew a deep breath and took the plunge. "But you, Mrs. Mitchell, would notice it sooner and far more deeply than others."

Mrs. Mitchell gave a bewildered laugh at the compliment. "What makes you say so?"

"Oh come – I think you know." Morwenna's smile was a challenge.

"But I haven't the faintest notion . . ."

"You cannot have lived so long – not that I'm implying you have one foot in the grave, you understand! – but you must have known by the time you were twenty that you are gifted with . . . certain *powers?*"

Mrs. Mitchell stared at her in astonishment. "Powers?" she echoed faintly.

"Something more than mere intuition, more than sympathetic guess-work. Call it second sight, call it clairvoyance, call it what you will, my dear, but you have it!"

Mrs. Mitchell laughed, in a kindly way, as women do when they reject praise but accept the intentions of the praiser. "I never heard anything so preposterous, Miss Troy!"

Morwenna shook her head knowingly. "All too often, Mrs. Mitchell, those who possess it think it so natural, they haven't the slightest notion of its true value. They pooh-pooh what others envy."

"Stop!" Mrs. Mitchell gave a tinkling peal of silvery laughter. "I shall leave if this goes on."

"But the evidence is all around us. Think how well you understand all our moods in this house. Why, not five minutes ago I was on the point of suggesting a little stroll – but you read my mind and got there first. And on your first visit to this house, you had not met Hamill three minutes before you saw how it would delight him to 'teach' you about our treasures – though the truth is you could probably teach him far more. Admit it now!"

"Oh dear, Miss Troy. I hope you don't think it a wicked deception? It was just that I suspected . . . that is, I felt his need to . . ."

"You see! Every word confirms it. And again, when you say you can *feel* Bill's presence in the house – ever since you spoke those words, I have to confess that I, too, feel him here. But it is only since you came. I suspect, you see, that your powers go beyond mere clairvoyance. I believe you to be that far rarer soul, Mrs. Mitchell: a true medium!"

Elizabeth's mother tried to laugh but fear won the contest. "No!" she said emphatically. "Absolutely not! That I shall never believe – never!"

Morwenna smiled knowingly. "It will take time," she said soothingly. "You yourself will realize it soon. Never fear."

A few weeks later – it was the day before Lilian's and George's wedding – a distraught Aunt Petty called at Wheal Lavender. The event was sufficiently rare for Oenone to get out the best china teaset.

Elizabeth wasted no breath on small talk. "What's my mother done now?" she asked.

"Well, curiously enough, dear, this time it's not so much your mother as Morwenna. Indeed, your mother seems very reluctant to acquiesce in it."

"In what? Do take some cinnamon toast. I'm not eating today because I know we'll all make pigs of ourselves tomorrow."

"Thank you. It looks delicious. Morwenna has conceived this outrageous notion that your mother is – a medium."

"A medium? D'you mean a medium . . . like . . . surely not?"

"Yes, like ghosts. That sort of medium. Morwenna . . . well, I don't like to say this, but I begin to fear she has become a little unhinged on the subject. She's possessed by this strange notion that Bill's spirit is very strongly present at Pallas House and . . ."

Elizabeth laughed. "But it isn't just at Pallas House, Aunt Petty. Surely the Dragon realizes it's over the whole of Pallas Estate. I feel him everywhere."

Petty swallowed and went bright red. "Oh dear! Perhaps I'm speaking out of turn."

"No. Go on. I'm sorry — I shouldn't have interrupted."

"Well" — Petty was hesitant now — "they have some notion of arranging a séance."

"They *what?*" Elizabeth flared up.

"Yes, dear. Table rapping . . . spirit voices — that sort of thing."

"Who is 'they'? Surely Hamill isn't duped by . . ."

"Duped is exactly the word, Elizabeth. She has him eating out of the palm of her hand. I'm sorry to take this tone, my dear. I know she's your mother. But she is false. And he can't see it."

"False would be the kindest word, Aunt Petty. I'm astonished that Hamill's taken in by her. Well, he'll be at the wedding tomorrow. I shall certainly have a word with him."

"Your mother will be there, too," Petty warned.

"But I thought Lilian put her foot down."

"I suspect Hamill talked her round."

Elizabeth frowned. "This idea that my mother is a medium — you say it comes from the Dragon, not my mother?"

"Oh yes. Your mother laughs at the very notion. It's Morwenna who's insisting on it."

"It's just her cunning. If I thought there was anything in it . . " She paused.

"What, dear?"

"I will not have Bill's spirit disturbed like that. It's one thing to know that he's still around us in a general sort of way. But it's quite another to summon him up like a defaulter and poke questions at him."

Oenone, who had been unashamedly listening in, said, "If they did call Master Bill up, he'd soon put Miss Morwenna in a dalver! Oh my gidge — what he'd tell she!"

"That's enough, Oenone," Elizabeth warned.

Petty looked at the two of them. "*You* haven't been holding séances, I hope?"

"I trust you know me better than that," Elizabeth replied.

"Didn't need no séance," Oenone said. "There was that letter what he wrote."

"That's quite enough, Oenone. You may fetch some more hot water."

"Bill wrote a letter?" Petty asked. "When was this?"

Oenone paused in the doorway and said, "Kick I out if you mind to, missis, but I think she should know. Everyone should know."

Elizabeth shrugged hopelessly. "If I stop you now, you'll only meet behind my back." She turned to Petty. "Oenone's referring to a letter from Bill to Randolph Haskins, his lawyer, the one in Brighton who drew up the will. It wasn't too complimentary about Morwenna. That's all."

Petty smiled broadly. "Oh, do tell me what it said!"

Elizabeth looked daggers at Oenone. "Just that she had more or less ruined the estate. That's all. But listen. Morwenna is *never* to hear of it. She's never to know Bill said that of her. Promise me, now!"

Petty was shocked. "Elizabeth! How can you be so protective? How can you bear to shield her from the plain truth. Just think of all she's done to blackguard you and ruin you! If she could put you in the gutter, she'd laugh for a month. You . . ."

"Tin't no good talking to she, Miss Smallwood," Oenone cut in. "I do tell she, 'twould be like water on a quilkin – telling the truth to Miss Morwenna."

"Exactly!" Petty said. "She'd just turn round and say it's one more proof of how you twisted Bill's mind."

"You're probably right," Elizabeth admitted. "If the letter had come to light in the beginning, when she was still angry at Bill for marrying me, when he was still her silly little boy . . . well, then I might have agreed. But over these years she's made him her demigod. She never speaks of *her* distress at what I'm doing to Pallas – only of how Bill must be turning in his grave. To read that letter now would shatter her life. Anyway" – she saw they were both preparing to argue – "I'm not willing to take the risk. I'd far rather endure her spite and ridicule. And on this topic – be warned – my mind is absolutely closed."

Oenone and Petty exchanged glances; there were flashes, hints of a most unlikely alliance in the offing. Elizabeth saw it but felt she had laid down enough law for one day; she said only that she'd take Hamill aside at the wedding tomorrow and discover how far this tomfoolery had gone.

"Randolph Haskins, eh?" Petty said. "Of Brighton."

CHAPTER FORTY-TWO

THE WEDDING BREAKFAST was at Yeol Parc, which Courtenay had completely redecorated. Gone was the Retired Colonial style; the master was now a Georgian Squire – a huntin' man, to judge by the sporting prints; a shootin' man, by the look of his trophies; a fishin' man, if you took note of the lugubrious pike, the surly trout, the somnolent carp that lurked about the house among weeds of starched linen in glass-cased sections of waters that never were. In such company even the delicate proportions and pastel shades of the striped wallpapers seemed plain and manly; it was a bluff, rural Georgian that would have set the dogs upon the baroque, and flogged the rococo to the bone.

It was also no more Courtenay-like than his earlier style.

It did, however, provide a slightly more fitting background for Lilian's reception; and for that she was glad.

All Helston had turned out to see the wedding. The tightly packed crowds in Church Street had forced the newlyweds to take the long way round, down an almost equally thronged Cross Street and up Almshouse Hill to Coinagehall Street, which was even more populous than it would have been for one of Will Tyacke's royal progresses. All agreed that never in their day had they seen so lovely a bride. Rough old farmers who would rather wake up dead (and usually did) than be caught in possession of a soft emotion were halted in mid-oath and held transfixed until the carriage had passed. Matrons fished out delicate kerchiefs to soak up small tears, wrung from them by a loveliness only their daydreams could share. When she had gone, young men recovered their breath and made ribald mock of their own envy. Their sisters preferred to remember the time Lilian went to live in London . . . the predictions of the brilliant match she was sure to make there – a duke or a marquis at least; it did not displease them that in the end she had managed to ensnare no one better than Lawyer Ivey. They gazed upon her now-neutralized beauty with a kindlier, more tolerant eye.

The breakfast was a seven-course marathon with a speech between each course. Best man Courtenay gave the wittiest, but George's was the bombshell.

After all the proper thank-yous and dedications, he said, "Today I unite my life, my so-far undistinguished life, with one who above all others deserves that most overworked epithet in love's dictionary: *angel*."

"George!" Lilian protested.

"Were it not for her, for the encouragement she has given me, for the support she has promised, I could not begin to contemplate the changes I intend making in my life – in *our* lives."

David murmured to Elizabeth, "He's going to nail his colours to the mast."

Full of foreboding she replied, "To every mast in the harbour, by the sound of it."

"Among my earlier thank-yous," George was saying, "was one omission." He turned toward his mother and father, who were close to him at the high table. "To my parents – thank you for the gift of my life. Thank you for my upbringing, for my education, for my training in the law – all of which, I know, cost you dearly, and not just in your purse. But above all I must thank you for something that cost you nothing to give, for you gave it as easily as one child gives another the mumps."

Everyone laughed, but he held up a finger. "The comparison is not accidental. I refer, dearest mama, dearest papa, to your love of beauty. I shall never forget the day you infected me with it, though I can hardly have been more than eight or ten at the time. We walked out past Culdrose Farm onto Helston Downs. I, of course, was interested only in trying to fly my kite, to catch a frog, and to find a cowpat dry enough to hurl at my sister. But on our way home you paused and turned. I saw a wonder in your eyes and I looked about us to see what the cause might be.

"The fading light of the setting sun touched the whole scene with gold. A wonderful stillness hung over the world. I remember the brightly coloured flowers. I saw them with a clarity that almost hurt, as if I had never seen such things before. And in a way, I hadn't. I needed your sense of wonder and awe to reveal them to me. But that wasn't the end of it. You, papa, must have seen my eyes sharing your discovery. You bent down at my side and said something to me. I wonder if you remember it now?"

His father shook his head and looked comically alarmed at what revelations might follow.

"You said, 'Yes, George – you couldn't buy it if you were the richest man in the world. Nor sell it if you were the neediest. You can't put it in a bottle and carry it away. You can't freeze it where it is, and keep it there forever. It's useless alike to man and beast. Yet to those with eyes to see, it's what makes all the rest of life worth living.' I've never forgotten that: the untouchable, unreachable, unusable, unencashable, unexploitable, unpossessable *wonder* of beauty.

"Since meeting Lilian, you will all readily understand, I have become obsessed with the very idea of beauty. It calls me – very much, I imagine, as the religious are called. It heaps me. It allows me no . . ."

He paused, either because he could think of no word grand enough or because he realized he was being carried away. He smiled and let an apologetic gesture finish the sentence.

"Superb!" David murmured to Elizabeth. He could not take his eyes off George.

"In short, I feel a conviction that I was really meant to be . . . not a lawyer but an artist. And so, from this day forth, that is what I shall be. Quite simply – I shall be an artist. *By these presents*, as we lawyers say, know ye that I herewith and forthwith renounce, cast off, set aside, and abjure my practice of the law."

A thunderstruck silence greeted his words. "I know! You all think I'm mad. You think I've been hearing voices. Well, so I have. I'll tell you about that. Last year I did some conveyancing work on a large estate. The fee ran up to fifty guineas. It was beef and claret *that* Sunday! But all my pleasure turned to dust when I learned that an artist was once paid eight pounds for painting the principal mansion. His name was John Constable. That's when I heard voices. They asked me: 'What gallery in all the world will one day hang your brilliant deed of conveyance?'

"I longed to give up then, but I lacked the courage to face this odyssey alone. That courage did not come to me until after Lilian and I were engaged. Other lovers may write letters or poems about their feelings but I could think of only one way to let Lilian see and understand mine: I determined to paint her portrait."

Lilian silently beckoned Mary, one of the maids, and whispered in her ear.

George continued: "How can I describe that liberation? From the moment the first astonished marks sang out upon that canvas, I have never felt even a momentary twinge of doubt. In Lilian's face I saw the world, the entire landscape of humanity. From the tip of my brush there poured one endless hymn of love and praise, for her, for the earth, for light, for colour . . . for the tumbling, tossing, restlessness of *things*."

Mary returned and nodded discreetly at Lilian.

George gave an embarrassed laugh. "Well, that's all I have to say. I had to tell you these things. When we come back from our honeymoon and I start winding down my practice in earnest, when we start spending more time in our studio in Mousehole than here in Helston, I wanted you to know it was not some sudden notion I sprang on poor Lilian after I got her safely to the altar. I told her – some time ago now – and she . . . gave me the blessing. And now I've told you . . . and I don't know how to end this speech."

"I do!" Lilian nodded to Mary, who went out and returned, bearing – of course – the portrait George had spoken of. Lilian took it and held it up for all to see.

There was a gasp. Lilian flushed with joy and pride.

Then Joel Harvey said, "Had the scarlet fever, did'ee, maid?"

There was laughter. There were shushes – but even those who shushed were suppressing smiles rather than expressing anger.

Elizabeth stared at the picture and her heart fell – or rather, it went out to George and Lilian. What had possessed them? Some mutually encouraged madness, a *folie à deux*. The woman in the portrait was Lilian, anyone could see that. And the colours were quite pleasing, too. But it was so flat and childish, as if it were made out of bits of cut-up wallpaper. It was textures-gone-mad. And there was no *solidity* in it; the shadows were almost as pale as the highlights, and just as strongly coloured. She wouldn't have given twopence for such a daub. Why, it hadn't even got a frame!

Lilian went on holding up the canvas, crying, "But look! Look at it properly!"

Hubert Tredwell shouted, "That's the best trick you ever played, George, boy! Took me in, proper job!"

George just stared at them, a terrible anger in his eyes. David murmured to Elizabeth, "Now – the refiner's fire! Will he melt or is he the genuine article?"

Elizabeth was astonished to see that her mother had risen from the table and was approaching Lilian, beckoning her to lower the painting. She took it from her and held it toward the light. She touched it reverently. She was transfixed.

The good-natured banter continued for a while but fell away as the general interest in Mrs. Mitchell grew. Lilian had joined George by the cake, which was yet to be cut. There they stood, two poor hunted animals at bay. At last Mrs. Mitchell set the painting down on the piano and turned to them. She stretched forth both her hands and took one of each of theirs.

Since George and Lilian were already holding hands, Joel Harvey called, "Ringaroses!" But now the laughter was scanty.

"You are right, Mr. Ivey," she said simply. Then, turning to Lilian, she added, "And so are you, my dear." She looked around the assembly. "And you are all wrong."

Then she smiled sweetly and sat down.

"Come on, George – cut the cake!" Courtenay shouted.

Disaster was averted.

"She has her uses, after all," Elizabeth said to David.

He nodded curtly. "She spoiled it."

Elizabeth realized he would have judged George as a painter not by the physical evidence – the painting itself – but by seeing how well he stood up to criticism and mockery. Perhaps that was the right way. She envied his singlemindedness, that he could contemplate the ruin of such an occasion simply for the chance it gave him to judge the man.

"Can't blame people, I suppose," George said to Elizabeth some time later. "No one's ever taught them how to look at the world."

"I thought the colour was . . . pretty," she told him.

He burst into laughter. "Oh, I'll teach *you*," he promised. "I have you marked down as my most important patron."

They had passage on a tramp steamer out of Falmouth, sailing for Cherbourg the following morning. They were to spend the night at the Greenbank Hotel. When their carriage had departed – amid the usual farrago of tearful farewells, daubed messages, and a trailing mass of battered tinware, the traditional Cornish "Shall-I" band – the party continued. Everyone now said aloud and freely what they had been constrained to say gently, jokingly before: that George and Lilian were a pair of betwattled scalliocks, that an artist was about as much use in the world as a stepladder on a yacht, and that the portrait of Lilian was a gert, gashly, shimshanking edjack of a thing.

"The boy'll see sense when they get back," George's father promised everyone – loud enough, he hoped, to drown out the suggestion that he had anything to do with his son's strange aberration.

"You saved the day," Elizabeth told her mother, glad for once to be able to praise.

"Why do people feel so threatened by something so innocent?" she asked.

"They were just sorry for George's incompetence, I suppose."

"But he's not incompetent. He's quite brilliant, in fact."

Elizabeth held her tongue. Her mother would naturally have to be contrary.

"Why d'you call it innocent?" Hamill asked impishly. "If photography has taught us anything it is that only the artist can penetrate the surface of reality and find its inner meaning. The artist is our lightning conductor between the sober, superficial world and the bolts of orgiastic electricity that are always threatening to rip it apart."

"He never stops writing his articles," Mrs. Mitchell explained affectionately, as if she had known Hamill for years and her daughter were new to the district.

David, who had to prepare for an important constituency meeting, left the party early; he told Elizabeth to stay and enjoy herself. He would sleep in his dressing room so that his early rising would not disturb her.

When she returned to the company, she found everyone gathered around the piano for a singsong. At the back of the crowd stood her mother and Hamill. Since the disappointments of her honeymoon she had developed a kind of sixth sense; she could feel passion and desire like an aura around certain people. She knew whether they were united by that particular bond or whether their marriage was like her own – busy, warm with friendship, admiring, comfortable, filled with intellectual challenge and interest ... . but always with that void at the heart of it. She felt such an aura now, between – of all people – her mother and Hamill.

They were both facing the piano, side by side, with the crowd in front of them, both singing. She watched Hamill's hand as it strayed near her mother's derrière; with the backs of his knuckles he lightly grazed the corseted flesh. Her mother looked up sharply, prepared to be outraged; then she saw who it was and, like some courtesan, responded with a subtle, catlike offering of herself.

In a panic Elizabeth spun about and went into the morning room, where the maids were clearing away some of the party debris.

"You all right ar'ee, missis?" one asked.

She took a grip of herself. "Thank you, Mary – just a little hot. I'll sit down here awhile."

The girl's smile said she knew better – wasn't the whole district waiting to be told that Pallas Estate had a new heir on the way?

It was becoming an obsession for Elizabeth – the image of the tiny baby who would never suckle at her breast. She carried that aching, empty space before her, day and night; sometimes she caught herself stupidly avoiding door jambs in case she bumped its precious little body; sometimes she woke up in the night, sweating with the fear of finding it overlaid beside her. She wondered if it wasn't driving her mad.

Why had she been so panic-stricken at the sight of her mother and Hamill? It was more than the fear of being caught spying on them. In a way she had fled from herself. She was bound so deeply to both of them. To Hamill by something beyond mere affection – by love. She loved his dotty warmth, his eccentric dedication to a culture that was surely gone forever; she loved the vulnerability he never sought to hide. To her mother she was bound by blood – and by a different kind of love – an exasperated love that all the woman's faults could never bury. And now, to find this *other* bond growing between those two, owing nothing to her, excluding her, even in some strange way *accusing* her . . . she did not wish to know of its existence. She went back and joined in the singing; but she stayed well away from them. Hamill questioned her once or twice with his eyes; she smiled reassuringly. Toward the end he found occasion to ask her if all was well.

She took her chance: "What's this tale I hear about ghost raising and table tapping at Pallas House?"

His smile was seraphic. "Your mother is an amazing woman. She has Morwenna distracted."

"My mother is a chameleon, Uncle Hamill. But it's absurd for someone my age to be warning you."

In any event Mrs. Mitchell herself arrived at that moment and the conversation had to be turned.

When they had all gone, Courtenay said casually, "I'll just see you home, shall I?"

She smiled. "That would be kind."

The night air was damp, promising rain. Thin, loose clouds scudded high across the sky though strangely enough the air at ground level hardly stirred. A narrow moon lighted their path. "Which way – Tregathennan or Wheal Pallas?" he asked at the gate.

"You decide."

"It's months since I was at Wheal Pallas," he said.

She closed her mind to thought. *I'll plan nothing*, she told herself. They turned toward Wheal Pallas.

"What d'you think of George?" she asked. "This wanting to be an artist?"

"I hope he gets it out of his system soon. Lilian ought to make him see sense."

"But you *heard* her – she's all for it."

"Well then, she must lie in whatever bed she chooses to make. He's got quite a bit of money put by, she says. They can last for years if they're frugal."

"But it's wrong. What sort of world would it be if people went about doing just whatever they liked?"

He took it as an empty question. After a pause he mused, "I don't suppose it'll affect people's opinion of me."

There was a further easy silence before he went on: "Talking of public opinion, would it surprise you to hear that the general verdict on your choice of husband is favourable?"

"Including yourself?"

More silence; she repeated the question.

"How do we stand now, Beth?" he asked slowly. "I mean, I quite accept that our mésalliance, our dalliance, had to end. But we shared a certain intimacy of mind, too. Must that also be killed off?"

"What d'you want to know?"

He chuckled. "You'll never answer a general question, will you. You know very well what I'd be curious about – what sort of a hand is David when it comes to carving the Sunday roast?"

"There's a tale going about that you've found a good lode on Little Tregathennan."

"Promising," he admitted. "Kindly and promising. And let's get the other red herring out of the way – I hear you've still found nothing very big at Deepwork."

He let the renewed silence press his question.

This dark was kindly, too, she thought – kindly and promising. You could talk by just thinking aloud. She tried it: "I suppose it was absurd to imagine that all men would be the same."

"Or all women."

"I mean, David was never *ardent*."

"Oh? Not in *any* way?"

"It's hard to tell. Sometimes he seems to be. I feel that sort of . . . tremble in him. And then I don't know whether it fizzles out or if he deliberately checks himself."

There was another silence before he said, "I don't want to keep pressing you with questions, Beth. I wouldn't like you to feel I'd tricked you into talking. But, on the other hand . . . anything you feel like confiding . . .?"

"What makes you think there might be?"

"You looked a bit glum today."

"I must be more careful in future."

"Yes, a politician's wife must learn to do without facial expressions."

"You may sneer, Courtenay, but life with David is rich and fulfilling."

"And ardent?"

They left the road and took the path over the moor north of Wheal Pallas. Their footfall softened, became less intrusive. They seemed to glide among the ling on the wide, pale, dusty pathways.

"I hate this sort of self-examination," she said.

"Why? What does it reveal?"

"You remember that first night when we . . . you know. When I came back to Yeol Parc with you?"

"I'll never forget it."

"I was so . . . naive. Every girl gets told that men only want one thing. And if you let them, they'll just cast you aside."

"Hah! That was David's tale – Mary Curnow. It's a convenient fiction for the moralists, isn't it."

"Never mind that. The thing is, next morning it was I who wanted to cast you aside! I didn't want to share my neat, orderly, busy, dutiful life with the sort of woman who could do a thing like that. And demand it again and again."

"It was exactly the same for me."

"I don't know why David married me," she said suddenly.

"D'you know why you married him? Let me guess. At the most impersonal level, the mistress of Pallas could provide the aspiring member of parliament with an excellent platform. The elected member would, in turn, make the wife's position socially unassailable."

"Lilian told you I said that."

"All Cornwall's been saying it, my lover. But, leaving aside such practicalities, I suppose there's also . . ."

Talk was useless. If she wanted talk she'd turn to David, who was worth ten of Courtenay. She looked up at him. The feeble light of the crescent moon was gentle to his features. She halted and put her arms around him. He fell silent. His embrace folded her into that old, familiar warmth of his body, which was the warmth of the fierce, dark half-love they uniquely shared.

"What is it?" he asked.

She clung more tightly to him. "Give me a baby," she begged.

END OF PART FOUR

PART FIVE

HOME IS WHERE . . .

CHAPTER FORTY-THREE

OR A MAN, loneliness is a fact of life, of the world; he discovers it "out there." For a woman it is a fact of herself; she nurtures it like a child in a second, secret womb whose term is silent, whose births are internal.

When Elizabeth at last mustered the courage to tell David she was expecting a child, he laughed for joy. "See!" he cried, "Oh ye of little faith! Did I not tell you: The Lord will find a way."

"But are you not . . . surprised?"

"Of course not. Only the godless scientist mocks at miracles."

Does he really believe such things? she wondered. *Or has he an infinite capacity to adjust to uncomfortable truths – the way he can assimilate party policies that run against all his previous convictions?* She almost risked telling him that the baby would be Courtenay's but she held back for fear that it would only take him about ten seconds to readjust his entire understanding of biology, not to mention morality.

The speed of his response had one unexpected effect: It shut her out of his life even more firmly than his now-permanent self-exclusion from her half of the bed; for, just as that left her body bereft of him, so this denied her any true contact with his mind. She became aware of that second growth within her, that essentially female loneliness, seeded by David's twin withdrawal.

And yet their lives were filled with laughter, friendship, good humour, warmth. They were dedicated to each other, loyal in every sense but one; they were even, it could be said, wrapped up in their marriage. All these blessings they had in greater abundance than many whose attachment was more passionate. In a way, her loneliness lay too deep, it was too inward, to affect the surface of her life in the slightest degree. Courtenay made her more aware of it than David.

She now became almost reckless in her demands on him, taking advantage of every possible encounter. Now that he no longer needed to "finish like a gentleman," he was more relaxed, more sensual with himself and her. There were times when she could simply lie there after the storm, drawing together the havoc of her body and senses, luxuriating in their continuing contact, observing the different nature of his ecstasy.

How opposite they were, this *man*, this *woman*. Like their different brands of loneliness, their joys also were exterior or internal: He entered her body, lay inside it, renewed his vigour there, emerged reborn, went back into the world; she held him within her and the peak of her joy was in that very act of holding him; she felt no rebirth, no emergence, no loss, no change of state. She was among the eternal, exactly as she was; his was the mutable part; he undertook that endless cycle of entry and rebirth, coming and going, rising and falling. Without it, some part of him would die. She felt for him an infinite pity; it was their closest brush with true love.

Yet women could die, too, while their bodies lived on. Betrayal could kill them. Oenone, for instance, would seek no further encounter with love, with men; she had shrivelled up inside after Courtenay's betrayal of her. Even the news of Elizabeth's pregnancy — which she had been the first to share — had hardly raised a smile.

One day, when Oenone had gone on some errand to her brother, Elizabeth brought Courtenay up to her old bedroom, now spare, the one that had been Bill's mother's — where she had vowed he would never enter.

"We've got hours and hours," she said happily. "Oenone always spends half the evening with her brother, and David has a meeting of the Borlase School governors tonight, so he probably won't come home at all."

But less than an hour later they heard the back door slam. Elizabeth's blood froze. Courtenay held his breath and fell limp inside her.

"Get up," she hissed. "Get dressed — quick! I'll have an appendicitis or something and you can pretend you just . . ."

"Listen!" He laid a finger over her lips.

Footsteps, the swish of a dress on the stair.

"What did you tell Oenone?"

"That I was going up to the mines."

"I'll swear that's her tread. No one else would just walk in like that."

The visitor reached the stairhead; the swish of the dress grew ever louder.

"Oh God!" Elizabeth's heart seemed to be leaping out at her throat. "Please, please don't let her come in here!"

Courtenay dived beneath the sheets and huddled tight against her.

The door opened. It was, indeed, Oenone. She saw Elizabeth and hastily tugged at the door, three-quarters closing it, leaving only her disembodied head inside the room. "You are all right ar'ee, missis?" she asked. Her eyes scanned the disorder of clothing . . . the man's jacket . . . the trousers . . . "Oh my gidge!" she cried. Her head vanished and she slammed the door.

Elizabeth sprang from the bed and struggled into her dressing gown —

the old one, which she had left here, thinking it too unfeminine, too unattractive, to be pleasing to David!

"What on earth are you doing?" Courtenay asked.

"It was Oenone. She saw all your clothing, probably even recognized it. I've got to go and talk to her."

He began to dress, too.

As she ran downstairs, four at a time, she heard the back door slam again. But when she arrived at the kitchen she found Oenone there, putting the kettle on the hob.

"Who was that?" Elizabeth asked.

"Who was what?"

"I heard the back door slam."

"Oh, I was going out to the pump but then I thought there was enough in the kettle."

It sounded reasonable, yet Elizabeth was sure there had been someone else – otherwise, why had Oenone pulled the bedroom door like that, until it almost throttled her?

Oenone looked at her and smiled. "I 'speck there's enough – even for three on us."

Angered but vulnerable Elizabeth countered: "I'm quite sure you came upstairs with someone else behind you. But I don't suppose you'd welcome me prying into your life – any more than I wish you to pry into mine."

Oenone smiled impregnably.

"I expect you recognized the clothes?" Elizabeth asked.

The woman sniffed. "Didn't 'zackly need to."

"Meaning?"

"Well, I didn't think you belong to go couranting with more'n one shiner, anyway."

Elizabeth sat down, aghast. "You mean – you already knew?"

"Well, afore you was married I . . . guessed, like. I never thought you and that one was still carrying on, though."

Courtenay gave a cough at the door. "In that case, there's no point in me hanging around outside." He entered, fully dressed. Elizabeth, in dressing gown and carpet slippers, felt like a slut.

"Now listen, you!" Courtenay went threateningly close to Oenone, wagging a ridiculous, schoolmasterly finger in her face. "If you so much as . . ."

Oenone did an extraordinary thing. She put her hands each side of his face and pulled him to her, kissing him fully on the lips. His alarmed eyes stared past her at an equally astonished Elizabeth.

All at once it struck her that Oenone was trying to hide something – throw them off the scent by this strange, erratic behaviour.

"There now!" Oenone said as she let Courtenay go. "Forgotten! That's what you always wanted, innit? Forgiven and forgotten, all right, my lover?"

Elizabeth had never seen such a transformation. In less than a minute the woman, usually so taciturn – and lately so moody – had changed into a flighty, carefree, impish young girl.

"What's come over you?" she asked.

The kettle began to sing. Oenone went to the cupboard and took down the teapot. "One, two, or three?" she asked gaily.

"I'm going to get dressed," Elizabeth said.

She had a feeling that Courtenay might extract more of the truth if they were alone.

When she returned, the pair of them were chatting away like old friends. Five minutes later Courtenay rose and took his leave.

"Well?" she asked as she saw him to the door.

"Nothing. She said nothing – or very little. I'll tell you next time we meet."

"When will that be?"

"Soon."

But Elizabeth could not wait. She went directly back to the kitchen and said, "Now tell me, Oenone – why have you been so miserable lately, and why are you suddenly like this – so happy?"

Oenone had no real guile, only a sort of peasant cunning. Elizabeth could see her trying and rejecting half a dozen implausible tales. "Because I was a-deceiving of'ee, missis," she said at last.

"In what way?"

"I got a peeching young feller, that's what. And we've been a-couranting together here when you've been gone."

"In my old bedroom?"

She answered with a guilty smile.

"Who is it, Oenone?"

"I aren't saying. He's beknown to'ee, I'll tell'ee that. And he do live overnigh here, anist Tregathennan. There now – that's already more'n what I ought to tell'ee."

"It still doesn't explain why you're so glad all of a sudden."

"'Course it do. I aren't so guilty, like."

It almost rang like the truth – but not an *Oenone* kind of truth.

"I'm not cheating Mr. Troy, you know," Elizabeth told her.

Oenone blushed and looked away.

"We've got to talk about it," Elizabeth went on. "We can't just let the accusations hang in the air."

"I aren't accusing of'ee, missis. Honest."

"Don't be absurd. You *must* be. So I have to tell you this: Courtenay takes nothing that Mister values. Mister has never touched me in that way. I think he's one of those men who are so interested in spiritual things and things of the mind that he doesn't . . . well, understand ordinary people like us, with ordinary feelings and ordinary needs. That's all."

Oenone, still distressed, merely stared at her boots.

"Listen, I was going mad – I honestly thought I was going mad – until . . . well, I wanted a baby, you see. Can you understand? Haven't you ever . . .?"

Her voice tailed off as she saw a big, fat tear roll down Oenone's cheeks and darken the collar of her dress.

"Oh my dear! I'm so sorry – what is it?"

"Babby," she snuffled. "When you said . . . that about wanting a babby."

Elizabeth put her arms awkwardly about her. "I'm sorry, my dear. Oh, I'm so sorry. It was thoughtless of me. But you'll see – this fellow of yours – you'll get married and . . ."

"No!" It was one long, soft call of anguish.

"Why not?"

"'Cause he've already got a wife, that's why!"

Elizabeth closed her eyes tight and shook her head, unable to find the words to express the sympathy she so deeply felt.

"He've already got a wife and he've been and gone and fixed a babby inside I! There now!"

CHAPTER FORTY-FOUR

MRS. MITCHELL, MORWENNA, and Hamill sat around the green baize card table, hands spreadeagled upon it, thumbs to thumbs, little fingers to little fingers.

"And now?" Mrs. Mitchell asked.

"I suppose we ask if there's anybody there?" Morwenna suggested. "Isn't that what they do?"

"We wait and gather the Power," Hamill told them.

They waited five minutes. Stays creaked. Digestive tracts gurgled. The wind soughed among the branches outside. Nothing happened.

Surreptitiously, Mrs. Mitchell stared at the other two, weighing them up. "Perhaps if we turn down the lamp a little?" she suggested timidly.

"Wait!" Hamill barked. "I feel it!"

Still nothing happened.

"It's as I told you, dear." Mrs. Mitchell gave Morwenna a sad, gentle smile. "Whatever these powers may be, I simply don't possess them."

"Can't you feel it!" Hamill almost shouted.

There were three distinct knocks; it was hard to locate them but they came from just beneath or just above the table.

"Now," Hamill said triumphantly. "We must each put a finger to the glass."

The two women obeyed. "Such nonsense," Mrs. Mitchell said.

An hour later the others had to agree. Once and once only the glass had visited the letters: B . . . I . . . L . . . L. For the rest they had spelled out long and at times frenzied sequences of gibberish.

"It must mean something," Hamill said crossly, looking at the reams of rubbish he had scribbled down at the glass's 'dictation.' He folded the paper carefully. "It's a code. I'll try and break it."

"Powers!" Mrs. Mitchell scoffed affectionately. She turned to Morwenna. "It's you I'm sorry for, dear. Your hopes must have been cruelly raised by this nonsense."

But Morwenna merely smiled. "We must give the poor boy time."

Petty reported these goings-on to Elizabeth, who felt more certain than ever that her mother was playing some devious game. She said as much.

"Well, she'll find she's not the only one who can play games," Petty replied. But no matter how Elizabeth pressed her, she would explain no further.

The second year of the Archipelago was even better than the first. The profit went straight into improvements on the farms, which enabled them to raise the rents once more. This time it was only three shillings – and, though there were grumbles aplenty in the best rural tradition, there was no revolt. A half-dozen or so of the older farmers either couldn't or wouldn't go in for the newer, more profitable crops; they gave up their tenancies and took other farms from more obliging landlords. Pascoe seized the chance to redistribute the land, making the neighbouring farms larger and even more profitable. Down in Helston market the grumbles about the Pallas Estate took on a grudging admiration. The rent rise brought in a further three hundred odd a year, some of which went into yet more improvements; the rest vanished into the bottomless pit of Deepwork.

When David saw the balance sheets his voice joined Pascoe's in telling her she was foolish not to raise a mortgage and improve the estate properly. "I know Pallas is none of my business," he said, "but this piecemeal patching-up – trying to pay for the improvements out of income –won't do at all. We'll both be tilled in our graves by the time the job's done. On the present rents, the arable land alone is worth over seventy thousand. And if what your mother says is true, the heirlooms would be valued at over a quarter of a million. It's absolutely absurd to be scratching around for a few thousand to improve the farms."

"I just have a dread of debt, that's all. And Pascoe *ought* to feel the same. I don't know why he's in chorus with you."

David eyed her shrewdly. "A fear of debt? Or a fear of the trouble Morwenna might make about it?"

"It's just too much of a risk, David."

"I can take care of Morwenna, you know. I can stick a crowbar in *her* spokes. Just say the word."

But Elizabeth held out against any mortgage on the land. She had a suspicion, which she dismissed as unworthy, that David wanted to see some loose cash in the bank; he would soon have need of it.

In that one respect she dreaded his election. While he remained a candidate he was very little drain on her purse. He went everywhere by pony and trap when the weather was good, and he travelled second class on the trains when it was not. He took pasties and fruit rather than buy meals out; and he had no extravagant tastes. The greatest expense was in the list of charities they now had to patronize.

But when he became the sitting member for St. Ives, that would all change. An MP receives no salary yet he must keep up a certain style in London. There would be the rent of an apartment to find, travel to and from Cornwall, postage, the wages of a secretary, meals out, clothes . . . where would it all come from?

From cash-in-hand – if there was any.

Her baby, she thought, would be born in July, but that guess was based on the moralist's certainty that every carnal act lights a nine-month fuze; biology is a less vengeful science. In fact, as the high summer of 1892 drew on, it became clear that August was a more likely month.

July, then, found her with time on her hands. She decided to pay George and Lilian a visit in Mousehole. She had met them often in Helston since their return from Paris but, for one reason or another, she had put off several invitations to their studio.

David protested that she was much too close to her time, but from the start she had refused to be treated as an invalid. The baby was at least a month, if not six weeks, away.

Mousehole is one of those Cornish fishing villages just made for artists – though George had chosen it for the more practical reason that his uncle owned a row of fishing cottages there, plus a few acres at the end of the lane. George had taken a lease on the last three cottages in the row, one of which had a great sail loft that had converted easily into a studio. He had also rented the fields – all for a song.

Mousehole itself stands on the western curve of Mount's Bay, where the rising sun warms it early. At the other end of the day, when even the most sluggish artist is up and about, the light spills down over the cottages, full into the natural basin of the harbour; it soaks into the water, the old stone walls, the bobbing fishing boats, the limewashed houses, giving them an intensity and depth of colour that always seems more Mediterranean than English.

"It makes me feel I'm twenty again," George often said.

Elizabeth left her pony and trap down at the inn and walked up the hill to the cottage. As she approached it, she was filled with envy for the simplicity of their life.

Lilian appeared at the gate of the field, recognized her, vaulted it like a gymnast, and came running down the lane to greet her.

"You should have sent word! I have nothing baked – oh dear, but how lovely to see you! Are you sure you ought to be out?"

Elizabeth laughed and assured her she was fine. However, she was grateful to take the weight off her feet and let herself be cosseted into a soft, chintzy seat in the back garden. She had loved the feeling of the baby inside her during the early months, but now the heaviness had become wearisome. The day was fine and warm and a stout hedge of escallonia kept the onshore breeze at bay.

George's greeting was just as effusive. He went back indoors to stand his brushes in turps. Lilian sat in the grass and began to shell peas. "Our second crop," she said proudly. She threw the empty pods over a stockade of rejected fishing net behind which a dozen hens fretted and darted for the spoils. "I know I ought to make soup from them," she added defensively. "But it's good for the fowls, too – and we eat the eggs."

Elizabeth laughed. "If the Lilian of three years ago could see you now!"

"Or if I could see her – we'd both scream."

"You once brazenly scolded me for going brown in the sun. Look at you now!"

"That's what I mean."

"No regrets?"

Lilian shook her head. Her long, fair hair was unrestrained by comb or band of any kind; she reminded Elizabeth of some wild, moorland filly, tossing her mane, free as the wind.

Fine while the money lasts, she told herself.

George returned. "A glass of wine?" he suggested.

"It's home-made," Lilian added quickly, with an incongruous blend of pride and warning in her tone.

"Heavens above – you're both very Kelmscottish and utopian here, aren't you!"

"We found a grove of elderberry down Lamorna valley. We simply couldn't pass them by."

Elderberry wine did not go particularly well with dressed crab, but that was their lunch. Crabs were a penny a piece on the quays below.

The pair of them plagued Elizabeth for all the latest Helston talk; one would have imagined they were exiles on some remote South Sea island instead of living just fourteen miles away.

Inevitably there came the moment she had been dreading, when Lilian asked, "Would you like to see George's latest?" But much to her surprise Elizabeth found that fifteen or more paintings, all in the same "textures-gone-mad" style, as she called it, had quite a different effect from one seen in isolation. She began actually to like the blurred outlines, the exaggerated colours, the obsession with pattern, the oddly snapshot-like points of view, the octopussy shadows with their intense, pale colours.

"It's *paint*, you see?" Lilian said. "No tricks. No pretence."

It pleased Elizabeth that she could now dimly grasp what their excitement was all about. "The tumbling, tossing restlessness of things," he had said at the wedding breakfast. That was so exactly right. All his canvases were full of the energy that is always *there* – the energy that photographs can never capture because all they can do is freeze the world.

"And these over here are what he's working on now," Lilian said offhandedly, leading her to the far end of the studio. The mingled aromas of turpentine and poppyseed oil were heady, the next best thing to a village bakery at dawn.

When she saw the pictures she understood why Lilian's offhandedness had sounded too careful: They were all paintings of her – naked.

There were enough classical nudes staring down from the walls of Pallas to make the coy, sculptural display of flesh seem acceptable to Elizabeth. But here was no coyness, no pale marble. Here was hot flesh, sensual in colour, oriental in its languor. They showed Lilian partly dressed – half-wrapped in a gorgeous silk shawl; lying ripe and stupefied with her blouse open to a caressing sunlight; standing before a tall looking-glass, hands sensuously on her hips, frankly admiring herself – and again the sun was spread upon her like butter.

A certain sadness filled Elizabeth, an undefinable sense of loss. She turned to see how Lilian was reacting, only to find her gone. She was sitting on a couch, up near George's easel, wearing nothing but a great straw hat stuck with everlasting flowers about its brim. Her only other clothing was one dark red stocking. "Come and sit up here and talk to me," she called.

"As long as I don't have to undress, too."

"We'll let you off this time," Lilian promised.

"I'd paint you like fruit," George said. "Wonderful ripe fruit. A hymn to fruitfulness, that's what you'd be. Don't you think it's about time the mistress of Pallas had her portrait painted? Something *real* to hang beside those sickly old masters?"

"Morwenna and my mother would only stick pins in it."

While they chatted she watched George at work. The painter did not overrule the lover. He stood there, peering hungrily through his half-closed eyes at Lilian's body; every stroke on the canvas was an act of love.

George must have guessed her thoughts. "Experience is a good thing," he said, "but not very important. Unless it brings about a change in attitude. Attitude is all."

When he rested the pose Lilian stretched like a cat. The sun caressed her flesh. Her hooded eyes stared out of the pale shadows, filled with a contentment beyond measure.

Once again, Elizabeth was suddenly filled with that almost unbearable sense of loss.

CHAPTER FORTY-FIVE

TREVANION TROY WAS BORN on the morning of the twenty-seventh of August, 1892. As births go, it was neither very hard nor very easy. At the time it felt like the end of the world. Pain was a liquid in her veins; it made the sweat sprout from every pore. But when it was over, even in those first few moments, when Doctor Reeves put the lusty little fellow on her slack, exhausted belly, she was filled with waves of forgetful gratitude. And within five minutes it was only her mind that sustained the memory.

Oenone went into labour that same afternoon; the doctor stayed on, and the child, Davina, was born before midnight, also with no complications.

David, who was over the moon with his son, could hardly bring himself to touch her for fear that she might collapse, shatter like a porcelain rose.

On the second day, Courtenay called. Elizabeth nodded to the nurse and she left them alone.

He stared down at Trevanion a long time in silence.

She watched him. *We did that*, she thought. *We made that funny little creature between us*. But the notion stirred nothing very profound within her; Courtenay did not really exist at those depths of her life. In some inexplicable way, Trevanion was already much more David's son than he ever would be Courtenay's.

Did Courtenay feel that too? Was that why he now turned to her and said, "Well done! By God, Beth, you must be the proudest woman alive."

She stretched out her hand and gave his a squeeze, not trusting her voice.

Keeping a hold of her hand he sat beside her bed and said, "So now you have everything." There was a flatness behind his words, a sadness, as if the sight of the boy had at last borne home to him all that he was missing, could never share. It would not be the magical bonds of fatherhood, which David had already forged; Courtenay's loss would lie in the physical, practical things: telling stories, playing bears, sailing toy boats, going on walking holidays. Those moments, too, would all belong to David.

She did not want him to dwell on such thoughts. "It's marvellous," she agreed. "You know when you're very young and you get the Christmas present you've always wanted? That ecstasy which fills you for about ten minutes and then slowly fades? Well it's like that except it *doesn't* fade. It goes on and on and on. What's happening outside – civil war? Floods? Seven plagues? It wouldn't matter, you know." She laughed.

"There must be something in it," he observed. "Oenone, too, is looking happier than I've ever seen her."

"You went to her first?"

She wondered if *he* could possibly be the unknown father. No – of course, he had been with her that day.

"They weren't going to let me see you at all."

"Oh, this is ridiculous, Courtenay. They're all behaving as if I'm ill. Will you do something for me?"

"If it's legal."

"Get one of the carriers in Helston to go down Porthleven harbour and fill two big kieves with salt water and bring them up here. Actually, you could ask Zakky Gilbert – he owes me a favour."

"May I inquire what you want it for? That business about drinking seawater – it's all been disproved, you know."

"I want to heat up one of them and bath in it. Followed by a cold plunge in the other kieve. Then I shall rise from my non-sickbed."

He gave an affectionate shake of the head. "Doc Reeves'll shoot you."

"I won't stay still long enough. What did Oenone say? Who does Davina look like?"

"The image of Oenone, actually. The same as Trevanion and you. We're two lucky men, Mr. A.N. Other and me." He laughed. "There's not one grain of romance in her soul, is there! I said to her what a coincidence it was – both being born on the same day. And she told me some tale of two sows her father once owned who both farrowed the same afternoon in the same corner of the same field – and lying in such a way that one sow's litter was born directly onto the other sow's teats! They completely swopped litters. She stood there and watched it happen, and she thought it was the funniest thing ever."

"Charming, I must say! You been over to Mousehole lately, have you?"

He wiped the corners of his mouth as if wondering how much to tell her. "I bought a couple of George's paintings, as a matter of fact."

An instinct made her say, "Not those ones of Lilian!"

He nodded, not letting his eyes stray from her.

"It doesn't seem decent, Courtenay."

"Why not?"

"You know very well. You won't be able to hang them."

"I already have – halfway up the stair. Pride of place. I don't think of them as Lilian. They're more than just her. When you look at them, don't they make you feel good to be a woman?"

Her tongue rested playfully on her lip. "I don't need one of George Ivey's pictures to do that to me."

"You!" He grinned conspiratorially. "The astonishing thing to me is that your mother saw it at once, at the wedding breakfast – in that portrait everyone thought was one of George's jokes."

"My mother saw nothing," Elizabeth told him. "My mother is all things to all people. That's how she makes her way in the world."

"You oughtn't to be so ungrateful. She's doing a splendid job for you at Pallas House."

"And you have her own word to prove it – I know!"

"More than that. What you probably don't know is that the executors of old Bishop Chavasse have at long last decided to sell up the contents of Trengrouse Hall. Vesey's of Old Bond Street are coming down from London to conduct the auction, which'll be a three-day affair. The whole district can talk of nothing else. The list of lots will take up four pages in the *Vindicator*, so you can just imagine the size of it. But the point is: old Vesey himself is coming down here – and guess where he'll be staying?"

"At Pallas?" She didn't believe it.

He nodded. "Courtesy of your mother."

"Oh, she's up to something, Courtenay. I just know it. You get that sea water up here as fast as Zakky can carry it!"

CHAPTER FORTY-SIX

THAT SAME AUGUST the Conservative administration of Lord Salisbury resigned after six years in office. The Queen sent for Gladstone, who agreed to form a new Liberal government that would tackle once and for all the question of Irish Home Rule. The sitting member for the St. Ives division, who had long intimated to his colleagues that he had tired of politics – and especially of Irish Home Rule – took advantage of the new Liberal tide to tender his resignation and leave what looked like a clear run for his successor, David Troy.

Elizabeth, not knowing when she might be able to enjoy her next peaceful day, went to visit George and Lilian. She took Oenone with her. After their own lunch they retired to feed their babies. Lilian's emotion as she watched them was tinged with a certain temporary gratitude that she was not yet a passenger in that particular boat. Perhaps after the winter exhibition of the Newlyn Society . . . if the paintings began to sell . . .?

"I wish you'd let George come in and sketch the pair of you," she said.

"Oh my gidge!" Oenone giggled and looked daringly at Elizabeth. Her response to the paintings of Lilian, nude, had been in the same vein.

"Now what d'you mean by giggling like that, Oenone?" Lilian asked with cool amusement.

"Stop it, Lilian," Elizabeth intervened. "You know very well. You only want to stir up an argument with me. George can stay in his studio until we've finished, and that's that."

"But it's not as if you're doing anything unnatural, or shameful. The madonna-and-child theme is . . ."

"It's just something private, dear. One day you'll understand these things."

"*I* shouldn't mind," Oenone chipped in. "I never had my photey painted."

The word was a red rag to Lilian. "It's not a photo," she cried. "It's . . ."

Elizabeth laughed. "Poor darling! You have so many battles to fight on behalf of that man – and on so many fronts at once!"

Trevanion was gorged. He fell away and lay comatose. His milk-mottled lips were slack, parted in the rictus of indulgence – no smile of thank-you, no acknowledgement of her part in his gratification. *Oh Courtenay – why does no one see the slightest trace of you in him when it is all I see?*

She lifted him to her shoulder to get up his wind. "Oh, may I?" Lilian asked.

Elizabeth handed him over eagerly. Those sudden, curdy eruptions at her ear were not among her favourite moments with the child. Trevanion made no complaint, though he usually permitted no one to take him from his mother. *Do they have some primitive awareness of kinship?* she wondered.

They chatted on about nothing in particular until Elizabeth made some remark about Lilian's unconventional behaviour. Lilian grew indignant. Elizabeth's behaviour, she said – carrying the baby around everywhere, keeping Oenone on when all the county expected her to be dismissed – was far more unconventional. "I don't know how you get away with it," she concluded.

Oenone then made an astonishing interruption. "They cried wolf too often," she told them.

Elizabeth turned to her in surprise. "Cried wolf?" The phrase – and the idea – was not one that would occur naturally to Oenone. She had come out with several novel thoughts recently; whoever A.N. Other (as Courtenay called him) might be, he was enlarging her horizons more successfully than Elizabeth had ever managed.

"They said as you'd bankrupt Pallas inside a year," Oenone pointed out. "They said as how the Dragon'd get the bettermost of'ee. They was certain as how the frost'd finish off all they lent lilies when you planted them first. And as for a farm all scudded about the parishes like the Archipelago – weel, that was just daw-brained! They swore as Cap'n Body'd feck every penny off of'ee for Pallas Consols. And Preacher Troy, he'd grab the reins once he got his ring around thy finger. They said as how you'd surely settle down fitty once you was wed proper. Their tongues have put you in your box and carried you down the lych-way so often now, no one's willing to open his mouth agin'ee no more. That's how I do see it."

Elizabeth was too surprised to answer.

"I think it's simply that they've got the whiff of prosperity," Lilian said. "There's new money on the breeze that blows out of Pallas toward Helston – and Helston folk have never let *anything* stand in the way of money. Talking of which, Beth, I need a new frock. When are you going to let George paint your portrait?"

Trevanion gave a great belch of agreement. Elizabeth took him back and laid him down to sleep. "Well, the election campaign starts in earnest next week. Why doesn't George follow us round sketch the hustings? I like his sketches – he draws beautifully. Much better than he paints. I'll pay four shillings for each sketch I like."

"Four!" Lilian protested.

"I think four is generous. He could easily knock off five sketches an hour. That's a pound – enough to live on for a week. I wish my income was as easy got! We'll pay ten shillings for any we use in the *Vindicator*."

Lilian was appeased. "But what about a proper portrait?"

"We'll see."

"I know what you're scheming, Beth, but you haven't a hope of persuading him to do an academic-salon painting, you know."

"I'm not against all impressionistic painting, but . . ."

"I know – you like the pretty-pretty kind. Well, you won't get it from George."

"Not even for ready money?"

Lilian stared back haughtily.

The bye-election, which was held in mid-October, was a lifeline to Elizabeth. Ever since that first visit to Mousehole she had felt despondent. Until then she had been convinced that George and Lilian had ruined their lives with a disastrous choice; but after seeing them together she suspected that the honour might, in fact, be hers. The rough and tumble of the campaign left no time for such gloom.

David, remembering her performance at the Central Hall, Westminster, set her name down to speak at half a dozen meetings. She suddenly ceased to be a porcelain rose. His only acknowledgement of her condition was to say, "You probably don't feel up to taking on more than that at the moment, do you?"

"I'll tell you after the first of them," she said warily.

That first meeting, in a crowded Temperance Hall at St. Just, heart of the Land's End mining district, found her absolutely petrified. David was not there; he had engagements in St. Ives itself and at Carbis Bay. George was with her, of course – that is, he was in the hall – but as a speaker she was alone up there on the platform.

Alone she stood up and alone she died.

Most of those present were Labour supporters. They sat in stony silence and let her flounder. She forgot David's advice – to have no more than four simple points, all linked by one chain of logic, and to make each point three times in different ways. She forgot the speech they had rehearsed together. She caught George's eye; he gave her a huge smile of encouragement, but it did not help. She just stood there and searched those granite faces while she hemmed and hawed and took endless sips of water and waited for something to strike her – inspiration . . . memory . . . anything.

Even a rotten cabbage.

The brickbats came, but in verbal form. Tom Jenkins, secretary of the Penzance Labour Party, stood up to deliver what he must have thought would be the coup de grace. He asked if she were the same Mrs. Troy who owned the *Vindicator*.

"You know perfectly well that I am, Mr. Jenkins."

"And you think 'tis fair, do you, that your paper gives your husband so much free support?"

She felt better at once – a concrete issue at last. "You surprise me," she said. "For your sake I hope your party leader, Mr. Keir Hardie, doesn't hear that you asked such a question."

A more experienced man would have pressed her to answer. Tom Jenkins said, "Why?"

"Because only yesterday he was reported in *The Times* as complaining about those Tory candidates who persuaded their friends the brewers to 'accidentally' let barrels of beer fall off their drays as they pass down working-class streets at election time. 'We have no fear of well-reasoned argument,' says your leader, 'but free beer is no argument at all. It merely shows up the bankruptcy of the Tory case.' However, Mr. Jenkins, it now seems you can't take well-reasoned argument either. I'm beginning to wonder about the bankruptcy of *your* case!"

The analytical part of her mind knew she had not answered his point. But the sudden buzz of approving laughter excited a tiny swirl of victory blood in her veins. She had grasped the first essential of an election meeting: It is not a tutorial in logic.

After that she rediscovered the thread of her speech and it went down well. She doubted if she swayed many minds in that Labour stronghold, but she gave as good as she got and, most important of all, she had cut her teeth.

"Thanks for that smile," she told George as they drove back through the dark, along the narrow lanes to Penzance. "It lifted me up just when I needed it. What did you think?"

"Very good!"

"No, George, that's sheer flattery. But I'll be better next time. What was the best bit?"

"Oh, from the front. No doubt of it. Where you can see all their faces. Degas has done some good ones of people in theatres. And Sickert. But I think elections almost beat the theatre."

She laughed. "In fact, you didn't hear a word I said!"

He cleared his throat. "Was I supposed to?"

"Never mind."

"I have some beauties for the paper. You couldn't make it a pound apiece, could you? That's still dirt cheap."

She ignored the provocation. After a pause she said, "You've changed so thoroughly, George, I don't know where I am with you now."

"Which of us d'you like better, lawyer or artist?"

"There was something never quite right about Lawyer Ivey."

"My feelings exactly."

"The thing is, did you *know* you wanted to be an artist, or did you just know that being a lawyer was wrong, without having the first idea what the right thing might be? D'you see what I mean?"

His answer came softly out of the dark: "I see what you mean, Beth. You mean you're in the same pickle as I was."

That idea had not occurred to her. She was about to protest when she realized it was true. "It's all so random, isn't it," she said. "I stood up there tonight, facing all those people, and I suddenly thought, *What on earth am I doing here? Why me? What a ridiculous and improbable chain of accidents has brought me to this unlovely hall at the end of England!* Droning away at the back of my mind I could hear the speech I ought to give . . . Home Rule, local control of drink-licensing hours, industrial insurance, Welsh disestablishment, and so on . . . and I just kept saying to myself, 'Surely I can tell them something *better* than that!' But nothing came to me. Isn't that awful?"

He didn't answer.

"Don't you think it's awful?" she pressed.

He spoke with reluctance. "I fear the awful bit is yet to come. When you talk of that improbable chain of events, it's a chain about your ankles, with the other end welded to Pallas. You didn't forge it. You didn't fasten it there. You're like an actor, imprisoned inside other people's scripts. First Bill's and now David's." He chuckled at a sudden memory. "That New Year's Eve party at Courtenay Rodda's – remember? Lilian told me how her brother had planned your dumb crambo on 'wedlock.' And halfway through it you and she suddenly tore up his script and started acting your own. Isn't that right?"

"Yes, but I don't see the connection."

"Don't you? It poses the question: What happens when you can no longer tolerate the weight of that chain – when you can't speak another word of Bill's script and David's script? When you suddenly see your own promised land before you? I'll answer your original question now – did I always know I needed to be an artist? Looking back, yes. But at the time, no. And I can tell you the exact moment when the change came. I was in Paris and I met a chap there, a painter, who'd just come back from a sketching holiday near Arles, with another painter. He'd been a banker or a stockbroker – something highly respectable, anyway. He had a wife and two or three children, and he'd simply thrown it all over and gone off to be a painter."

"Did he leave them well provided?"

There was a pause before George answered, "To be quite candid, I didn't even think to ask. I was so overwhelmed at the magnificence of what he'd done – and so ashamed at my own cowardice. And I went on being ashamed, and a coward, until Lilian gave me the courage." He put an arm about her and gave her a brotherly squeeze. "Will you have the courage, Beth, when your moment comes? That's going to be the awful bit."

CHAPTER FORTY-SEVEN

IF THE FATES had overheard George on the drive back to Penzance, it must have spurred them into reminding Elizabeth that they, too, had a hand in what he had called "the script." Their manner of showing it, though, had more in common with the boxing ring than the dramatic stage: They feinted with the right, and came in with a series of piledrivers from the left.

The right feint was David's election victory. His margin, though smaller than that of his predecessor, was big enough to celebrate – which they duly did in great style at dinners in St. Ives, Penzance, Hayle, and, of course, Helston. The following week Elizabeth accompanied him to London, where they found rooms in a temperance hostel in Lambeth, just over the river from the Palace of Westminster.

"The best gentleman's club in the world," it was called, and she could well believe it. Most of it was barred to her, of course – though in an apron and mob cap, carrying a carpet sweeper, she might have wandered anywhere unchallenged. The building was modern but, like the Law Courts, it had been faked to seem ancient; half a century of city grime and male usage had done wonders to abet the forgery. Not even the most fiery radical could enter those lofty gothic chambers without feeling in some way diminished by the weight of history; for though the building was new, these were, after all, the selfsame precincts where the common people of England had fought and won their centuries-long battle to curb the despotism of kings.

"It takes little imagination to see them all here," David murmured when he first showed her around the public chambers. "Cromwell, Hampden, Pym, Wilberforce . . ."

"Troy?" she joked.

"Who can say?" He was only pretending to joke.

When they parted, when she saw him walking off into the members-only heart of the palace, she knew she had finally lost him. It would be unfair to say that she and Pallas had been mere stepping stones for him, that he was now embarked on a grander journey that would leave her, as now, standing in some outer court of his life. He had been destined for Westminster long before they met. Their marriage, and the income he could now enjoy, had merely shortened his road. Nevertheless, his life had moved into realms that lay for ever beyond her; from now on, even though he came home every weekend, he would always be a visitor.

But she was never one to mope over what could not be helped. On that journey back to Cornwall she dwelled instead on her pride in their achievement; she relived the excitements of the campaign, the raucous public meetings, the joy of routing a heckler, the agony of the count, and the thrill of the declaration. She returned to Wheal Lavender resolved to dedicate herself even more strongly to the rescue of the estate and the reversal of its fortunes.

That was the feint. The first piledriver came from Pallas Consols.

The sump at Deepwork had been extended below two hundred and twenty fathoms. Despite the savings from using the old Wheal Fortune adit, the extra cost of forking dry to the new depth was horrifying. Two more exploratory drifts had been started at the 210 Level; both had gone toward Wheal Vor without discovering the slightest trace of the Great Lode. They could not drift all the way to the boundary of the abandoned mine, of course, because it was flooded up to its adit. They had to leave a two-fathom wall of rock to hold back all that water.

Early in 1893, when the latest drift had reached that safe limit, the miners came up against a section heave that dipped westward. At last it became clear why no one had found the Great Lode on the Pallas side: The whole country had dropped. The Lode was to be found lower down.

Excitement ran like fire through the whole district. The search was over – or very nearly. Now, anyone who could add or subtract two simple numbers could tell you where the Great Lode would be found. Old-timers who could still remember the levels in Wheal Vor were taken below to examine the strata revealed in the walls of the new drift. The angle of those strata was shallow, almost horizontal – a sure sign that they must lie somewhere in the region of the Great Lode – whose other name, after all, had been the Great Floor, because (almost uniquely in Cornwall) it was practically horizontal.

The old timers were unanimous in their opinion that the strata revealed on the Pallas side at two hundred and ten fathoms were identical to those at the 180 Level in Wheal Vor. So the heave had dropped all the strata by thirty fathoms on the Pallas side. The calculation was now child's play. The "back" or ceiling of the Great Lode had been at two hundred and sixteen fathoms; therefore the Great Lode would be discovered at $216 + 30 = 246$ fathoms – only another thirty-six fathoms to go.

"Only!" Elizabeth said despairingly when Captain Body brought her the good news.

The cost of it would be at least another £500, assuming the country was dry all the way down. If they struck a spring or a cistern, or worst of all, a fault that allowed Wheal Vor to drain out into Deepwork, it could bankrupt her.

The financial ice on which she was skating grew thinner by the week.

"Do we sink a new winze, missis?" the captain asked.

"Of course we do. I've already thrown the best part of eight thousand pounds down that hole. What's another one!"

"You shall have it all back inside a month," he promised.

". . . or two," she said. "I know."

The new winze was sited a good distance from Wheal Vor, just in case the vast charge of floodwater in the abandoned mine decided to flow out along the line of the heave. Naturally, once the Great Lode was located, the cost of forking out Wheal Vor and keeping it dry would be the merest nibble into the expected profits. But first find the Great Lode!

By March the search had cost almost a thousand and had yielded nothing but rock. By mid-May they were well below the level at which they had been certain-sure to find the Lode. The old timers went back for another look. All the strata dipped steeply; there was no sign of a horizontal layer. It reminded them of the country at the northern edge of the Wheal Vor sett, within thirty fathoms of the surface.

"What does that mean?" Elizabeth asked Captain Body.

"It means there must have been a second slide that we haven't come to yet."

"I don't understand all that," she said impatiently. "What does it mean in practical terms?"

"Well, missis, if we're down more'n two hundred fathom and finding what Wheal Vor found at twenty fathom, then there must have been a monster slide equal to the difference."

"Two hundred fathoms?" Elizabeth was aghast.

He nodded unhappily. "And the line of the slide must lie close to the boundary of the two setts, else one or other of us would surely have found 'n afore now."

"In other words, the Great Lode could be *another* two hundred fathoms below where we're now looking for it?"

He nodded again, reluctant to put the confirmation into words.

She raised her hands in a gesture of hopelessness. "Then we must abandon all further exploration at once, Captain Body. There can be no question of going another *twenty* fathoms, let alone two hundred."

He could not disagree with her.

All work on the new winze was stopped. The best part of ten thousand pounds simply had to be written off. Elizabeth lived in a sick daze; half a dozen times a day the enormity of the figure would strike her and she would think of all the other uses to which the money might have been put. The entire agricultural side of the estate could have been transformed . . . every single smallholding amalgamated . . . modern buildings erected. Her home farm could have added dairying to its market-garden activities; she could be the owner of a good-sized herd of pedigree Jerseys by now. Why had she ever heeded the siren voices that promised fortunes beyond reckoning from those exhausted levels?

To add to her chagrin, May was also the month in which Courtenay's venture on Tregathennan found the lode they called Chigwidden's Glory — six fathoms wide at only twenty fathoms below the adit! In June, three weeks after exploration was abandoned at Pallas Consols, Chigwidden himself came to see her. She did not know it, but that was the second piledriver; at the time he seemed like an angel of rescue.

"I wanted to tell'ee how grateful I was, Mrs. Troy, for you giving out my name to Mr. Rodda like that."

"Not at all, Mr. Chigwidden. You were very kind to me during those dreadful days. One good turn deserves another."

"Well, that was what I was thinking," he said with a canny smile. "I might be in the way to do'ee a good turn."

"Oh?"

"Yes. I'd like for'ee to come out Carleen and have a look at one particular part of the old Wheal Vor sett."

Intrigued, she agreed to join him. They set out from the village of Carleen across a ruined, wasted countryside, walking toward Deepwork. Within the first few paces, at the foot of a giant halvan of tumbled rock, he pointed to a broad swath of ground in which nothing flourished but chickweed and Great King Harry.

"Now that do belong to be a sign of arsenical poisoning," he told her. "I once thought that's where they must have tipped out soot from the old callaciner chimbley. But now you come and look at this here."

And so he led her across the old halvans and the pocket-handkerchief fields, pointing out further patches of the same two weeds. There were other signs, too — a different tinge to the green of the furze, a stunted habit in its growth. Taken together, they defined a line almost a mile long and running slightly south of due west. But there it stopped, just on the Pallas side of the common boundary with Wheal Vor.

"Now, missis," he said, "See where it've stopped? Do that recall anything to'ee?"

The penny dropped. "This is the slide we never found — right on the boundary of the two setts. Well — isn't that clever of you, Mr. Chigwidden! I only wish you'd shown me this two years ago."

He raised a cautionary finger. "That's the half of it," he said. "Now I'll tell'ee another thing. About a furlong and a half from here" — he pointed toward Poldown — "there's a patch of Great King Harry, starting on this very same line and running away to the east." He stood along the line and raised his arms like a scarecrow's. "There's only one explanation. That patch of King Harry over to Poldown is a continuation of this — or it *was* before the slide moved it over there, see?"

He seemed to have reached the end of his demonstration. She was bewildered. Where was the "good turn" he had promised?

"So," she said, "over near Poldown I've got a deposit of arsenic to do what I like with! I'm glad I didn't know it three weeks ago when we stopped the exploration, or I might have been tempted."

He nodded his head shrewdly. "I don't think it *is* arsenic, missis. My belief, now, is that you've got copper here. Copper and arsenic do often go together."

Yet more gloom. "You don't mean that I should now start a new mine over near Poldown?"

"One day, one day – yes. But I reckon as you've an easier way to prove the lode. There's another place, see."

"I'm a fool even to be listening to this – but go on."

"That lode do dip down, see – down into Pallas Consols. He's down there underneath our feet right now."

"Where?"

"Why, I'll bet he's within ten fathom of where you stopped your exploration!"

She closed her eyes, buried her face in her hands, and gave a silent scream.

"A twenty-fathom lode of copper!" he added. "Why, that's worth *three* Great Lodes put together."

"Worse and worse!" she cried.

He chuckled, thinking she was joking.

CHAPTER FORTY-EIGHT

WHOM THE GODS WILL DESTROY they first let find copper. They extended the privilege to Elizabeth that August, just before parliament went down. Captain Body's note reached Wheal Lavender at midnight. "Great King Harry is crowned," it read.

Next morning's dawn found her impatiently driving up the narrow lane to the mine buildings. Captain Body saw her coming and ran out to greet her; she had never seen him so animated. "You never clapped eyes on such bunches!" he shouted before she had even pulled up.

"How thick is the lode?"

"My dear soul, we haven't hardly begun to go down through 'n yet.

But there's everything there — native copper, sulphuret . . . come and look-see!"

He beckoned her inside. The table in the centre of his office had been cleared of all its usual bric-à-brac; in its place was ranged what looked like the booty from a raid on a museum of geology.

"There now!" he said as, from the middle, in pride of place, he picked up a lump of native copper. He was no weakling but it was as much as his right arm could lift. Its base was almost circular; the top expanded in a series of rough, spiky excrescences.

"Why it *is* a crown!" She laughed with delight.

"That's how I writ that to'ee. That's King Harry's crown right enough." He laid it back in the collection. "Fifty-two pounds o'native copper. And I'll tell'ee this — that's the first bit what they found. 'Tis an omen."

"What depth?"

"Two hundred and thirty eight below the adit. But they'll be deeper now. The gozan is as kindly as a man could wish."

She looked at the other minerals — red crystals, bunched like gems, green ones, gray ones . . . crystals that looked like tarnished gold. It was an Aladdin's cave.

He reeled off the names to her — sulphuret, tennantite, arseniate, carbonate . . . cubed ruby . . . olive copper. They meant nothing but they sounded like a million pounds.

The long search was over. The nailbiting could stop. She wanted to kiss someone, dance, drink too much, do something outrageous.

"Get me a pair of breeches," she said. "I must go down and see this with my own eyes."

His good humour vanished at once. He shook his head.

"I must," she insisted.

"I can't tell'ee not to, missis, but I'd advise'ee agin it."

"Just because I'm a woman?"

"'Tis bad luck."

"You don't believe in that rubbish."

"Maybe not, but the men do."

"Such nonsense! Anyway, I've been told old Mrs. Hosking was down Wheal Rocket almost every other day. And she lived to be ninety and the mine kept her all her life. So there!"

"In the first place, Wheal Rocket wasn't no more than a lil' ol' rabbit hole. And in the second place no one every thought of she as a woman — she were more like one o' Will Tyacke's hosses."

"Nonetheless, Captain Body, I wish to go down, and there's an end to it!"

Still he resisted. "No one never went all the way down the man-engine on their maiden trip."

"What's wrong with the way I went in last time, with Clifford Chigwidden – the Long Stope?"

"Well that's all right to the Seventy Level. How are you proposing to go the next hundred and ten fathoms? Down they ladders?"

"All right. Why couldn't I be winched down in the ore kibble? Men go down that way every day."

"If I catch them, they're off this working afore their feet can touch the grass."

In the end, of course, he had to agree it was the only way. Still rumbling, he left her to change into trousers while he made the arrangements. He would go one descent ahead of her to warn any men working naked.

For all her brave words, her spirit sank at the approach to the head of the whimshaft. A kibble filled with ore had just been winched up. It hung, twisting a degree or two on its wire rope, about six feet above the shafthead, which was capped by a heavy timber floor with a trap-doorway in the middle. The whim-boss threw a lever. Compressed air hissed as the trapdoors swung down and closed. Light tram rails bolted to their upper surface completed a railway line that ran in an endless loop between the shafthead and the dressing sheds. A bal boy pushed an empty dram forward along this line, bringing it to a halt on the trapdoors, over the centre of the shaft and immediately beneath the kibble. He picked up a hammer and clouted a lever on the side of the kibble. This released its bottom plate, which, being hinged, fell open, dropping the full charge of ore neatly into the dram. With the weight of the ore gone, a cunning counterweight automatically re-closed the bottom, which, in turn, tripped the lever back into place, locking the kibble once more.

Elizabeth watched in fascination. *What a debt we owe to human laziness,* she thought.

The captain then leaped onto the dram and shinned up the side of the kibble. At the top he stood, straddling the rim, lightly clasping the wire rope to him with both arms. The boss gave four deliberate pulls on a rope that hung beside him. It produced four distant clangs on the bell in the engine house. Captain Body plummeted from sight. Even he looked surprised.

Had he forgotten to tell the engine winder that a man was going down? Evidently so, for the boss was staring in fascination at the trapdoor hole and fanning his face as schoolboys do when someone else is getting it in the neck. The wire rope was so shiny it was impossible to tell the rate of descent. The boss threw the lever that closed the trapdoors; the rope went on paying down into the shaft through a small hole cut half into each door.

The descent was over surprisingly quickly. The boss laughed. "Nigh on two hundred fathoms in a dozen seconds!" he said. "I hope the cap'n and his breakfast is still all of a piece."

I must be mad, Elizabeth thought.

While the kibble was being refilled the boss went over to the engine shed to tell the winder he'd have Mrs. Troy for a passenger next time. No doubt they had a good laugh at the thought of the descent Captain Body must have endured.

She didn't need to shin up the kibble as he had done; they opened the trapdoors and lowered it until the top was level with the wooden floor that capped the shaft. The boss and the boy manhandled a plank across the gap so that she had a sure footing all the way. Even so, it took every ounce of her nerve to step out upon it, trying unsuccessfully to forget that some twelve hundred feet of emptiness yawned beneath her.

She grasped the rope. Never in her life, in childhood, in love, in ecstasy, in pain, had she clutched anything to her so tightly as she clutched that bundle of wire. But once she felt hard iron beneath her feet she began to relax. She had expected the kibble to swing wildly when she first stepped upon it, but its massive weight, even unladen, gave it a comforting inertia and it hardly stirred.

"Ready, missis?" the boss asked.

"Right-ho!" The voice was strangely alien.

Her senses were so peeled to everything around her that she actually heard the steam complaining as it dribbled into the cylinder in the engine house a hundred yards away. The start of her descent was so gentle that a spider dropping on its own silk would have overtaken her.

The first surprise was the long twilight of the upper levels; she had expected to be plunged into darkness almost at once. But until the boss closed the trapdoors, when she was about twenty fathoms down, she was able to see the walls of the shaft in amazing detail. Mostly it was bare elvan rock but here and there, where it passed through "killas," or clay shale, there was timber shoring to hold it in place; she could even see the nailheads in the timber.

The smell of wet rock and dust and residual smoke from recent blasting carried her back at once to the time of the man-engine disaster. She found it hard to connect that tumbled, ruined Deepwork of her memory with the present-day mine, where everything was shored-up and shipshape.

The momentum of her descent gathered pace until the apparent updraught of warm air made a moaning in her ears, and stray wisps of hair fluttered freely. There were other sounds, too. The groan of the winding wheel at the top of the shaft was transmitted down the ever-lengthening rope as it paid out; she felt the murmur of it directly through her body. Then came a sudden roaring blast that took her by surprise. At first she assumed it was a real blast — someone bringing down the back of a stope in a nearby level; but then she realized the roar must have been the new compressed-air drills.

She felt secure enough now to risk peeping over the edge of the kibble, trying to see the foot of the shaft. It was a little ring of fairy lights so far below that her eyes could hardly resolve it into separate points. She ought to have been horrified to see how much emptiness still separated her from shaft bottom. She looked up. The light that leaked in around the wooden staging was now dim to the very limits of visibility; even as she watched, it faded into total darkness. She peered down again; the ring was markedly closer, she must be falling at quite a rate.

As she neared shaft bottom a new note was added to the strange, ringing, sighing quietude of the mine — a deep rumble, groaning, complaining. That would be the bottom end of the man-engine, of course, rising and falling over its rollers; also the offset water pumps connected to its foot. They were all within a hundred yards of the whimshaft bottom, though they descended diagonally, following the lode.

The most frightening moment came at the very end, when the winding engine braked. The wire rope was fully an inch in diameter. And though twelve-hundred feet of it was now paid out, she would never have believed there was so much elasticity in it. The kibble bobbed up and down, two or three feet each way; it felt like two or three fathoms.

"Hold fast!" she heard Captain Body shout.

She clung on grimly. In the corner of her eye she saw someone operate a lever. There was a hiss and the kibble lurched as some powerful piece of machinery pushed it a little to one side and locked it against the staging.

"Keep a hold."

Another hiss as the grip of the machine relaxed. The kibble sank ten or twelve inches until the top was level with a tramway that projected out over the foot of the shaft. The captain walked out along it and offered her his hand. At last she felt safe enough to let go of the wire rope and walk with him to the haven of solid ground — not, in fact, the shaft bottom (that was several fathoms below them, to allow a sump for dead rock and flooding) but the floor of the bottom level in Deepwork. There was spontaneous applause as she reached it.

So much, she thought, for the men's alleged dislike of seeing a woman underground! It was women *workers* they didn't want there — because the wage would fall by half. And that was fact, not superstition. They had no objection at all to Mrs. Troy below ground; handclapping was, after all, less arduous than shovelling rock.

"You want to see the new pewmatic drill at work, do'ee?" the captain asked her. "Just so well now you'm down here."

"On our way back, perhaps. I can't wait to see this copper."

He nodded toward a tunnel mouth, the largest of several drifts that pierced the western cheek of the shaft. A balcony of wooden staging led round to them.

"Are those all the abandoned exploratory drifts?" she asked.

"Yes, missis. You're looking at the best part of four hundred pounds' worth there."

"Four thousand, more likely."

Though its mouth was wide, the drift they now entered was the smallest a man and a wheelbarrow could easily negotiate – thirty-six inches wide, seventy-five high. It was, she knew, almost half a mile long. If she suffered from hidden claustrophobia, this was the tunnel to reveal it.

For a moment she hesitated. "How does fresh air get in there?" she asked. "Especially all the way to the end?"

He pointed to a hose of rubberized canvas that ran round the balcony and vanished into the drift. "That's another advantage of compressed air," he said. "'Tis reduced pressure in that, see. They do open 'n up every time the air do grow foul."

The fresh air, of course, pushed the foul, sulphurous air back along the drift. They met several pockets of it on that long trudge through the tunnel. The top of the winze, when they finally reached it, was not hard to recognize. A ladder poked up into the drift and beside it was a hand winch for hauling up the dead rock. The feeble rays of the captain's lantern picked out the spoil the miners had been dumping farther on, in the cul-de-sac end of the drift.

The sight of the hole itself was a shock. "I expected something bigger," she said.

"At five guineas a fathom?" he asked sarcastically.

"Is it deep?"

"Johnny Matthews heard a cock crow down there last week, and he'll swear 'twas in Chinese."

She laughed. "But seriously?"

"'Tis three stages of thirty foot each. You want to turn back, do'ee?"

She put a foot to the ladder.

"I'd best go first," he said.

As she followed him down she tried not to picture the narrow thread of empty space that now linked her with the surface. The bottom of this winze was almost a quarter of a mile *beneath* the level of the sea. But she felt exhausted past caring by the time they finally arrived. The heat was overpowering. How was she ever going to climb up again – a hundred feet up those ricketty, swaying ladders?

Then suddenly it no longer mattered. By the light of the three oil lanterns that lit the exploration she saw such a wealth of ore that even her untrained eyes knew this was the end of the rainbow. Almost literally, for the colours were as rich and varied as any she had ever seen in plain rock in such dim light – reds, greens, blues, grays of every subtle tint, black, bronze, brown . . . and, of course, the glint everywhere of nuggets of native copper. All glistened in crystalline purity, virgin bright.

"Arthur Cousins and Johnny Matthews, ma'm," the captain introduced the two miners.

Their delight encouraged hers. Since yesterday's discovery they had enlarged the cavern to about six feet and were now driving a trial hole at right angles to the dip, so as to gauge the thickness of the lode.

"What do'ee think to 'n, boys?" the captain asked.

Johnny Matthews answered. "I'm betting six fathom. But Cousins, he's sure 'tis more'n seven." He patted the hanging wall. "See that? The angle of that would carry'ee straight up to just this side the Carleen road at Poldown. That's where this lode do dip up to grass."

Just in case she didn't grasp the point, Captain Body said, "So every bushel of 'n do lie inside the Pallas sett."

"Let's start at once on a trial shaft up at Poldown," she suggested.

He did not dismiss the idea. "I'd be happier to prove the width and assay down here first."

"Will you be looking for other venturers now, missis?" Johnny Matthews asked.

"Now there's no risk? D'you take me for a fool?"

He laughed. "That's right. You keep 'n to yourself now."

She stooped and picked up a loose nugget. "Memento," she said. "Captain Body, we're delaying the two most valuable men in the mine." To them she said, "The prosperity of four parishes during the next twenty years may depend on what you find here. So good luck, eh?"

They helped her up the first few rungs of the ladder, but all their chivalry could not ease the remaining hundred and thirty-odd steps back to the drift. By the time she reached the top she thought the heat would kill her and her heart was beating so fast she wondered how it had time to refill between the pulses. When Captain Body joined her she gasped, "Next time . . . you want to . . . dissuade me . . . just remind me . . . of this."

He was fairly out of breath, too. "We'll stop a minute if you mind to."

She accepted gratefully.

The walk back to the whimshaft bottom seemed only half as long as the inward journey. All the way they made excited plans for mining the new ore body. They'd need to build a new smelter. Tin could be half-smelted and sent away for finishing but it wouldn't pay to treat copper in that fashion. Also, there was a good market for arsenic and flowers of sulphur and other by-products. There might even be a small assay of silver in the ore.

He took her to see one of the new rock drills, powered by compressed air. "They ones we'm using up the One-thirty Level are shifting so much ore we was choking the ways. We've had to open up more backs into the lower stopes, so that's how we'm using this one down here," he explained.

The old system of hand boring had been done by a "pare" of two men and a boy. The boy held the borer while the two men hammered at it alternately with sledges. Even in the rock-boring contests, with extra-sharp tools and working out in daylight, a champion pare took up to ten minutes to bore a foot of hole; in everyday mining conditions it could take the same pare four times as long. But in those same eight minutes a pneumatic drill could accomplish what a pare would do in an hour. It consisted of a stout, adjustable leg that spanned from floor to ceiling, or wall to wall. The drill was fastened to it and driven forward on a wormscrew by turning a handle at its back end. In the earliest models the exhaust air had been led down the centre of the drill bit, which was hollow; this blew out the waste and kept the hole clean but it made such a fearful dust that the miners were choked and blinded. Now a certain amount of water was fed in along with the exhaust air so that the waste came out as mud.

What with the percussion of the drill and the fact that the miners were usually boring over their heads, everyone was soon spattered from head to foot in oily shale-mud. Every now and then the boy whose chief task it was to keep tapping the drill bit with a hammer to stop it from wedging fast had to go and fetch a hose and sluice down the men in his pare. Sweat, mud, and sluicing kept them wet from the first to the last minute of their daily core.

"Now you see how we raised our output so much," the captain said.

"I also see why the compressor station burns up an extra hundred tons of coals each month," she answered tartly. "We're making more money here but most of it is going back out so as to keep Welsh miners in beer and tobacco."

"Gusson, missis! He'll pay for hisself soon enough."

There was the sudden piercing shrill of an alarm siren. Captain Body shouted, "Keep behind me as best you may." He ran at once for the floor of the bottom level. She leaped after him and managed to keep up. The bottom of the whimshaft, obviously his destination, was only a couple of hundred yards away.

When they arrived, an appalling sight met their eyes. Water was pouring in a torrent from one of the abandoned exploratory drifts – not the one that led to the copper ground but one that had gone within a few feet of the old Wheal Vor sett. "Damn!" Captain Body cried. "It must have bursted through. That's all Wheal Vor to drain into us now."

"What about Arthur Cousins and Johnny Matthews?" she asked, trying not to sound querulous and panicky. The water had filled the whimshaft sump and was already backfilling into the drift that led to the copper.

"Yes. I got to get you out, too."

"Oh damn about me! How can we warn them and get them out?" She tried not to imagine a death by drowning at the bottom of a winze at the end of a dead-end drift.

"What slope did we put on that drift?" he asked a nearby miner.

A pair of carpenters waded around the balcony, up to their knees in water. When they reached the drift they began trying to shore off the mouth of it, to delay the inflow of the water.

"One in two hundred," the man replied.

"Hell!" Captain Body said. "'E isn't enough. At one in one fifty that drift would seal hisself afore the water reached the winze."

"'E's rising a foot a minute."

"Fair 'nuff," the captain said. "How much vein-rock is in that kibble?"

"'E's near-on full."

"Perfect!" He turned to her. "You get in that kibble now, Mrs. Troy. Sit inside of it mind, 'cause he'll go up full speed. When you do get up to grass, tell they what's happened. Say they'm to stop the whim and couple in the big fifty-four to the idle pump and go at it like Gunwalloe geese."

There were so many questions she wanted to ask, but she obeyed without a word.

As soon as he saw her on the tramway leading out to the kibble he sprinted for the balcony and waded over to the carpenters, who were already almost waist-deep. She saw him gesturing that they were to leave a gap of about fifteen inches at the top of the drift. Also not to pinch off the compressed-air line, which he now lifted above the bit of the threshold they had already managed to build and were just about to nail in place.

She understood then that he intended to run back into the drift, to warn the two miners. "Captain Body!" she shouted.

He just managed to hear her above the roar of the water. He paused and looked up.

"Don't!" she called.

He grinned and waved.

The whim plucked her up at a sickening pace. "Good luck!" she cried. The roaring dwindled until she was marooned in the eerie, windrushing silence of the shaft. In just a few seconds, as it seemed, she popped out into a blinding daylight.

The whim-boss turned pale to see her but she was already shouting the news. He wanted to help her out but she insisted that he run at once to the engine house and tell them to couple in the big pump.

The lad helped her down. She sent him to fetch the mine surgeon before she returned to Captain Body's office, where she changed back into her own clothes.

She sent another man on a fast horse to the post office in Breage. He was to telegraph the harbourmaster in Falmouth, asking him to send over a diver and whatever means of underwater lighting they might have.

And then, unable to think of any other useful activity, she began the most agonizing wait she had ever been forced to endure.

CHAPTER FORTY-NINE

THE THREE CORPSES were brought out the following day – Captain Body, Johnny Matthews, and Arthur Cousins. The diver found them in the drift, about half way to the whimshaft. The end of the air hose was near by, still bubbling. It had not helped save them.

The whole community was stunned. Captain Body was one of the most loved and respected mine captains in living memory. David came down from Westminster and went directly to Pallas Consols.

Elizabeth could not stop talking about the disaster; scenes of it played themselves over and over in her mind. "I hindered him," she told David. "He was going into the drift and I called out to wish him luck. I know it only delayed him a few seconds, but perhaps that was all the margin he had."

"Don't torment yourself, now."

"Hamill's right. There are *forces* in that mine. Why should that drift have sprung a leak at just that moment?"

"Such things happen."

"Yes, but it's the timing of them. That first inrush of water looked fierce enough to me, but actually it was only a trickle. The abandoned drift was full of wedged rock and rubble. When it cleared itself the inrush was ten times as fast. I was standing at the top of the whimshaft. I've never heard such an eerie sound."

Her obsessive reliving of the disaster was like a ritual, something that could not be avoided.

"In just twelve hours the whole of Wheal Vor equalized its floodwater with us. It was coming in so fast that some of the men at the Ninety Level, whom we thought were safe *whatever* happened, only just got out in time. It didn't stop until after midnight. By then . . ." She buried her face in her hands.

He stood behind her and caressed her neck. "You mustn't blame yourself, dearest."

"I shall blame myself until my dying hour, David."

"But why?"

"For going down there at all, for insisting on it, for forcing him to go down. And all because . . ."

"How much water is there?"

"We're flooded up to within ten fathoms of the adit — despite the fact that we've had every available pump going full blast all night. We plumbed Wheal Vor an hour ago and the level there has dropped no more than twenty fathoms. Twenty fathoms of Wheal Vor has almost filled us to the adit! Until today I never realized Wheal Vor actually incorporated so many other mines. We'll be forking out water for a year before we reach the Two-hundred again. In fact, I don't think we'll ever go back down."

"The last mines in this district, eh."

"I don't want to think about it."

"All those people out of work!" He shook his head. "At least it didn't happen during the election. Even in the midst of our tragedies we must look to the Lord for such mercies."

The engineers continued forking out at full blast round the clock, but the rest of the mine was closed until after the funerals. In three days' pumping they achieved little more than a fathom; come the winter and they wouldn't even keep pace with the inflow.

It spelled the end of Pallas Consols. "I have no choice but to knock the whole mine," she told Clifford Chigwidden.

He nodded unhappily. "I speck you'm right enough there, missis. Start again, will'ee?"

"Start again! For heaven's sake — apart from the ten thousand I spent on exploration, there's over four thousand pounds' worth of equipment lost down there. All we managed to rescue were the rock drills."

"No, I mean start over to Poldown. We know where the copper do dip out to grass, see. And 'tis inside the Pallas sett. All you need do is sink a caunter whimshaft down the lode, and a manshaft, and you could be back in business inside a month."

"Or two at the most," she said. There was a sudden catch in her throat.

"Yes, mebbe two," he said, not catching the allusion.

Later that week, at ten in the forenoon, the two miners were buried in Breage new churchyard; the same afternoon Captain Body was laid to rest in Helston, not far, in fact, from Bill's grave. David spoke orations at both services. In Breage he dwelled upon the unsung courage of those who daily take their lives into their hands, deep in the bowels of the earth, winning the raw materials on which the rest of civilization depends. In Helston he praised courage of an even higher order.

"If these had been military miners," he pointed out, "if their tunnels had been designed to sap the defences of some impregnable hilltop fortress, if William Body's captaincy had been by the queen's commission, and if he had risked his life in her service, who can doubt but that the illustrious initials *V.C.* would grace the headstone that will soon stand here? Deeds of military heroism are engrossed in the annals of our nation; but the valour of an ordinary man is enshrined in a memorial grander by far — in the grateful

hearts and the uplifted lives of all who knew him. Simply by knowing
William Body and by seeing what great courage was in him when the
occasion called, we are all of us ennobled in some small measure. For his clay
was our clay, and whatever was writ there in him is to some degree written
in us all. If we, like him, can show it when we are called, then he will not
have died in vain."

The captain left no close family. His modest savings were divided
among a number of squabbling cousins and nephews but Elizabeth insisted
on paying for his funeral and headstone. The design included a horizontal
kerb into which was fastened the crown-shaped nugget of native copper; the
stone bore the legend: A KING IS CROWNED. On the underside, where it
would not be seen, she got the mason to carve the message:

> We shall stand together in a year.
> Or two.

"A bit morbid?" David suggested.

"He'll understand. It's a kind of prayer for a long, long life."

A week after the funeral Clifford Chigwidden came to her with an offer
to take up the venture for the Body Lode (as the Great King Harry Lode was
now renamed). He had the bounty Courtenay Rodda had given him for the
discoveries at Little Tregathennan. He would start in a small way, hoping
to win enough metal to finance further work before the cash ran out. She saw
then how deep the gambling spirit of the Cornish miner had etched its way
into her soul, for she could not say him an outright yes; she could not be
shot of the business for ever, merely collecting her rent as lord of the
minerals.

She told him she'd think it over, already knowing in her heart that
she'd go into the venture with him — though Lord knew where the money
would come from.

Next day he was back. She told him if he'd take the active fifty-one
percent, she'd be the forty-niner. He seemed to expect her reply for he said
at once that if she'd re-erect the Pallas Consols' fifty-four-inch engine at
Poldown, she could come in at forty-nine.

No sooner had Chigwidden left than a somewhat agitated Hamill
came to her door.

"Who's your lawyer these days?" he asked the moment he was inside.

"Why?"

"Have you heard nothing from Coad and Coad?"

"Oh no! Has Morwenna started up all over again?"

He nodded. She poured him a brandy, he looked so shaken.

"She couldn't have picked a worse time," Elizabeth said. "Or a better
one from her point of view. I've thrown away a lot of good money there.
Perhaps I deserve to lose."

But Hamill shook his head. "That's not her chosen ground. Some amateur archivist (and Lord forgive me but I suspect your mother) has been sleuthing around at Somerset House and you'll never guess what she's discovered?"

Elizabeth held her breath. She felt sick. "I think I can," she said at length. "Has this anything to do with old Sir William's will?"

"You know about it then!"

"David looked it up once. It leaves Pallas in tail-general. Does she think that entitles her to inherit?"

He nodded. "Apparently."

"But that entail was broken by Bill's father and grandfather, Robert and Samuel Troy, surely?"

"She claims it wasn't."

At that moment David came into the room. Elizabeth told him Hamill's news. It surprised him less than she had expected. "I thought it wouldn't be long before some kind friend whispered in her ear," he said. "She must be relying on that action of Fine and Recovery in 1832."

"That's right," Hamill interjected. "Those were the very words I overheard — fine and recovery."

"What are her chances?" Elizabeth asked.

He shrugged. "Blank, I'd say. If the Fine was successful, Sir William's entail was barred; therefore she can't inherit. If the Fine was unsuccessful, then the later action between Robert and Samuel prevails — and once again the original entail is barred. She still doesn't inherit." He tapped his teeth with his thumbnail. "So what has Coad found that we've all missed?"

"Have you talked it over with Petty?" she asked Hamill. "The Dragon often lets slip . . ."

"Petty's gone away. Friends in Worthing. I don't understand her. She's spent the last twenty years saying she can't abide them and then suddenly she's fishing like mad for an invitation."

"Worthing!" Elizabeth smiled fondly. "Bill and I once walked from Brighton to Worthing, through Old Shoreham. That's where he proposed to me." She shook off the memory and became businesslike again, turning to Hamill. "But why d'you think my mother's behind it?"

"Your mother is not all she seems," he said stiffly.

"You do surprise me, Uncle Hamill. I thought she was supposed to be the most wonderful woman since Helen of . . ."

"I found a book beneath her mattress," he grunted. *"Tricks and Frauds of the Spiritualist Mediums Exposed!* Why would she keep such a book beneath her mattress if her interest in such fakery were genuine and above-board, eh?"

"I still don't see how we get from that to her being Morwenna's informer."

Hamill emphasized his disgust with a wave of his hand. "She's up to all sorts of deviltry. You know that Vesey fellow — Bond Street auctioneer?

He's been back to Helston a couple of times. Your mother spends *hours* closeted with him. They're up to something – you'll see. Plain as a pikestaff – Vesey's only interest in the heirlooms would be to auction them off."

Elizabeth could think of a far more plausible reason for those closeted hours, but she did not want to hurt Hamill by suggesting it. "What d'you think, darling?" she asked David.

"I think we must start taking a closer interest in the goings-on at Pallas House," he replied.

CHAPTER FIFTY

To PAY FOR HER reckless gamble at Pallas Consols, Elizabeth had to use the income from the estate. She had a perfect right to it, of course, but it left no finance for the improvements in progress. She therefore had to start mortgaging the land.

That, too, was within her rights, as set forth in the recent Settled Lands Acts; but because it diminished the market value of the estate, at least until the improvements were carried out, it gave Morwenna the chance for which she had been waiting. The moment she heard of it, she jumped into her carriage and drove over to Wheal Lavender. She found Elizabeth in the garden and began at once to shout abuse at her over the wall.

Elizabeth had no choice but to invite her in. "Only this time I warn you," she added, "if you strike me, I shall strike you back."

Morwenna ignored the reminder. "I knew this would happen," she crowed. "I warned everyone at the time. You and your bankrupt manager will destroy Pallas between you. No one would heed me, of course."

Elizabeth felt her fingernails in the palms of her hands. She said, "There's little point in our discussing the business in those terms, Miss Troy."

"I didn't come here to discuss anything. And certainly not business. You are not competent to discuss business. No, I came here to tell you that I shall – that is, we, the trustees – we shall be applying for the administration of the estate on the grounds of your reckless management."

"Not that you'll be granted it," Elizabeth told her, with more confidence than she felt. "Mortgages are not evidence of recklessness. Good heavens — nine settled estates out of ten are mortgaged these days. You're living in the past — as always."

"Ah!" Morwenna said triumphantly, "But Pallas has *never* been mortgaged before — until it fell under your disastrous hand."

"When we get to court," Elizabeth said calmly, "the account books and rent rolls will tell quite a different story. They will show rents abated and mounting delapidations . . . an estate in decline over many years. But, from the moment it fell under my disastrous hand, they will show improvements — all made out of income, mark you — and they'll also show the first rise in that income for thirty years. The first to be sustained, anyway. So now, to increase the pace of improvement, I am mortgaging one-twentieth part of the value. Recklessness, you call it? The judge will commend my restraint."

"Fiddlesticks!" Morwenna almost screamed.

"And I'll tell you what else will happen," Elizabeth went on in the same provokingly gentle tone. "Just like last time, you'll go into the witness box. Just like last time, you'll screech like a parakeet. Just like last time, you'll make an utter fool of yourself. And all you'll get from the judge is the offer of a glass of water — just like last time. You're a stupid old woman, Miss Troy. You can't learn from the past and you won't face the future. Why don't you just leave Pallas to those who understand it?"

For one frightening moment she thought the woman would die of an apoplexy. Morwenna turned bright scarlet, fought for breath . . . raised her hand.

Elizabeth steeled herself for the blow but at that moment David came running down the lawn. "Stop!" he called. "Ladies! For the love of heaven!"

Morwenna lowered her hand and began breathing as if she had just run a mile. She stared at David. "As for you — you've turned your coat so many times it's threadbare. I wonder the world doesn't see straight through it. And through you."

"There's no point in prolonging this exchange," he said coldly.

Morwenna's eyes flickered rapidly between the pair of them. "By God, but you deserve each other!" she said and, turning on her heel, stalked back up the lawn, scoring it deeply with her heels and her parasol.

David turned to Elizabeth. "What on earth were you thinking of?" he asked.

"Trying to make her behave irrationally. It's not difficult. I don't think she'll dare attack me on my weakest flank now."

He saw how angry she was, despite her surface calm. "My dearest — I've never known you like this."

"That's because you've never seen anyone try to take Pallas away from me before."

She soon learned what her mother and Mr. Vesey had been doing during those 'closeted hours.' With the help of her catalogue of the treasures of Pallas House, they had been putting a valuation on each item.

"It makes a grand total of five hundred and thirty-four thousand, seven hundred and sixteen pounds, thirteen shillings and ninepence," Mrs. Mitchell told her daughter when the reckoning was complete. "You're a very wealthy young lady, my dear."

It took a long time for Elizabeth to comprehend, much less believe, so large a sum. "But they're insured for only fifty thousand," she objected. "You must have made a mistake."

Her mother gave a long-suffering smile. "They cost fifty thousand when they were bought a hundred years ago. Many of the pictures were bought from the painter during his lifetime, and as everyone knows, the prices double as soon as he dies. And in some cases the prices have gone up tenfold, even a hundredfold. But your insurance value at Pallas hasn't changed in eighty years. You are hopelessly under-insured, my dear." She sighed – not too convincingly. "I'm afraid you're going to face a premium of something like a thousand a year."

Elizabeth gave a humourless laugh. "Which I can manage only by selling part of the collection!"

"Oh that would be such a shame!" The words were even less convincing than the sigh.

"That's your game, isn't it, mother – you and Vesey. A thousand pounds' worth of trinkets through his salerooms each year . . . nice bit of commission for you."

"My dear! You used to be such a happy child . . ."

"Sorry – call it cataloguing fee, then."

"You've become rough and unwomanly. It's unladylike to go about suspecting people like this."

"Talking of suspicions, I hope you've stopped all that nonsense with séances at Pallas?"

Mrs. Mitchell looked away uneasily. "They keep pestering me to try again, even Petty, now she's back from Worthing. And Hamill is worse. But I don't trust him. May I tell you a secret, dear? I suspect him of cheating!"

"Hamill?"

"Yes. At our first séance there were three distinct knocks. We all heard them. I certainly didn't cause them, and nor did Morwenna." She gave a knowing smile. "But don't worry – I'll catch him. Oh yes – I've studied all their tricks."

"I give up! Talk about second childhood!"

The most serious aspect of her mother's revelation, as Elizabeth soon realized, was that it gave Morwenna yet another flank to attack – the "reckless under-insurance" of the Pallas treasures. Fortunately, the Dragon was entirely preoccupied with her present suit, the grounds for which were quite extraordinary.

She was claiming that the abandoned Fine and Recovery of 1832 had stultified all later legal actions with regard to the real estate, which, of course, included the heirlooms. The Fine was recorded in Chancery, but so was the objection from David's father, George Troy. So, did the Fine stand or was it barred? None of the parties had withdrawn. The whole process was, as it were, frozen in time, unresolved. While that remained the case, no later actions by any of the parties, or their successors, were valid.

Morwenna had persuaded the trustees to bring the action because (she claimed) the uncertainty made the property valueless. David was sure the court would throw it out as vexatious and out of time. "But," he said, "just in case you come up before some old pedant who'd be thrilled to waste five years of everyone else's time and money in arguing the point, I think I'll enter as *amicus curiae*."

"Meaning?"

"They could argue that, despite all the legal actions that have governed the descent of Pallas, the line down to Bill has actually been the same as it would have been if Sir William's original will had spoken throughout. Therefore the issue only became live when you inherited. And as that was only four years ago, the issue is not out of time. If the court allows that, they will effectively revive the 1832 Fine – in which case, I, as my father's successor, shall revive his objection and pursue it for all I'm worth." He laughed. "Or, rather, for all *you're* worth!"

"And if you win, the estate comes down to you?"

He looked at her reproachfully. "To us."

It struck her that even if Morwenna won, she being unmarried and past childbearing age, the estate would still pass to David on her death. She almost said as much but the words stuck in her throat. Her mother was right – she *had* become rough and unwomanly. David was a political man, used to making compromises to achieve the greater good of others; but he would never compromise his most fundamental principles when the only beneficiary was himself.

CHAPTER FIFTY-ONE

SHE TRIED TO DISCUSS her doubts and uncertainties with Courtenay but his exclusion from Trevanion's upbringing had also, in ways she could not explain, barred that old intimacy of their minds. In any case, he had lately begun to court the daughter of a mine owner in Redruth. The only other people she could buttonhole were George and Lilian. Having resisted Lilian's blandishments for most of that year, she finally yielded and agreed to commission George to paint her portrait – fully clothed, full length, and for a fulsome fifty guineas.

Lilian rubbed in the salt. "Last year you could have had it for thirty, but you can thank your mother for the increase."

"Oh?"

Lilian explained that Vesey, the fine-art auctioneer, had a nephew called Ralph Devery who owned a small gallery for modern art in a mews behind the Bond Street saleroom. "Your mother put him on to Geo. He's a rare man – with a wonderful head for business and a keen eye for genius." She held up crossed fingers. "I think our nail-biting days are over, at least as far as the money is concerned."

"Why d'you call him Geo, now?"

"Oh, that's Devery's idea, too, but I agree. Geo is much more artistic than George."

"Geo" himself appeared at that moment. "Has Lilian told you she's pregnant?" he asked.

"George!" Lilian said. "Don't use that word, *please!*"

"Pregnant?" he asked provokingly. "Is it against nature?"

"It's not decent," Elizabeth told him. "If you must talk about it at all, you should say *enceinte* or 'in a certain condition.' Anyway" – she turned to Lilian – "whatever the word, I'm so happy for you, my dear. For both of you."

Lilian gazed at George with a maternal fondness. Then, her eyes begging sympathy from Elizabeth, she said, "It's not at all certain yet."

"It's the only way I can get a mother-and-child model in these prudish days," George said. "Time you had another one, Beth."

"That, dear George, is in the lap of the gods."

He raised an amused eyebrow. "Dear me – how positively messianic!"

But as soon as she was in her pose he became serious. For half an hour, until he let her rest, there was complete silence. During the break he continued working, sketching in the background. Lilian brought a cup of tea.

Elizabeth told them of Morwenna's action; she looked expectantly at George, but he kept his own counsel.

She went on to the problem of the insurance.

"A thousand pounds!" Lilian said. "How can you even sleep at night? Where will you find it?"

"I shall have to apply to the trustees to sell off one or two things. Morwenna will have a field day."

George cleared his throat. "Not necessarily," he said.

They both turned to him.

"Would you consider setting up a charitable trust to house and exhibit the paintings and sculptures? I suppose they represent most of the value?"

"Some of the furniture came from the French court. They're worth quite a bit."

"All right – the art and the most expensive pieces of furniture? Would you?"

"Of course I would – I'd gladly give it away. It's absurd to think that six square feet of Rembrandt might be worth ten thousand pounds or more."

"Turn Pallas House into a public gallery?" Lilian asked.

"No, I was thinking of the Mines Institute in Camborne. Now they've moved into their new building there's a debate about what to do with the old place. It would make an ideal gallery."

Elizabeth laughed. George had found the answer. "And charge admission to pay for the insurance!" she said.

"Not at all. You'd set up a sister charity, called The Friends of the Pallas Collection, which would seek donations and bequests to pay the running costs, including the insurance. It would be a great attraction to visitors. I'm sure several chambers of commerce would contribute handsomely. It so happens that I know the secretary of the Mines Institute. Shall I sound out the ground?"

By the time Elizabeth came for her third sitting, the arrangements were well advanced. "You really ought to get some legal clothing around you now," George said. "You're a bit . . . exposed. Will you ask David to oblige?"

She dodged the question. "I don't like to bother him with estate matters when he's so busy in the House. I don't suppose *you'd* consider it?"

"I know someone in Penzance," he told her.

It was a month before David returned from Westminster. By then the preliminary agreements were drawn up and signed; the announcement was carried in that week's *Vindicator* and quickly taken up in the national papers.

Predictably, Morwenna was furious; but, as her only legal interest in the residual estate was the continuation of her portion – which was already well secured – she had no grounds for action. The only possible complainant was Elizabeth herself, the ultimate legatee, and she had waived her rights for the period of the bequest to the charity, which was fifty years.

But David's response was extraordinary. She had never seen him so furious.

"You had no right to do this without consulting me!" he shouted.

Rather than contradict him flatly she said, "But I can't see why it should upset you so."

"Upset! *Upset!* You go creeping behind my back and . . ."

"But I have never troubled you with estate business. Especially now that you're . . ."

"You don't deceive me one little bit, Mrs. Troy. You are as devious as you are disloyal. You know very well . . ."

She turned on her heel and left the room. He caught up with her in the garden, storming furiously toward the gate that led to the Wheal Pallas croft.

"You'll go into Penzance tomorrow," he said, already out of breath. "You'll tell Ivey he's no longer on our list of friends and you'll instruct him to undo the whole sorry business."

She leaped nimbly ahead of him through the gate, turning immediately and slamming it in his path. The blow winded him. "I shall do no such thing," she replied. "How dare you suppose you may order me about in that fashion!"

As he fought for breath his face turned scarlet; she could see bright arteries in his cheeks. "I shall do more than order you about," he gasped. "I shall chastise you. Aye – even unto seven times for your sins. You are my *wife*, woman!"

"I was never your wife!' she screamed. Then, taking a grip of herself, she added in a quieter tone. "And none knows it better than you!"

Suddenly the fight went out of him. It was as if his bones had begun to dissolve. His whole frame went slack. He seemed to hang upon the air like a wreath of smoke. "I suppose you're off to Courtenay Rodda," he said in a tone of deep disgust.

The space between them froze. She could not move. She could not speak.

He was the first to emerge from their trance. He cleared his throat. "I mean," he said weakly, "doesn't this path lead to Yeol Parc?"

She answered him in a voice barely above a whisper. "You were the man with the binoculars!"

He closed his eyes and shook his head violently. "I don't know what you may mean by that. Let's stick to the point – this Pallas Bequest . . ."

Still in a daze she turned and walked away from him. Not toward Yeol Parc. Not toward Wheal Pallas. Just away from him.

"Beth!" he called after her.

She paused and turned. In his eyes was the most piteous plea: *Unsay these things! Call back this last half-minute!*

"How *could* you!" she said.

For an hour she wandered the Wheal Pallas moors, visiting all the old haunts – the tunnels where she had first met Courtenay, the paths beside which they had laid and loved. Had he spied on them then, too? None of these places were familiar any more – or, rather, their very familiarity, their ties with her old life, seemed to mock her innocence. What could she do? How could she ever face David again?

Her wanderings brought her within sight of Yeol Parc but she heard the strains of a piano and the accompaniment of female laughter and turned instead toward Little Tregathennan.

The fields of Pallas no longer proclaimed their neglect, yet now they seemed more of a millstone than ever. You could put new heart into the soil. You could lime it and cull its weeds and enrich it with all manner of fertilizer; but the one thing you'd never manage was to neutralize the poison of family avarice.

It would be a terrible justice, she thought, if Morwenna won back everything. Then she and David would drink that poison all the days of their lives.

She remembered the mute plea in his eyes and began to soften. He was not a monster, not an evil man. As poor youngsters carry the rickets of their childhood always, so he had carried into adulthood the crippling marks of his own spiritual poverty. Surely the least she could do was try to understand? They could no longer live together – or, at any rate, they would have to arrive at some accommodation of social demands and their private needs – but at least she owed it to him to try and understand.

It was dark by the time she reached home. The whole house was silent. He, of course, would be sleeping in his dressing room. She lay awake for hours, trudging through the waste of her emotions, until, like a bewildered traveller in an ocean of sand, she recognized the footprints ahead of her as her own. In desperation she thought of Oenone. She had to talk to someone. Oenone's rough peasant sense might show the way forward.

She tiptoed past David's door and along the passage. No matter where she trod, every floorboard seemed to screech. And Oenone's door itself groaned like a churchyard gate.

The moonlight fell strongly across the bed. It revealed two sleeping forms beneath the blankets but it was several moments before she recognized the man as David.

Oenone turned toward her. She was not asleep. Their eyes met and dwelled in each other's. "I am in hell," Oenone murmured. The tears were streaming down her face but she made no sound.

Without a word Elizabeth turned and went back to her own bed. If the floorboards creaked, she did not hear it.

CHAPTER FIFTY-TWO

NEXT MORNING OENONE tried to behave as if nothing had happened. Elizabeth had spent the entire night wondering how to deal with this new situation; all Oenone said was, "Morning, missis. What'll I cook Mister for his breakfast?"

Elizabeth sat down at the kitchen table. "How long, Oenone?" she asked.

The woman would not look at her. "Bacon and egg, I suppose," she said.

"D'you *love* him?"

She stood stiffly for a moment and then, with a whispered "Yes," began to sob in the same quiet, almost effortless way as she had sobbed last night.

"And Davina is . . . his?"

She nodded. "He chose the name."

"Like a banner."

Oenone, seeing that Elizabeth was not angry, nor even sad, stopped crying; curiosity got the better of her. "Missis?" she prompted.

Elizabeth looked at her. The woman seated herself at the table opposite her. "What we going do?"

"I've been awake all night asking myself that. Why did he marry me?"

Oenone's tongue darted uncertainly around her lips. "Well, he do have funny notions about women."

Elizabeth closed her eyes. "I don't really want to know."

"Some is angels, like you. And the rest . . . well, they're like me."

"I'm sorry, Oenone."

"I believe he've fixed another babby inside I." She watched and waited, full of tension.

After a pause Elizabeth shrugged and said, "Nothing surprises me any more."

"What we going do?"

"Why should we *do* anything? We'll carry on as before, I suppose – except that we no longer need deceive one another." She stood up and turned toward the door. "Make whatever you want for his breakfast. You probably know what he likes better than I do."

Oenone reached down the frying pan and said with a giggle, "He do like chewing my stockings!"

Elizabeth fled back upstairs.

It was the day of her final sitting for George. She almost gave it a miss, for fear she would blurt out these dreadful revelations. But as she drove over to Mousehole she realized there was no point in telling anyone; she did not seek advice – and she certainly wanted no sympathy. In any case, what advice could they give her? Leave David? Stay? She could decide things like that for herself. George, as a man, and a former lawyer, presumably with some experience of depravity, might be able to explain David's behaviour; but she no longer felt much desire to understand it.

In the end she was glad she went, for George, without knowing it, handed her what looked like the answer to all her problems.

He approached the topic in a roundabout way by saying, "It's lucky you married David, Beth."

She laughed. "Is it? I'm sure you've never thought so."

He grinned complacently. "Well, it's true I always felt you could have done better for yourself – but I'm sure all the world said the same about Lilian. However that's all water under the bridge. The point I'm making is that even if Morwenna wins, Pallas will ultimately come to our David."

He stared at her keenly, with more than a painterly concentration. She decided to give him the hook he was seeking. After all, if she did break with David, it would be as well to prepare her friends. She said, "Oh yes – David always gets two bites at the cherry."

He smiled grimly. "You think it occurred to him before . . ."

"If you want to know the truth, George, I think he put the Dragon up to it. My most vulnerable flank was my stupid mismanagement of the capital outlay. I put far too much into the mines. She could have made out a very good case there – but, of course, that would have excluded him. So I'm sure he found some subtle, devious, roundabout way to let her think this other line of attack was copper-bottomed – which, as you say, it *is*. For him!"

George was staring at her, open mouthed. "I didn't mean . . ." he faltered.

She smiled. "I know you didn't. Why don't you stop beating about the bush?"

He swallowed. "Well – it makes it easier for me to tell you this. I've been doing a bit of digging among the statutes since last we met. Specifically" – he reached his hand to the shelf behind him and took down a slim paperbound volume – "the Settled Lands Act of 1884. I don't imagine it was constant reading matter in the offices of a radical young lawyer with an extensive police-court practice, but" – he gave a devilish grin – "it ought to have been! Especially if that same young lawyer is going to start meddling in affairs of estate!"

He threw the book at her feet. "Take a rest and cast your eye over that. Section six, subsection one."

The page was marked. Her eyes strayed down the neat columns of text. "What's a *lis pendens*?"

"Pending litigation. Literally 'litigation hanging.'"

She gave a mirthless laugh. "It should be *Liz pendens*!" After further, brief study of the document she said, "I can't make head nor tail of it. Just tell me."

"What it says is that in the ordinary course of events the trustees can sell without any reference to you. They don't need to consult you, inform you, get your consent – nothing like that. They can just sell. *But*" – he raised a triumphant finger – "if you take out an action against them and that action is registered as a *lis pendens*, then all the powers of the trustees immediately pass to you!"

"Say that again?"

"It's nice to think that sometimes even the parliamentary draftsmen make mistakes – sometimes they frame a law that accidentally permits a little bit of justice to emerge."

"Never mind that now. What did you say before?"

He laughed. "I said, all you have to do is take out an action against the trustees, and . . ."

"What sort of action?"

"Anything. It doesn't matter. Sue them for being dilatory with the sale, for instance. And the effect of section six is that all the powers of the trustees immediately pass to you!"

"I could sell it at once?"

"On the spot – provided you get 'a fair and reasonable price.' There now! What d'you say to that?"

"I say you were a fool to give up the law, George. You have the most brilliant legal mind in the country."

He laughed again. "I've finished here. Come and look – see if you still think so."

Until then he had not allowed her to see his painting. With her heart in her mouth she stepped down from the dias and came around his easel.

The portrait took her breath away. It was not a salon picture. It was not a pretty piece of impressionism. But nor was it one of his usual flat-pattern daubs. He had somehow gone beyond all his previous experience and skill and arrived at this strong, fluent . . . masterly – no other word occurred to her – masterly image.

"Well?" he asked.

She shook her head, still at a loss for words. Perhaps she was especially sensitive to such feelings that day but the woman who stared back at her from that canvas seemed filled with tension. Her pose was assured enough; her gaze held yours calmly. Yet there was something – the carriage of her head, the slight parting of her lips, the light in her eye – something that told of loss, of *un*fulfillment.

"How do you *do* that?" she whispered.

"I've wanted to paint you ever since that first day we met, Beth – when the hounds broke up that fox almost at your feet. D'you remember?"

She nodded.

"That was the look on your face then. It's haunted me ever since."

"D'you know what I was thinking?"

"I don't want to know. Please don't tell me."

"I'm ashamed at only paying you fifty pounds."

"Guineas, actually. But a bargain's a bargain. Tell you what, though – if you sell Pallas for a good price, now I've told you how to go about it, you can take Lilian and me on a painting holiday to the south of France."

"Done! But first I must find my buyer. Oh, I can't wait to get rid of it."

"My my!" He looked at her askance. "Here's a change indeed!"

"I'll tell you one day," she promised.

She returned to Wheal Lavender via the new copper workings at Poldown. They were driving a caunter shaft aimed at meeting the old adit from Deepwork through to Wheal Fortune; then if they chanced to meet a spring or cistern, it could be led away without pumping. For several years to come, it would free them of the necessity to keep the mine in fork.

The work was going well. Chigwidden himself was sinking the shaft; four tributers were working the copper body, which was proving as rich as they had all hoped.

There would be no profits to distribute for a year or so, but then it would start to pay handsomely.

Wondering how she could feel so contented, on a day that should have been the second-darkest in her life (if not the darkest, for on the day of Bill's death she had been mercifully unconscious), she pulled into the lane by Wheal Lavender.

A tall stranger, a gentleman by his dress, was standing before her garden wall, peering intently – or so it seemed – at the plants between the stones. When he heard the dogcart, he straightened, turned to face her, and took off his hat.

"Good afternoon, Mrs. Troy," he said affably. He sounded almost Cornish, but not local.

"You seem very interested in my wall, Mr. . . . ?"

He smiled broadly. He was a handsome man – and she suspected he knew it. He was in his thirties, perhaps even approaching forty. For all the gentlemanly cut of his clothes there was something rough about him.

A rough diamond?

Perhaps a kinder word would be rugged.

"Very interested," he agreed. "It's about the most interesting wall I ever saw. In fact, I was wondering if you'd sell it to me?"

"Sell it?"

He nodded. "I'm offering a thousand pounds." And while she floundered, he added, "Pardon me, I forgot to introduce myself. My name is James Troy – Jimmy to my friends."

CHAPTER FIFTY-THREE

ELIZABETH LAUGHED. "Those are two most interesting statements, Mr. Troy. I hardly know which to pursue first."

"Well, now" – he replaced his hat, at a more rakish angle than before – "as an honest American, I'd say go for the money first. I know that isn't exactly what your English gentry preach but it is exactly what they practice, or so I've observed."

"Ah, I remember now. You must be from the American branch of the family. James, wasn't it, who emigrated? You'd be his . . . grandson? Great-grandson?"

"Grandson. Willy Boy Troy was my father."

"I know the name, but very little else about him."

He smiled affably. "How many winter evenings can you spare? He was quite a man."

She descended from the dogcart; he sprang at once to help her. She liked him from the first. He was easy, relaxed, open, confident. But there was no boyishness in his charm. His manner suggested he had travelled the world in order to arrive at this remote Cornish lane on this particular evening; he had seen everything, done most things, none of life's surprises would take him unawares. Yet, despite the ease and humour of his talk, there was a cool watchfulness in his eyes, suggesting he was holding back far more than he was saying.

"About the wall," he continued. "I hear you're the local magnate in tin and copper, but . . ."

"Just recently I could have offered a better bargain in floodwater."

He chuckled. "Yes, I heard that, too. How are you on wolfram – or tungsten, as some call it?"

She shrugged. "One hears the name, of course. I've been told it used to contaminate the tin at Wheal Pallas very badly, until they found a way of separating it."

He pointed at her wall. "Is that where these stones come from? Wheal Pallas?"

Her pulse quickened but outwardly she remained calm. "It's a common sort of stone hereabouts. Why? D'you think they contain tungsten?"

As if it were proof, he picked a stone from the top of the wall, making a pantomime of its weight. "The words are Swedish, you know – *tung*, heavy, *sten*, stone. I have no idea what wolfram means." He replaced the stone and drew her attention to another, which sported an especially fine cluster of opalescent-grey crystals in a hollow on its surface. "And there it is. A small fortune in tungsten." He waved a hand to include the entire wall.

"It's growing dark," she said. "Will you come in and have 'a dish o' tay,' as we say?"

David had gone back to Westminster; it was, in any case, only ten days before the new session of parliament. Jimmy Troy had his 'dish o' tay' and then stayed to dinner, too. Elizabeth offered him a bed for the night but he said he had to get back to the Angel. He had come out by train so he borrowed their pony and trap, saying he'd be back with it on Monday morning.

"You'd better come tomorrow," she advised. "Monday is going to be . . . well, impossible."

During the hours he spent at Wheal Lavender he told her the story of his family. He was a second cousin to both Bill and David. His grandfather, James, was the younger brother of Robert, Bill's grandfather; James had been one of the first Cousin Jacks. Though he had not actually worked in the Cornish mines, his family involvement with the business had taught him more about deep mining than was then known in America, which, being virgin territory, was still able to strip what it needed rather than dig for it. James had managed deep mines all over the Americas, mainly in Mexico and Venezuela but toward the end of his life in California and Nevada, too.

His son, Willy Boy Troy, had grown up in the business. He had made and lost several fortunes; money just ran through his fingers – "mainly because he could never bother to analyze people," Jimmy said. "You'd ask him, 'What sort of a fellow is so and so?' and he'd answer you, 'Tall with a scar right here.' No, I'm exaggerating. That makes him sound stupid. He wasn't stupid. He had good intuitions about people but they never carried him far enough. For hiring and firing workmen he couldn't be beat. But for taking on partners – and wives – no sir!"

Jimmy himself had had an *interesting* upbringing, to say the least —
back and forth across America, from silver mines to sulphur wells to
goldfields – Alaska, the Yukon, California, Texas, Pennsylvania . . . each
was his boyhood state, and so was everywhere in between.

"Living down here," she said wistfully, "it's so easy to forget there's a
whole world beyond."

His gaze was intent; he took the remark far more seriously than she
had intended. "Is your father still alive?" she prompted.

No, his father had died only ten years ago. Fortunately Willy Boy's
last wife, Hazel (not Jimmy's mother but the one who had seen to most of
his rearing) had managed to steady him down a piece, persuading him to try
to lead only three lives at once instead of ten. She had also put aside a goodly
pile of gold from the glory days.

Willy Boy died rich, too. "That's one thing Hazel could never
forgive him for. The business that made him rich, the business he and I
built up together, actually grew out of the worst stretch of poverty they
ever endured – and all because they're both of them stubborn as mules.
How can a body plan a life! He hadn't a nickel and he was sore as a bear at
her because she wouldn't allow him to touch the gold – she wouldn't even
let on where it was hid. That was to help put me through college and then
start up some business that would keep him and her in their old age. So
just to spite her he lit out and took a job blacksmithing. This was in
Pennsylvania, right after the time when Drake started all that oil business
there. Those oil drills, you know, they are something! They can shake a
whole county. And Willy Boy Troy became the champeen smith at
forging and edging the bits for oil rigs. And we never looked back. I was
always interested in metals. You'd always catch me round the tinkers' fires
in any camp. Neighbors'd bring me their pans and kettles to fix. I never
did get to college. That was my college. I graduated on kettles, majored
in boilers, and took my master's in drill bits. You've heard of Eureka
Drills and Tools?"

"Of course! Is that you?"

"That's us. So now you understand my interest in tungsten. Our
tungsten-steel drills are the finest in the world." He laughed self-
mockingly, as if to say, *We both know that's how all Americans talk, but I'm a
man of the world, too.*

He was well accustomed, she thought, to having his cake and eating
it. "Are you married?" she asked.

He laughed at her directness and shook his head.

"And your stepmother, Hazel Troy, she's still alive?"

"Oh very much! She's here in Helston right now. In fact, we've both
spent a most enjoyable day at Pallas House. Of course, we were kind of sorry
so many of the pictures were packed in crates, but . . ."

"You know why?"

"Yes, your mother told us. She is *charming*." His eyes challenged her to respond.

"She knows more about the family heirlooms than any of us."

"She surely does! My mother adored it. But – as I was saying – when it comes to prospecting for tungsten, well, she kind of leaves that to me. She'll be mad to have missed meeting you, though."

"But do bring her with you tomorrow. Stay for lunch. Then you and I can walk over to Wheal Pallas afterwards and see how much tungsten there is among the deads there."

And so it was arranged. They came out after church.

Hazel Troy was a handsome, self-contained woman in her sixties. Her hair was silver, tightly wound in a plaited bun. She was at first wary with Elizabeth, which suggested that Jimmy had perhaps been rather too enthusiastic in the description his stepmother must have demanded. However, her native jollity soon broke through and then the house rang with her laughter – which she constantly excused, saying that people who couldn't laugh would never have survived around Willy Boy.

She adored Pallas House and just wished she could have seen it with all its treasures.

"But the exhibition will open soon," Elizabeth pointed out.

"Yes, but it's not the same thing, is it. Oh I do hope Jimmy decides to settle over here."

"Hay . . . zel!" Jimmy warned.

"Is that on the cards?" Elizabeth asked.

The answers flickered behind his eyes before he said, "It is one of several possibilities."

"My mouth!" Hazel laughed.

"I was very interested in the electrical installation at Pallas House," Jimmy said. "I understand your first husband was responsible for that?"

"Yes." He seemed to expect more so she told him, "I've never actually seen it. They told me he ripped up a lot of floorboards and laid solid copper rods underneath them. But that was as far as he got before he died. There were to have been electric platewarmers and a clothes press and lights in the corridors and so on. And there should have been some kind of generating machine and wet cells out in the stables. But apart from the copper conductors nothing was ever installed."

"The old boy – Mr. Hamill Oliver? – he took up a couple of loose boards and showed me. They're as thick as lightning conductors, those rods. He's trying to rig up some electrical devices but he wouldn't say what. He seems to think electricity is a mystic force."

"Uncle Hamill is a great local historian," she said diplomatically. "He'd be your second cousin, too, of course."

He gave her an odd, appraising sort of glance. "I really envy a man like that, don't you, Mrs. Troy? He's lived here all his life, either in this house or over there. I can't imagine what it must be like to wake up and go to sleep among the same hills and valleys for one entire lifetime."

"You're the one I envy," she answered. "Seeing so much of the world."

"There you go!" he chuckled. "The other man's grass is always greener. Maybe I should content myself with the wandering life."

As soon as lunch was over, Elizabeth, glancing out of the window, said, "If you wish to inspect the old halvans, Mr. Troy, we'd better put up our skates. That storm isn't going to wait for us."

He lingered. "I honestly don't think I ought to impose on you, Mrs. Troy. I can wait for a finer day. I'll be around in Cornwall for at least another . . ."

"This has to be settled today," she said. She knew he was testing her eagerness to do business but she had no time for such sparring. "And as for the weather, I've been out in worse. All day."

While they climbed into their oilskins and gumboots, it struck her as odd, uncharacteristic even, that she should be boasting to him. She supposed American women were tough, resourceful, pioneering sort of people; she didn't want him to imagine she stayed at home all day, practising Strauss and pressing wildflowers.

Yet why should his opinion matter a hoot to her?

The gathering storm darkened the day by a good two hours; they set off in what already seemed like late twilight. Fortunately the path to Wheal Pallas was by now well trodden.

Jimmy Troy noticed it. "You keep a good eye on everything, even the abandoned corners of your property," he remarked.

She pointed a thumb toward Crava Croft. "My neighbour that way, Zakky Gilbert, he was an ordinary labourer when I first came here. An ordinary labourer but an extraordinary stonemason. He rebuilt the gates and the lodge at Pallas House."

"Then he *is* good."

"He also built the wall you wish to buy off me. Anyway, the point is, I paid him in kind. He had ambitions to become a highway contractor — ambitions he has since fulfilled, I may say. I let him draw all the old deads he wanted off the Pallas halvans."

Jimmy Troy closed his eyes and said, "Oh God no!"

She laughed. "I think we'll be all right. Zakky's a hard worker but he wouldn't waste a muscle. This wolfram ore is twice the weight of ordinary rock — and brittle. He's been throwing it to one side from the beginning."

"Yet he used it for your wall."

"Partly because his pile of discards was beginning to get in his way, and partly because . . ." She hesitated.

"What?"

"Don't laugh. I know you're going to. I liked the pretty crystals!"

"Well that makes two of us." He laughed. "I'm relieved."

"Anyway, that explains how this path is so well worn. I've been keeping an eye on Zakky's men and their raiding parties on my halvans."

She kept edging away from him, to share as much of the path as possible. At last he took her elbow in a firm but gentle grip and pulled her back toward the middle. "You stay there now." He pretended to chide her. "This bitsy gorse and heather doesn't bother me a lick."

"It's called furze and ling down here."

"There's a difference?"

"So I'm told. I'm not the county's most avid presser of wildflowers."

He chuckled. "No, by heaven, I believe you there. You really love this, don't you."

"Love what?"

"Oh, you know what I'm talking about – the Pallas Estate, the farms, the mines, everything. You love picking up the bits and putting them all together again. Making them work better. Cousin Hamill told me about your fight with Miss Morwenna – though I'd already heard of it in Helston."

"I can imagine."

When they reached the halvans he gave one long whistle of delight. "Holy Mo!" he cried. "You don't have an abandoned tin mine here. You have a regular, right-down, full-blood wolfram quarry. Bring back the machinery!"

He found bunches of it everywhere he looked. "Didn't anybody ever tell you?" he asked.

"I suppose in Cornwall we've always thought of wolfram as a by-product of tin. I've never heard of a mine whose main product was wolfram."

"Well, don't go away." He laughed and then, pulling out his cheque book and unscrewing his pen, passed both to her, saying, "Just name your price there. I swear I won't quibble."

"That's a good trick." She smiled and passed it back to him. "But let's do it properly. First of all, you've only seen half the mine."

She led him through the tunnel to the inner working, where, once again, he found wolfram everywhere. "It's Eldorado," he kept saying. The rain began to fall, large drops of it, warm for October. They returned to the shelter of the tunnel mouth, where he stood awhile and mentally paced out the dimensions of the mine. They went back through the tunnel and he repeated the process at the other end.

Quietly, almost as if he were thinking aloud, he said, "I'll be settling down here, by the way. This makes it absolutely certain."

"Does it?"

"Surely does. Treat this in confidence, but one of my reasons for coming over here was to look into the possibility of expanding our business into . . ." He knew they were absolutely alone yet he could not avoid one quick check all about him before he said, ". . . armor plating. It sounds a far cry from mining drills, I know, but the metallurgy is almost identical. Europe's building up to a war. Maybe you need to be at a distance to see it. There may not actually be a war but there's no question of the build-up. Your navy, the German navy, the Russians, the French . . . they're all going to triple in size. And they're all going to need armor plating. Just look around you, Mrs. Troy. You're the best friend every sailor's mother ever had! What are you asking for it?"

She laughed. "Yesterday I'd have given you all of this for that thousand you offered, on condition I kept my wall."

"Keep your wall anyway, now I've seen this. I wouldn't dream of disturbing those beautiful plants. But this! I wouldn't insult you with a thousand for this. What are you asking?"

There was a loud peal of thunder. While she waited for it to die she saw how clever he had been, with his apparently unbusinesslike wonder at the riches all about them . . . handing her his chequebook like that . . . she could easily have said, "Fifteen thousand pounds," thinking it a fortune, and he'd have pretended to haggle but finally consented — and it could really be worth ten times at much.

"I'll tell you exactly what I want," she said. "I want to sell Pallas Estate, farm by farm, to its tenants. My husband and I have long wished to do this, but lack of money has always held us up."

"How much?" His tone was flat, his face expressionless.

"It may not even be a matter of cash. A guarantee might do."

"In return for the mineral rights?"

She shook her head. "There's one thing about us Troys, you know — we're never content merely to be mineral lords. We like to be venturers as well. So I'll go into a venture with you, half and half, and the rent for the sett will be a peppercorn. I put in the land and the roads. You put in the plant. And Eureka can underwrite a guarantee on mortgage default up to thirty thousand pounds."

He whistled. "Too much."

"Good." She turned on her heel. "I like a man who can make a quick decision. Now I know where I stand."

"Surely we can adjust the terms, Mrs. Troy?" He trotted to catch her up.

She stopped and turned to him. "But I've already told you my minimum terms. I have the courts on my back, looking over my shoulders. I need to be prudent to a quite ridiculous degree."

After a pause he said, "There's more, isn't there. I can feel it. Why all the hurry?"

She hesitated.

"Sometimes," he added, "*you* have to make the quick decision — about trusting people."

She told him then – of her suspicion that David was behind Morwenna's action, and how, if she acted quickly, she could beat them both. "But I can't even take the first step," she concluded, "without that guarantee behind me."

He listened throughout impassively. When she had finished he said without hesitation, "I'll give you that guarantee, Mrs. Troy, if you'll give me sixty-forty on the wolfram."

"I'll split the difference," she conceded reluctantly. "Fifty-one, forty-nine."

Eventually they settled on fifty-five, forty-five. They began walking back to Wheal Lavender. He was so genial and expansive she knew he'd driven a fine bargain for himself.

Somehow she did not mind.

CHAPTER FIFTY-FOUR

THE WIND HAMMERED at the old sash windows, rattling them in their frames, stirring even the heaviest of the velvet drapes. Outside, in the long-neglected demesne, a mighty elm came crashing down, taking with it three sound younger trees. The potting-shed chimney fell through its roof in a splintered shower of cloam and slate. In the stables a frightened groom held the head of a terrified pony and spoke to it, trying to pacify its fear, which, bad as the storm might be, seemed out of all proportion.

Oblivious to the outside world, Morwenna, Hamill, and Mrs. Mitchell spread the letters in a circle on the polished mahogany table, bickering as ever.

"Where's the X?" Morwenna asked. "You've lost the X."

"*I* lost it! I like that, I must say. You were the one who put them away last time."

"Considering how long ago 'last time' was, I don't see how you can possibly remember."

"Well I do." Hamill put the crystal tumbler in the middle of the circle.

Just as they were about to take their seats, in walked Petty. "Oh," she said.

Morwenna and Hamill stared at her uneasily. She used not to approve of Spiritualism. Indeed, once she had threatened to tell the vicar. But now she asked eagerly, "D'you think I might join you?"

They looked at Mrs. Mitchell, who nodded. "Let her have your chair, Hamill, there's a dear."

"No!" he replied firmly. "I have to sit here, facing east – the sunrise, you know. The Power is in the sunrise."

She laughed. "But you're facing north, dear."

"That's right," he said crossly. "My right hand side must face the Power, draw on it."

In the end Petty sat opposite Hamill, who caught her eye as she settled. She looked at him pugnaciously. "What's the matter? Isn't this what you've always wanted?"

"Why have you changed your mind? You used to be so utterly against all this."

"Never you mind."

"Oh, it's only harmless fun," Mrs. Mitchell chided him. "We'll give ourselves a lovely fright and exhaust ourselves thoroughly and then fall sound asleep in our beds until this dreadful storm passes. You'll see."

He smiled at her, anticipating a triumph. "You're the one who's going to see – you just wait!"

"This isn't the right spirit at all," Morwenna complained. "We've got to be more serious."

Mrs. Mitchell chuckled affectionately. "Very well. Let's get it over and done with."

There was no need to turn down the wicks on the lamps; the disturbed air made them flicker and dwindle and flare to a suitably atmospheric degree. They all leaned forward and placed the forefingers of their right hands upon the foot of the upturned glass. The three of them looked at Mrs. Mitchell, who smiled back indulgently and asked the air in general, "Is anybody there?"

Nothing happened.

"Is there anybody there?"

Still nothing happened.

Mrs. Mitchell closed her eyes. The table shivered. She opened them at once and stared accusingly at Hamill. He pushed his chair back a foot or two and sat leaning awkwardly forward so they could all see his knees.

Mrs. Mitchell closed her eyes again. "Anybody?" she called. "Anyone at all?"

"Bill?" Morwenna whispered.

There was a thump from somewhere near the door, followed by a dry sort of whirring noise that was slow to die.

"There!" Hamill said excitedly.

Petty stared daggers at him.

The tumbler stirred uneasily. They all took their fingers off in a fright.

Then they laughed sheepishly and put them back.

At once it began to move . . . toward the lower end of the alphabet
. . . toward the numerals . . . up toward the *As* and *Bs* . . . then it
stopped, marooned half way to nowhere.

"What is it, dear?" Morwenna asked.

Mrs. Mitchell looked at all three of them. *Someone* – and she didn't
mean a ghost – was trying to move the glass. She knew it, because she
herself was at the game, too.

The tumbler resumed its wanderings. Round and round, back and
forth, halting, moving, hesitating . . . never touching a letter or numeral.

"I shall be severe with you in a minute," Morwenna said, in a tone that
made both Hamill and Petty look at her sharply.

She stared back at them. "These are his old tricks," she reminded
them . "I won't have it." She stared about the darkened room and called out
sternly, "Bread and water for you!"

The glass began to move again, but this time without any dithering.
Uneeringly, as if it ran on rails, it crossed the circle and stopped before the
B.

"Yes?" Morwenna encouraged it excitedly.

I

L

"Oh yes!" Morwenna was ecstatic. "My darling! My darling boy!"

L

"Are you all right, my precious? Is all well with you?"

Y

"And mother and father? Are they with you? D'you see them?"

1

"One question at a time," Mrs. Mitchell interpreted.

"Do you see them often?"

Y

"Are they there now?"

N

"D'you know what's happening to us?"

+

"Be more precise," Mrs. Mitchell said.

"D'you know about the court case, about me and . . . Elizabeth?"

Y

"Have you anything to say about it? D'you want to tell me anything?"

If a simple crystal tumbler might be said to have a mind of its own,
this one now seemed to have two. It went into a positive battle with itself,
shuddering and turning in tight spins, darting one way, then another . . .

But Petty lost – Mrs. Mitchell was sure it was Petty. The tumbler at
last spelled out: *Leter*.

"D'you mean 'letter,' dear?" Morwenna asked. "A letter on the table?"

She understood then: "The missing *X!*" She turned to Hamill. "I told you!"

But the tumbler, almost unnoticed by them, raced across the table and stopped unerringly before the *N*.

Petty gave Mrs. Mitchell a conspiratorial smile. "You mean the other letter," she asked the 'spirit.' "The sort people write?"

Y

Now Petty and Mrs. Mitchell were no longer fighting each other.

"What letter?" Morwenna asked eagerly.

There was another thump from near the door. Hamill looked toward it eagerly, and then at the others. But they paid it no heed.

The glass now rested on *B*.

"Bank! A letter from the bank – Bolitho's Bank!"

U

"*B*, *U*, – what begins with . . . I have it! Burden! Mr. Burden – he's my barrister's clerk. There's a letter coming to me from Mr. Burden. What does it say? Are we going to win?"

R

"See – it is Burden."

O

And there the glass stopped.

"*Buro?*" Morwenna looked at the others in bewilderment.

Petty risked the faintest hint of a wink at Mrs. Mitchell.

Morwenna was still guessing: "D'you mean Burhos, dear? The village?"

More thumps came from the door, followed by a clanking sound, as if fingers wearing thimbles were being dragged over a washboard.

"Listen!" Hamill prompted.

"Oh, shut up!" Mrs. Mitchell told him crossly. The three women were staring intently at the glass, which, in swift sequence, now spelled: *EUA*.

"That doesn't make sense at all. The boy never could spell for toffee. Start again!"

The glass moved obediently: *BUR* . . .

"I'm hopeless at spelling, too," Petty told Mrs. Mitchell. She gave the slightest possible twitch of her head to the right.

Mrs. Mitchell's followed up the gesture. Then the glass unerringly spelled: *Bureau*.

"Bureau?" Morwenna repeated, still mystified.

"French for 'office,' " Hamill said testily.

"I don't suppose . . . ?" Mrs. Mitchell glanced toward the bureau in the room; it stood against the wall facing Morwenna.

"Of course! Of course!" Morwenna cried. "All his papers were kept there." She paused. "But what can he mean? I've been through it a hundred times. I felt sure he must have left another will . . ."

Bursting with impatience, Petty rose and began to cross the room.

"No!" Morwenna cried and raced ahead of her. "I shall open it."

Petty turned back with a smile of triumphant relief. Mrs. Mitchell quizzed her with raised eyebrows.

There was suddenly a paroxysm of knocking from the direction of the door. Both women turned on Hamill and told him to stop it.

His eyes were all innocence. "Stop what?" He held up both hands to show they were empty.

"And move your right foot," Mrs. Mitchell said.

"My what?"

"You heard."

The thunder rolled. There was lightning all around the house now.

With a sheepish grin Hamill moved his right foot. But the knocking continued. Bewildered, he stared toward the door. A thin wisp of smoke was seeping between two of the floorboards.

"Damnation!" he cried and sprang toward it.

The floorboard was loose. He raised it and kicked it to one side. The hammering stopped. A contraption of copper and ivory was now revealed, flailing away at the air. It was wedged between the copper conductors Bill had installed all those years ago. Dense pale smoke was coming from its innards.

Hamill grasped at it and flung it to one side. There was an almighty cascade of sparks and the smoke burst into flames.

With considerable presence of mind Mrs. Mitchell swept a small cloth off a nearby table and, picking up the flaming machine, flung it straight out through the window. The noise as the pane shattered was almost drowned by the storm. The wind now came howling in; around the room it swirled, billowing out the curtains, scattering the alphabet.

By the guttering light of the oil lamp they now saw Morwenna. She was standing at the bureau holding in her hand a sheet of blue notepaper. She was no longer reading it but staring into the emptiness before her.

"What have you found, dear?" Petty asked brightly.

Morwenna gave a tight-lipped little smile. "An outrageous forgery," she rasped.

She walked over to the oil lamp and held the letter above the glass chimney. At once it turned brown and began to smoulder.

"No!" Petty ran over to her. "I want to read it, too."

In the ensuing struggle they knocked over the oil lamp. Its reservoir burst, spreading a long tongue of yellow flame across the bare, polished floor. They stood and stared, aghast at what they had done.

Hamill and Mrs. Mitchell wrestled a carpet through from the next room but, although it put out the above-board flames, the oil had by then dripped through to the space below, where it burned merrily, and beyond their reach.

"We must get out . . . rouse the servants . . . fetch buckets," Hamill cried. He shepherded them out, along the corridor, and down the stairs. Fingers of smoke billowed behind them, as if nudging them on.

He looked over his shoulder and saw how well advanced the fire now was. "We must save the pictures," he cried. "The rest is lost."

As soon as they reached the main hall they began to drag and roll the packing cases toward the door. Morwenna worked as hard as anyone. The servants came running downstairs, shouting "Fire!" Hamill set them on, too. And the groom and the gardener's boy when they came running up. No one fought the fire; their only thought was to rescue the treasures.

They tore the few remaining pictures from the walls and hurled them out through the wide-open windows. Tapestries were wrapped around great vases and hurled out after them. Out went occasional tables, escritoires, chaises longues, butterfly cases, barometers, clocks, Dresden shepherdesses . . . The rain fell on crated Rembrandt and naked Zuccarelli indifferently. Smithereens of Wedgwood shivered in the gale among miraculously unscathed wax fruit. All gave back a myriad ghastly reflections of the fire that now engulfed the whole top floor of the great house.

"What's that noise?" the gardener's boy asked.

"That's the rain on the roof," the groom told him. "They slates is red hot, see."

"Weel! You'd swear the old house was screaming!"

A myth was born.

"Come on! Come on!" Hamill yelled at them.

When there was nothing left downstairs to save but the odd, minor Picturesque–Pastoral he suddenly remembered the library. Burning fragments of curtain, carpet, shards of collapsing floor were already falling down the stairwell. Soon the whole ground floor would be alight, too.

"The library!" he shouted. "Bring buckets. Every bucket you can lay hands on!"

But even as he opened the library door, part of the roof collapsed upon the floor above. With it came a section of wall that should have been repointed half a century ago. The ceiling fell in, being already ablaze in half a dozen places. The flames licked hungrily at the carpet, the bookcases, the library ladder, the floorboards, the desk, the curtains. The heat drove him back.

It was Mrs. Mitchell who dragged him from the inferno, out through the hall, stepping among a dozen fires, down the steps, out into a downpour that was powerless to halt the march of those ravenous flames.

Soon they had to withdraw half across the lawn, so fierce was the heat. Paint on those canvasses nearest the fire began to heave and blister; but for the rain they would have burst into spontaneous combustion. A monstrous ring of steam now curtained the blazing house. They could do nothing more but stand in a huddle beneath the trees and watch it burn to a shell.

That was the moment when Morwenna broke free of them and ran straight for the heart of the inferno.

CHAPTER FIFTY-FIVE

IT COULD NOT HAVE BEEN the smell of burning alone that woke Elizabeth; her own chimneys were transformed into flutes by the storm, and puffs of smoke constantly dipped out at the fire breasts. It must have been the skyglow as well. Certainly that was the first sign to penetrate her consciousness as she surfaced: The wall above her bed was suffused bright orange.

Suddenly she was wide awake. She sat up, throwing the bedclothes aside, feeling for her slippers with her toes. Not finding them, she rose and hastened barefoot to the window. The sight that greeted her when she drew aside the curtain was by then a confirmation of her fears. Flames were leaping above the trees that formed her southern skyline. The entire quarter was aglow. Clouds of smoke, touched with a lurid scarlet, billowed upward into the black of the rain-drenched night. Lightning flickered opaquely in the clouds, most especially around the house, as if its destruction required some special brand or token in the sky.

She raced back to her bedside and pulled on her outer garments. Moments later she was hurrying along the corridor to Oenone's room.

"Wake up! Wake up!" she cried, shaking hard.

Oenone woke like a woman drugged.

"Pallas House is on fire," Elizabeth told her. She had to repeat it before Oenone fully grasped the words. "Fire?"

"Yes. Come down and help me harness up the pony."

In the nursery next door, Trevanion and Davina both began to cry. For once Elizabeth ignored them, taking the steep back stairs three at a time.

Before they could harness the pony, there came the sound of a carriage, being driven furiously down the lane from Pallas. Moments later it turned into the courtyard, where a disconsolate trio dismounted – Hamill, Petty, and Mrs. Mitchell. All talking together they told her of the fire, the saving of the pictures, the collapse of the roof, the inferno, the human impossibility of doing more. She herded them into the kitchen, where Oenone set to at once, brewing up a go of tea.

Now they were all strangely silent.

"Where's Morwenna?" Elizabeth asked.

"Dead," her mother said wearily.

"No one could stop her," Hamill explained. "The heat . . ."

"She just walked back into it," Mrs. Mitchell cut in. "I still can't believe it."

"How?" Elizabeth asked.

Petty said quietly, "It was my fault."

"The fire?" Elizabeth asked.

"No. The letter. The letter was my fault."

Elizabeth raised inquiring eyebrows at Hamill.

"The library's lost," he said.

"Oh no!" Elizabeth's eyes went large. "Oh Hamill – all your papers! Your books! Your lifetime's work!"

"Funeral pyre." Though he was answering her points he was not actually talking to her but rather to some unseen gathering in the air about him. "A dead language. A dead culture." He nodded reassuringly. "Funeral pyre."

Elizabeth turned to her mother. "Can you make sense of any of this? What has been happening over there tonight?"

Her mother sighed. "Morwenna insisted on another séance. I was going to make it appear that Bill was telling her to drop the court case . . . leave you alone. Bill was going to tell her to cooperate with you."

Petty looked at her aghast. "But I had no idea!"

Mrs. Mitchell nodded. "I know – but I couldn't fight you."

"I thought you were determined to ruin your daughter."

Mrs. Mitchell smiled at Elizabeth. "Ever since I came down here I've only had the one idea – that I should hold a séance and Bill would tell her to stop, to leave you alone."

Elizabeth closed her eyes. "Oh, mother!"

"If only I'd known," Petty said.

Elizabeth turned to her. "What did you do?"

"If I'd fought you," Mrs. Mitchell said, "Morwenna would have seen it."

"Let her tell me," Elizabeth insisted.

"It was all my fault," Petty repeated.

"Tell me."

Tonelessly Petty went on, "When I went to stay in Worthing, dear – remember? Well, it's so close to Brighton I couldn't resist it. I paid that solicitor's clerk ten pounds to purloin that letter."

Elizabeth sat down, facing her. "Go on."

"I didn't ever mean to show her, I promise you – only if one of her actions against you ever looked like succeeding. Originally I just meant to hand it over to her and make her read it. But when they suggested a séance tonight . . . well, it seemed like the ideal opportunity."

Elizabeth closed her eyes and sighed. "You mean you hid Bill's letter somewhere about the room and then made it seem that his spirit was directing Morwenna towards it? Oh, Aunt Petty!"

"I'd do it again, dear," Petty said.

"It was my fault," Hamill said suddenly. "I put an electrical hammering device under the floor. That's what started the fire."

Mrs. Mitchell touched his arm. "That wasn't it, my love. Don't you remember? I threw that out. I think it was my fault. The wind came in by the broken window and the curtain knocked the lamp over."

Elizabeth sighed. "If it's anybody's fault, it's mine. I was going to win without any of this. I ought to have told you. We all ought to have talked to each other." After a pause she asked, "Was that it? The curtain knocked the lamp over?"

"That was it, dear." Mrs. Mitchell looked firmly at Petty.

Through the kitchen window Elizabeth could see that the fireglow was dying. "I suppose it's useless my going over there? If you couldn't even get near it . . ."

Her mother answered. "The Helston fire brigade is there, doing what they can. Oh, and James Troy came out, too. He was wonderful. He's the one who made us come over here. He got everybody organized, wrapping wet sacks around them and dashing in to pick up the paintings and things nearest the fire. I expect he's got everything carried into the outhouses by now."

When Elizabeth heard Jimmy Troy was there, all her anxiety eased. "Come on, then," she told them. "Let's get you into your beds."

As soon as they were all tucked up, she got dressed properly and set off for Pallas. The stench of wet smoke was awful but there was no skyglow now. When she came to the part of the drive that looks down over the house she was dazzled by the carbide lanterns and fire-brigade storm lamps. Then she began to make out a few details – men moving, the hoses running down to the lake, a few shrubs, and, of course, the house itself. At first it seemed the damage was slight. The walls stood; the windows, though dark, seemed crisp and rectangular. But then she saw the gaping hole where the roof had been, the steam rising; as she drew still closer, she could make out the glowing embers through the downstairs windows and inside the front door.

She had never liked the house, but this destruction was so complete, so irreversible, she could not prevent a lump from rising in her throat.

A figure detached itself from a small group standing near the door; he came straight to her. It was Jimmy Troy. "I was just coming over to you," he said. "We're about through here. There's nothing more to do tonight."

He saw the tears in her eyes. "I wouldn't linger here," he murmured. "I'll walk you back. Take my arm if it'll help."

He was strong; she imagined she could hang all her weight on his arm and it would hardly dip.

"Morwenna?" she asked.

"Taken care of."

"I ought to thank everybody."

"They'll understand."

"Is it . . ."

"It's a total ruin, yes. But the outbuildings don't seem too bad. We managed to save almost all the pictures and an amazing amount of furniture. A lot of the porcelain is smashed, but they can fix those things nowadays."

"I'd give them all not to have Morwenna dead."

After a pause he said, "You're quite a lady!"

When they reached the bend in the drive she turned back for a final look. He said, "Cousin Hamill will be pleased. Some of his papers were saved. It was an incredible fluke, really. Did you ever go up beneath the roof at Pallas?"

"No. I doubt if I've been in that house more than half a dozen times."

"Oh really?" He assimilated that before he continued. "Well, it seems there was an old slate water tank up there, right above that end of the library, and when the roof caved in, it shed its load over his desk and papers. They're all wet, of course, but mostly legible. He had the good sense to write in pencil."

"He thinks they're lost. He pretended he was resigned to it but I'm sure it would have killed him." She gave his arm a squeeze. "We all of us owe you a great debt, Mr. Troy."

"Oh!" He gave an awkward laugh. "It's family."

"That's too simple."

There was a smile in his voice as he said, "What explanation would you prefer?"

"The truth. You're a good man."

They walked on. After a while she added, "I'm surprised you never married."

"Well, I wasn't quite forthcoming on that topic when you raised it the other day, but . . ."

"Did I raise it? I thought it was you."

"You're right. I knew it was one of us. Anyway, the truth is I married twice."

"And American law allows that?"

"Well, naturally, I divorced Hilda – number one – before I married Elise." He waited to make sure she was holding her breath, before he added, "And I divorced Elise, too. Or she divorced me." He cleared his throat. "I have an unfortunate tendency to liaisons."

CHAPTER FIFTY-SIX

WITH MORWENNA GONE, the disposal of Pallas Estate went ahead without hindrance. Not every farmer took up her offer to sell, of course. Some were unwilling, others unable – especially the smaller ones without savings. But such farms were all eventually sold, chiefly to nearby farmers with sons too young to manage them yet. Courtenay bought two of them to add to his pocket-handkerchief estate. The rest went to an extraordinary motley of buyers – a Dutchman who wanted to breed bulbs . . . an Irishwoman who had brought over a promising new variety of anemones, called "St. Brigid," from her native County Wicklow . . . a young-retired Gunner officer who had been advised to pursue a quiet life ("Ha-ha!" thought Elizabeth) . . . "all in all, quite a goodly crop of furriners," Pascoe commented. He himself bought two hundred acres, on a no-interest mortgage, and settled to rebuild his fortunes.

The mineral lordship was sold by public tender. The highest bidder turned out to be Eureka. People cried foul, of course, but the auction had been scrupulously conducted by Coad & Coad. Elizabeth's own ventures in Wheal Body, the copper mine at Poldown, and in the new Wheal Pallas wolfram mine were not part of the estate. She and Jimmy Troy became firm friends as well as partners; she relied on his advice a great deal.

She sold off the Archipelago, too, each field to its neighbouring farmer. Courtenay persuaded her to dedicate one four-acre patch to his naturalists' club. They would fence it off against human trespass and record its gradual return to untouched wilderness. "I can do an article on it for *Nature* each summer," he said. "It'll be one of the most important scientific experiments in the entire country. I'll take all the pictures."

"That man," Jimmy commented, "has what we call the buckshot approach to fame."

Hamill moved his rescued papers and books to the gatelodge. Mrs. Mitchell always referred to him as "my P.G." Gossips tried to fan a scandal out of their liaison, but they weren't the right material. Elizabeth settled a good annuity on her mother, appointed Hamill its trustee, and left them to get on with it – or bicker on with it, which is what they seemed to prefer. Aunt Petty came to live at Wheal Lavender.

The great bulk of the treasures of Pallas had been saved and went on semi-permanent loan as planned. There remained the question of what to do with the ruins of the house.

This was, of course, the most delicate question of all, for it was not just a simple matter of a ruin on a hundred or so acres of parkland — it involved the future of her marriage. A divorce was out of the question. Elizabeth wanted to stay in Cornwall and David still had his parliamentary career; even a separation would finish them both socially. In the circumstances the best they could do was preserve the outward form of their marriage while they pursued their own separate lives as far as possible — and within the bounds of social good sense. Elizabeth decided she would continue to farm. She would level the ruins and plough up the parkland.

It required the special leave of the court for a trustee to sell to herself, but in the circumstances it was readily granted. Thus was Pallas Farm born.

All her market-garden activities were now concentrated within the old walled garden of Pallas, where she put up new hothouses. Mr. Vivyan rented the ones she had built in Helston. His son was not gifted in the academic line but was green-fingered and fairly practical. Vivyan sleeping-partnered him in the cut-flower trade and they made a go of it for many years.

As for the American Troys, they soon became local fixtures.

"There's no justice," Elizabeth complained. "I shall be a furriner to the day I die, but you can come back after two generations away and within a year you're accepted as Cornish."

Hazel fell in love at first sight with the Helford River, whose steep, densely wooded banks, framing delightful vistas of sheltered water, made such a contrast to the open, almost treeless landscape on the Pallas side of Helston. She took a ninety-nine-year lease from the Duchy of Cornwall on a rather grand cottage just below the headland overlooking Helford; it was not large but parts of it were Elizabethan, which meant a lot to her. Jimmy stayed with her at first but he found the roads tiresome in the February of '94 and moved back into Helston, taking a suite of rooms in Angel Passage, one of which he used as an office; he ate his meals at the hotel. He had another office at Wheal Pallas, of course, specifically for the wolfram business. Elizabeth's share of the venture made ten thousand pounds profit within nine months of being capitalized.

"You should start playing the stock market," Jimmy advised.

She laughed.

"Seriously. Put nine thousand into something secure — government stock or something — and play with the remainder."

"I couldn't possibly do that."

"What then? You can't put it *all* somewhere safe. That wouldn't be like you."

"I think I have a better idea. It's still a gamble, but I may go into the greengrocery business. I noticed this spring that when we were selling cabbage at eight to a penny they were twopence each in the shops. One expects the merchant to make *some* profit, but sixteen hundred percent?"

He nodded shrewdly. "I can see why you'd want to enrol in that club. Where will your shop be? Let's call it your *first* shop. Right here in Helston?"

"No, I'd tread on too many neighbours' corns in Helston. I thought I might start up in Falmouth. In fact, I'm going over there all next week to rent some premises and get them done up."

He looked at her sharply. "But I'm in Falmouth next week."

She smiled. "I know."

CHAPTER FIFTY-SEVEN

THEY BECAME LOVERS the very first night. And again, many times, during the week that followed; it was the honeymoon she had never had.

"I've known some women in my time," Jimmy said.

"I suspected that."

"But you're *all* of them. If I'd met you first, I'd have known what monogamy is all about."

Their bodies seemed made for each other; from the very first moment there was nothing alien in the sight and touch of him, no fear, no awkwardness to overcome. She did not resent his experience, nor even his calm way of talking about it, which seemed to hint that everyone, all over the world, was making love all the time, every chance they got. Perhaps they were. He certainly knew all the ways of giving a woman pleasure, how to anticipate the first wave of it and use its power, and his skill, to lift her up to plateaux whose existence she would never have suspected.

They returned to Helston as they had come, by train. On the Helston branch from Gwinear Road they had the carriage to themselves. "What a week it's been!" she said. "Why did we hold ourselves apart so long? All these months."

"Because this is no idle *affaire* for us, Beth. You know that. We now have some serious thinking to do."

She was silent.

He combed his fingers through her hair, making her tingle again. "What's on your mind?"

"Oh . . . a friend . . . some years ago now. She had her life all mapped out in advance. She was determined to marry an ambitious man, well launched into his career. She'd give him his family and dutifully see them through their childhood, and then, when she was thirty, she was going to embark on an astonishing series of discreet but passionate *affaires* with all the most interesting men she could reach."

"And her husband?"

"He'd be getting on with his career – and be rather glad she didn't bother him with demands for love and attention."

"Sensible woman. Hers is the system that's served me pretty well – the other way about, if you see what I mean."

"What's so funny is that she is now married – soul, spirit, mind, and body . . . day and night . . ."

"Is this Lilian Ivey?"

"Oh, you're too quick, Jimmy." She raised her head and looked at him. A furtive edge to his smile made her add, "By God – you've had your eye on her!"

"What man wouldn't! Ever since I saw her picture hanging in Yeol Parc. I understand why you laugh at her life-plan, though."

"You understand half of it. The rest of the joke is that I told her no one can play their life like that . . . and anyway, it was a tawdry ambition. I didn't put it so bluntly, of course. Yet look at me! Look at us."

"And?"

"And what?"

"*Is* it tawdry?"

She nuzzled him affectionately. "No. The difference is I never planned it."

"Our being in Falmouth was a coincidence?"

"That's different."

"In what way?"

"It just is."

He smiled and let it drop. "How about David?" he asked. "I guess he'll be civilized about us?"

"He wants to be prime minister one day."

"And you?"

His persistent questioning annoyed her. "What d'you want, Jimmy? A contract?"

"Well, Beth, in an ideal world I'd love you to be *my* Mrs. Troy, not his. We'd have a marvelous life together, don't you think?"

It hardly seemed possible that he was seeking reassurance from her. "I no longer believe in soul mates," she said. "I know quite a few men with whom – if we still lived in an age of arranged marriages – I could lead a tolerably happy life."

He gave her chin a playful punch. "You'd lead the *same* tolerably happy life with each of them. Men are only incidents to you."

"But how can you say that — after such a week as this!"

He nodded confidently. "Especially after such a week."

"I know what you really think of me," she said crossly.

"I doubt it."

"You think I'm a coward. I ought to go to America, live in one of those easy-divorce states until I can end my marriage with David, and then marry you."

"I'm never going to marry again — which is all you're fishing to hear."

She chuckled, despite herself. "What would you like to do?"

"Seriously?"

He wasn't teasing now. She gave his hand a squeeze. "Yes."

"Well then, seriously, in a couple of years' time, maybe three, depending how the business pans out, I'd like to put it all in the hands of a manager — and you do the same with your farm — and then we'd take off around the world. Just you and me. Not on those luxury liners, but little cargo boats with four cabins for passengers. Think of the people we'd meet! All the shady characters flitting from country to country . . . all the odd little out-of-the-way ports we'd see. And we'd have no plan. If we liked a place, why, we'd stay there — a month, a year! What the heck! We'd see civilizations that were old when men were running over these fields in skins. We'd see places where no white men have ever been. Trace the footsteps of Alexander! Stand where Tigris and Euphrates meet! Make love in the Forbidden City! Oh Beth! Am I mad even to think it?"

It was so beautiful she was close to tears; all she could do was shake her head.

"What d'you say?" he pressed.

She leaned her head on his shoulder once more. "You know I'm going to say yes. Why can't we go now?"

"You know why."

"Tell me, even so. I no longer trust my own opinion. I was so convinced George Ivey was heading for disaster when he made that change — yet look how things have turned out for them!"

"Are you saying you think it's possible for him but not for you? Or — to ask an even more pertinent question — are you afraid if you start in on this change-my-life business, it'll become just another habit? D'you want us to run away together *now* because you're scared you'll change your mind again by tomorrow?"

She nuzzled his ear.

"That's a feeble answer," he said.

Still she made no response; he pressed her: "Will you change your mind?"

"You know I won't," she murmured.

"Sure, *I* know it — but do you?"

She nodded; her nose nuzzled his ear again, incidental to the movement. She went on doing it, knowing how sensual he found the caress.

He shivered and pulled himself away with some reluctance. "Then we have no need of haste. This is the final choice for both of us. Like George Ivey, we're never going to do anything so momentous again, not ever. Not if we lived nine lives. So we'll take our time and do it right."

She chuckled. "Go on. More."

"What d'you mean — more! That's it. We'll settle our affairs here in Cornwall and then, in our own good time, we'll slip quietly away and spend the rest of our lives together. Right?"

She hated to hear it set out like that, all cut and dried. "How can you be so sure it *is* the final choice for me?" she teased.

She felt the tension leave him. His whole body relaxed, filled with the ease of certainty. "Ancient folk wisdom." His voice betrayed some secret amusement. "After all, I'm the third Troy in your life."

She sat up, frowning in bewilderment. "I don't follow."

Solemnly he prompted her: "You know the old saying, surely? 'If at first you don't succeed . . . Troy, Troy . . .'"

Her elbow caught his Adam's rib and halted him. Pretending to be far more winded than he was, he laughed and spluttered, "Aiee — I've been trying to work that into the conversation all week. God, I thought my chance would never come!"

"I hate you!" she laughed.

They drew in to Pallas Halt.

She became businesslike again. "Are you going on to Helston?"

He rose and helped her to her feet. "No, I'll go to Wheal Pallas and leave in the details of these shipments. I'll cut across the fields from the gatelodge. I'll walk you as far as there."

When the train had gone, dragging its soot and sulphur with it, she took a deep breath of fresh air and stretched luxuriously. "On just such a day as this," she told him, "five years ago almost to the month, I stepped off that very train and wandered up this lane in search of Pallas House."

"Nobody came to meet you here?"

"They were waiting in Helston. I was too frightened to face them. All I wanted was to peep at the house and then run away. What a ninny I was!"

"No, you never were that. It seems to me . . ."

"Oh Jimmy, d'you mind? I don't want to talk about me any more. Or us."

"When then?"

"I don't know. Just amuse me."

"Last time I tried that you cracked a rib. *My* rib."

"I don't mean like that. I mean *really* amuse me. Tell me about the first woman you ever made love to."

He pulled a face. "I need to hold a glass of whiskey and have six men about me for that."

"I'd really like to hear it."

"Very well." He paused and closed his eyes, as if he had to fight to remember. "I guess I was fourteen. Yeah – it was weird. We were passing through Philadelphia and our rooming house was two down on the block from a Jewish girls' boarding school. And as I was walking by there one afternoon I saw this one particular girl upstairs, looking at her breasts in the glass. She was . . . what? – fifteen? Then she saw me and she just turned and showed them to me, too – with this lovely smile."

"You had time to notice the smile as well!"

He laughed. "That night I went over the rooftops and in through her window. She was in some kind of quarantine but she wasn't ill. And so we showed ourselves to each other and played around . . . you know. Just touching each other. We didn't actually make love." He sighed. "But it set the pattern for my life. I've been a fool for it ever since." After a moment of reverie he went on: "The first woman I ever actually made love to . . . now that happened on the back platform of a train to South Fork, Indiana. I was seventeen. I'd never seen her before in my life. We just had a couple of drinks and went straight out there and did it. I wanted her to tell me about other men she'd done it with. Was I better? Did they do things I didn't know about? But she wouldn't talk about them. I got so mad I almost threw her off the platform." He laughed.

"Before you went out there with her, did you ask her if she'd let you? Or did you just know."

"I just knew. I always know – almost always. It's the curse of my life, Beth."

They had reached the gatelodge.

"The parting of the ways," he said.

"Only for today." She wet her lips and kissed them toward him.

He took her hand. "I love you, Beth. You're going to be the last woman in my life. That should be sad, but it isn't."

They did not dare risk a proper kiss. But he laughed for joy, like a bird singing, as he walked away.

She took off her gloves and wandered on toward Wheal Lavender. Though the garden wall was new, and the garden itself completely restored, the place was in all its essentials still the same charming, peaceful country lodge she had seen on that first day, six years ago. The same bourbon roses grew beside the path; the sage and lavender still made the air drowsy with their mingled scent. The space in which the house existed had not cast off that magical quality of seeming lost, drowned in its own peace. She wandered up the old flagstone path.

As she drew near the front door it seemed to her that time had slipped, for she distinctly heard, coming from the back, the sound of the yard pump being cranked. But there the similarity ended. No vigorous, manly cry of joy followed it — only shrieks of childish laughter.

As quietly as she could she went to the side of the house, keeping behind the cover of the trellis until she could peep among the fronds of clematis and jasmine.

Trevanion and Davina, now both two years old, were standing naked beneath the spout of the pump, fighting each other — with much laughter — to occupy the most favoured spot, directly in the path of the outflow. Oenone was gripping the handle, staring down at them, pretending to threaten them; she held her second baby, Zelah, easily, confidently, on her hip. Every now and then she gave the handle a quick, powerful thrust and the crystal water, ice-chill from the well, came gushing out, making them scream and laugh and scream again.

Sometimes she halted the crank just as the water was about to pour out, but they screamed all the same, first in anticipation, then in disappointment.

As on that other afternoon, the sun was beyond the courtyard, gilding the old cobbles and putting a halo of shimmering iridescence around everything that moved.

Baby Zelah, not yet a year old, could only just have woken up. She blinked at the sunlight and the noise, trying to discover where all the fun might be. When the pump again disgorged its silvered waters, and the two older children shrieked and laughed as if it were still the biggest surprise in all the world, she burbled and reached a chubby little hand toward it. Oenone leaned over to oblige, giving the crank another tug.

Zelah felt the water and looked up at her mother as if to say, *Is that all?* Then she thought better of it and opened her mouth to give vent to the most forced, insincere scream ever.

Oenone laughed and, putting her lips to the child's neck, behind her ear, blew a rasp, to give her something to really scream and laugh at.

"She's spoiling it," Trevanion complained, pushing at Oenone's skirts with his wet hands.

Watching them, Elizabeth felt a sudden, sharp pang of loss. She had lost Wheal Lavender. The marriage it was intended to adorn had carried it from her, breaking all those ties that turn a house into a home. Oenone was now its true inheritor, for it *was* home to her, and her children — and their father.

Perhaps there was a pattern in it, after all?

Who lived at Pallas House now?

Only the old gardener and the stable servants.

And who now owned the Pallas acres?

Their former tenants, by and large.

Had she been directed here for this? With the millennium at hand, were the meek at last inheriting the earth?

She smiled then, to imagine what Jimmy would make of such wild fancies. He would be the first to point out that only five years ago she would have ranked *herself* among "the meek." Anyone could make patterns if they were allowed to change the elements as blatantly as that!

Nevertheless, it helped her bear the loss, which was still acute – this thought that a pattern might exist, justifying all that she had done down here.

She crept away from her vantage behind the trellis and tiptoed back toward the front door.

She pushed it open, stepped inside, and – testing herself – drew breath to call out, "I'm home everybody!"

But the words were lost.

THE END